TARKIN

STAR WARS

TARKIN

James Luceno

DEL REY • NEW YORK

Star Wars: Tarkin is a work of fiction. Names, places, and incidents either are products of the author's imagination or are used fictitiously. Any resemblance to actual events, locales, or persons, living or dead, is entirely coincidental.

2015 Del Rey Mass Market Edition

Published in the United States by Del Rey, an imprint of Random House, a division of Penguin Random House LLC, New York.

DEL REY and the HOUSE colophon are registered trademarks of Penguin Random House LLC.

Originally published in hardcover in the United States by Del Rey, an imprint of Random House, a division of Penguin Random House LLC, in 2014.

This book contains excerpts from the forthcoming books *Star Wars: Dark Disciple* by Christie Golden and *Star Wars: Battlefront: Twilight Company* by Alexander Freed. These excerpts have been set for this edition only and may not reflect the final content of the forthcoming editions.

ISBN 978-0-553-39290-6
eBook ISBN 978-0-553-39287-6

Printed in the United States of America

www.starwars.com
www.delreybooks.com
Facebook.com/starwarsbooks

9 8

Del Rey mass market edition: July 2015

For my elder son, Carlos,
frequently my sounding board,
who this time provided a plot point
just when I needed one;
and for Pablo Hidalgo,
who led me down a couple of paths
I had never explored.

In loving memory of Rosemary Savoca,
my aunt and most forgiving fan.

THE DEL REY
STAR WARS™
TIMELINE

A long time ago in a galaxy far, far away. . . .

TARKIN

Five standard years have passed since Darth Sidious proclaimed himself galactic Emperor. The brutal Clone Wars are a memory, and the Emperor's apprentice, Darth Vader, has succeeded in hunting down most of the Jedi who survived dreaded Order 66. On Coruscant a servile Senate applauds the Emperor's every decree, and the populations of the Core Worlds bask in a sense of renewed prosperity.

In the Outer Rim, meanwhile, the myriad species of former Separatist worlds find themselves no better off than they were before the civil war. Stripped of weaponry and resources, they have been left to fend for themselves in an Empire that has largely turned its back on them.

Where resentment has boiled over into acts of sedition, the Empire has been quick to mete out punishment. But as confident as he is in his own and Vader's dark side powers, the Emperor understands that only a supreme military, overseen by a commander with the will to be as merciless as he is, can secure an Empire that will endure for a thousand generations . . .

1

THE MEASURE OF A MAN

A SAYING EMERGED during the early years of the
Empire: *Better to be spaced than based on Belderone.*
Some commentators traced the origin to the last of
the original Kamino-grown soldiers who had served
alongside the Jedi in the Clone Wars; others to the
first crop of cadets graduated from the Imperial academies. Besides expressing disdain for assignments on
worlds located far from the Core, the adage implied
that star system assignment was a designator of worth.
The closer to Coruscant one was posted, the greater
one's importance to the Imperial cause. Though on
Coruscant itself most effectives preferred to be deployed far from the Palace rather than anywhere
within range of the Emperor's withering gaze.

For those in the know, then, it seemed inexplicable
that Wilhuff Tarkin should be assigned to a desolate
moon in a nameless system in a remote region of the
Outer Rim. The closest planets of any note were
the desert world Tatooine and equally inhospitable
Geonosis, on whose irradiated surface the Clone

Wars had begun and which had since become a denied outlier to all but an inner circle of Imperial scientists and engineers. What could the former admiral and adjutant general have done to merit an assignment most would have regarded as a banishment? What insubordination or dereliction of duty had prompted the Emperor to exile one he himself had promoted to the rank of Moff at the end of the war? Rumors flew fast and furious among Tarkin's peers in all branches of the military. Tarkin had failed to carry out an important mission in the Western Reaches; he had quarreled with the Emperor or his chief henchman, Darth Vader; or his reach had simply exceeded his grasp, and he was paying the price for naked ambition. For those who knew Tarkin personally, however, or had even a passing familiarity with his upbringing and long record of service, the reason for the assignment was obvious: Tarkin was engaged in a clandestine Imperial enterprise.

In the memoir that was published years after his incendiary death, Tarkin wrote:

> After much reflection, I came to realize that the years I spent at Sentinel Base were as formative as my years of schooling on Eriadu's Carrion Plateau, or as significant as any of the battles in which I had participated or commanded. For I was safeguarding the creation of an armament that would one day shape and guarantee the future of the Empire. Both as impregnable fortress and as symbol of the Emperor's inviolable rule, the deep-space mobile battle station was an achievement on the order of any fashioned by the ancestral species that had unlocked the secret of hyperspace and opened the galaxy to exploration. My only regret was in not employing

a firmer hand in bringing the project to fruition in time to frustrate the actions of those determined to thwart the Emperor's noble designs. Fear of the station, fear of Imperial might, would have provided the necessary deterrent.

Not once in his personal writings did Tarkin liken his authority to that of the Emperor or of Darth Vader, and yet even so simple a task as overseeing the design of a new uniform was perhaps a means of casting himself in garb as distinctive as the hooded robes of the former or the latter's signature black mask.

"An analysis of trends in military fashion on Coruscant suggests a more tailored approach," a protocol droid was saying. "Tunics continue to be double-breasted with choker collars, but are absent shoulderboards or epaulets. What's more, trousers are no longer straight-legged, but flared in the hips and thighs, narrowing at the cuffs so as to be easily tucked into tall boots with low heels."

"A commendable alteration," Tarkin said.

"May I suggest, then, sir, flare-legged trousers in the standard-issue gray-green fabric, of course— accented by black knee boots with turndown topside cuffs. The tunic itself should be belted at the waist, and fall to mid-thigh."

Tarkin glanced at the silver-bodied humaniform couturier. "While I can appreciate devotion to one's sartorial programming, I've no interest in initiating a fashion trend on Coruscant or anywhere else. I simply want a uniform that *fits*. Especially the boots. The stars know, my feet have logged more kilometers aboard Star Destroyers than during surface deployments, even in a facility of this size."

The RA-7 droid canted its shiny head to one side in a show of disapproval. "There is a marked difference between a uniform that 'fits' and a uniform that suits the wearer—if you take my meaning, sir. May I also point out that as a sector governor you have the freedom to be a bit more, shall we say, *daring*. If not in color, then in the hand of the cloth, the length of the tunic, the cut of the trousers."

Tarkin considered the droid's remarks in silence. Years of shipboard and downside duties had not been kind to the few dress and garrison uniforms he retained, and no one on Sentinel Base would dare criticize any liberties he might take.

"All right," he said finally, "display what you have in mind."

Dressed in an olive-drab body glove that encased him from neck to ankles and concealed the scars left by wounds from blasterfire, falls, and the claws of predators, Tarkin was standing on a low circular platform opposite a garment-fabricator whose several laser readers were plying his body with red beams, taking and recording his measurements to within a fraction of a millimeter. With his legs and arms spread, he might have been a statue mounted on a plinth, or a target galvanized in the sights of a dozen snipers. Adjacent to the fabricator sat a holotable that projected above its surface a life-sized hologram of him, clothed in a uniform whose designs changed in accordance with the silent commands of the droid, and which could be rotated on request or ordered to adopt alternate postures.

The rest of Tarkin's modest quarters were given over to a bunk, a dresser, fitness apparatus, and a sleek desk situated between cushioned swivel chairs and two more basic models. A man of black-and-white tastes, he favored clean lines, precise architecture, and an absence of clutter. A large viewport looked out across an illuminated square of landing field to a massive shield generator, and beyond to the U-shaped range of lifeless hills that cradled Sentinel Base. On the landing field were two wind-blasted shuttles, along with Tarkin's personal starship, the *Carrion Spike*.

Sentinel's host moon enjoyed close to standard gravity, but it was a cold forlorn place. Wrapped in a veil of toxic atmosphere, the secluded satellite was battered by frequent storms and as colorless as the palette that held sway in Tarkin's quarters. Even now an ill-omened tempest was swooping down the ridge and beginning to pelt the viewport with stones and grit. Base personnel called it "hard rain," if only to lighten the dreariness such storms conjured. The dark sky belonged chiefly to the swirling gas giant that owned the moon. On those long days when the moon emerged into the light of the system's distant yellow sun, the surface glare was too intense for human eyes, and the base's viewports had to be sealed or polarized.

"Your impressions, sir?" the droid said.

Tarkin studied his full-color holo-doppelgänger, focusing less on the altered uniform than on the man it contained. At fifty he was lean to the point of gaunt, with strands of wavy gray streaking what had been auburn hair. The same genetics that had bequeathed him blue eyes and a fast metabolism had also granted him sunken cheeks that imparted a masklike quality to his face. His narrow nose was made to appear even longer than it was courtesy of a widow's peak that had grown more pronounced since the end of the war. As well, deep creases now bracketed his wide, thin-lipped mouth. Many described his face as severe, though he judged it pensive, or perhaps penetrating. As for his voice, he was amused when people attributed his arrogant tone to an Outer Rim upbringing and accent.

He turned his clean-shaven face to both sides and lifted his chin. He folded his arms across his chest, then stood with his hands clasped behind his back, and finally posed akimbo, with his fists planted on his hips. Drawing himself up to his full height, which was just above human average, he adopted a serious expression, cradling his chin in his right hand. There were few beings to whom he needed to offer salute, though there was one to whom he was obliged to bow, and so he did, straight-backed but not so low as to appear sycophantic.

"Eliminate the top line collars on the boots, and lower the heels," he told the droid.

"Of course, sir. Standard duranium shank and toes for the boots?"

Tarkin nodded.

Stepping down from the platform, out from inside the cage of laser tracers, he began to walk circles around the hologram, appraising it from all sides. During the war, the belted tunic, when closed, had extended across the chest on one side and across the midsection on the other; now the line was vertical, which appealed to Tarkin's taste for symmetry. Just below each shoulder were narrow pockets designed to accommodate short cylinders that contained coded information about the wearer. A rank insignia plaque made up of two rows of small colored squares was affixed to the tunic's left breast.

Medals and battle ribbons had no place on the uniform, nor in the Imperial military. The Emperor was scornful of commendations for sand or pluck. Where another leader might wear garments of the finest synthsilk, the Emperor favored robes of black-patterned

zeyd cloth, often concealing his face within the cowl—
furtive, exacting, ascetic.

"More to your liking?" the droid asked when its
cordwainer program had tasked the holoprojector to
incorporate changes to the boots.

"Better," Tarkin said, "except perhaps for the belt.
Center an officer's disk on the buckle and a matching
one on the command cap." He was about to elaborate when a childhood recollection took him down a
different path, and he snorted in self-amusement.

He must have been all of eleven at the time, dressed
in a multipocketed vest he thought the perfect apparel
for what he had assumed was going to be a jaunt
on the Carrion Plateau. On seeing the vest, his grand-
uncle Jova had smiled broadly, then issued a laugh
that was at once avuncular and menacing.

"It'll look even better with blood on it," Jova had
said.

"Do you find something humorous in the design,
sir?" the droid asked in what amounted to distress.

Tarkin shook his head. "Nothing humorous, to be
sure."

The foolishness of the fitting wasn't lost on him. He
understood that he was simply trying to distract himself from having to fret over delays that were imped-
ing progress on the battle station. Shipments from
research sites had been postponed; asteroid mining at
Geonosis was proving unfeasible; construction phase
deadlines had not been met by the engineers and scientists who were supervising the project; a convoy
transporting vital components was due to arrive . . .

In the ensuing silence, the storm began to beat a
mad tattoo on the window.

Doubtless Sentinel Base was one of the Empire's
most important outposts. Still, Tarkin had to wonder
what his paternal grand-uncle—who had once told

him that personal glory was the only quest worth pursuing—would make of the fact that his most successful apprentice was in danger of becoming a mere administrator.

His gaze had returned to the hologram when he heard urgent footsteps in the corridor outside the room.

On receiving permission to enter, Tarkin's blond-haired, clear-eyed adjutant hastened through the door, offering a crisp salute.

"A priority dispatch from Rampart Station, sir."

A look of sharp attentiveness erased Tarkin's frown. Coreward from Sentinel in the direction of the planet Pii, Rampart was a marshaling depot for supply ships bound for Geonosis, where the deep-space weapon was under construction.

"I won't tolerate further delays," he started to say.

"Understood, sir," the adjutant said. "But this doesn't concern supplies. Rampart reports that it is under attack."

2

BLOWS AGAINST THE EMPIRE

THE DOOR TO TARKIN'S QUARTERS whooshed open, disappearing into the partition, and out he marched, dressed in worn trousers and ill-fitting boots, with a lightweight gray-green duster draped over his shoulders. As the adjutant hurried to keep pace with the taller man's determined steps, the strident voice of the protocol droid slithered through the opening before the door resealed itself.

"But, sir, the *fitting*!"

Originally a cramped garrison base deployed from a *Victory*-class Star Destroyer, Sentinel now sprawled in all directions as a result of prefabricated modules that had since been delivered or assembled on site. The heart of the facility was a warren of corridors linking one module to the next, their ceilings lost behind banks of harsh illuminators, forced-air ducts, fire-suppression pipes, and bundled strands of snaking wires. Everything had an improvised look, but as this was Moff Wilhuff Tarkin's domain, the radiantly heated walkways and walls were spotless, and the pipes and feeds were meticulously organized and labeled with alphanumerics. Overworked scrubbers purged staleness and the smell of ozone from the recycled air. The corridors were crowded not only with specialists and junior officers, but also with droids of all sizes and shapes, twittering, beeping, and chirping to one another as their optical sensors assessed the speed and momentum of Tarkin's forward march and propelling themselves out of harm's way at the last possible instant, on treads, casters, repulsors, and ungainly metal legs. Between the blare of distant alarms and the warble of announcements ordering personnel to muster stations, it was difficult enough to hear oneself think, and yet Tarkin was receiving updates through an ear bead as well as communicating continually with Sentinel's command center through a speck of a microphone adhered to his voice box.

He wedged the audio bead deeper into his ear as he strode through a domed module whose skylight wells revealed that the storm had struck with full force and was shaking Sentinel for all it was worth. Exiting the dome and moving against a tide of staff and droids, he right-angled through two short stretches of corridor, doors flying open at his approach and additional personnel joining him at each juncture—senior officers, navy troopers, communications technicians, some of them young and shorn, most of them in uniform, and all of them human—so that by the time he reached the command center, the duster billowing behind him like a cape, it was as if he were leading a parade.

At Tarkin's request, the rectangular space was modeled after the sunken data pits found aboard *Imperial*-class Star Destroyers. Filing in behind him, the staffers he had gathered along the way rushed to their duty stations, even while others already present were leaping to their feet to deliver salutes. Tarkin waved them back into their swivel chairs and positioned himself on a landing at the center of the room with a clear view of the holoimagers, sensor displays, and authenticators. Off to one side of him, Base Commander Cassel, dark-haired and sturdy, was leaning across the primary holoprojector table, above which twitched a grainy image of antique starfighters executing strafing runs across Rampart's gleaming surface, while the marshaling station's batteries responded with green pulses of laser energy. In a separate holovid even more corrupted than the first, insect-winged Geonosian laborers could be seen scrambling for cover in one of the station's starfighter hangars. A distorted voice was crackling through the command center's wall mounted speaker array.

"Our shields are already down to forty percent, Sentinel . . . jamming our transmiss . . . lost communication with the *Brentaal*. Request immediate . . . Sentinel. Again: request immediate reinforcement."

A skeptical frown formed on Tarkin's face. "A sneak attack? Impossible."

"Rampart reports that the attack ship transmitted a valid HoloNet code on entering the system," Cassel said. "Rampart, can you eavesdrop on the comm chatter of those starfighters?"

"Negative, Sentinel," the reply came a long moment later. "They're jamming our signals net."

Peering over his shoulder at Tarkin, Cassel made as if to cede his position, but Tarkin motioned for him to stay where he was. "Can the image be stabilized?" he asked the specialist at the holoprojector controls.

"Sorry, sir," the specialist said. "Increasing the gain only makes matters worse. The transmission appears to be corrupted at the far end. I haven't been able to establish if Rampart initiated countermeasures."

Tarkin glanced around the room. "And on our end?"

"The HoloNet relay station is best possible," the specialist at the comm board said.

"It is raining, sir," a different spec added, eliciting a chorus of good-natured laughter from others seated nearby. Even Tarkin grinned, though fleetingly.

"Who are we speaking with?" he asked Cassel.

"A Lieutenant Thon," the commander said. "He's been on station for only three months, but he's following protocol and transmitting on priority encryption."

Tarkin clasped his hands behind his back beneath the duster and glanced at the specialist seated at the authenticator. "Does the effectives roster contain an image of our Lieutenant Thon?"

"On screen, sir," the staffer said, flicking a joystick and indicating one of the displays.

Tarkin shifted his gaze. A sandy-haired human with protruding ears, Thon was as untried as he sounded. Fresh from one of the academies, Tarkin thought. He stepped down from the platform and moved to the holoprojector table to study the strafing starfighters more closely. Bars of corruption elevatored through the stuttering holovid. Rampart's shields were nullifying most of the aggressors' energy beams, but all too frequently a disabling run would succeed and white-hot explosions would erupt in one of the depot's deep-space docks.

"Those are Tikiars and Headhunters," Tarkin said in surprise.

"Modified," Cassel said. "Basic hyperdrives and upgraded weaponry."

Tarkin squinted at the holo. "The fuselages bear markings." He turned in the direction of the spec closest to the authenticator station. "Run the markings through the database. Let's see if we can't determine whom we're dealing with."

Tarkin turned back to Cassel. "Did they arrive on their own, or launch from the attack ship?"

"Delivered," the commander said.

Without turning around Tarkin said: "Has this Thon provided holovid or coordinates for the vessel that brought the starfighters?"

"Holovid, sir," someone said, "but we only got a quick look at it."

"Replay the transmission," Tarkin said.

A separate holotable projected a blurry, blue-tinted image of a fantailed capital ship with a spherical control module located amidships. The downsloping curved bow and smooth hull gave it the look of a deep-sea behemoth. Tarkin circled the table, appraising the hologram.

"What is this thing?"

"Begged and borrowed, sir," someone reported. "Separatist-era engineering more than anything else. The central sphere resembles one of the old Trade Federation droid control computers, and the entire forward portion might've come from a Commerce Guild destroyer. Front-facing sensor array tower. IFF's highlighting modules consistent with CIS *Providence*-, *Recusant*-, and *Munificent*-class warships."

"Pirates?" Cassel ventured. "Privateers?"

"Have they issued any demands?" Tarkin asked.

"Nothing yet." Cassel waited a beat. "Insurgents?"

"No data on the starfighter fuselage markings, sir," someone said.

Tarkin touched his jaw but said nothing. As he continued to circle the hologram, a flare of wavy corruption in the lower left portion captured his attention. "What was that?" he said, standing tall. "At the lower— There it is again." He counted quietly to himself; at the count of ten he fixed his gaze on the same area of the hologram. "And again!" He swung to the specialist. "Replay the recording at half speed."

Tarkin kept his eyes on the lower left quadrant as the holovid restarted and began a new count. "Now!" he said, in advance of every instance of corruption. "Now!"

Chairs throughout the room swiveled. "Encryption noise?" someone suggested.

"Ionization effect," another said.

Tarkin held up a hand to silence the speculations. "This isn't a guessing game, ladies and gentlemen."

"Interval corruption of some sort," Cassel said.

"Of some sort indeed." Tarkin watched silently as the prerecorded holovid recycled for a third time, then he moved to the communications station. "Instruct Lieutenant Thon to show himself," he said to the seated spec.

"Sir?"

"Tell him to train a cam on himself."

The spec relayed the command, and Thon's voice issued from the speakers. "Sentinel, I've never been asked to do that, but if that's what it's going to take to effect a rescue, then I'm happy to comply."

Everyone in the room turned to the holofeed, and moments later a 3-D image of Thon took shape above the table.

"Recognition is well within acceptable margins, sir," a spec said.

Tarkin nodded and leaned toward one of the microphones. "Stand by, Rampart. Reinforcements are forthcoming." He continued to study the live holovid, and had begun yet another count when the transmission abruptly de-resolved, just short of the moment it might have displayed further evidence of corruption.

"What happened?" Cassel asked.

"Working on it, sir," a spec said.

Repressing a knowing smile, Tarkin glanced over his right shoulder. "Have we tried to open a clear channel to Rampart?"

"We've been trying, sir," the comm specialist said, "but we haven't been able to penetrate the jamming."

Tarkin moved to the communications station. "What resources do we have upside?"

"Parking lot is nearly empty, sir." The comm specialist riveted her eyes on the board. "We have the *Salliche*, the *Fremond*, and the *Electrum*."

Tarkin considered his options. Sentinel's *Imperial*-class Star Destroyer, the *Core Envoy*, and most of the flotilla's other capital ships were escorting supply convoys to Geonosis. That left him with a frigate and a tug—both vacant just then, literally parked in stationary orbits—and the obvious choice, the *Electrum*, a *Venator*-class Star Destroyer on loan from a deep-dock at Ryloth.

"Contact Captain Burque," he said at last.

"Already on the comm, sir," the specialist said.

A quarter-scale image of the captain rose from the comm station's holoprojector. Burque was tall and gangly, with a clipped brown beard lining his strong jaw. "Governor Tarkin," he said, saluting.

"Are you up to speed on what is occurring at Rampart Station, Captain Burque?"

"We are, sir. The *Electrum* is prepared to jump to Rampart on your command."

Tarkin nodded. "Keep those hyperspace coordinates at the ready, Captain. But right now I want you to execute a microjump to the Rimward edge of this system. Do you understand?"

Burque frowned in confusion, but he said: "Understood, Governor."

"You're to hold there and await further orders."

"In plain sight, sir, or obscure?"

"I suspect that won't matter one way or another, Captain, but all the better if you can find something to hide behind."

"Excuse me for asking, sir, but are we expecting trouble?"

"Always, Captain," Tarkin said, without levity.

The hologram disappeared and the command center fell eerily silent, save for the sounds of the sensors and scanners and the tech's update that the *Electrum* was away. The silence deepened, until a pressing and prolonged warning tone from the threat-assessment station made everyone start. The specialist at the station thrust his head forward.

"Sir, sensors are registering anomalous readings and Cronau radiation in the red zone—"

"Wake rotation!" another spec cut in. "We've got a mark in from hyperspace, sir—and it's a big one. Nine hundred twenty meters long. Gunnage of twelve turbolaser cannons, ten point-defense ion cannons, six proton torpedo launchers. Reverting on the *near side* of the planet. Range is two hundred thousand klicks and closing." He blew out his breath. "Good thing you dispatched the *Electrum*, sir, or it'd be in pieces by now!"

A specialist seated at an adjacent duty station weighed in. "Firing solution programs are being sent to downside defenses."

"IFF is profiling it as the same carrier that attacked Rampart." The spec glanced at Tarkin. "Could it have jumped, sir?"

"If the ship was even there," Tarkin said, mostly to himself.

"Sir?"

Tarkin shrugged out of the duster, letting it fall to

the floor, and stepped down to the holoprojector. "Let's have a look at it."

If the ship in the orbital-feed holovid was not the same one that had ostensibly attacked Rampart, it had to be her twin.

"Sir, we've got multiple marks launching from the carrier—" The spec interrupted himself to make certain he was interpreting the readings correctly. "Sir, they're *droid* fighters! Tri-fighters, vultures, the whole Sep menagerie."

"Interesting," Tarkin said in a calm voice. One hand to his chin, he continued to assess the hologram. "Commander Cassel, sound general quarters and boost power to the base shields. Signals: Initiate countermeasures."

"Sir, is this an unannounced readiness test?" someone asked.

"More like a bunch of Separatists who didn't get the message they lost the war," another said.

Perhaps that was the explanation, Tarkin thought. Imperial forces had destroyed or appropriated most of the capital ships produced for and by the Confederacy of Independent Systems. Droid fighters hadn't been seen in years. But it was even longer since Tarkin had witnessed HoloNet subterfuge of the caliber someone had aimed at Sentinel Base.

He swung away from the table. "Scan the carrier for life-forms on the off chance we're dealing with a sentient adversary rather than a droid-control computer." He eyed the comm specialist. "Any separate channel response from Rampart?"

She shook her head. "Still no word, sir."

"Carrier shows thirty life-forms, sir," someone at the far end of the room said. "It's astrogating by command, not on full auto."

From the threat station came another voice: "Sir, droid fighters are nearing the edge of the envelope."

And a thin envelope it was, Tarkin thought.

"Alert our artillery crews to ignore the firing solution programs and to fire at will." He pivoted to the holotable. A glance revealed Sentinel Base to be in the same situation Rampart appeared to have been in only moments earlier, except that the enemy ships and the holofeed were *genuine*.

"Contact Captain Burque and tell him to come home."

"Tri-fighters are breaking formation and commencing attack runs."

The sounds of distant explosions and the thundering replies of ground-based artillery infiltrated the command center. The room shook. Motes of dust drifted down from the overhead pipes and cables; the illumination flickered. Tarkin monitored the ground-feed holovids. The droid fighters were highly maneuverable but no match for Sentinel's powerful guns. The moon's storm-racked sky grew backlit with strobing flashes and globular detonations, as one after another of the ridge-backed tri-fighters and reconfigurable vultures was vaporized. A few managed to make it to the outer edge of the base's hemispherical defensive shield, only to be annihilated there and hit the coarse ground in flames.

"They're beginning to turn tail," a tech said. "Laser cannons are chasing them back up the well."

"And the capital ship?" Tarkin said.

"The carrier is steering clear and accelerating. Range is now three hundred thousand klicks and expanding. All weapons are mute."

"Sir, the *Electrum* has reverted to realspace."

Tarkin grinned faintly. "Inform Captain Burque that

his TIE pilots are going to enjoy a target-rich environment."

"Captain Burque on the comm."

Tarkin moved to the comm station, where Burque's holopresence hovered above the projector.

"I trust that this is the trouble you were expecting, Governor."

"Actually, Captain, most of this is quite unexpected. Therefore, I hope you'll do your best to incapacitate the carrier rather than destroy it. No doubt we can glean something by interrogating the crew."

"I'll be as gentle with it as I can, Governor."

Tarkin glanced at the holotable in time to see squadrons of newly minted ball-cockpit TIE fighters launch from the dorsal bay of the arrowhead-shaped Star Destroyer.

"Sir, I have Rampart Station Commander Jae on the comm, voice-only."

Tarkin gestured for Jae to be put through.

"Governor Tarkin, to what do I owe the honor?" Jae said.

Tarkin positioned himself close to one of the command center's audio pickups. "How is everything at your depot, Lin?"

"Better now," Jae said. "Our HoloNet relay was down for a short period, but it's back online. I've sent a tech team to determine what went wrong. You have my word, Governor: The glitch won't affect the supply shipment schedule—"

"I doubt that your technicians will discover any evidence of malfunction," Tarkin said.

Instead of speaking to it, Jae said: "And on your moon, Governor?"

"As a matter of fact, we find ourselves under attack."

"What?" Jae asked in patent surprise.

"I'll explain in due course, Lin. Just now we have our hands full."

His back turned to the holoprojector table, Tarkin missed the event that drew loud groans from many of the staffers. When he turned, the warship was gone.

"Jumped to lightspeed before the *Electrum* could get off a disabling shot," Cassel said.

Disappointment pulled down the corners of Tarkin's mouth. With the capital ship gone, the remaining droid fighters could be seen spinning out of control— even easier prey for the vertical-winged TIE fighters. A scattering of spherical explosions flared at the edge of space.

"Gather debris of any value," Tarkin said to Burque, "and have it transported down the well for analysis. Snare a few of the intact droids, as well. But take care. While they appear to be lifeless, they may be rigged to self-destruct."

Burque acknowledged the command, and the holo vanished.

Tarkin looked at Cassel. "Secure from battle stations and sound the all-clear. I want a forensic team assembled to examine the droids. I doubt we'll learn much, but we may be able to ascertain the carrier's point of origin." He grew pensive for a moment, then added: "Prepare an after-action report for Coruscant and transmit it to my quarters so I can append my notes."

"Will do," Cassel said.

A specialist handed Tarkin his duster, and he had started for the door when a voice rang out behind him.

"Sir, a question if you will?"

Tarkin stopped and turned around. "Ask it."

"How did you know, sir?"

"How did I know what, Corporal?"

The young, brown-haired specialist gnawed at her lower lip before continuing. "That the holotransmission from Rampart Station was counterfeit, sir."

Tarkin looked her up and down. "Perhaps you'd care to proffer an explanation of your own."

"In the replay—the bar of interval noise you noticed. Somehow that told you that someone had managed to introduce a false real-time feed into the local HoloNet relay."

Tarkin smiled faintly. "Train yourself to recognize it—all of you. Deception may be the least of what our unknown adversaries have in store."

COLD CASE

IN SENTINEL'S MAINTENANCE HANGAR, Tarkin paced the length of a high, blastproof partition. The storm had blown through and the base had resumed normal operations, but many of the soldiers and specialists were still parsing the fact that Sentinel had come under attack. For the youngest among them, recruits or volunteers, it was the first action they had ever seen.

On the far side of a series of massive transparisteel panels set into the partition, several hazmat-suited forensic technicians were examining wreckage from the battle and running tests on three droid starfighters grasped in cradles suspended from tall gantries. Elsewhere in the hangar loadlifters and other droids were sorting through piles of debris. The tang of lubricants and flame-scorched metals hung in the air, and the noise level created by the labor droids was grating. As Tarkin had warned, many of the vulture droids had transformed into bombs on losing contact with the warship's central control computer. Regardless, Captain Burque's salvage teams had managed to recover a droid whose auto-destruct mechanism had been damaged during combat.

Hung in walking configuration with its blaster cannon lateral wings split, the three-and-a-half-meter-long vulture looked less like its namesake scavenger than it did a long-legged alloy quadruped with an equine head. With the central nacelle open and the computer brain exposed and studded with instruments, the droid might have been undergoing torture rather than autopsy. The other two dangling captives—three-armed fighters that mirrored the appearance of the species that had designed them—were similarly exposed and quilled with probes.

Tarkin had lost count of how many back-and-forth meanders he had completed, and was standing opposite the vulture droid when a decontamination lock in the partition opened and a tech emerged, removing the hood of his anti-rad suit and wiping sweat from his face and balding pate with a bare hand.

Tarkin spun around to meet him halfway. "What have you learned?"

"Not as much as we'd hoped to, sir," the tech said. "Analysis of data received by the command center's friend-or-foe indicator confirms that the capital ship is a downsized version of a Separatist *Providence*-class cruiser-carrier, modified with modules taken from CIS frigates and destroyers. Ships of the sort made a name for themselves during the war by jamming signals and destroying HoloNet relays. Parts of the ship's sensor array tower, which the Seps usually mounted aft rather than forward, appear to have come from the cruiser *Lucid Voice*, which saw action at Quell, Ryloth, and in a couple of other contested systems."

Tarkin frowned. "How did the appropriation teams manage to miss confiscating that ship?"

"They didn't, sir. Records show that the *Lucid Voice* was dismantled at the Bilbringi shipyards four years ago."

Tarkin considered that. "In other words, some components of that vessel went missing."

"Lost, stolen, sold, it's impossible to say. Other sections of the warship appear to have come from the *Invincible*."

Tarkin didn't bother to mask his surprise. "That was Separatist Admiral Trench's ship—destroyed during the Battle of Christophsis."

"Partially destroyed, in any case. The ship was modular in design, and the modules that survived must have been worth salvaging and putting on the open market. Parts dealers in the Outer Rim are desperate for supplies, so the modules may have ended up in the Tion Cluster or the like." The tech removed his other elbow-length glove and wiped his face again. "The Idellian scanner isolated thirty life-forms— a crew of humans and near-humans—which is in keeping with the practice of placing sentients in command of most *Providence*-class ships. But for a ship of that size and armament, thirty sentients is virtually your definition of a skeleton crew. Sometimes the Seps substituted OOM pilot battle droids, and I'm guessing our skittish warship had some of those as well, because whoever cobbled the thing together retrofitted it with a rudimentary droid-control computer— possibly a redundant comp of the sort you used to find on first-generation Trade Federation Lucre-hulks."

"*Whoever*, as you say."

"*Lucid Voice* was built by the Quarren Free Dac Volunteers Engineering Corps—much to the displeasure of the Mon Cals who share their planet with the Quarren. We're checking to see if QFD or their erstwhile partners, Pammant Docks, might have supervised the reassembly. TradeFed and Separatist technology has been showing up lately in the Corporate Sector, so we're also looking into the possibility that the ship was built there. The Headhunter starfighters seen in the holovid could have come from anywhere. Tikiars are produced in the Senex, but it's not uncommon to encounter them in this sector of the Rim."

Tarkin nodded and motioned toward the hangar. "The droids?"

The specialist turned to face the viewports. "Relatively few modifications to the vulture. Same fuel slug propulsion, same weapons system. Alphanumeric identification indicates that this one belonged to a Confederacy battle group known as The Grievous Legion."

"And also managed to find its way onto the black market . . ."

"So it appears, sir."

Tarkin moved farther down the partition. "And the tri-fighters?"

"Unremarkable. But we've no evidence regarding their origin. Not yet anyway."

Tarkin forced an exhalation through his nose. "Were you able to retrieve data regarding the warship's point of origin?"

The specialist shook his head. "Negative, sir. The memory modules of the droids don't log jump information."

"All right," Tarkin said after a moment. "Continue with the analysis. I want every weld and rivet investigated."

"We're on top of it, sir." The tech pulled the hood back over his head, slipped his hands into the long gloves, and disappeared through the lock.

Tarkin watched him enter the hangar, then resumed pacing, replaying the attack in his mind.

Harassment of Imperial installations by pirates and malcontents was nothing new, but in almost all cases the assaults had been hit-and-run sorties, and none had taken place so close to heavily defended Geonosis. The counterfeit real-time holotransmission had been designed to draw ships from Sentinel to Rampart Station, in the hope of leaving the former vulnerable. But the attack was clearly calculated to be suicidal from its inception. Even if he had dispatched the *Electrum* to the marshaling station—even if he had been taken in by the distress call and dispatched half his flotilla—the energy shields and laser cannons that protected Sentinel would have been sufficient to ward off any strikes, let alone from droids. The warship seen in the holovid the attackers had transmitted through the local HoloNet relay had shown up at Sentinel, but where were the modified starfighters, which had to have been flown by living pilots? Despite being crewed by sentients, the mysterious cruiser hadn't discharged any of its point-defense or ranged weapons. If destruction of the base was the goal, why hadn't whoever was behind the attack used the ship as a bomb by reverting from hyperspace in closer proximity to the moon? Planetary bodies larger than Sentinel had been shaken to their core by such events.

Equally worrisome was the question of how the counterfeiters had known about Lieutenant Thon, whose recent posting to Rampart should have been top secret. The creators of the false holovid had been able to improvise by transmitting a real-time hologram of the young officer in response to Tarkin's order that he show himself. Was Thon involved in the conspiracy, or had the attackers merely doctored existing footage of him, lifted perhaps from the public HoloNet or some other source?

As troubling as it was to accept that the locations of

Sentinel and Rampart bases had been compromised, he still couldn't make sense of the attack itself. What would pirates or privateers stand to gain by launching an ill-fated drone attack? What, for that matter, would political dissidents stand to gain?

Was it a case of vengeance?

One group fit the bill: the Droid Gotra, a lethal band of repurposed battle droids with what some considered legitimate grievances against the Empire for having been abandoned after their service during the Clone Wars. But recent intelligence reports stated that the Droid Gotra was still confined to an industrial complex in the bowels of Coruscant, serving as muscle for the Crymorah crime syndicate in robberies, protection, kidnapping, illegal salvage, and extortion. It was possible that the Gotra was branching out—it was even possible that the group had learned about Sentinel Base—but it was unlikely that the droids would make use of obsolete weapons to send a message to the Empire.

Tarkin shook his head in aggravation. In part, the deep-space mobile battle station was meant to put an end to harassments of any sort, whether driven by greed, political dissent, or revenge for acts committed during the Clone Wars or since. Once everyone in the galaxy grasped the weapon's capabilities, once the fear of Imperial reprisal took hold, discontent would cease to be a problem. But just now—and notwithstanding the covert nature of the Geonosis project—the Imperial Security Bureau and Naval Intelligence were continually trying to quash rumors and prevent information leaks. In the three years Tarkin had been commanding Sentinel and hundreds of nearby supply and sentry outposts, as well as administering a vast slice of the Outer Rim, no group had been successful in penetrating Geonosis space.

The chance that that could change shook *him* to the core.

If establishing the identity of Sentinel's enemies was already proving daunting, getting to the truth of the battle station's origin was nearly impossible. Everyone from celebrated ship designers to gifted engineers wanted to take credit for the superweapon. Tarkin himself had discussed the need for such a weapon with the Emperor long before the end of the Clone Wars. But no one outside the Emperor knew the full history of the moonlet-sized project. Some claimed that it had begun as a Separatist weapon designed by Geonosian Archduke Poggle the Lesser's hive colony for Count Dooku and the Confederacy of Independent Systems. But if that was the case, the plans had to have somehow fallen into Republic hands *before* the Clone Wars ended, because the weapon's spherical shell and laser-focusing dish were already in the works by the time Tarkin first set eyes on it following his promotion to the rank of Moff—escorted to Geonosis in utmost secrecy by the Emperor himself.

All the same, he had no compelling reason to solve the enigma of the battle station's beginnings. What bothered him was that, compliant with a strategy that no base commander—Moff, admiral, or general— should have unrestricted access to information regarding shipments, scheduling, or construction progress, no single person was in charge of the project, unless of course the Emperor was considered to be that person. But the Emperor's visits had been few and far between, and it was anyone's guess just how much information was getting past the Imperial Ruling Council the Moffs and others answered to and actually reaching the Emperor's ear. Certainly he was being briefed, but briefings were no longer enough. The project had reached a point where it had to rely on countless suppliers; and though each was being kept in the dark regarding the final destination of their contributions, millions of beings, perhaps tens of millions of beings galaxywide, were now involved with the battle station in one capacity or another. Yes, the project required the on-site presence of a think tank of scientists, weapons specialists, and habitat architects, but what did any of them know about *protecting* the station from saboteurs?

If Tarkin had his way, and at this point it was uncertain he ever would, he would adopt the hegemonic arrangement that was in place on Coruscant and elsewhere, and appoint an overseer to coordinate all construction and defense considerations. A single overseer to whom others would answer—or be damned if they didn't.

If whoever was responsible for the dubious attack on Sentinel was simply hoping to get his attention, then that part of the plan had succeeded, for in the end he was left with more questions than answers.

His restless pacing subsided as his adjutant hurried into the maintenance hangar's safe area.

"A communiqué from Coruscant, sir."

Tarkin assumed that it was Military Intelligence, responding to the after-action report he had filed, and said as much.

"No, sir. Higher up the chain of command."

Tarkin arched an eyebrow. "How high?"

"Nosebleed altitude, sir."

Tarkin stiffened slightly. "Then I'll take the transmission in my quarters."

Where Tarkin's own uniformed holopresence had stood two days earlier, the holotable now projected a towering apparition of Vizier Mas Amedda, swathed in rich maroon robes, the cyan tint of the holofield darkening the Chagrian's natural blue pigmentation. From bulging extrusions of flesh on either side of Amedda's thick neck dangled tapered horns that matched the pair crowning his hairless cranium.

"We trust all is well at Sentinel Base, Governor."

Tarkin couldn't be certain if or how much Amedda knew about the recent attack. On Coruscant information was closely guarded, if only as a means of maintaining one's cachet, and even the head of the Ruling Council might not have been made privy to details known to Military Intelligence and the Admiralty.

"Rest assured, Vizier," Tarkin said.

"No surprises, then?"

"Only the expected ones."

The ambitious amphibian vouchsafed a tight-lipped smile at his end of the duplex holocomm. Obstructive and fault finding during his years as vice chancellor of the Republic Senate, he had become one of the Emperor's most valued advisers, as well as the Empire's most formidable intermediary.

"Governor, your presence is required on Coruscant," Amedda said after a moment.

Tarkin moved to his desk and sat down, centering himself for the holocam. "I'll certainly try to make time for a visit, Vizier."

"Permit me, Governor, but that will not suffice. Perhaps I should have said that your presence is *urgently* required."

Tarkin waved a hand in dismissal. "I'm sorry, Vizier, but that doesn't alter the fact that I have my priorities."

"Priorities of what sort?"

Tarkin returned Amedda's mirthless smile. There was probably no harm in sharing with Amedda information about the expected shipments of matériel from Desolation Station to Geonosis—including vital components for the battle station's complex hyperdrive generator—but he was under no obligation to do so.

"I'm afraid my priorities are on a need-to-know basis."

"Indeed. Then you are refusing the request?"

Tarkin glimpsed something in the thick-skulled Chagrian's pink-rimmed cerulean eyes that gave him pause. "Let's say that I'm reluctant to abandon my post at this time, Vizier. If you wish, I'll provide the Emperor with my reasons personally."

"That's not possible, Governor. The Emperor is presently engaged."

Tarkin leaned toward the cam. "So engaged that he can't speak briefly with one of his Moffs?"

Amedda affected a bored tone. "That's not for me to say, Governor. The Emperor's concerns are on a need-to-know basis."

Tarkin stared into the hologram. What his granduncle Jova wouldn't have given to be able to mount a Chagrian head on the wall of his cabin in the Carrion.

"Perhaps you're willing to clarify the need for such urgency?" he asked.

Amedda tilted his massive head to one side. "That's a matter for you to discuss with the Emperor, since it was he who issued the order that you report to Coruscant."

Tarkin concealed a grimace. "You might have said as much at the start, Vizier."

Amedda adopted a haughty look. "And deprive us of such verbal sport? Next time, perhaps."

Tarkin remained at his desk after Amedda ended the transmission and the hologram vanished. Then he signaled for the protocol droid.

"I'm going to need that uniform as soon as possible," he told the RA-7 as it entered.

The droid nodded. "Certainly, sir. I'll instruct the fabricator to begin at once."

Tarkin summoned the uniformed 3-D image of himself from the holotable and regarded it, thinking back to Eriadu and recalling Jova's comment once more.

"It'll look even better with blood on it."

4

A BOY'S LIFE

CYNOSURE OF THE Greater Seswenna sector of the Outer Rim, Eriadu could trace its history to the earliest era of the Republic. At that time, the galaxy's dark age had ended, the Sith had been defeated and driven into hiding, and a true republic had emerged from the ashes. With a member of House Valorum presiding as Supreme Chancellor, a pan-galactic Senate had been created, and the military had been disbanded. Revitalized, the populations of the Core Worlds, ravenous for new resources and not above exploiting every opportunity to enhance the quality of their lives, were eager to expand their reach.

The planet was transformed from just another Outer Rim wilderness to a civilized world worth considering for inclusion in the Republic by adventurous pioneers who had been granted permission by Coruscant to procure and settle new territories, either by cutting deals with indigenous populations or simply by overrunning them, and finally to establish trading colonies capable of furnishing the Core with much-needed resources. It was a scenario played out in many remote regions, and in Eriadu's case the resource happened to be lommite ore—essential to the production of transparisteel—rich deposits of which had been discovered on worlds throughout the Greater Seswenna. Lacking funds to mine, process, and ship the crude, Eriadu's settlers had been forced to secure high-interest loans from the InterGalactic Banking Clan, but in an era when hyperspace travel between the Seswenna and the Core required astrogating by hyperwave beacons—with numerous reversions to realspace necessary to ensure safe passage—shipments of ore were frequently delayed or lost due to one catastrophe or another. As debts mounted, Eriadu risked becoming a client world of Muun bankers until entrepreneurs from the Core world Corulag had intervened, rescuing the planet from servitude. It was likewise through Corulag's influence with the Republic Senate that the fledgling Hydian Way had been routed through Eriadu space and the planet placed on the galactic map.

Corulag's motives, however, were not altogether altruistic; the Core entrepreneurs forced Eriadu to increase the lommite supply and had demanded the bulk of the mining profits. Amplified operations led to rampant growth and an influx of impoverished workers from neighboring worlds. Eriadu's once lush mountains were soon stripped of cover, a pall of pollution hung over the major cities, and the standard of living plummeted. Still, there was prosperity for a few; quick credits to be made in ore processing, local and deep-space transport, and usury.

For the Tarkins, wealth came by providing security. Their climb to the top had been hard won. Among Eriadu's earliest pioneers, the ancestral Tarkins had had to function as their own police force and defend-

ers, countering attacks first by the ferocious predators
that thrived in Eriadu's forests and mountains, then
by offworld rogues and scoundrels who preyed on
the exposed populations of the struggling settlements. Under Tarkin leadership local militias evolved
slowly into a sector military. As a result, and despite
his celebrated ancestors having had their start as
hunters, freelance pilots, and mining contractors, Tarkin thought of himself as the product of a military
upbringing, in which discipline, respect, and obedience were held in the highest regard. Avowed tech-
nocrats as well, the family held a view that it was
technology—more than Corulag—that had rescued
Eriadu from savagery and had allowed Eriaduans to
forge a civilization from a murderous wasteland.
Technology in the form of colossal machines, swift
starships, and potent weapons had helped convert the
hunted into the hunters, and it would be technology
that would one day usher the planet into the elite
of the modern galaxy.

While Tarkin had been raised with all the advan-
tages that came with wealth, it was a curious kind of
privilege. In mansions that strived to emulate the architectural fashions of the Core but were little more
than gaudy imitations of the originals, the Tarkins
and others like them did their best to mimic the customs of the affluent, without ever succeeding. Their
hardscrabble roots were far too apparent, and life on
Eriadu seemed barbaric compared with life on cos-
mopolitan Coruscant. Tarkin understood this at an
early age, particularly when dignitaries from the Core
visited and made his parents feel smaller than he knew
them to be; less evolved for living on a wild world
whose outlands were racked by seismic quakes, whose
rough cities lacked weather control and opera houses,
and whose residents were still battling pirates and ra-

pacious nature for supremacy. And yet he felt no need to search outside his own family for childhood heroes, since it was his ancestors who had fought back the wilderness, survived the odds, and brought order and progress to the Seswenna.

Even in relaxed and safe surroundings, then, Tarkin was not the entitled child one might have imagined judging by his tailored clothes or rambling home. As proud as his parents were of their achievements, they were also well aware of their low social standing among people who mattered. They never missed an opportunity to remind their son that life was inequitable, and that only those with an appetite for personal glory could succeed. One needed to be willing to crush underfoot anything or anyone. Discipline and order were the keys, and law was the only unanswerable response to chaos.

At every opportunity Tarkin's parents would emphasize what it meant to live in deprivation. Their sermons were designed to drill into their son the fact that everything they owned was the product of having overcome adversity. Worse, affluence could vanish in an instant; without constant vigilance and the drive to succeed, everything one had could be wrested away by someone stronger, more disciplined, more committed to personal glory.

"How do you imagine we came to the point where we have so much," his father might say over dinner, "while so many outside the gates of this elegant home have to struggle to survive? Or do you imagine that we have always resided in such luxury, that Eriadu was accommodating from the start?"

Early on, young Wilhuff would only stare down at his plate of food in silence or mutter that he had no answers to his father's questions. Then, during one supper, his father—tall and straight-backed, with deep forehead creases that curved down past his eyes like parentheses—ordered the family's servant to remove Wilhuff's meal before he'd had a chance to take so much as a bite from it.

"You see how easy it is to go from having everything to having nothing?" his father asked.

"How would you fare if we now banished you to the city streets?" his mother added. Nearly as tall as her husband, she dressed in expensive clothes for every meal and affected elaborate hairstyles that were sometimes hours in the making. "Would you do what you needed to do to survive? Could you bring yourself to wield a club, a knife, a blaster, if weapons were what it took to keep you from starving?"

In an effort to calculate the expected response, Wilhuff glanced between the two of them and puffed out his chest. "I would do whatever I had to do."

His father only grinned in disdain. "A brave one, are you? Well, you'll have that bravery put to the test when you're taken to the Carrion."

The Carrion.

There it was again: that strange word he had heard so often growing up. But just then he asked: "What is the Carrion?"

His father seemed pleased that his son had finally wondered aloud. "A place that teaches you the meaning of survival."

In the quiet comfort of the family dining room, rich with the heady odors of exotic spices and long-simmered meats, the statement had no meaning. "Will I be afraid?" he said, again because he sensed he was meant to ask.

"If you know what's good for you."

"Could I die there?" he said, almost in self-amusement.

"In ways too numerous to count."

"Would you miss me if I did die?" he asked them both.

His mother was the first to say, "Of course we would."

"Then why do I have to go there? Have I done something wrong?"

His father placed his elbows on the table and leaned toward him. "We need to know if you are simply ordinary or larger than life."

To the best of his ability, he mulled over the notion of being *larger than life*. "Did you have to go there when you were young?"

His father nodded.

"Were you afraid?"

His father sat back into his tall, brocaded armchair, as if in recall. "In the beginning I was. Until I learned to overcome fear."

"Will I have to kill anything?"

"If you wish to survive."

With some excitement, Wilhuff said: "Will I get to use a blaster?"

His father shook his head in a grave manner. "Not always. And not when you'll need one most."

Wilhuff grappled with imagining the place, this Carrion. "Does everyone have to go there?"

"Only certain Tarkin males," his mother said.

"So Nomma never had to go?" he asked, referring to their diminutive, heavily jowled near-human servant.

"No, he didn't."

"Why not? Are Tarkins different from Nomma's family?"

"Who serves whom?" his father responded with force. "Have you ever placed a meal in front of Nomma?"

"I would."

His mother's expression hardened. "Not in this house."

"What you learn on the Carrion will one day allow you to show Nomma how to be content with his station," his father went on.

Wilhuff struggled with the word *station*. "To be happy about serving us, you mean."

"Among other things, yes."

Still on unsure ground, Wilhuff fell silent for an even longer moment. "Will you be taking me there— to the Carrion?" he asked finally.

His father narrowed his eyes when he smiled. "Not me. Someone else will come for you when the time is right."

A more delicate, impressionable child might have lived in fear of that day, but to Wilhuff the threat of sudden change, the abrupt undermining of his effortless life, and the need to forge his own future eventually became a promise: a parable, an adventure on which he yearned to embark, made real in his imagination long before it actually came to be.

The day arrived shortly after his eleventh birthday; Wilhuff was, by then, a shipshape kid burning with desire for bigger things, already something of a dreamer, an actor, an exaggerator. He was seated with his parents for the evening meal. The litany of harsh reminders was about to commence when three men looking as if they had just crawled out from beneath a mine collapse barged through the front door and into the dining room. Tracking mud across the polished stone floors, they began to stuff the pockets of their ragged longcoats with food snatched from the dinner table. When Wilhuff looked to his suddenly silent parents, his mother only said, "They've come for you."

But if his parents and the three intruders thought

they had taken him by surprise, he had one of his own in store for them. "First I need to get my gear," he said, hurrying up the curving stairway as expressions of puzzlement began to form on the faces of the uninvited guests.

The looks were still in place when he returned a moment later, dressed in cargo pants and a multipocketed vest he had stitched together in secret over many weeks. Dangling from his neck was a pair of macrobinoculars that had been a birthday gift. His gear, his outfit, his uniform for when it would be needed.

Scanning Tarkin from head to toe, the tallest and grimiest of the three launched a short laugh that shook the anteroom chandelier. Then he stepped forward to take the boy by shoulders that would remain bony and narrow throughout his life, shaking him as he said: "That's a beauty, it is. A uniform fit for a future hero. And you know what? It'll look even better with blood on it."

His father stepped forward to say: "Wilhuff, meet my father's brother, your grand-uncle Jova."

Jova grinned down at him, showing even teeth, whiter than Wilhuff would have expected considering his uncle's dirt-streaked face.

"Time to go," Jova announced.

So: whisked from his home without a reassuring embrace from either parent, the two of them standing instead in each other's arms, expressions of sad resolve on their faces. This was something he needed to experience. And through the gate into Eriadu's pitch-black pall, safe for the moment within the uniform, exhilaration stifling the hunger he was already feeling. Whisked not only from the manicured grounds but also from the city itself in an aged airspeeder, on a shaky flight across the finger-shaped bay and up

into the hills beyond to follow the meandering Orrineswa River to a region he had never known to exist
on his homeworld, one that seemed more the stuff of
holodramas and escapist literature: an untamed expanse of flat-topped mesas separated by surging
boulder-strewn rivers, and in the far distance volcanic
mountains that were perhaps still active. Even more
shocking was Jova's explanation that while vast areas
of Eriadu were much like this one, everything the
boy's wide blue eyes could take in from horizon
to horizon was family land—Tarkin land, procured
twenty generations earlier and never allowed to fall
into the hands of developers, miners, or anyone with
designs on the region. A protected place and more: a
natural monument, a reminder of what the planet
could devolve into should sentient beings lose their
grip and surrender their superiority to nature, to savagery. For young Wilhuff, a place of initiation; and
central to it all, the Carrion Plateau.

A rickety speeder listing to one side because of a
faulty repulsorlift carried them up onto the tabletop
summit: Wilhuff, Jova, two other headclothed elders,
and a pair of elderly Rodians who worked as guides,
caretakers, trackers, all six of them perched atop the
ailing machine and Wilhuff's five keepers carrying
long-barreled slugthrowers. His hunger partially staved
by dried meat almost too tough to swallow, Wilhuff
was beginning to have serious misgivings, though he
refused to let them be known. This was a much darker
and more dangerous place than the one his imagination had conjured. Fixed on masking his unease and
on seeing an actual animal in the wild, he sat with
the macrobinoculars glued to his eyes as the speeder
navigated immense stretches of grassland and forest,
passing thick-boled ten-thousand-year-old trees with
skinny, near-leafless limbs; monolithic ruins and cliff-

side petroglyphs ten times older; and shallow seasonal lakes dotted with flamboyant birds.

At length that first twilight he spotted something: a stately quadruped two meters tall, striped in black and white and crowned with graceful, curving horns. *My first animal in the wild.* The others spied it, as well, without the aid of magnifying lenses, and Jova brought the speeder to a jarring halt. But not, as it happened, to gaze on the beauty of the beast. In unison, the antique rifles came up and half a dozen shots rang out. Through the glasses, Wilhuff watched the majestic creature leap up, then fall heavily onto its side. And a moment later they were all hurrying through the sharp grass in an effort to reach their kill before other predators or scavengers could arrive—and also to get to it while it was still warm.

Wilhuff asked himself what the creature had done to deserve such a fate. If it, too, had come to the Carrion to learn the meaning of survival, it had failed miserably.

The Rodians rolled the animal onto its back, and from a sheath strapped to his thigh Jova drew a well-used vibroblade.

"Cut straight up from between the legs to the throat," he said, handing Wilhuff the knife. "And take care not to make a mess of the innards."

Fortifying himself—worried as much about fainting as about disappointing his elders—Wilhuff plunged the point of the weapon through the creature's fur and flesh and tasked the vibroblade to cut. Hot maroon blood spurted, striking him full in the face. The Rodians seemed almost gleeful as it dripped from the tip of his nose to his chin and down the front of his pristine vest, saturating the seams and pockets he had stitched with such care.

"Good cut," Jova said when the carcass had parted,

the smell of the beast's entrails nearly overwhelming Wilhuff. "Now, you reach deep in there"—he indicated a place in the torso—"and follow the rear curve of the breathing muscle until your hands find the liver. Then you pull it out. Go on: Do it. Do it, I said!"

In went his hesitant, shaking hands, maneuvering through squishy bulbous organs until they found a heavy lump rich with blood. He had to yank several times before the liver broke free of its fibrous net of blood vessels and ligaments, and he nearly fell backward when it did. Then Jova took the slippery, uncooperative thing into his callused hands and began tearing chunks from it.

"This one's for you," his uncle said, placing the largest of the pieces in the palm of Wilhuff's already bloodied hand. He motioned with his chin: "Go ahead now. Down it goes."

Once more Wilhuff focused on living up to expectations, and when he had gotten past his revulsion and devoured the chunk, his uncles and the Rodians celebrated his act with a short song in a language Wilhuff didn't understand; celebrated Wilhuff's first step, the opening stage in an initiation that wouldn't conclude until years later at the Carrion Spike.

While Eriadu didn't have indigenous creatures as large as the rancor or as unusual as the sarlacc, it did boast ferocious felines, carnivorous crustaceans, and a species of veermok far more fierce and cunning than others in its primate family. For the next month Wilhuff did little more than follow in the tracks of his elders, observing predators of many varieties killing and devouring one another, and learning how to keep himself from being similarly devoured. There was no denying that witnessing death up close was a far more

visceral experience than watching such events tran-
spire in holodramas viewed in the airy tranquillity
of his bedroom. Still, he struggled to understand just
what he was supposed to be taking away from the
close encounters. Could daily brushes with death
transform a simply ordinary person into one who was
larger than life? Even if that was possible, how could
that transformation have an impact on the lives of
Nomma and others like him? He might have been
able to puzzle out the answers were he less preoccu-
pied day to day with being set upon and eaten by the
beasts they stalked.

Gradually the routine changed from merely observing kills to *stealing* them. Frequently the Rodians
would use their vibro-lances to drive killer beasts
back from their quarries and hold them at bay while
Wilhuff rushed in to complete the theft. Other times
it would be Wilhuff's turn to wield a vibro-lance, and
someone else who would make the grab.

"We're teaching them how to behave in the presence of their betters," Jova said. "The ones who learn,
profit from the laws we lay down; the rest die." He
wanted to make certain Wilhuff understood. "Never
try to live decently, boy—not unless you're willing to
open your life to tragedy and sadness. Live like a
beast, and no event, no matter how harrowing, will
ever be able to move you."

When his uncle decided that Wilhuff had experienced enough stealing, it came time to do the actual
hunting. And so Jova and the others began to teach
him tactical methods for taking advantage of the
wind or the angle of the light. They taught him how
to defend against attacks by groups of beasts by confounding them with unexpected moves. They taught
him to kill by concentrating all his power on one
point. All the while the vest became more bloodied

and tattered, until ultimately it was useless except as a rag, and he was on his own, without a uniform or costume to hide within.

The routine of tracking, hunting, killing, and cooking over fire continued as the land surrendered the last of its moisture to the blinding sky. His feet turned raw and his sunburned skin blistered, his mind given over to memorizing the names of the Carrion's every tree, animal, and insect—all of them serving one purpose or another. Late one evening the speeder's powerful forward lamps illuminated a rodent as it leapt from the saw grass, and with a carefully aimed collision Jova sent it flying. Wilhuff was instructed to use his vibroblade to excise a scent gland buried where the animal's thin, hairless tail met its plump body. From that gland the Rodians prepared a musky gel that they then used in their hunts for more of the same rodents. Similarly, they prepared stimulant concoctions from residue drained from the stomach of long-necked ruminants or the droppings of felines that had ingested certain plants. Wilhuff grew accustomed to eating every part of an animal and to drinking blood on its own or mixed with mind-altering plants gathered during treks across the plateau.

Over time he became so inured to the sight, smell, and taste of blood that even his dreams ran red with it. He kept waiting for the adventure to conclude at some log-walled shelter stocked with prepared food and soft beds, but the days grew only more harrowing, and at night half-starved scavengers would circle and howl at the edge of a meager cook fire, their eyes glowing furiously in the dark, waiting for a chance to rush in and steal back what food they could.

The tight-knit band of humans and Rodians didn't always succeed at remaining at the top of the food chain. Jova's cousin Zellit was killed during a night-time raid by a gang of reptiles whose saliva contained a powerful poison. By midseason Wilhuff knew real hunger for the first time, and came close to dying of an illness that caused him to shake so violently he thought his bones would break.

Sometimes even the smallest of the plateau's creatures would catch them unprepared and get the better of them. One night, when they had been too exhausted to set up a perimeter of motion detectors, he dreamed that something was feasting on his lower lip, and what his numb fingers found there was a venomous septoid, its pincers anchored in his soft flesh. Waking with a start, he hurried through the open flap of the self-deploying tent only to land in a stream of the segmented critters, which were all over him in a moment, hungry to find purchase wherever they could. By then his pained cries had woken the others, who themselves became targets, and shortly all of them were all hopping around in the dark, yanking septoids from themselves or plucking them off one another. When at last they had retreated to safety, it became clear that the assailants comprised only a narrow tributary of the insect river; the principal torrent had gone up and over the tent to where the Rodians had stored pieces of the beasts the group had slaughtered and dressed earlier in the day—all of it now devoured to the bone.

But regardless of whether they had won or lost the day, Wilhuff would be treated to tales of his ancestors' exploits: the lore of the early Tarkins.

"All of Eriadu was similar to the Carrion before humans arrived from the Core to tame it," Jova told him. "Every day, on their own, as pioneers and settlers, they waged battles with the beasts that ruled the planet. But our ancestors' eventual triumph only altered the balance, not the reality. For all that sentients have achieved with weapons and machines, life remains an ongoing battle for survival, with the strong or the smart at the top of the heap, and the rest kept in check by firepower and laws."

Jova explained that the Tarkin family had produced a succession of mentors and guides through the many generations. What made him unique was his decision to make the Carrion his home following his initiation in young adulthood. That was how he came to have tutored Wilhuff's father, and why he might even live long enough to tutor Wilhuff's son, should he have one.

They spent the remainder of the dry season on the plateau, leaving only when the rains came to that part of Eriadu. Wilhuff was a different person when the speeder carried them down from the mesa and back into civilization. Jova had no need to lecture him on what technology had allowed his ancestors to achieve in the planet's handful of cities, since it was evident everywhere Wilhuff looked.

But Jova had something to add.

"Triumphing over nature means better lives for sentients, but dominance is sustained only by bringing order to chaos and establishing law where none exists. On Eriadu, the goal was always to rid the planet of any creature that hadn't grown to fear us, so that we could rule supreme. Up the well, outside Eriadu's envelope, the goal is the same, but with a different caliber of predators. When you're old enough to be taken there, you're going to find yourself faced with prey who are every bit as quick thinking, well armed, and determined to succeed as you are. And unless you've taken the lessons of the Carrion to heart, only the stars themselves will bear witness to your cold airless death, and they will remain unmoved."

Returned to his comfortable bedroom, Wilhuff

wrestled with what he had been put through, the experiences on the plateau infiltrating his sleep as vivid dreams and night terrors. But only for a short time. Little by little, the experiences began to shape him, and would become the stuff of his true education. Each of the next five summers would find him on the Carrion, and each season his education would widen, right up until the day he had to endure his final test at the Spike.

But that was a different story altogether.

5

PREDACITY

TARKIN WAITED UNTIL the *Carrion Spike* was in hyperspace to announce an impromptu inspection of the officers and enlisted ratings who were accompanying him to Coruscant. In the starship's austere main cabin, furnished only with a round conference table and chairs for half a dozen, eighteen of his crew were standing smartly in two rows, arms at their sides, shoulders squared, chins held high. Each wore a uniform similar to his, though the tunics were slightly longer and the trousers slimmer and more threadbare than those the fabricator had produced for him. The officers wore brimmed caps studded with identity disks, and displayed code cylinders in their appropriate pockets.

Hands clasped behind his back and looking stylish in his new garments, Tarkin had reached the last crew-member in the second row—a midshipman—when he stopped to peer down at the instep of the junior officer's left boot, where a smudge of what looked like grease or some other viscous substance had left a large circular stain.

"Ensign, what is *that*?" he asked, pointing.

The young man lowered bloodshot eyes to follow Tarkin's forefinger to the spot. "That, sir? Must have spilled some hair product I was applying in preparation for the inspection." His gaze was unsteady when he looked up at Tarkin. "Permission to wipe it off, sir?"

"Denied," Tarkin said. "To begin with, it's obviously a *stain,* Ensign, not some blemish you can simply rub out." He paused to scan the midshipman from head to toe. "Remove your cap." The youth's brown hair was regulation length, but it did indeed have the stiff look that hair gel might have imparted.

"Attempting to train it, are you?"

The midshipman stood stiffly, eyes front. "Exactly, sir. It can be unruly."

"No doubt. But that blot on your boot is not hair product."

"Sir?"

"One can tell simply by the way it congealed that it is lubricant—lubricant of a type used almost exclusively in the repulsor generator of our T-Forty-Four landspeeders." Tarkin's eyes narrowed as he focused on the stain. "I see, too, that the lubricant is impregnated with grit, which I suspect came from outside Sentinel's auxiliary dome, almost certainly from where the landing platform is undergoing renovation."

The youth swallowed. "I don't know what to say, sir, I could have sworn—"

"One of our landspeeders was recently sent to the repair bay of the vehicle pool after having become fouled by construction dust," Tarkin said, as if to himself. "There are areas in the bay that are not entirely accessible to our security holocams. However, I often tour the vehicle pool to review repairs, and recently have chanced upon envelopes of a sort that have become fashionable for the storage of a particular class of stimulant spice." His gaze bored into the youth's face. "You're sweating, Ensign. Are you certain you're fit for duty?"

"A touch of hyperspace nausea, sir."

"Perhaps. But nausea doesn't account for the fact that the thumb and index finger of your right hand bear yellow-ocher stains, which are often the result of pinching plugs of spice that hasn't been sufficiently processed. I observe, too, that your left eyetooth reveals what appears to be a nascent cavity, such as might be caused by dipping spice. Finally, your record indicates that you have recently been late in reporting for duty, as well as inattentive when you deign to report." Tarkin paused for a moment. "Have I forgotten anything?"

Embarrassment mottled the midshipman's face.

"Nothing to say for yourself, Ensign?"

"Nothing at this time, sir."

"I thought not."

Tarkin swung to a female officer standing at the opposite end of the row. "Chief, Ensign Baz is relieved of duty. See to it that he is escorted to the crew berth and confined to quarters for the remainder of the voyage. I will decide his fate once we reach Coruscant."

The petty officer saluted. "Yes, sir."

"Also, alert Commander Cassel that the vehicle pool has become a rendezvous area for spice users. Tell him to perform a flash inspection of all barracks and personal lockers. I expect him to confiscate all inebriants and other illicit substances."

"Sir," she said.

Dismissed, the rest of the crew scattered with haste, and Tarkin blew out his breath in irritation. The conversation with Mas Amedda had left him on edge, and he was taking his frustration out on his crew. He understood and fully supported the idea of a chain of command, but he took it personally when power plays interfered with his duties. He trusted Cassel to attend to Sentinel's responsibilities in his absence, but he wasn't comfortable with being summoned away at such a critical time, much less without full explanation. If the purpose of the visit was to discuss the recent attack, then perhaps he should have delayed filing the report. If not about the attack, what matter could be so vital that it couldn't wait until after the looming shipments were safely escorted to Geonosis?

What was done was done, however, and he was determined to present the best possible face to the Emperor.

Leaving the main compartment, he walked forward through two hatches to the ship's command cabin, which he had designed to be more spacious than those found on similar ships, as it was here that he spent most of his travel time. Immediately he found himself relaxing, and let out his breath in slow reprieve. If exasperated by Coruscant's demands, he should at least be able to find some solace in the ship.

At just under 150 meters in length, the corvette fit neatly between the old Judicial cruisers and Corellian Engineering's new-generation frigates. Heavily armed with turbolasers, ion cannons, and proton torpedo tubes, and featuring a Class One hyperdrive that made it the fastest ship in the Imperial Navy, the *Carrion Spike* had been designed specifically for him—and to meet many of his personal specifications—by Sienar Fleet Systems. Based on a prototype stealth corvette that had been introduced during the Clone Wars at the Battle of Christophsis to counter Separatist Admiral Trench's blockade of the planet, the triangular-shaped ship was unique in having cloak technology. Powered by rare stygium crystals, the stealth system rendered the ship essentially invisible to ordinary scanners.

Hearing Tarkin enter, the captain—a slim, dark-complected man who had served under Tarkin during the war—swiveled in his acceleration chair.

"Sir, do you wish to assume the controls?"

Tarkin nodded and replaced him in the command chair, running his hands over the instruments as he settled in. The *Carrion Spike*'s ion turbine sublight arrays, countermeasures suite, and navicomputer were also state-of-the-art, the latter allowing the ship to make the jump from Sentinel Base to Coruscant without exiting hyperspace to retrieve routing data from relay stations or primitive hyperwave beacons.

Gazing into the nebulous swirl of hyperspace, he decided that, yes, he could take comfort in having such a ship. In many respects the *Carrion Spike* was a sign of just how far he had come, and where he now stood in the Imperial hegemony.

And what Eriadu wouldn't have given for such a vessel in the decades leading up to the Clone Wars! At that point the sector's problems were pirates lured by sudden wealth, privateers hired by Eriadu's competitors in the lommite trade, and resistance factions protesting the unjust practices of shipping conglomerates operating with impunity in the free trade zones. Eriadu would eventually triumph with the defenses it had at its disposal; but a ship like the *Carrion Spike* might have granted the Seswenna the edge it needed to vanquish its enemies with greater efficiency and added flourish.

In the absence of a Republic military, and as punishment for refusing to provide the Core Worlds with profitable deals, Judicials—the Republic's non-Jedi law enforcers—were often withheld from intervening in disputes, leaving the Seswenna little choice but to create its own armed forces. A loosely knit group that came to be known as the Outland Regions Security Force, the sector's response to pirates and privateers had to make do with second-rate ships built on Eriadu or at Sluis Van, and with laser and ion cannons purchased from arms merchants who for a century had been ignoring the Republic's ban on the sale of weaponry to member worlds.

Not six standard months after passing his ultimate test on the Carrion Plateau, sixteen-year-old Wilhuff was sent up the well to begin his training in space combat, his tutelage supervised by an entirely new cast of characters, some of them Tarkins, but others from worlds as distant as Bothawui and Ryloth. Jova had neither a taste nor the tolerance for space, but would sometimes sedate himself with anti-nausea drugs and accompany his grand-nephew, less to offer hands-on instruction in astrogation, combat maneuvering, and weapons training than to make sure that Wilhuff was applying in zero-g the lessons he had learned on the plateau.

"More than fifty Tarkins have lost their lives to marauders," his uncle told him, "and the number of Eriaduans who've been killed is beyond estimation."

To drive home the point, their first stop was a colony world of Eriadu that had suffered a recent attack by pirates. Wilhuff had had ample time to grow accustomed to the sight, scent, and taste of blood, but he had never seen so much human blood spilled in one place. The mining colony had been attacked without warning, thoroughly plundered, and burned to the ground. Those settlers who hadn't died of laser wounds or been incinerated in the fires had been mercilessly butchered and left to be picked over by scavengers or consumed by insects. It was clear to Wilhuff that many of them had been tortured. Hundreds of settlers had been abducted and perhaps already sold into slavery.

Wilhuff was sickened, physically and spiritually, in a way he had never experienced on the Carrion, and the disgust he felt gave rise to despair and a hunger for revenge.

"This is the way of things among the lawless," Jova said as they moved grimly through the destruction, not so much to defuse Wilhuff's outrage as to anchor the massacre in a moral context. "Pirates, privateers, or activists, they're no different from the vermin and predators we dealt with on the Carrion. They need to be educated, and acquainted with our notion of law and order. So you treat them just like the ones we hunted or forced into submission, striking fast and in full commitment. You make use of asteroid fields, nebulae, star flares, whatever you find, to intensify the havoc. You keep them off balance with unexpected maneuvers, and you let your starfighters function like vibro-lances in the hands of our Rodians. You establish supremacy like we showed you, by concentrating all the force at your command on one point, hammering away like you would with a vibroblade, through armor like you would through scales or cartilage or bone, and you show no quarter. You stay on your quarry until you've found the soft spot that brings death, and you put the fear into the rest by gutting your victim, ripping out his liver, and devouring it."

As he was expected to, Wilhuff took his uncle's instructions to heart, by demonstrating in space the mettle he had shown on the Carrion.

The incident that would garner the most attention in the academies he would later attend was one involving Eriadu's ore convoys and a Senex sector pirate group known as Q'anah's Marauders. Loans from offworld financiers had enabled the Greater Seswenna to create the Outland Regions Security Force, but the militia had far too few vessels to protect every lommite shipment traveling between Eriadu and the Core. Making the most of the shortage, several pirate groups had forged an alliance wherein some would monitor or engage Outland's warships while others preyed on the unguarded convoys.

The titular head of the alliance was a human female known only as Q'anah, whose audacious raids throughout the Senex sector had made her something of a folk hero. A native of the Core world Brentaal IV, she was the only daughter of a former bodyguard for House Cormond, who had accepted a lucrative offer to leave the Core to oversee security for House Elegin on the world Asmeru. Trained in combat by her father and eager for adventure, Q'anah became the mistress of the youngest son of the noble house, who was himself leading a secret life as a pirate and whose group Q'anah eventually joined. Fighting alongside the members of her lover's crew, Q'anah lived a colorful and bawdy life until the young Elegin was captured, sentenced to death, and executed on Karfeddion. Having by then given birth to Elegin triplets, Q'anah dedicated herself to avenging the death of her paramour by targeting ships and settlements strewn across the Senex-Juvex sectors.

At the point she became a nuisance to Eriadu, she had already become the subject of breathtaking HoloNet tales and scandalous rumors, having survived starship collisions and starfighter crashes, blaster-bolt and vibroblade wounds, and countless fistfights and

personal duels. Said to be as fast on the draw as a
circus sharpshooter and as talented on the dance floor
as a double-jointed Twi'lek, Q'anah had chewed off
her own infected hand while awaiting rescue on an
isolated moon, and was known to wear artificial arms
and at least one leg—from the knee down—in addition to an ocular implant and who knew what else.
Twice she had been captured and sentenced to lengthy
terms in maximum-security prisons, and had escaped
from each thanks to daring rescues mounted by her
soldiers, who all but worshipped her. Only her link
to House Elegin had saved her from execution. But
following an encounter with Judicial Forces, during
which she destroyed six ships, the Republic also put
a high price on her head, and it was that bounty that
had landed her in the Greater Seswenna, a sector rarely
if ever patrolled by Judicials, notwithstanding repeated entreaties by Eriadu and other harassed worlds.

Lommite convoys typically comprised up to a score
of unpiloted container ships slave-rigged to a crewed
shepherd vessel, now and then with an armed gunboat trailing. Each container was capable of jumping
to hyperspace, but during those years before the era
of affordable and reliable navicomputers, the convoys
had to navigate by hyperspace buoys located along
the route, and experience had proved that jumping in
single file was safer than going to hyperspace in clusters, even though the maneuver left the containers
vulnerable to attack on their reversions to realspace.

Outland capital ships would ride herd on valuable
shipments, but ordinary convoys frequently found
themselves targeted by Q'anah's flotilla of deadly
frigates and corvettes. With the swiftest ships engag-
ing the shepherd vessel, the rest would deliver boarding parties to some of the containers and separate
them from the pack. Once the slave-rigs of the ore

carriers were disabled, the boxy vessels would be slaved to a dedicated pirate frigate and jumped in line to hyperspace. By the time Outland could respond to the distress calls, Q'anah's crews were already selling the stolen ore on the black market or turning it over to the companies that had hired them to carry out the raids.

The convoys became easier and easier pickings, and Eriadu Mining began to accept that it was more cost-effective to surrender the containers than to risk having their overpriced lead or follow ships destroyed in defensive engagements. The company attempted to trick the pirates by placing empty container ships among the fully loaded ones, but the dummy ships only prompted an increase in the number of raids. The company also tried concealing explosive devices and even, on a few occasions, parties of armed spacers in some of the containers. Not once, however, did Q'anah's raiders take the bait, and over time the strategy of including dummy containers and armed troopers was also deemed too expensive. Attempts were made to predict which containers the pirates would target, but in the end Eriadu Mining's battle analysts decided that Q'anah was choosing containers at random.

Just coming into his own as a lieutenant in Outland's anti-piracy task force, Wilhuff refused to accept the disheartening analysis and devoted himself to a detailed study of the raids in which Q'anah had participated—failures and successes both—in the hope of deciphering her method for choosing containers. Her attacks weren't at all like the hunts he had witnessed on the Carrion Plateau, where solitary predators or prides would select the stragglers, the young, or the weakest of the herd animals, and for some time it indeed appeared that her choices had neither rhyme nor reason. But Wilhuff remained convinced that a pattern existed—even if Q'anah herself wasn't consciously aware of having created one.

The scheme that ultimately emerged was so deceptively simple, he was surprised no one had unraveled it. Q'anah turned out not to be the pirate's original name, but rather one she had adopted after her father had relocated the family to Asmeru. In the ancient language of that mountainous world, the word referred to an ages-old festival that always fell on the same day of the planet's complex calendar: the 234th day of the local-year, in the 16th month. Q'anah had assigned each of the five numbers to a letter of her name, and had used that sequence as her basis for choosing targets. Thus on her initial attack on an Eriadu Mining convoy, she had targeted the second container ship counting back from the lead ship; then the third from that one, then the fourth from that one, and so on, until she had grabbed five containers. On subsequent attacks the sequence might commence substituting the last targeted container for the lead vessel. Sometimes she would reverse the sequence, or move forward in the line rather than toward the rear. Occasionally a pattern would begin in one convoy but wouldn't conclude until the next convoy or even the one after that. The numeric sequence itself, however, never changed. Q'anah was essentially spelling out her sobriquet over and over, as if leaving her mark on every convoy she attacked.

Once Wilhuff had grasped the pattern and persuaded Outland's commanders that his months of obsession hadn't driven him completely mad, Eriadu Mining agreed to sacrifice several container ships to the pirates as a means of confirming the theory. Emboldened by the results, the company urged Outland to stock the predicted convoy targets with soldiers, but Wilhuff's paternal cousin, Ranulph Tarkin, proposed an alternative method for exacting revenge by secreting a computer virus in the containers' hyperdrive motivators. One of Outland's most respected commanders, Ranulph—who so resembled Wilhuff's father they could have passed for twins—had designed the ploy years earlier, but Eriadu Mining had balked, based on the cost of having to outfit countless containers with the virused computers. With a lead on which containers Q'anah would target, however, the company agreed to finance the measure, even though the strategy entailed dispatching only one convoy at a time and often operating at a loss.

To make matters worse, the attacks suddenly ceased. It was almost as if the pirates had learned of the ploy, and with increasing pressure from Core buyers for added shipments and wasting funds on attempts to ferret out spies in their midst, Eriadu Mining was on the brink of financial ruin when the Marauders finally struck, targeting precisely those containers Wilhuff had predicted. No sooner did the pirates slave the containers to their frigate than the virus wormed its way into the ship's navicomputer, overriding the requested jump coordinates and delivering it to a realspace destination where Outland warships were lying in wait. Once the frigate had been crippled and boarded, and Q'anah and her crew rounded up and shackled, Ranulph—always the gentleman—insisted on introducing the pirate queen to her eighteen-year-old "captor."

Her sneering expression ridiculed the very idea of it. "Barely a whisker on his chin, but luck enough for a professional sabacc player."

"It was your vanity that turned out to be a laudable substitute for luck," Wilhuff told her. "Your need to leave your signature all over Eriadu's convoys."

Her real eye opened wide and she quirked a grin that told him she understood what he had accomplished, but she followed up the begrudging grin with a snort of contempt. "There isn't a prison that can contain me, boy—even on Eriadu."

Wilhuff offered the sly smile that would later become a kind of signature. "You're confusing Eriadu with worlds that have noble houses and trials by jury, Q'anah."

She searched his youthful face. "Execution on the spot, is it?"

"Nothing so straightforward."

She continued to appraise him openly and defiantly. "There's hardly a part of me that hasn't been replaced, boy. But take my word: I'm not the last of my kind, and your convoys will continue to suffer."

He allowed a nod. "Only if we fail to discourage your followers."

Outland had Q'anah and her crew transferred to one of the stolen containers, whose sublight engines were programmed to send the ship slowly but inexorably toward the system's sun. The plight of the captives was broadcast over the pirates' own communications network, and several of Q'anah's cohorts succeeded in determining the point of origin of the transmission and hastening to her rescue. Their ships were destroyed on sight by Outland forces. The rest were wise enough to go into hiding.

Wilhuff demanded that the container ship's audio and video feeds be kept enabled to the very end, so that Outland's forces and any others who might have been listening could either savor or lament the agonized wails of the pirates as they were slowly roasted to death. In the end, even the notorious Q'anah succumbed to the torture and wailed openly.

"Your task is to teach them the meaning of law

and order," Jova would hector his nephew. "Then to punish them so that they remember the lesson. In the end, you'll have driven the fear of you so deeply into them that fear alone will have them cowering at your feet."

IMPERIAL CENTER

BRIGHT-SIDE CORUSCANT air traffic control directed the *Carrion Spike* to the Imperial Palace, and there into a courtyard landing field that was large enough to accommodate *Victory-* and *Venator*-class Star Destroyers. As repulsors eased the ship down through the busy skyways and into the court, Tarkin realized that the Emperor's current residence had once been the headquarters for the Jedi—though practically all that remained of the Order's elegant Temple complex was its copse of five skyscraping spires, now the pinnacle of a sprawling amalgam of blockish edifices with sloping façades.

At the edge of the landing courtyard, centered among a detail of red-robed Imperial Guards armed with gleaming force pikes, stood Mas Amedda, dressed in voluminous shoulder-padded robes and carrying a staff that was taller than him, its head ornamented by a lustrous humaniform figure.

"How charitable of you to make time for us, Governor," the Chagrian said as Tarkin approached from the corvette's lowered boarding ramp.

Tarkin played along. "And for you to welcome me personally, Vizier."

"We all do our part for the Empire."

With crisp turns, Amedda and the face-shielded guards led him through elaborate doors into the Palace. Tarkin was familiar with the interior, but the expansive, soaring corridors he walked years earlier had contained a rare solemnity. Now they teemed with civilians and functionaries of many species, and the walls and plinths were left unadorned by art or statuary.

Tarkin felt curiously out of step, perhaps because of the increased gravity, the pace, the crowds, or a combination of all those things. For three years the only non- or near-humans he had seen or had direct contact with had been slaves or recruited laborers at outlying bases or at the battle station's construction site. He had heard that one needn't have been absent from Coruscant for years to be startled by the changes, in that each day saw buildings raised, demolished, incorporated into ever larger and taller monstrosities, or merely stripped of Republic-era ornamentation and renovated in accordance with a more severe aesthetic. Curved lines were yielding to harsh angles; sophistication to declaration. Fashions had changed along similar lines, with few outside the Imperial court affecting cloaks, headcloths, or garish robes. By most accounts, though, Coruscanti were satisfied, especially those who lived and worked in the upper tiers of the fathomless cityscape; content if for no other reason than to have the brutal war behind them.

Tarkin's most carefree years had been spent on Coruscant and neighboring Core Worlds before he had been elected governor of Eriadu, with some help from family members and influential contacts. He had a sudden desire to sneak outside the Palace and explore the precincts he had roamed as an adventurous young adult. But perhaps it was enough to know that law and order had finally triumphed over corruption and indulgence, which had been the hallmarks of the Republic.

Someone called his name as he and Amedda were moving down a colonnaded walkway, and Tarkin turned, recognizing the face of a man he had known since his academy years.

"Nils Tenant," he said in genuine surprise, separating himself from the Chagrian's retinue to shake Tenant's proffered hand. Fair-skinned, with a prominent nose and a downturning full-lipped mouth, Tenant had commanded a Star Destroyer during the Clone Wars, and displayed on his uniform tunic the rank insignia plaque of a rear admiral.

"Wonderful to see you, Wilhuff," Tenant said, pumping Tarkin's hand. "I came as soon as I learned you were coming."

Tarkin affected a frown. "And here I thought my arrival would be a well-kept secret."

Tenant sniffed in faint amusement. "Only some secrets are well kept on Coruscant."

Clearly bothered by the delay, Mas Amedda tapped the base of his staff on the polished floor and waited until the two had joined the retinue before moving deeper into the Palace.

"Is that the new uniform?" Tenant asked as they walked.

Tarkin pinched the sleeve of the tunic. "What, this old thing?" then asked before Tenant could respond: "So who let it be known that I was coming? Was it Yularen? Tagge? Motti?"

Tenant was dismissive. "You know, you hear things."

He moved with purposeful slowness. "You've been in the Western Reaches, Wilhuff?"

Tarkin nodded. "Still hunting down General Grievous's former allies. And you?"

"Pacification," Tenant said in a distracted way. "Brought back to attend a Joint Chiefs meeting." Abruptly he clamped his hand on Tarkin's upper arm, bringing him to a halt and encouraging him to fall back from Amedda and the guards. When they seemed to be out of earshot of Amedda, Tenant said: "Wilhuff, are the rumors true?"

Tarkin adopted a questioning look. "What rumors? And why are you whispering?"

Tenant glanced around before answering. "About a mobile battle station. A weapon that will—"

Tarkin stopped him before he could say more, glancing at Amedda in the hope that he and Tenant were, in fact, out of the Chagrian's range.

"This is hardly the place for discussions of that sort," he said firmly.

Tenant looked chastised. "Of course. It's just that . . . You hear so many rumors. People are here one day, gone the next. And no one has laid eyes on the Emperor in months. Amedda, Dangor, and the rest of the Ruling Council have taken to dispatching processions of Imperial skylimos simply to maintain an illusion that the Emperor moves about in public." He fell briefly silent. "You know they commissioned an enormous statue of the Emperor for Senate—I mean, Imperial Plaza? So far, though, the thing looks more terrifying than majestic."

Tarkin raised an eyebrow. "Isn't that the idea, Nils?"

Tenant nodded in a distracted way. "You're right, of course." Again he regarded the nearby columns with wariness. "The scuttlebutt is that you're scheduled to meet with him."

Tarkin shrugged noncommittally. "If that's his pleasure."

Tenant compressed his lips. "Put in a word for me, Wilhuff—for old times' sake. A great change is coming—everyone senses it—and I want to be back in the action."

It struck Tarkin as an odd request, even a trifle audacious. But in considering it, he supposed he could understand wanting to be in the Emperor's good graces, as he was certainly grateful to be there.

He clapped his fellow officer on the shoulder. "If the occasion arises, Nils."

Tenant smiled weakly. "You're a good man, Wilhuff," he said, falling back and vanishing as Tarkin hurried to catch up with Amedda and the retinue turned a corner in the hallway.

Tarkin attracted a good deal of attention as the group climbed a broad stairway and debouched into a vast atrium. Figures of all stripe and station—officials, advisers, soldiers—stopped in their tracks, even while trying not to make an obvious display of staring at him. Subjugator of pirates; former governor of Eriadu; graduate of Prefsbelt; naval officer during the Clone Wars, decorated at the Battle of Kamino and promoted to admiral after a daring escape from the Citadel prison; adjutant general by the war's end, and named by the Emperor one of twenty Imperial Moffs . . . After years of absence from the Imperial capital, was Tarkin here to be forgiven, rewarded, or punished with another mission that would send him chasing Separatist recidivists through the Western Reaches, the Corporate Sector, the Tion Hegemony?

He sometimes wondered where fate might have taken him if he *hadn't* entered the academy system after his years with Outland, when a move to civilian instruction had seemed the best strategy for introducing himself to the wider galaxy. Perhaps he would still be in pursuit of Outer Rim pirates or mercenaries, or slaved to a desk in some planetary capital city. No matter what, it was unlikely that he would ever have crossed paths with the Emperor—when he was still known as Palpatine.

It was while Tarkin was attending the Sullust Sector Spacefarers Academy that they met—or rather that Palpatine had sought him out. Tarkin had just returned to the academy's orbital facility from long hours of starship maneuvers in an Incom T-95 Trainer when someone called his name as he was crossing the flight deck. Turning to the voice, he was astonished to find the Republic senator walking toward him. Tarkin knew that Palpatine was part of Supreme Chancellor Kalpana's party, which included his administrator Finis Valorum and several other senators, all of whom were on station to attend the academy's commencement and commissioning day ceremonies. Most of the graduates would be moving on to positions in commercial piloting, local system navies, or the Judicial Department. Dressed in fashionable blue robes, the red-haired aesthete politician flashed a welcoming smile and extended a hand in greeting.

"Cadet Tarkin, I'm Senator Palpatine."

"I know who you are," Tarkin said, shaking hands with him. "You represent Naboo in the Senate. Your homeworld and mine are practically galactic neighbors."

"So we are."

"I want to thank you personally for the position

you took in the Senate on the bill that will encourage policing of the free trade zones."

Palpatine gestured in dismissal. "Our hope is to bring stability to the Outer Rim worlds." His eyes narrowed. "The Jedi haven't provided any support in dealing with the pirates that continue to plague the Seswenna?"

Tarkin shook his head. "They've ignored our requests for intervention. Apparently the Seswenna doesn't rate highly enough on their list of priorities."

Palpatine sniffed. "Well, I might be able to offer some help in that regard—not with the Jedi, of course. With the Judicials, I mean."

"Eriadu would be grateful for any help. Stability in the Seswenna could ease tensions all along the Hydian Way."

Palpatine's eyebrows lifted in delighted surprise. "A cadet who is not only a very skilled pilot, but who also has an awareness of politics. What are the chances?"

"I might ask the same. What are the chances of a Republic senator knowing me on sight?"

"As a matter of fact, your name came up in a discussion I was having with a group of like-minded friends on Coruscant."

"My name?" Tarkin said in disbelief as they began to amble toward the pilots' ready rooms.

"We are always on the lookout for those who demonstrate remarkable skills in science, technology, and other fields." Palpatine allowed his words to trail off, then said: "Tell me, Cadet Tarkin, what are your plans following graduation from this institution?"

"I still have another two years of training. But I'm hoping to be accepted to the Judicial Academy."

Palpatine waved in dismissal. "Easily done. I happen to be personal friends with the provost of the academy. I would be glad to advocate on your behalf, if you wish."

"I'd be honored," Tarkin managed. "I don't know what to say, Senator. If there's anything I can do—"

"There is." Palpatine came to an abrupt halt on the flight deck and turned to face Tarkin directly. "I want to propose an alternative course for you. Politics."

Tarkin repressed a laugh. "I'm not sure, Senator . . ."

"I know what you must be thinking. But politics was a noble enough choice for some of your relatives. Or are you cut from so different a cloth?" Palpatine continued before Tarkin could reply. "If I may speak candidly for a moment, Cadet, we feel—my friends and I—that you'd be wasting your talents in the Judicial Department. With your piloting skills, I'm certain you would be an excellent addition to their forces, but you're already much more than a mere pilot."

Tarkin shook his head in bewilderment. "I wouldn't even know where to begin."

"And why should you? Politics, however, is my area of expertise." Palpatine's relaxed expression became serious. "I understand what it's like to be a young man of action and obvious ambition who feels that he has been marginalized by the circumstances of his birth. Even here, I can imagine that you've been ostracized by the spoiled progeny of the influential. It has little to do with wealth—your family could buy and sell most of the brats here—and everything to do with fortune: the fact that you weren't born closer to the Core. And so you are forced to defend against their petty prejudices: that you lack refinement, culture, a sense of propriety." He stopped to allow a smile to take shape. "I'm well aware that you've been able to make a name for yourself in spite of this. That alone, young Tarkin, shows that you weren't born to follow."

"You're speaking from personal experience," Tarkin risked saying after a long moment of silence.

"Of course I am," Palpatine told him. "Our home worlds are different in the sense that mine wished no part of galactic politics, while yours has long sought to be included. But I knew from early on that politics could provide me with a path to the center. Even so, I didn't get to Coruscant fully on my own. I had the help of a . . . teacher. I was younger than you are now when this person helped me realize what I most wanted in life, and helped me attain it."

"You . . . ," Tarkin began.

Palpatine nodded. "Your family is powerful in its own right, but only in the Seswenna. Outland forces will soon have the sector's pirate pests on the run, and what will you do then?" His eyes narrowed once more. "There are larger fights to wage, Cadet. When you graduate, why not visit me on Coruscant? I will be your guide to the Senate District, and with any luck I'll be able to change your mind about politics as a career. Unlike Coruscant, Eriadu hasn't been corrupted by greed and the welter of contradictory voices. It has always been a Tarkin world, and it could become a beacon for other worlds wishing to be recognized by the galactic community. You could be the one to bring that about."

As it happened Tarkin wouldn't enter politics for many years, though he did accept Palpatine's help in gaining admission to the Judicial Academy. There—and precisely as the senator from Naboo had predicted—his fellow cadets had initially viewed him as a kind of noble savage: a principled being with abundant energy and drive who had the misfortune of hailing from an uncivilized world.

In part, Tarkin's father and the top echelon of the Outland Regions Security Force were to blame. Eager to impress the Core with their achievements and the fact that they were willing to contribute one of their finest strategists to the Republic, Outland's leaders had personally delivered Tarkin to the academy in one of its finest warships, its glossy hull emblazoned with the symbol of the fanged veermok and Tarkin himself turned out in the full regalia of an Outland commander. His arrival caused such a stir that the academy's provost marshal had mistaken him for a visiting dignitary—which, while certainly the case on worlds throughout the embattled Seswenna sector, carried no weight in the Core. Were it not for Palpatine's influence once more, Tarkin might have been dismissed from the academy even before he had been enrolled as a plebe.

Tarkin understood that he had neglected to heed the lessons he had learned at Sullust and had committed a tactical blunder of the worst sort. Both on the Carrion Plateau and in Eriadu space he had grown so accustomed to flying boldly into confrontation and announcing himself with flourish and dash that he hadn't stopped to consider the staid nature of his new testing ground. Instead of sowing chaos of the sort that had so often served his purposes on land and in deep space, he had succeeded only in rousing the instant scorn of his instructors and the ridicule of his fellow plebes, who took every chance to refer to him as "Commander" or to offer facetious salutes when- and wherever possible.

Early on, the derisive teasing led to brawls, which he mostly won, and also to disciplinary action and demerits that sentenced him to remain at the bottom of the class. That a plebe could be expelled from the Judicials for standing up for himself was something of a revelation, and perhaps he should have seen it as emblematic of the stance the Republic itself would adopt in the coming years, when its authority would be challenged by the Separatists. But he couldn't keep himself from answering fire with fire. Gradually he came to suffer the mockery of his peers without resorting to retribution, though demerits would continue to accrue owing to mischief making and impulsive outbursts. Even so, he refused to allow himself to be cut down to size, choosing instead to bide his time and wait for an opportunity to show his peers just what he was made of.

Halcyon would prove to be that opportunity.

A Republic member world located in the Colonies region, Halcyon was suffering a crisis of its own. A cold-blooded group of would-be usurpers clamoring for the planet's right to manage its own affairs had abducted several members of the planetary leadership and was holding them hostage at a remote bastion. After attempts at negotiation had been exhausted, the Republic Senate had granted permission for the Jedi to intervene and, if necessary, to employ "lightsaber diplomacy" to resolve the crisis. Tarkin was chosen to be one of the eighty Judicials the Senate ordered to attend and reinforce the Jedi.

Never having seen let alone served alongside a Jedi, he was fascinated from the start. His theoretical grasp of the Force was as keen as that of most of his academy peers, but he was less interested in furthering his understanding of metaphysics than in observing the aloof Jedi in action. How adept were they at tactics and strategy? How quick were they to wield their lightsabers when their commands fell on deaf ears? How far were they willing to go to uphold the authority of the Republic? As a self-considered expert in the use of the vibro-lance, Tarkin was equally captivated by their lightsaber skills. Watching them train during the journey to Halcyon, he saw that each had an individual fighting style, and that the techniques for attacks and parries seemed unrelated to the color of the energy blades.

At Halcyon the Jedi divided the Judicials into four teams, assigning one to accompany them to the fortress and inserting the others on the far side of a ridge of low mountains to block possible escape routes. While Tarkin saw a certain logic in the plan, he couldn't quite purge himself of a suspicion that the Jedi merely wanted to rid themselves of responsibility for law enforcement personnel they clearly thought of as inferiors.

What the Jedi hadn't taken into account was the fact that Halcyon's usurpers were a tech-savvy group who had had ample time to prepare for an assault on the bastion. No sooner were the Judicial teams inserted into the densely forested foothills than the planet's global positioning satellites were disabled and surface-to-air communications scrambled. In short order, Tarkin's team lost touch with the two cruisers that had brought them to Halcyon, their Jedi commanders, and the other Judicial teams. The prudent response would have been to hunker down while the Jedi attended to business at the fortress and wait for extraction. But the team's commander—a by-the-numbers human with twenty years of Judicial service whose piloting and martial skills had earned him Tarkin's reluctant respect—had other ideas. Convinced that the Jedi, too, had fallen prey to a trap, he got it in his head to strike out overland, traverse the ridge, and open a second front on reaching the fortress. This struck Tarkin as pure arrogance—no different from what he

had seen in some of the Jedi he had come to know—
but he also realized that the commander likely
couldn't abide being stranded in a trackless wilderness with a group of raw trainees.

Tarkin was immediately aware of the potential for
disaster. The commander's datapad contained re-
gional maps, but Tarkin knew from long experience
that maps weren't the territory, and that triple-canopy
forests could be confounding places to negotiate. At
the same time, he realized that the opportunity for
finally proving his worth couldn't have been more
made to order if he had designed it himself. Mission
briefings had acquainted him with the local topogra-
phy, and he was reasonably certain he could follow
his nose almost directly to the bastion. But he decided
to keep that to himself.

For three days of foul weather, mudslides, and sudden tree falls, the commander had them stumbling
through thick forest and bogs, occasionally circling
back on themselves, and growing increasingly lost.
When on the fourth day their blister-pack rations ran
out and exhaustion began to set in, all semblance of
team integrity vanished. These scions of wealthy Core
families who thought nothing of journeying across
the stars had forgotten or perhaps never known
what it meant to stand or sleep beneath them, far
from artificial light or sentient contact, in an isolated
wilderness on a far-flung world. The frequent, intense
downpours disspirited them; the hostile-sounding but
innocuous calls of unseen beasts unnerved them; the
overhead roar of swarming insects left them huddling
in their confining shelters. They grew to fear their own
shadows, and Tarkin found his strength in their distress.

The chance to show just what he was made of
came on the pebbled shore of a wide, clear, swift-

flowing river. Off and on for some hours, the team had been moving parallel to the river, and Tarkin had been studying the current, making parallax observations of objects on the bottom and observing the shadows cast by Halcyon's bashful suns. Hours earlier, downstream of a waterfall, they had passed a stretch they would have been able to ford without incident, but Tarkin had held his tongue. Now, while the commander and some of the team members stood arguing about how deep the water might be, Tarkin simply waded directly into the current and trudged to the middle of the river, where wavelets lapped at his shoulders. Then, cupping his hands to his mouth, he yelled back to the team: *"It's this deep!"*

After that, the commander kept him by his side, and eventually surrendered point to him. Navigating by the rise and set of Halcyon's twin suns, and sometimes in the sparing illumination of the planet's array of tiny moons, Tarkin led them on a tortuous forest course that took them through the hills and into more open forest on the far side. Along the way he showed them how to use their blasters to kill game without burning gaping holes in the most edible parts. For fun, he felled a large rodent with a hand-fashioned wooden lance and entertained the team by dressing and cooking it over a fire he conjured with a spark-stone from a pile of kindling. He got his fellow plebes used to sleeping on the ground, under the stars, amid a cacophony of sounds and songs.

At a time when the Clone Wars were still a decade off, it became clear to his commander and peers that Wilhuff Tarkin *had already tasted blood.*

When they had walked for three more days and Tarkin estimated that they were within five kilometers of the usurper's fortress, he fell back to allow the commander to lead them in. The Jedi were astounded.

They had only just put an end to the insurrection—
somehow without losing a single eminent hostage—
and they had all but given up on finding any members
of the Judicial team alive. Search parties had been dispatched, but none had managed to pick up the team's
trail. Relieved to be back on firm ground, the cadets
were at first reserved about revealing the details of
their ordeal, but in due course the stories began to be
told, and in the end Tarkin was credited with having
saved their lives.

For those Judicials who knew little of the galaxy
beyond the Core, it came as a shock that a world like
Eriadu could produce not only essential goods, but
also natural champions. A clique of congenial cadets
began to form around Tarkin, as much to bask in
the reflected glow of his sudden popularity as to be
taught by him, or even to be the butt of his jokes. In
him they found someone who could be as hard on
himself as he could be on others, even when those
others happened to be superiors who shirked their responsibilities or made what to him were bad decisions. They had already witnessed how well he could
fight, scale mountains, pilot a gunboat, and succeed on
a sports field, and—as crises like the one at Halcyon
grew more common—they grew to realize that he had
a mind for tactics, as well; more important, that Tarkin
was a born leader, an inspiration for others to overcome their fears and to surpass their own expectations.

Not all were enamored of him. Where to some he
was meticulous, coolheaded, and fearless, to others
he was calculating, ruthless, and fanatical. But no
matter to which camp his peers subscribed, the stories
that emerged about Tarkin in the waning days of the
Judicial Department were legendary—and they only
grew with the telling. Few then knew the details of his
unusual upbringing, for he had a habit of speaking

only when he had something important to add, but he had no need to brag, since the tales that spread went beyond anything he could have confirmed or fabricated. That he had bested a Wookiee in hand-to-hand combat; that he had piloted a starfighter through an asteroid field without once consulting his instruments; that he had single-handedly defended his homeworld against a pirate queen; that he had made a solo voyage through the Unknown Regions . . .

His strategy of flying boldly into the face of adversity was studied and taught, and during the Clone Wars would come to be known as "the Tarkin Rush," when it was also said of him that his officers and crew would willingly follow him to hell and beyond. He might have remained a Judicial were it not for a growing schism that began to eat away at the department's long-held and nonpartisan mandate to keep the galaxy free of conflict. On the one side stood Tarkin and others who were committed to enforcing the law and safeguarding the Republic; on the other, a growing number of dissidents who had come to view the Republic as a galactic disease. They detested the influence peddling, the complacency of the Senate, and the proliferation of corporate criminality. They saw the Jedi Order as antiquated and ineffectual, and they yearned for a more equitable system of government—or none at all.

As the clashes between Republic and Separatist interests escalated in frequency and intensity, Tarkin would find himself pitted against many of the Judicials with whom he had previously served. The galaxy was fast becoming an arena for ideologues and industrialists, with the Judicials being used to settle trade disputes or to further corporate agendas. He feared that the Seswenna sector would be dragged into the rising tide of disgruntlement, without anyone

to keep Eriadu and its brethren worlds free of the
coming fray. He began to think of his homeworld as
a ship that needed to be steered into calmer waters,
and of himself as the one who should assume command of that perilous voyage. The time had come to
accept Palpatine's invitation to join him on Coruscant, for his promised crash course in galactic politics.

Entering one of a bank of turbolifts that accessed the
centermost of the Palace's quincunx of spires, Tarkin
was surprised when Mas Amedda charged the car to
descend.

"I would have expected the Emperor to reside
closer to the top," Tarkin said.

"He does," the vizier allowed. "But we're not pro-
ceeding directly to the Emperor. We're going to meet
first with Lord Vader."

7

MASTERS OF WAR

TWENTY LEVELS DOWN, in a courtroom not unlike the one in which Tarkin had tried to make a case against Jedi apprentice Ahsoka Tano for murder and sedition during the Clone Wars, stood the Emperor's second, Darth Vader, gesticulating with his gauntleted right hand as he harangued a score of nonhumans gathered in an area reserved for the accused.

"Was this where the Jedi Order held court?" Tarkin asked Amedda.

In a voice as hard and cold as his pale-blue eyes, the vizier said, "We no longer speak of the Jedi, Governor."

Tarkin took the remark in stride, turning his attention instead to Vader and his apparently captive audience. Flanking the Dark Lord was the deputy director of the Imperial Security Bureau, Harus Ison—a brawny, white-haired, old-guard loyalist with a perpetually flushed face—and a thin, red-head-tailed Twi'lek male Tarkin didn't recognize. Bolstering the commanding trio were four Imperial stormtroopers with blaster rifles slung, and an officer wearing a black uniform and cap, hands clasped behind his back and legs slightly spread.

"It appears that some of you have failed to pay attention," Vader was saying, jabbing his pointer finger in the chill, recirculated air. "Or perhaps you are simply choosing to ignore our guidance. Whichever the case, the time has come for you to decide between setting safer courses for yourselves and suffering the consequences."

"Wise counsel," Amedda said.

Tarkin nodded in agreement. "Counsel one dismisses at one's own peril, I suspect." Glancing at the Chagrian, he added: "I know Ison, but who are the others?"

"Riffraff from the lower levels," Amedda said with patent distaste. "Gangsters, smugglers, bounty hunters. Coruscanti scum."

"I might have guessed by the look of them. And the Twi'lek standing alongside Lord Vader?"

"Phoca Soot," Amedda said, turning slightly toward him. "Prefect of level one-three-three-one, where many of these lowlifes operate."

Vader was in motion, pacing back and forth in front of his audience, as if waiting to spring. "The liberties you enjoyed and abused during the days of the Republic and the Clone Wars are a thing of the past," he was saying. "Then there was some purpose to turning a blind eye to illegality, and to fostering dishonesty of a particular sort. But times have changed, and it is incumbent on you to change with them."

Vader fell silent, and the sound of his sonorous breathing filled the room. Tarkin watched him closely.

"The Tarkin heritage will grant you access to many influential people, and to many social circles," his father had told him. *"In addition, your mother and I*

will do all within our power to help bring your desires within reach. But nothing less than the strength of your ambition will bring you together with those who will partner in your ascension and ultimately reward you with power."

Since the end of the war, Vader had on occasion been such a partner in Tarkin's life, both in Geonosis space and in political and military campaigns that had taken them throughout the galaxy. Tarkin had long nursed suspicions about who Vader was beneath the black face mask and helmet, as well as how he had come to be, but he knew better than to give open voice to his thoughts.

"Lest any of your current activities infringe on the Emperor's designs," Vader continued, "you may wish to consider relocating your operations to sectors in the Outer Rim. Or you may opt to remain on Coruscant and risk lengthy sentences in an Imperial prison." He paused to let his words sink in; then, with his gloved hands akimbo and his black floor-length cape thrown behind his shoulders, he added: "Or worse."

He began to pace again. "It has come to my attention that a certain being present has failed to grasp that his recent actions reflect a flagrant disrespect for the Emperor. His brazen behavior suggests that he actually takes some pride in his actions. But his duplicity has not gone unnoticed. We are pleased to be able to make an example of him, so that the rest of you might profit at his expense."

Vader came to an abrupt stop, scanning his audience and certainly sending shivers of fear through everyone—Toydarian, Dug, and Devaronian alike. As his raised right hand curled slowly into a fist, many of them began nervously tugging at the collars of their tunics and cloaks. But it was the Twi'lek prefect, standing not a meter from the Dark Lord, who unexpectedly gasped and brought his hands to his chest as if he had just taken a spear to the heart. Phoca Soot's lekku shot straight out from the sides of his head as if he were being electrocuted, and he collapsed to his knees in obvious agony, his breath caught in his throat and blood vessels in his head-tails beginning to rupture. His eyes glazed over and his red skin began to pale; then his arms flew back from his chest as if in an act of desperate supplication, and he tipped backward, the left side of his head slamming hard against the blood-slicked floor.

For a long moment, Vader's breathing was the only sound intruding on the silence. Without bothering to gaze on his handiwork, the Dark Lord finally said: "Perhaps this is a good place to conclude our assembly. Unless any of you have questions?"

The stormtrooper commander made a quick motion with his hand, and two of the white-armored soldiers moved in. Taking hold of the prefect by his slack arms and legs, they began to carry him from the room, tracking blood across the floor and passing close to Tarkin and Amedda. The vizier's blue face was contorted in angry astonishment.

Tarkin hid a smile. It pleased him to see Amedda caught off guard.

"Lord Vader," the vizier said as the Emperor's deputy approached, "we've refrained from requesting that you grant stays of execution to those in your sights, but is there no one you are willing to pardon?"

"I will give the matter some thought," Vader told him.

Amedda adopted a narrow-eyed expression of exasperation and withdrew, leaving Tarkin and Vader facing each other. If Vader was at all affected by the Chagrian's words, he showed no evidence of it, in either his bearing or the rich bass of his voice.

"We haven't stood together on Coruscant in some time, Governor."

Tarkin lifted his gaze past Vader's transpirator-control chest plate and grilled muzzle to the unreadable midnight orbs of his mask. "The needs of the Empire keep us elsewhere occupied, Lord Vader."

"Just so."

Tarkin directed a glance at the exiting storm-troopers. "I am curious about Prefect Soot."

Vader crossed his thick arms across the illuminated indicators of the chest plate. "A pity. Tasked with controlling crime in his sector, he succumbed to temptation by hiring himself out to the Droid Gotra."

"Well, clearly his heart wasn't in it," Tarkin said. "Strange, though, that the Crymorah crime syndicate had no representation in your audience."

Vader looked down at him—blankly? Perturbed?

"We have reached an accommodation with the Crymorah," Vader said.

Tarkin waited for more, but Vader had nothing to add, so Tarkin dropped the matter and they set out for the turbolifts together, with Amedda and his retinue of Royal Guards trailing behind.

Nothing about Vader seemed natural—not his towering height, his deep voice, his antiquated diction—yet despite those qualities and the mask and respirator, Tarkin believed him to be more man than machine. Although he had clearly twisted the powers of the Force to his own dark purposes, Vader's innate strength was undeniable. His contained rage was genuine, as well, and not simply the result of some murderous cyber-program. But the quality that made him most human was the fierce dedication he demonstrated to the Emperor.

It was that genuflecting obedience, the steadfast devotion to execute whatever task the Emperor as-

signed, that had given rise to so many rumors about
Vader: that he was a counterpart to the Confederacy's
General Grievous the Emperor had been holding in
reserve; that he was an augmented human or near-
human who had been trained or had trained himself
in the ancient dark arts of the Sith; that he was nothing more than a monster fashioned in some clandestine laboratory. Many believed that the Emperor's
willingness to grant so much authority to such a being
heralded the shape of things to come, for it was beyond dispute that Vader was the Empire's first terror
weapon.

Tarkin didn't always agree with Vader's methods
for dealing with those who opposed the Empire, but
he held the Dark Lord in high esteem, and he hoped
Vader felt the same toward him. Very early on in their
partnership—soon after both had been introduced
to the secret mobile battle station—Tarkin grew convinced that Vader knew him much better than he let
on, and that behind the bulging lenses of his face
mask, whatever remained of Vader's human eyes regarded him with clear recognition. More than anything else it was those initial feelings that had provided
Tarkin with his first suspicion as to Vader's identity.
Later, observing the rapport the Dark Lord shared
with the stormtroopers who supported him, and the
technique he displayed in wielding his crimson lightsaber, Tarkin grew more and more convinced that his
suspicions were right.

Vader might very well be Jedi Knight Anakin Skywalker, whom Tarkin had fought beside during the
Clone Wars, and for whom he had developed a grudg-
ing appreciation.

"How is life on the Sentinel moon, Governor?"
Vader asked as they walked.

"In a week we'll be back on the bright side of the gas giant, where security is improved."

"Is that the reason you were opposed to coming to Coruscant?"

Vader shouldn't have known as much, but Tarkin wasn't surprised that he did. "Tell me, Lord Vader, does the vizier always share confidences with you?"

"When I ask him to, yes."

"Then he should have qualified his statement. I may have been reluctant to leave my post, but I wasn't opposed to doing so."

"Certainly not when you learned that the request originated with the Emperor."

Tarkin smirked. "Why not simply call it an order, then?"

"It is unimportant. I might have done the same."

Tarkin looked at Vader askance, but said nothing.

"Will your absence affect the construction schedule?"

"Not at all," Tarkin was quick to say. "Components for the hyperdrive generator will be shipping on schedule from Desolation Station, where initial tests have been completed. Work continues on the navigational matrix itself, as well as on the hypermatter reactor. At this point I'm not unduly concerned about the status of the sublight engines or shield generators."

"And the weapons systems?"

"That's a bit more complicated. Our chief designers have yet to reach an agreement about the laser array, and whether or not it should be a proton beam. The designers are also debating the optimum configuration for the kyber crystal assembly. The delays owe as much to their bickering as to production setbacks."

"That will not do."

Tarkin nodded. "Frankly, Lord Vader, there are simply too many voices weighing in."

"Then we need to remedy the situation."

"As I've been proposing all along."

They fell silent as they entered a turbolift that accessed the Palace's primary spire, leaving Amedda and the Royal Guards no choice but to wait for a different car. The silence lingered as they began to ascend through the levels. Vader brought the lift to a halt one level below the summit and exited. When Tarkin started to follow, Vader raised a hand to stop him.

"The Emperor expects you above," he said.

The turbolift carried him to the top of the world. He stepped from the car into a large circular space with a perimeter of soaring windows that provided a view for hundreds of kilometers in every direction. A curved partition defined a separate space that Tarkin assumed was the Emperor's personal quarters. Prominent in the main area was a large table surrounded by oversized chairs, one of them with a high back and control panels set into the armrests. Alone, Tarkin wandered about admiring artworks and statues positioned to catch the light of Coruscant's rising or setting sun, some of which he recognized as having been moved from the Supreme Chancellor's suite in the Executive Building, in particular a bas-relief panel depicting an ancient battle scene. A circular balcony above the main level contained case after lofty case of texts and storage devices.

The Emperor emerged from his quarters as Tarkin was regarding a slender bronzium statue. Dressed in his customary black-patterned robes, with the cowl raised over his head, he moved as if hovering across the reflective floor.

"Welcome, Governor Tarkin," he said in a voice

that many thought sinister but to Tarkin sounded merely strained.

"My lord," he said, bowing slightly. Gesturing broadly, he added: "I like what you've done with the place." When the Emperor didn't respond, Tarkin indicated the bronzium statue of a cloaked figure. "If memory serves, this was in your former office."

The Emperor laid a wrinkled, sallow hand on the piece. "Sistros, one of the four ancient philosophers of Dwartii. I keep it for sentimental value." He gestured broadly. "Some of the rest, well, one might call the collection the spoils of war." His glance returned to Tarkin. "But come, sit, Governor Tarkin. We have much to discuss."

The Emperor lowered himself into the armchair and swiveled away from the window-wall so that his ghastly face was in shadow. Tarkin took the chair opposite and crossed his hands in his lap.

As Nils Tenant had reaffirmed, there were as many rumors circulating about the Emperor as there were about Darth Vader. The fact that he rarely appeared in public or even at Senate proceedings had convinced many that the Jedi attack on him had resulted not only in the ruination of his face and body, but also in the death of the sanguine politician he had been before the war, betrayed by those who had served him and had supported the Republic for centuries. Some Coruscanti even confessed to having fond memories for ex-chancellor Finis Valorum, about whom they could gossip to no end. They yearned to see the Emperor strolling through Imperial Plaza or attending an opera or officiating at the groundbreaking of a new building complex.

But Tarkin didn't speak to those things; instead he said: "Coruscant appears prosperous."

"Busy, busy," the Emperor said.

"The Senate is supportive?"

"Now that it serves rather than advises." The Emperor swiveled slightly in Tarkin's direction. "Better to surround oneself with fresh loyal allies than treacherous old ones."

Tarkin smiled. "Someone once said that politics is little more than the systematic organization of hostilities."

"Very true, in my experience."

"But do you even need them, my lord?" Tarkin asked in a careful, controlled voice.

"The Senate?" The Emperor could not restrain a faint smile. "Yes, for the time being." With a dismissive gesture, he added: "We've come far, you and I."

"My lord?"

"Twenty years ago, who would have thought that two men from the Outer Rim would sit at the center of the galaxy."

"You flatter me, my lord."

The Emperor studied him openly. "I sometimes wonder, though, if you—born an outsider, as I was—feel that we should be doing more to lift up those worlds we defeated in the war? Especially those in the Outer Rim."

"Turn the galaxy inside out?" Tarkin said more strongly than he intended. "Quite the opposite, my lord. The populations of those worlds wreaked havoc. They must earn the right to rejoin the galactic community."

"And the ones that waver or refuse?"

"They should be made to suffer."

"Sanctions?" the Emperor said, seemingly intrigued by Tarkin's response. "Embargoes? Ostracism?"

"If they are intractable, then yes. The Empire cannot be destabilized."

"Obliteration."

"Whatever you deem necessary, my lord. Force is the only real and unanswerable power. Oftentimes, beings who haven't been duly punished cannot be reasoned with or edified."

The Emperor repeated the words to himself, then said, "That has the ring of a parental lesson, Governor Tarkin."

Tarkin laughed pleasantly. "So it was, my lord— though applied in a more personal manner."

The Emperor swiveled his chair toward the light, and Tarkin glimpsed his sepulchral visage; the molten skin beneath his eyes, the bulging forehead. After all these years, he was still not accustomed to it. *"When one consorts with vipers, one runs the risk of being struck,"* the Emperor had told Tarkin following the attack on him by a quartet of Jedi Masters.

There were many stories about what had occurred that day in the chancellor's office. The official explanation was that members of the Jedi Order had turned up to arrest Supreme Chancellor Palpatine, and a ferocious duel had ensued. The matter of precisely how the Jedi had been killed or the Emperor's face deformed had never been settled to everyone's satisfaction, and so Tarkin had his private thoughts about the Emperor, as well. That he and Vader were kindred spirits suggested that both of them might be Sith. Tarkin often wondered if that wasn't the actual reason Palpatine had been targeted for arrest or assassination by the Jedi. It wasn't so much that the Order wished to take charge of the Republic; it was that the Jedi couldn't abide the idea of a member of the ancient Order they opposed and abhorred emerging as the hero of the Clone Wars and assuming the mantle of Emperor.

"I thank you for remaining in service to the Empire

and not turning your hand to writing," the Emperor said, "as some of your contemporaries have done."

"Oh, I still dabble, my lord."

"Doctrinal writings?" the Emperor said in what seemed genuine interest. "Examinations of history? A memoir perhaps?"

"All those things, my lord."

"Even with your obligations as sector governor, you find the time."

"Sentinel Base is remote and mostly tranquil."

"It suits you, then. Or is it that you are well suited to it?"

"Sentinel isn't exactly privation, my lord."

"Even when attacked, Governor?"

Tarkin restrained a smile. He knew when he was being goaded. "Is this the reason you summoned me, my lord?"

The Emperor sat back in the chair. "Yes and no. Though I am familiar with the report you transmitted to the intelligence chiefs. Your actions at Sentinel bespeak a keen intuition, Governor."

Tarkin adopted an expression of nonchalance. "The important thing is that the mobile battle station remains secure."

The Emperor imitated Tarkin's affected indifference. "This isn't the first time we've been forced to deal with malcontents, and it won't be the last. From both near and far." He paused. "There is no refuge from deception when adversaries remain."

"All the more reason to safeguard the supply lines, especially through sectors that aren't under my personal control."

The Emperor placed his elbows on the table and steepled his long fingers. "Clearly you have thoughts about how to rectify the situation."

"I don't wish to be presumptuous, my lord."

"Nonsense," the Emperor said. "Speak your mind, Governor."

Tarkin compressed his lips, then said: "My lord, it's nothing we haven't discussed previously."

"You are referring to the need for oversector control."

"I am. Each oversector governor would then be responsible for maintaining control beneath him—if only as a means of policing districts without having to request guidance from Coruscant."

The Emperor didn't reply immediately. "And who might assume your position if I were to remove you from Sentinel?"

"General Tagge, perhaps."

"Not Motti?"

"Or Motti."

"Anyone else?"

"Nils Tenant is very competent."

Again the Emperor fell briefly silent. "Are you certain that Sentinel's unknown assailants managed to override the local HoloNet relay station?"

"I am, my lord."

"Have you some notion as to how they achieved this?"

Tarkin wet his lips. "Travel to Coruscant prevented me from carrying out a complete investigation. But yes, I have some ideas."

"Ideas you are willing to share with our advisers and intelligence chiefs?"

"If it will serve your purpose, my lord."

The Emperor exhaled forcibly. "We will see at length just whose purpose it serves."

8

THE EMPEROR'S NEW SPIES

SIMILAR IN DESIGN to the pinnacle room, the audience chamber on the penultimate level of the central spire was a circular space, but without partitions and featuring a ten-meter-tall podium reserved for the Emperor, who accessed it by private turbolift from his residence. Tarkin arrived by means of the more public turbolift, entering the vast room to find nearly a dozen people waiting, all of whom he knew or recognized, loosely divided into three groups that made up the Empire's uppermost tiers. First, and positioned closest to the podium, was the Ruling Council, represented just then by Ars Dangor, Sate Pestage, and Janus Greejatus, all three dressed in baggy costumes of riotous color and floppy hats more befitting a night at the Coruscant Opera. More or less on equal footing, the two other groups were made up of members from the Imperial Security Bureau and the more recently created Naval Intelligence Agency, with Harus Ison and Colonel Wullf Yularen speaking for the former, and Vice Admirals Rancit and Screed for the latter. Feeling like the odd man out, Tarkin gravitated to where Mas Amedda and Darth Vader were standing, off to one side of the podium.

Tarkin acknowledged his military comrades with a friendly nod to each. Some he had known since his academy days; others he had served with during the Clone Wars. Interestingly, the Emperor's advisers were also a kind of clique, having attached themselves to the Emperor since his early years as an untested senator from Naboo. Perhaps their outlandish garb was in some sense a tribute to the sartorial extravagance of Naboo's nobility. Even those who should have known better tended to dismiss Dangor, Greejatus, and Pestage as sycophants, when in fact members of the Ruling Council oversaw the everyday affairs of the Empire and wielded wide-ranging and sometimes menacing powers. Even the Empire's twenty Moffs were obligated to answer to the Imperial cadre.

On receiving a signal from the Emperor, Amedda banged his statue-tipped staff on the floor as a sign that the briefing should commence. First to step forward was white-haired ISB deputy director Ison, who bowed to the Emperor before turning to address everyone else in the chamber.

"My lords, Moff Tarkin, Admirals . . . With your permission, and for the benefit of those of you who may not be fully conversant with the matter at hand, I offer a brief summary. Three weeks ago, one of our intelligence assets reported a startling find on Murkhana."

Tarkin came to full alert at Ison's mention of the former Separatist stronghold world.

"Due to the nature of the find, ISB wasted no time in bringing the matter to the attention of the Ruling Council, as well as to our counterparts in Military Intelligence." Ison glanced at Rancit and Screed. Having lost an eye in the war, Screed was sporting a cybernetic implant. "Normally ISB would have pursued an investigation on its own, but on Vizier Amedda's recommendation we are opening it up to discussion, in the hope of resolving how best to proceed."

Tarkin wasn't surprised by Ison's equivocal introduction. ISB functioned under the auspices of COMPNOR, the Commission for the Preservation of the New Order, which itself had arisen from the dregs of the Commission for the Protection of the Republic, and the deputy director was determined to spearhead the investigation without appearing overly proprietary and ambitious. And so he was generously "opening the matter up to discussion," when it was clearly his hope that the Ruling Council would grant ISB full oversight, exempting the bureau from having to share sensitive information with Military Intelligence or anyone else.

"Please don't leave us hanging, Deputy Director," Amedda said in his most sniping voice, "and come to the point."

Tarkin watched Ison's square jaw clench. The deputy director was surely biting his tongue, as well.

"The Murkhana discovery consists of a cache of communications devices," Ison said. "Signal interrupters, jammers, eradicators, and other apparatus, which, to ISB, suggests evidence of a potential stratagem to incapacitate the HoloNet, as was temporarily achieved by the Separatists during the Clone Wars."

Obviously in the dark about the find, advisers Greejatus and Dangor traded looks of bewilderment. Where Greejatus's dark sunken eyes and puffy face granted him an ominous look, Dangor's long, braided mustachios and broad, furrowed brow imparted a bit of élan to an otherwise surly aspect.

"Director Ison," Dangor said, "perhaps these

devices—though recently discovered—are nothing more than a cache left over from the war. They may even have been discovered elsewhere by beings unfamiliar with such devices, and relocated to their present site."

Ison had an answer ready. "That's entirely possible. The cache is so large that our agent didn't have time to inspect every crate and container, much less catalog every component. However, his preliminary report suggests that some of the devices may not have been available to the Confederacy during the war."

"Accepting that at face value for the moment," Dangor went on, "what importance do you attach to this technological trove?"

Colonel Yularen took over for Ison. "My lords, ISB fears that political dissenters may be planning to launch a propaganda operation similar to the wartime Shadowfeeds but directed, of course, against the Empire."

Close to Tarkin's age—though with more gray in his hair and especially in his bushy mustache—Yularen had traded a distinguished career in the Republic Navy for a position in Imperial Security, heading a division devoted to exposing instances of sedition in the Senate. He now served as a liaison between ISB and Military Intelligence. But not everyone in the audience chamber was touched by the colonel's justified concerns. In fact, Greejatus appeared to be *cackling*.

"That's a bit far-fetched, Colonel," he managed to say, "even for ISB."

"Has there been any evidence of HoloNet tampering that might support such a claim?" Dangor asked in a more serious tone.

"Yes, there has," Yularen said, though without explanation or so much as a glance in Tarkin's direction.

Vice Admiral Rancit stepped forward to speak. "My lords, while Naval Intelligence agrees with ISB regarding the possibility of HoloNet sabotage, we feel that Deputy Director Ison is understating the importance of the evidence and the real nature of the threat. Yes, Count Dooku succeeded in using the HoloNet for Separatist propaganda purposes, but Republic forces were quick to shut down those Shadowfeeds." He looked at Ison. "If memory serves, COMPOR itself was established as a result of the navy's actions at the time."

"No one in this chamber needs a history lesson, Vice Admiral," Ison interrupted. "Do you actually intend to go down that path?"

Rancit made a calming gesture. Exceedingly tall, he had a full head of jet-black hair and the symmetrical facial features of a HoloNet idol. The fit of his uniform was equal to if not superior to the fit of Tarkin's.

"I'm merely pointing out that Naval Intelligence should not be left out of the loop here," Rancit said. "For all anyone knows, this newly discovered cache is merely part of a much more sinister plot—one that could require military intervention."

Ison shot Rancit a polar look. "You weren't worried about the cache when it was first brought to your attention. Now all of a sudden you're convinced that it's part of a plot against the Empire?"

Rancit spread his hands theatrically. "What became of opening the matter to discussion, Deputy Director?"

Tarkin smiled to himself. His history with Rancit went back even farther than his history with Yularen. Rancit had been born in the Outer Rim, had graduated from the naval academy on Prefsbelt, and served as an intelligence case officer and station chief during the Clone Wars, dispatching operatives to Separatist-occupied worlds to foment resistance movements. After the war, he had commanded Sentinel Base during the mobile battle station's initial stage of construction, while Tarkin had been busy doling out punishments to former Separatist worlds. Replaced at Sentinel by Tarkin—a circumstance Rancit's rivals enjoyed interpreting as a demotion—he had been reassigned by the Emperor himself to head Naval Intelligence. Fond of art and opera, he was a very visible presence on Coruscant, though few were aware of the covert nature of his work.

As the backbiting between Rancit and Ison continued, Tarkin was tempted to raise his eyes to the podium to see if the Emperor was smiling, since it was his policy to encourage misunderstanding as a means of having his subordinates keep watch over one another. A form of institutionalized suspicion, the policy had proven an efficient fear tactic. He recalled Nils Tenant's wariness in the Palace corridors. The competition for status and privilege and the jockeying for position brought to mind the waning years of the Republic, but with one major difference: Where during the Republic era cachet could be purchased, present-day power was at the whim of the Emperor.

"Now who's understating the risk," Ison was saying, "despite abundant evidence to the contrary?"

Rancit kept his head. "We would have been glad to step aside and allow ISB full oversight if not for recent events." He made no secret of looking directly at Tarkin.

"What recent events?" Dangor asked, glancing back and forth between Rancit and Tarkin.

Mas Amedda banged his staff on the floor in a call for quiet. "Governor Tarkin, if you please," he said.

Tarkin stepped out from between Amedda and Vader

to place himself where everyone in the chamber could see him.

"As regards the matter of whether ISB, Naval Intelligence, or some combination of our various intelligence agencies should be tasked with the investigation, I offer no opinion. I will allow, however, that the concerns of Deputy Director Ison and Vice Admiral Rancit are warranted. A base under my command was recently attacked by unknown parties. The attack followed the successful sabotaging of a HoloNet relay station and the insertion of both prerecorded and real-time holovids, in an attempt to mislead us into dispatching reinforcements to a secondary base. The details of my after-action report are available to anyone here with proper clearance, but suffice it to say that if a connection exists between the discovery on Murkhana and the sneak attack on the base, then it stands to reason that something more nefarious than anti-Imperial propaganda may be in the works."

Ison nearly groaned, and the Emperor's advisers conferred in confidence before Dangor said: "With all due respect, Governor Tarkin, it is my understanding that this base you go to some lengths to leave unidentified is far removed from Murkhana—on the order of several sectors."

Tarkin gestured negligently. "Irrelevant. Communications devices are cobbled together in one place to be deployed elsewhere. What's more, we've seen incidents of attack in many sectors these past five years."

"By pirates and outlaws," Greejatus said.

Tarkin shook his head. "Not in every instance."

"The Separatist war machines were shut down," Dangor went on. "Their droid warships were confiscated or destroyed."

"Most were," Tarkin said. "Clearly, some escaped

our notice or were made available by insiders to a host of new enemies."

Ison glared at him. "Are you accusing ISB—"

"Review my report," Tarkin said, cutting Ison off.

"Furthermore, not every Separatist warship was crewed by droids," Rancit said. "As Governor Tarkin can attest, our navy was still chasing Separatist hold-outs as late as a year ago."

Sate Pestage, who had remained silent throughout the meeting, spoke up. "Governor Tarkin, we're curious to know how you knew you were being deceived at your base of operations." With his shaved head, pointed chin beard, and raking eyebrows, Pestage resembled some of the pirates Outland had chased through the Seswenna.

Rancit stepped forward before Tarkin could utter a word. "May I, Wilhuff?"

Tarkin nodded and stepped back.

"Governor Tarkin—*Moff* Tarkin," Rancit began, "back when he was merely *Commander* Tarkin, was personally instrumental in frustrating Count Dooku's propaganda efforts. I know this to be fact because I was the case officer who supplied him with counterintelligence operatives. No doubt he was able to identify specific elements of corruption in the false holofeed—corruption even the Separatists were unable to purge from their intrusion signals." He turned to Tarkin. "How am I doing?"

Tarkin nodded in appreciation. "My lords, that is the long and short of it. I recognized telltale noise in the holovid and knew then that the feed was originating at the HoloNet relay station and not being transmitted from our auxiliary base." He paused to glance around the chamber. "Regardless, my first recommendation to the Joint Chiefs would be to issue an advisory to our base commanders that they should double-check the encryption codes of all Imperial HoloNet transmissions."

Again the advisers leaned toward one another to confer, while Ison exchanged rancorous looks with Rancit and Screed. Tarkin returned to where he had been standing with Vader, who simply cast a downward gaze at him. After a long moment, Mas Amedda's staff struck the floor with finality.

"The Emperor will take the matter under advisement."

9

AS ABOVE, SO BELOW

"RISE, LORD VADER."

Vader stood from his genuflection and joined his Master, Darth Sidious, at the railing of the central spire's west-facing veranda. Roofed but otherwise open to the sky, the small balcony—one of four identical overlooks, each oriented to a cardinal direction—crowned a finlike architectural projection located several tiers below the spire's rounded summit. The air was thin, and a persistent wind tugged at Sidious's robes and Vader's long cape.

The briefing in the audience chamber had ended hours earlier, and just now that part of Coruscant was tipping into night. The long shadows of distant cloudcutters seemed to reach in vain for the gargantuan Palace, and the sky was swathed in swirls of flaming orange and velvety purple.

When the two Sith Lords had stood in silence for some time, Vader said, "What is thy bidding, Master?"

Sidious spoke without turning from the view. "You

will accompany Moff Tarkin to Murkhana to investigate this so-called cache of communications devices.
You will report your findings directly to me, and I
will decide what if any information needs to be conveyed to our spies and military. I won't have Ison and
the others muddying the waters by conducting their
own inquiries."

Vader took a moment to reply. "The governor's
presence is unnecessary, Master."

Sidious swung to his apprentice, his eyes narrowed
in interest. "You surprise me, Lord Vader. You have
carried out previous missions with Moff Tarkin. Has
he done something to prompt your disfavor?"

"Nothing, Master."

The Emperor exhaled with purpose. "A reply that
conveys nothing. Provide me with a satisfactory reason."

Vader looked down at him, the sound of his regulated
breathing diminished by the howl of the high-altitude
wind. "Moff Tarkin should be ordered to return to Sentinel Base and resume his duties there."

"Ah, so you're arguing on Tarkin's behalf, are you?"

"For the Empire, Master."

"The Empire?" Sidious repeated, miming surprise.
"Since when do you put the needs of the Empire before *our* needs?"

Vader crossed his gauntleted hands in front of him.
"Our needs supersede all, Master."

"Then why do you contradict me?"

"I apologize, Master. I will do as you have commanded."

"No—not good enough," Sidious snapped. "Of
course you will do as I command, and of course Moff
Tarkin needs to resume his duties on the Sentinel
moon. The sooner the battle station is completed, the
sooner you and I can devote ourselves to more press-

ing matters—matters *only* you and I can investigate and that have little to do with the *Empire*."

Vader allowed his hands to hang at his sides. "Then why is Murkhana important, Master?"

Darth Sidious moved from the railing to a chair snugged up against the spire's curved wall and sat down. "Do you not find it intriguing that both you and Moff Tarkin have ties to the very planet where this newly discovered cache of jamming devices has been found? Tarkin, to quash Dooku's Shadowfeeds, and you—in one of your first missions, I seem to recall—to effect an execution. Or perhaps you feel that no connections exist, that this is mere coincidence."

Vader knew the reply. "There are no coincidences, Master."

"And *that*, my apprentice, is why Murkhana matters to us. Because the dark side of the Force has for whatever reason brought that world to our attention once more—as you should well understand."

Vader turned his back to the railing, and the wind wrapped his cape around him. "Which of us would be in command of the mission, Master?"

A sudden glint in his eye, Sidious shrugged. "I thought I would allow you and Moff Tarkin to work that out."

"Work that out."

"Yes," Sidious continued. "Reach a compromise, of sorts."

"I understand, Master."

Sidious's tortured face was a mask. "I wonder if you do . . . But let us return to Moff Tarkin for a moment. Has it never struck you that all three of us—you and Tarkin and I, the Empire's architects, if you will—hail from worlds that occupy but a narrow slice of galactic space? Naboo, Tatooine, Eriadu . . . all within an arc of less than thirty degrees."

Vader said nothing.

"Come, Darth Vader, you of all people should accept that some are born for greatness. That some are larger than life."

Vader remained silent.

"Yes, Lord Vader—*Tarkin*." Sidious softened his tone. "You are a true Sith, Lord Vader. Your dedication is unerring and your powers unparalleled. Perhaps, however, you are under the misimpression that only Sith and Jedi have trials to pass."

"What trials has Governor Tarkin passed?"

"Have you never been to Eriadu?"

"I have."

"Then you know what that world is like. Venture outside the safe haven of Eriadu City and the land is every bit as bleak and hostile as Tatooine. That land forged Tarkin in much the same way Tatooine forged you."

Vader shook his head. "Tatooine did not forge me."

Sidious stared at him, then grinned faintly. "Ah, I see. Slavery and the desert forged Skywalker. Is that what you mean?"

Vader left the question unanswered. "What trials did Tarkin endure?"

Sidious took a long moment to respond. "Trials that helped transform him into the military mastermind he has become."

Vader was silent for a moment. Then he said, "We will go to Murkhana, Master, as you command."

Sidious tilted his head to regard Vader. "Sometimes there is more to be gained by stepping into a trap than by avoiding it. Particularly when you're interested in learning who set it."

"Are you suggesting that Murkhana is a trap?"

"I'm suggesting that you pay close attention to what you and Moff Tarkin uncover there. Getting to the heart of this matter may require us to peel away layer upon layer of purpose."

Vader bowed his head in a gesture of obedience.

Sidious pressed the tips of his fingers together. "Do you know why Tarkin's ship is named the *Carrion Spike*?"

"I do not, Master."

Sidious looked past Vader to the darkening sky. "You should ask him."

On being informed of the Murkhana mission by Mas Amedda, Tarkin had contacted Commander Cassel to say that he would be delayed in returning to Sentinel Base, and had sent everyone but the *Carrion Spike*'s captain and communications officer back to the moon. For the moment, the crew would be limited to the dozen stormtroopers Vader had handpicked to accompany them. Amedda hadn't said whether he or Vader had command of the mission, and Tarkin was trying to puzzle that out on his own. Vader held an invisible rank. But the *Carrion Spike* was Tarkin's ship, which gave him authority. Tarkin was also a Moff, but the title alone didn't grant him jurisdiction in the sector to which Murkhana belonged. Disdain crept into his thoughts. That Vader was a Sith shouldn't factor into the question of authority, and yet how could Vader's dark side powers and crimson light-saber *not* factor into the matter?

The whole business had the taint of *politics*.

Twenty years earlier, Tarkin had been on a career track to be appointed provost marshal of the Judicial Department when he resigned his rank and position. Coruscant at the time had been in the throes of an economic upswing for those senators, lobbyists, and entrepreneurs who had placed themselves at the ser-

vice of the galactic industrial conglomerates. Availing
itself of loopholes built into the free trade zone legislation, the monolithic Trade Federation was expanding its reach into the Outer Rim, as well as its influence
in the Republic Senate. Against expectation, Finis
Valorum's supporters had managed to secure his reelection to the Republic chancellery, but Valorum
was scarcely a year into his second term when the
citizens of Coruscant began to place bets on whether
he would be able to hold on to his office. Palpatine's
name was already being whispered as someone who
might replace Valorum as Supreme Chancellor.

Tarkin and Palpatine had had only sporadic in-
person contact during the years of Tarkin's service
with the Judicials, but they had been faithful correspondents, and Palpatine had remained a staunch
supporter of legislation that benefited Eriadu and the
Seswenna sector. When Tarkin asked to meet with
him on Coruscant, Palpatine made the travel arrange-
ments. Tarkin was one of few people to be on a first-
name basis with the senator, but out of respect for his
elder and mentor of a sort, he most often referred to
him by his title.

"You need a new battlefield," Palpatine said after
he had listened in silence to Tarkin's tale of disillu-
sionment. "I sensed from the moment we met that the
Judicial Department was too insular to contain a man
of your talents—despite your having garnered a following superseding the one you attained at Sullust."

They were sitting in stylish chairs in the senator's
red-roomed apartment in one of Coruscant's most
prestigious buildings.

"The Judicials are at the end of their tenure, in any
case, as the Jedi seem to have become the Senate's
arbiters of choice." Palpatine shook his head ruefully.
"The Order has been given approval to intercede in

matters it normally would have avoided. But complicated times beget wrongheaded decisions." He blew out his breath and looked at Tarkin. "As I told you so many years ago at Sullust, Eriadu will always be a Tarkin world, no matter who resides in the governor's mansion. Now more than ever, your homeworld needs the guidance of a leader who is astute in both politics and galactic economics."

"Why now?" Tarkin asked.

"Because something dangerous is brewing in our little corner of the Outer Rim. Discontent is on the rise, as are criminal enterprises and mercenary groups in the employ of self-serving corporations. In the Seswenna sector, several lommite mining concerns are vying for the attention of the Trade Federation, which is determined to forge a monopoly in the free trade zones. Even on my own Naboo, the king finds himself embroiled with the Trade Federation and offworld bankers with regard to our plasma exports."

Palpatine held Tarkin's gaze. "Ours are remote worlds, but what transpires in those sectors of the Outer Rim could very well have galactic repercussions. Eriadu needs you, and, perhaps more to the point, we need someone like you on Eriadu."

Palpatine's use of the plural was more than an affectation, and yet as close as their relationship had become, the senator never spoke in detail of those like-minded friends and allies he frequently alluded to. Not that that had kept his political opponents from speculating. Aside from the cabal of senators with whom he was often grouped—along with a following of devoted aides who had followed him from Naboo—Palpatine was rumored to have wide-ranging links to a host of shadowy beings and clandestine organizations that included bankers, financiers, and industrialists representing the most important sectors of the galaxy.

"I've been away from Eriadu for many years," Tarkin said. "The Valorum dynasty enjoys an influential presence there, and a political victory by me can hardly be assured. Especially given what happened on Coruscant."

Palpatine waved his thin hand in negligence and what seemed annoyance. "Valorum didn't *win* the election; he was merely *allowed* to win. The Senate's special-interest groups require a chancellor who can be easily entangled in bureaucratic doubletalk and arcane procedure. That is how loopholes are maintained and illegalities overlooked. But as regards your doubts, we have sufficient funds to counter the Valorums and guarantee your victory." He fixed Tarkin with a gimlet stare. "Perhaps you and I could serve each other, as well as the Republic, by taking Valorum down a notch." His shoulders heaved in a shrug of uncertainty. "With the backing of your family, you may not even need our help, but rest assured that we will bolster you if necessary." Palpatine quirked a sly smile. "You will be Eriadu's finest leader, Wilhuff."

"Thank you, Sheev," Tarkin said, with obvious sincerity, and using Palpatine's given name. "I will do what's best for my homeworld, and for the Republic—in any manner you deem fit."

Palpatine's words about Naboo and Eriadu turned out to be prophetic.

After the Naboo Crisis and Palpatine's election as Supreme Chancellor, many of Tarkin's former Judicial peers would pin their hopes on Palpatine to keep the Republic from splintering. But the Separatist movement grew only stronger, and Tarkin and others were forced to accept that Palpatine, for all his talents, had come to power too late. Social injustices and trade

inequities prompted hundreds of star systems to secede from the Republic, and local skirmishes became
the norm. And then came war—a war that soon raged
across the galaxy.

Owing to its strategic location in the Outer Rim
and its geopolitical alliances, Eriadu found itself in
a thorny situation with regard to the Republic and
the Separatists. Perhaps Governor Tarkin, too, should
have found himself in a quandary. But in fact, there
was never a question as to whose ambitions he was
ultimately going to serve.

Dawn the following morning, Tarkin went to the
Palace landing field to ready the *Carrion Spike* for
the voyage to Murkhana, only to find Vader and a
contingent of stormtroopers already on the scene.
Unencumbered by helmets or armor, most of the body-
suited soldiers were engaged in overseeing the transfer of a featureless black sphere from a *Victory*-class
Star Destroyer into one of the larger of the *Carrion
Spike*'s cargo holds. Some three meters in diameter,
the sphere was flattened on the bottom, and evidently
made to nestle in a hexagonal base that was also
being lifted toward the corvette. Vader was pacing
beneath the repulsorlift cranes in what was either
agitation or concern. When the stormtrooper operating the equipment accidentally allowed the flattened
sphere to bang against the edge of the cargo hold's
retracted hatch, Vader stamped forward with his
gloved hands clenched.

"I warned you to be careful!" he shouted up at the
trooper.

"My apologies, Lord Vader. Wind shear from—"

"Excuses won't suffice, Sergeant Crest," Vader cut

him off. "Perhaps you are aging too quickly to remain on active duty."

Tarkin couldn't make sense of the remark until he realized that Crest's was a face he had seen countless times during the war—the face of an original Kamino clone trooper. The bare-headed others comprising Vader's squad were human regulars who had enlisted after the war.

"It won't happen again, Lord Vader," Crest said.

"For your sake it won't," Vader warned.

Tarkin turned his gaze from Vader to the dangling black sphere, unsure about just what he was looking at. A weapon, a laboratory, a personal toilet, a hyperbaric chamber—some merger of the three? Had Vader become reliant on the sphere in the same way he was on the transpirator and helmet? Perhaps the chamber was nothing more than a private space in which he could temporarily free himself from the confines of the suit.

Whatever the sphere was, it lacked a proper hatch, though two longitudinal seams appeared to indicate that the device was capable of parting. Tarkin glanced at Vader again: gauntleted fists on his hips, black cloak snapping in the wind whipped up by departing warships, the morning light reflecting off the top of his glossy, flaring helmet. He was being as short with his men as Tarkin had been with his during the jump to Coruscant. Worse, Vader was clearly as irritated as Tarkin was about having been tasked to head for Murkhana.

Vader seemed to regain his composure as the sphere and its platform were successfully lowered into the cargo hold. A trio of stormtroopers was already uncoiling cables with which to link the device to the *Carrion Spike*'s power plant. Passing close to Tarkin on his way to the ship's boarding ramp, Vader paused to say, "This shouldn't take a moment, Governor. Then we can be on our way."

Tarkin nodded. "Take as long as you need, Lord Vader. Murkhana isn't going anywhere."

Vader stared at him before marching off.

That look again, Tarkin thought—or at least that *suggestion* of a look that always made him feel as if Vader knew him from some previous life.

"We no longer speak of the Jedi," Mas Amedda had said when they had watched Vader issue his warnings to members of Coruscant's underworld. It struck Tarkin now that the Chagrian's attitude wasn't one that was confined to the Emperor's court. In the five short years since the Order had been eradicated— Jedi Masters, Jedi Knights, and Jedi Padawans wiped out by the very clone troopers they had commanded and fought beside—the Jedi already seemed a distant memory.

Despite their refusal to come to Eriadu's aid against pirates, Tarkin had respected the Jedi as peacekeepers, but as generals they had proven failures. The Jedi Master with whom he had served most closely during the Clone Wars was Even Piell, to whom Tarkin's cruiser had been assigned. Brusque and bellicose, the Lannik excelled in lightsaber combat, seeming to have integrated every possible fighting style, but he, too, had his flaws as a strategist. If Piell had deferred to Tarkin during their mission to investigate a hyper-lane shortcut into Separatist-held space, they might have avoided capture and imprisonment, and perhaps the Lannik would have survived at least until the end of the war.

The Force had endowed the Jedi with wondrous powers, but their biggest failing was in not having used the Force in all ways possible to bring the war to a quick end. By remaining faithful to their ethical code, they had allowed the war to drag on and spiral downward into a meaningless bloodbath. The conflict's sudden conclusion and the Order's decision to depose Supreme Chancellor Palpatine had taken nearly everyone by surprise. But Tarkin suspected that even if the Jedi had restrained themselves from rising against Palpatine in his moment of glory, the esoteric Order had doomed itself to extinction. Where their flame had burned bright for a thousand generations, technological might was the new standard.

Tarkin had never been able to make sense of the Clone Wars, in any case. A battle on Geonosis, an army of clones springing up out of nowhere . . . Almost from the beginning he had suspected that an elite outsider, or a group of elite outsiders, had been tampering with or manipulating events; that the battles had been waged in support of a surreptitious agenda. In the meandering prewar conversations Tarkin had had with Count Dooku, the former Jedi had never made a convincing case for Separatism, much less for galactic war. If, as some claimed, Dooku had never actually left the Jedi Order, why then hadn't the Jedi thrown in with the Separatists from the start?

In their final meeting, only weeks before the Battle of Geonosis and the official outbreak of the Clone Wars, Dooku had tried to persuade Tarkin to bring Eriadu into the Confederacy of Independent Systems.

By then Tarkin's homeworld had transformed itself into a major trade center along the Hydian Way. With the Trade Federation monopoly on Outer Rim shipping broken as a result of the Naboo Crisis, and the loss of prestige suffered by Valorum Shipping as the result of scandals and Finis Valorum's truncated term as supreme chancellor, Eriadu Mining and Shipping was prospering beyond the wildest dreams of the Tarkin family. Tarkin himself was just completing his second term as planetary governor and was being urged by many to run for a seat in the Republic Senate, even while many of his academy friends—convinced that a war between the Republic and the Separatists was inevitable—were urging him to leave himself open to the possibility that the Military Creation Act could be pushed through the Senate, and a Republic Navy instated.

Count Dooku of Serenno had been most responsible for bringing the galaxy's disenfranchised worlds under one umbrella. Tarkin had never known him when he had been one of the Jedi Order's most dashing duelists, but they had met shortly after the count's quiet disaffiliation, introduced to each other on Coruscant by Kooriva senator Passel Argente, who would himself go on to become a member of the Separatist leadership. Tarkin was intrigued by the tall, charismatic count, not so much because he had been a Jedi but because he had surrendered a family fortune that would have guaranteed him a place among the galaxy's most powerful and influential beings. During that first meeting, however, they had spoken not of wealth but of politics and the escalating tensions that had been stirred by trade inequities and intersystem conflicts. Tarkin agreed with Dooku that the Republic was in danger of imploding, but he held that a supervising government—even if ineffectual—was preferable to anarchy and a fractured galaxy.

For some eight years following his leave-taking from the Jedi Order, Dooku was scarcely heard from. Amid rumors about his fomenting political turmoil on a host of worlds, most people were convinced that he had gone into self-exile, intent on founding an offshoot of the Jedi Order. Instead he had staged a theatrical return to public life by commandeering a HoloNet station in the Raxus system and delivering a rousing speech that condemned the Republic and essentially set the stage for the Separatist movement. Moving about in secrecy—some said one step ahead of assassins hired by Republic interests—Dooku became the focus of galactic attention, backing coups on Ryloth, meddling in the affairs of Kashyyyk, Sullust, Onderon, and many other worlds, and spurning all opportunities to negotiate with Supreme Chancellor Palpatine.

Chiefly because of its location at the confluence of the Hydian Way and the Rimma Trade Route, Eriadu became something of a contested world early on, and as adjacent and neighboring sectors seceded or joined the Separatists, Tarkin found himself pressured by both sides to declare his loyalties. Dooku went out of his way to meet with Tarkin on several occasions, as if to demonstrate that he had taken a personal interest in Eriadu's future. In fact, having already laid the groundwork for the creation of a southern Separatist sphere by bringing Yag'Dhul and Sluis Van over to his side, he needed Eriadu to seal the deal. If Dooku could achieve in the Greater Seswenna what he had achieved elsewhere, he could effectively collapse the Core back into itself, reversing the expansion that had resulted from millennia of space exploration, conquest, and colonization.

At each meeting Dooku had emphasized that for most of its history Eriadu had either been ignored by or been at the economic mercy of the Core. Having forged its own destiny, it owed no allegiance to Coruscant. But on the occasion of their final meeting, threat replaced persuasion. Recent turmoil at Ando and Ansion had left the galaxy staggered, and Dooku seemed caught up in the feverish rush of events. Still, he had arrived on Eriadu in his usual caped finery, elegant and urbane. At Tarkin's residence overlooking the bay and the glittering lights of the distant shore, they dined on foods prepared by Tarkin family chefs and rare wines provided by the gray-bearded count. Even so, Dooku was restless throughout, ultimately dropping his guise to storm from the long table to the balcony railing, where he whirled on Tarkin.

"I need an answer, Governor," he began. "This is a pleasant evening and I have always enjoyed your company, but circumstances demand that we conclude the matter of Eriadu's commitment."

Tarkin set his napkin and wineglass down and joined him at the balcony. "What has happened to bring this to a head?"

"An imminent crisis," Dooku allowed. "I can't say more."

"But I can. I suspect that you are now close to persuading your secret allies to initiate an economic catastrophe."

Dooku's response was limited to a faint smile, so Tarkin continued.

"Eriadu's friendships are wide ranging. Nothing happens in this or any other sector without our knowledge."

"Which is precisely why your world is so important to our cause," Dooku said. "But sometimes economic pressures are not enough to guarantee success—as you well know, Governor. Or do you believe you could simply have bought off the pirates who harassed this sector for so long? Of course not. Eriadu established the Outland Regions Security Force to deal with them. You went to war."

"Is war what you have in the works?"

Instead of answering the question directly, Dooku said, "Consider Eriadu's current situation. I realize that you have been successful in shipping lommite through Malastare, and circling around Bestine to reach Fondor and the Core. But where will Eriadu be when Fondor opts to join the Confederacy?"

"Opts to join, or falls to you?"

"Join us and you can continue to transact business in Confederacy spheres—through Falleen, Ruusan, all the way to the Tion sectors." He paused. "Is your friend and benefactor on Coruscant in any position to offer you a similar guarantee, with the Core contracting around him?"

"The Supreme Chancellor is not required to bribe me into remaining loyal to him."

"As a complement to previous bribes, you mean. In allowing your illegal actions in the Seswenna to go completely unchecked since you abetted in the undermining of Finis Valorum." Dooku snorted in scorn. "A strong leader would never have allowed galactic events to reach a point of crisis. He is weak and inadequate."

Tarkin shook his head negatively. "He is hemmed in by a corrupt and incompetent Senate. Otherwise the Republic would have already raised a military to oppose you."

"Ah, but the end of his second term is upon him, Governor, with no one of any merit to succeed him. Unless, of course . . . some crisis results in his term being extended."

Tarkin tried to decipher the count's inference. "One might almost conclude that you're positing an *advantage* to going to war. But how would that work? The volunteer security forces of the Confederate worlds against—what, Judicials and ten thousand of your former Jedi brethren?"

Dooku adopted an arrogant expression. "Don't be too surprised, Governor, if the Republic has access to secret forces."

Tarkin regarded him in open astonishment. "Mercenaries?"

"*Proxies* is perhaps a more accurate term."

"Then you have already committed to war."

"I am committed to the idea of a galaxy ruled by an enlightened leader, with laws that apply universally—not one set for the Core Worlds, another for the Outer Rim worlds."

"An autocracy," Tarkin said. "Guided by the count of Serenno."

Dooku gestured in dismissal. "I am ambitious, but not to that degree."

"Who, then?" Tarkin pressed.

"We'll leave that for another day. I'm simply trying to keep you from finding yourself on the losing side."

Tarkin studied him. "Will there actually be a losing side for men like you and me? I sometimes suspect that this crisis is a mere charade."

Dooku appraised him. "Would you be opposed to being part of a charade if it meant that the galaxy could be brought under the rule of one?"

Tarkin regarded him for a long moment. "I wonder what you mean, Dooku."

The count nodded in assessment. "I may not be able to forestall repercussions, Governor, but should this situation escalate to war between the Confederacy and the Republic, I will do my best to see that no lasting harm comes to your homeworld."

Tarkin's brows beetled. "Why would you?"

"Because in the end, you and I are likely to find ourselves under the same roof."

Tarkin had long wondered why Dooku's prophecy had never come to pass. It was the Separatists who had wound up on the losing side, along with Dooku and, most unexpectedly, the entire Jedi Order, and the Emperor and Tarkin who had found themselves under the same roof.

"The *Carrion Spike* has launched, Your Majesty," 11-4D told Darth Sidious.

The droid resembled a protocol model, except for its several arms, only two of which terminated in what might be considered hands; the rest were devoted to tools of varied purpose, including computer interface and power charge extensions. The droid had once been the property of Sidious's tutor, Plagueis, and had been in Sidious's possession since his former master's death, though in several different guises.

The announcement roused Sidious from meditation, and he took a moment to reach out to Vader, his perturbed apprentice.

"Alert me when the ship makes planetfall on Murkhana," Sidious said.

The droid bowed its head. "I will, Your Majesty."

The two of them were in Sidious's lair, a small rock-walled enclosure beneath the deepest of the Palace's several sublevels that had once been an ancient Sith shrine. That the Jedi had raised their Temple over the shrine had for a thousand years been one of the most closely guarded secrets of those Sith Lords who had perpetuated and implemented the revenge strategy of the Jedi Order's founders. Even the most powerful of Dark Side Adepts believed that shrines of the sort existed only on Sith worlds remote from Coruscant, and even the most powerful of the Jedi believed that the power inherent in the shrine had been neutralized and successfully capped. In truth, that power had seeped upward and outward since its entombment, infiltrating the hallways and rooms above, and weakening the Jedi Order much as the Sith Masters themselves had secretly infiltrated the corridors of political power and toppled the Republic.

Save for Sidious, no sentient being in close to five thousand years had set foot in the shrine. The room's excavation and restoration had been carried out by machines under the supervision of 11-4D. Even Vader was unaware of the shrine's existence. But it was here that they would one day work together the way Sidious and Plagueis had to coax from the dark side its final secrets. In the intervening years he had actually come to appreciate Plagueis for the planner and prophet he had been. Such perilous machinations required two Sith, one to serve as bait for the dark side, the other to be the vessel. Success would grant them the power to harness the full powers of the dark side, and allow them to rule for ten thousand years.

Sidious found himself unable to return to his meditations. Stretching out with his feelings, he endeavored to assess the mood aboard the *Carrion Spike*. Vader had made clear his thoughts about the mission, but Sidious had learned from Vizier Amedda that Tarkin, too, was displeased with the assignment. During the Clone Wars, Sidious had made every attempt to promote a rapport between Skywalker and Tarkin, but the relationship had never prospered to his satisfaction. Then came that business with Skywalker's Togruta apprentice, Ahsoka Tano, which, while it had provoked further disaffection in Skywalker, had also created a rift between him and Tarkin that perhaps had yet to mend. Yes, they had partnered since the end of the war, but—to Sidious's own annoyance—absent a true appreciation for each other's talents.

Well, if they were going to continue to serve him, Sidious thought, it was long past time that they found a way to work out their differences.

The fact that Sidious held Tarkin in such approbation made the matter all the more wearisome. They had met several years after Sidious—still an apprentice of Darth Plagueis at the time—had been appointed Naboo's representative to the Republic Senate. Despite the fact that Naboo and Eriadu were very different Outer Rim worlds, Sidious had recognized Tarkin, some twenty years his junior, as a fellow colonial. And more: a human who had the potential to become a powerful ally, not only with regard to Sidious's political ambitions, but also in helping to implement his true agenda of destroying the Jedi Order.

Toward that end, Sidious had brought Tarkin into the fold early on, even facilitating a meeting between Tarkin and many influential Coruscanti, if only to solicit their opinions of Eriadu's local hero. The more Sidious investigated Tarkin's past—his unusual upbringing and exotic rites of passage—the more he grew to feel that Tarkin's thinking about the Republic and about leadership itself was in keeping with his own, and Tarkin hadn't disappointed him. When Sidious had asked for help in weakening Supreme Chancellor Valorum so that Sidious himself could win election to the position, Tarkin had stonewalled Valorum's attempts to investigate the disastrous events of an Eriadu trade summit, thereby helping to foment and hasten the Naboo Crisis. Tarkin had remained loyal during the Clone Wars as well, enlisting in the military on the side of the Republic, despite repeated entreaties by Count Dooku—which Sidious had arranged as a test of Tarkin's dedication.

Sidious assumed that Tarkin had puzzled out that Vader had once been Anakin Skywalker, under whom Tarkin had served during the war. Tarkin may also have determined that Vader was a Sith. If so, it followed that he accepted that Sidious was Vader's dark side Master. But Tarkin's intuitions were important only in the sense that he never revealed them and never allowed them to interfere with his own ambitions.

For his own sake as much as Tarkin's, Sidious had been careful to keep those ambitions in check. He understood that Tarkin was frustrated with his current position as sector governor and base commander, but overseeing construction of the mobile battle station was too grand an undertaking for any one person, even one of Tarkin's caliber. As powerful as the battle station might become, its real purpose was to serve as a tangible symbol and constant reminder of the power of the dark side, and to free Sidious from having to portray that part.

Darth Plagueis had once remarked that *"the Force can strike back."* The death of a star didn't necessarily curtail its light, and indeed Sidious could see evidence of that sometimes even in Vader—the barest flicker of persistent light. Attacks like the one directed against Tarkin's moon base and discoveries like the one on Murkhana were distractions to his ultimate goal of making certain that the Force *could not* strike back, and that whatever faint light of hope remained could be snuffed out for good.

10

A BETTER WOMP RAT TRAP

LIKE MANY FORMER Separatist bastions, Murkhana was a dying world. The lingering atmospheric effects of years of orbital bombardment and beam-weapon assaults had raised the temperature of the world's seas and killed off coastal coral reefs that had once drawn tourists from throughout the Tion Cluster. What had been wave-washed black beaches were now stretches of fathomless quicksand, and what had been sheltered coves were stagnant shallows, rife with gelatinous sea creatures that had risen to the evolutionary fore when the fish had died. Battered by relentless squalls of acid rain, the once graceful, spiraling structures of Murkhana City were pitted and cracked, and had turned the color of disease-ridden bone. Even when the rains ceased, menacing clouds hung over the bleached landscape, blotting out light and leaving the air smelling like rancid cheese. Descending through the atmosphere was like dropping into a simmering cauldron of witch's brew.

Below was what remained of the seaside hexagonal spaceport and the quartet of ten-kilometer-long bridges that had linked it to the city; the Corporate Alliance landing field was slagged and tipped on the massive piers that had supported it, and the bridges had collapsed into the frothing waters. Arriving starships were now directed to the city's original spaceport at the base of the hills.

"Governor Tarkin, we have a visual on the landing zone," the captain said as the ship pierced a final low-lying layer of dirty cloud, revealing the ravaged city spread out beneath them from sea to surrounding hills like some terrain exported from a nightmare. "Spaceport control says that it's up to us to find a place to set down, as their guidance systems are no longer in service and the terminal has been shut down. Immigration and customs have relocated to the inner city."

Tarkin shook his head in disgust. "I suspect no one makes use of them. What do our scanners tell us of the atmosphere?"

"Atmosphere is a mess, but breathable," the comm officer said, her eyes fixed on the sensor board. "Background radiation is at tolerable levels." Swiveling to Tarkin, she added, "Sir, you might want to consider wearing a transpirator."

Tarkin watched smoke pour into the sky from fires that might have been burning for six years. He considered the specialist's advice for a moment, gradually warming to the idea of being the only one among the mission personnel to be bare-headed, thus appearing more the commanding officer.

"Looking for an adequate site, Governor," the captain said.

Tarkin leaned toward the viewport to assess the landing field. It was impossible to tell the bomb craters from the circular repulsorlift pits that had once functioned as service areas for the Separatists' spherical core ships. The edges of the field were lined with ruined hemispherical docking bays and massive rectangular hangars, their roofs blown open or caved in. The façade of the sprawling terminal building had avalanched onto the field, and the interior had been gutted by fire. Ships of various size and function were parked at random, though most of them looked as if they hadn't seen space in a long while.

"Twenty-five degrees east," Tarkin said finally. "We'll have just enough room."

Vader entered the command cabin as repulsors were lowering the corvette toward the cracked permacrete.

"A world I never expected to see again," Tarkin said.

"Nor I, Governor," Vader said. "So let us be quick about it."

Tarkin scanned the immediate area as *Carrion Spike* began to settle on her landing gear and the instruments were shut down. Only a handful of starships occupied their corner of the uneven field, including a decrepit forty-year-old Judicial cruiser and a sleek and obviously rapid black frigate bristling with weapons, its broad bow designed to suggest slanting eyes and bloody fangs thrusting from a cruel mouth.

"Charming," Tarkin said. "And very much in keeping with the surroundings."

Wedging a brimmed command cap into the pocket of his tunic, he joined Vader and eight of the stormtroopers as they were filing from the ship. Barely through the air lock, he could already taste acid on his tongue. They had just reached the foot of the boarding ramp when a teetering low-altitude assault transport soared into view, its wing-mounted repulsorlift turbines straining as it dropped from the sky to hover alongside the *Carrion Spike*. Two Imperial storm-troopers in scratched and dented armor leapt from the open side hatch, while well-armed door gunners kept watch over the field.

"Welcome to Murkhana, sirs," their squad leader said, offering a lazy salute.

Tarkin heard stifled laughter from someone inside the gunship. Adorning the vehicle's vaned sliding hatch was the faded insignia of the Twelfth Army.

His posture reflecting obvious displeasure, Vader appraised the noisy gunship. "Are you certain that this relic is capable of carrying us, Squad Leader, or might *we* end up carrying *it*?"

The stormtrooper glanced over his shoulder at the gunship. "Sorry to report that we've no choice, Lord Vader. The rest are in even worse shape."

"Why is that?" Tarkin stepped forward to ask.

"Sabotage, sir. We're not well liked by the locals."

"No one asked them to like you, Squad Leader," Vader snapped. With a swirl of his cloak, he climbed aboard the gunship, followed by his personal storm-troopers.

Tarkin paused to comlink *Carrion Spike*'s captain. "We're leaving four stormtroopers to guard the ship. Keep the comlink open and contact me at the first sign of trouble."

"Acknowledged, Governor," the comm officer said.

Vader extended a hand to Tarkin and pulled him up onto the deteriorated deck plates of the gunship's deployment platform.

"Go," the Dark Lord shouted to the cockpit crew.

The gunship lifted shakily off the landing field and began to wheel toward the heart of Murkhana City. Placing himself behind one of the door gunners, Tarkin grabbed hold of an overhead strap and peered out the open hatchway.

He wasn't surprised to see that most of the city's charred, devastated buildings had yet to be demolished. Facing sanctions, the local government had not been able to grow the economy, and the substantially reduced population had been forced to rely on black marketeers for goods and resources. Rusting remnants of the war, carbon-scored Hailfire, spider, and crab droids stood idle in the desolate streets, picked clean of usable parts by gangs of scavengers. Scattered among them were a couple of burned-out Republic AT-TE and turbo tanks, along with a Trident transport. The hulk of a Commerce Guild warship protruded like a broken tooth close to what remained of the Argente Tower, which was itself a husk.

Breath-masked residents scurried for cover as the gunship raced over glass-littered avenues, past boarded-up storefronts, toppled monuments, and gloomy cantinas. Packs of famished animals roved the alleyways, and nearly every street corner hosted crews of smugglers and hoodlums. Tarkin caught glimpses of limping war veterans—Koorivar with broken cranial horns, Aqualish with missing tusks, and Gossams with crooked necks—along with children stricken with hideous birth defects.

As the gunship veered through a turn, a hunk of twisted metal slammed into the hatch's retracted door, hurled by a young woman who had stepped boldly from a lopsided doorway and stood in the street, hands on hips, as if challenging the Imperials to reply.

"Permission to exterminate, sir," one of the stormtroopers said, his blaster rifle braced against his shoulder.

Vader stretched out his gloved hand to lower the weapon. "We haven't come all this way to instigate a riot."

And yet two city blocks later, catching sight of defaced military recruitment posters and walls vandalized by hand-scrawled insults aimed at the Emperor, he turned to Tarkin to say: "We should put this place out of its misery."

"Too magnanimous," Tarkin said. "Though it may come to that."

The gunship began to shed velocity as it crossed a cratered plaza; it came to a hovering halt in the middle of a broad concourse obstructed by a collapsed coral archway.

"We're here, sirs," the squad leader said.

"Which building?" Tarkin asked, then followed the line of the stormtrooper's extended hand to see a squat structure with rounded corners three blocks away.

"Originally the property of the Corporate Alliance, sir," the squad leader continued. "A medcenter, until it was used to house a deflector shield generator that protected a vital Separatist landing platform."

"And the current proprietor?"

"Unknown, sir. The place has changed hands several times since the end of the war. Identities of the various owners are buried under layers of phony documentation."

"You have been maintaining surveillance?" Vader asked.

"Continuous since receiving orders from Coruscant three weeks back, Lord Vader. But we haven't observed anyone coming or going. The locals tend to steer clear of this entire area."

"Then you have no one in custody."

"No one, Lord Vader."

Tarkin's eyes clouded over with suspicion. "Yes, but who might have been watching you while you were watching the building?"

Vader nodded. "Yes, Governor, it might very well be a trap."

The stormtrooper indicated several nearby buildings. "We've installed rooftop snipers there, there, and there, Lord Vader."

"Are you carrying remotes?"

"We have a couple of AC-ones onboard, along with an ASN retrofitted with a holotransmitter."

"Those will do. Prepare them."

The gunship touched down and Vader stepped from the deployment platform, all but floating to the buckled street. When his stormtroopers had followed, he turned to Sergeant Crest.

"Take four of your men and trail the remotes inside. We will monitor the holofeeds from here. Perform a full reconnaissance of the building, but do not enter the room where the devices are said to be located until we follow on your all-clear."

Crest saluted and pointed to four of the stormtroopers. By then the spherical remotes had already been tasked and were whirring off toward the building. The squad leader placed a handheld holoprojector on the deployment platform deck plates and enabled it. A moment later the device began receiving transmissions from one of the remotes. While Vader paced, Tarkin watched as illuminated views of narrow hallways and short staircases resolved above the holoprojector. The squad leader shifted feeds from one remote to the next, but the views and sounds remained largely unchanged: puddled hallways, dark stairwells, dripping water, creaking doors, indistinct noises that may have come from still-working machines.

Almost an hour passed before the voice of Sergeant Crest issued from the comlink of one of his subordinates. "Lord Vader, the building is clear. We're holding at the head of a corridor leading to the device storage room. I've tasked one of the remotes to guide you to our position."

Leaving the local stormtroopers to establish a perimeter outside the building, Tarkin, Vader, and the remainder of the Coruscant contingent entered, glow rods in hand as they trailed the tasked remote through some of the corridors and up and down some of the stairways they had been shown earlier. In short order they had rendezvoused with Crest and the others, fifty meters from massive, retrofitted sliding doors that appeared to seal the storeroom.

Vader gestured for the squad leader to send one of the remotes down the final stretch, then to follow with four of his troopers. Tarkin tracked their wary advance on the sliding doors, which Crest parted just widely enough to allow passage for the remote. When after a long moment the remote exited, Crest signaled for Vader, Tarkin, and the others to proceed.

First to reach the sliding doors, Vader came to a sudden halt.

"The remote found nothing untoward?" he asked Crest.

"Nothing, Lord Vader."

Vader's breathing filled the corridor. "Something . . ."

Tarkin watched him closely. Vader's exceptional instincts had alerted him to a threat of some sort. But what? He began to think through the holotransmissions of the remotes' dizzying exploration of the confused interior of the building. On every level the surveillance droids had reached dead ends similar to the one he, Vader, and the stormtroopers now faced. Did that mean that the storeroom was several stories high? Perhaps it had been an atrium before it became a storage space. Tarkin thought back to the squad

leader's description of the building: "*A medcenter . . .
Housed a deflector shield generator . . .*"

Tarkin couldn't imagine such an enormous piece of
machinery having been assembled in place. Which
could mean—

"Lord Vader, this isn't the primary entrance," he
said.

Vader turned to him.

"Who would be fool enough to haul communications devices through these corridors and up and
down these stairways?" Tarkin gestured upward with
his chin. "I suspect they were delivered here through
a rooftop access. The sliding doors could lead to an
ambush of some sort."

Vader took a moment to consider it, then looked at
Crest. "You've failed me again, Sergeant."

"Lord Vader, the remote—"

"The rooftop," Tarkin interrupted.

Vader glanced at him but said nothing.

They exited the building by the same route they
had taken earlier. Once outside, Vader ordered the
squad leader to call for the gunship, and all of them
scampered up onto the deployment platform. On the
building's flat roof they discovered a well-concealed
and functional turbolift shaft, five meters in diameter,
transparent, and safe to use. Surveying the vast room
while they were descending, Tarkin spotted the remains of a reception counter centered among stacks
of metal shipping containers and exposed machines.

"No one touches anything until I've had a look,"
he told the stormtroopers. "And take care where you
walk. The doors may not be alone in being rigged."

While Vader, Crest, and some of the others moved
off to investigate the secondary entrance, Tarkin, feeling as if he were stepping back in time, began to me-

ander through the rows created by the stacked containers and devices.

It had been just nine months after the Battle of Geonosis that Count Dooku's scientists had succeeded in slicing into the Republic HoloNet by seeding the spaceways with hyperwave transceiver nodes of a novel design. The Separatists could have kept quiet about the infiltration and tasked the nodes to gather intelligence about Republic military operations. Instead, Dooku—as if suddenly intent on winning hearts and minds rather than defeating the Republic with his droid armies—began using the HoloNet to broadcast propaganda Shadowfeeds, providing Separatist accounts of battle wins and disinformation about Republic war crimes, and in the end spreading apprehension among the populations of the Core Worlds that a Separatist victory was imminent.

It was, however, Separatist success in jamming Republic communication relays that had brought Tarkin into play. Together with operatives of the Republic's fledgling cryptanalysis department and elements of the Twelfth Army, Tarkin had been sent to Murkhana both to spearhead the invasion and to oversee the dismantling of the Shadowfeed operation.

Running his hands now over S-thread jammers, signal eradicators, and HoloNet chafing devices, he recalled being among the first wave of clone trooper platoons to fight their way into the building that was the source of the Shadowfeeds; then, on overpowering the Separatist forces, torturing the captive scientists into revealing the secrets of their jamming and steganographic technology, and putting to death thousands of beings who had contributed to Dooku's scheme. The mission had constituted the first of Tarkin's covert operations undertaken for then supreme chancellor Palpatine. Murkhana had kicked off a year of similar successes—though it had ended in Tarkin's capture, torture, and incarceration in Citadel prison.

With the Emperor's proclamation of the New Order, some aspects of the HoloNet had come under strict Imperial control, as much to provide the military with exclusive communications networks as to censor unauthorized news feeds.

Tarkin was completing his initial survey of the components when Vader sought him out.

"The sliding doors were engineered to trigger a blast when opened fully," he said. "Odd that the remote failed to register the explosives."

Tarkin gestured to the stacks of devices. "Whoever assembled this array found a way to blind the remotes."

Vader looked around. "Imperial Security's operative made no mention of a rigged entrance."

Tarkin pinched his lower lip. "That could mean that the explosives were only recently installed."

"With the building under constant surveillance?"

"The street entrances, yes," Tarkin said. "Probably not the roof."

Vader absorbed that in silence, then said, "Puzzling, even so. All this merely to lure and murder an investigative team?"

"I doubt that the door trap was meant for us, Lord Vader."

"Intruders of a more ordinary sort? Would-be thieves, black marketeers?" Vader gazed about him in what struck Tarkin as mounting vexation. "Have you found any unfamiliar devices?"

"Not yet," Tarkin said.

"Then it is all too obvious. These devices were deliberately placed where they could be discovered. This is a stage set."

"Perhaps," Tarkin said. "But we're going to need to

investigate every container to be certain there's nothing new among the devices. This cache may date from the war, but that doesn't negate that the components appear to be fully functional and capable of interrupting or corrupting HoloNet signals."

Vader was dismissive. "Technology that has been available for nearly a decade, Governor."

"The question is, why are these devices here?"

"Someone found them elsewhere and moved them here for safekeeping until their value could be determined."

"That would explain the rigged doors . . . ," Tarkin said. "But it's also possible that whoever originally found the cache made use of some of the components to engineer the false distress call transmitted to Sentinel Base."

Vader fell silent for a long moment, then said, "I agree. Your proposal, then?"

Tarkin glanced around. "We cam everything and record and transmit to Coruscant any serial numbers or markings we find. Any suspect components should be relocated to the *Carrion Spike* and also returned to Coruscant for further analysis. The rest should be destroyed."

Vader nodded in agreement.

Tarkin glanced around again and sighed with purpose. "We have our work cut out for us."

"The stormtroopers can see to most of it," Vader said. "There is someone I wish to speak with before we return to the Core."

Tarkin showed him a questioning look.

"The Imperial Security Bureau asset who first reported the find."

11

FAIR GAME

AS THE GUNSHIP SPED back toward the center of the city, Tarkin, gazing on the devastation, thought: *This might have been Eriadu had he not warned the planetary leadership that supporting Dooku would have meant inviting cataclysm.*

Not every member of the planet's ruling body had agreed with him, but in the end he'd gotten his way and Eriadu had remained loyal to the Republic. For Tarkin, though, the stewardship of his homeworld had come to an end. When word of his decision not to seek reelection became known, his aging and by then ailing father had summoned him to the family compound for a frank conversation.

"Politics hasn't been enough of a battleground for you?" his father had asked from the bed to which he was confined, his body punctured by feeding tubes and shunts. The view out the large window took in nearly all of the calm bay.

"More than enough," Tarkin said from a chair beside the bed. "But the immigration issues are solved, the economy is back on track, and our world is now thought of as a Core world in the Outer Rim." The adjoining room of the master suite had been transformed into a kind of intensive care unit, with a bacta tank and a team of medical droids standing by in the event the elder Tarkin should desire resuscitation.

"Granted," his father said. "That, however, does not mean that your work is done. A lot of people worked very hard to get you in office."

"I've done what I set out to accomplish and paid them back in full," Tarkin said more harshly than he intended. "Some more than they even deserve." He fell silent for a moment, then added: "I'm exasperated by having to appease so many separate interests and fight to have laws passed and enacted. Politics is worse than a theater of war."

His father snorted. "This from someone who has always preached the importance of law and rule by fear."

"That hasn't changed. But it has to be on my terms. What's more, Eriadu's internal problems scarcely matter in the present scheme of things. When I met last with Dooku, he made it sound as though galactic war is both inevitable and imminent."

"And why wouldn't he? In his determination to persuade you to throw in with his Separatists, he would make use of enticement, threats, whatever it takes."

Tarkin thought back through his recent conversation with the count, and shook his head. "There was something else on his mind, but I couldn't pry it from him. It was almost as if he was offering me an opportunity to join some secret fraternity of beings who are actually responsible for this mess."

His father seemed to consider it. "What will you do, then? Wait for the Republic to instate a military and enlist?" He shook his head in disgust. "You served in Outland, you served in the Judicial Department. Enlistment would be a backward step just when Eriadu needs you most. *Especially* if this schism leads to war. Who will be able to keep Eriadu safe should it fall to Dooku's forces?"

"That's precisely the point. There's only so much one can do with words and arguments."

"So you'll race to the light of the lasers. Wasn't that what you used to exclaim as an Outland commander?" His father managed a rueful laugh. "You may as well adopt it as a personal motto."

"Death or renown, Father. I am, after all, your son."

"So you are," his father said, slowly nodding his head. "Has the supreme chancellor remarked on your decision?"

Tarkin nodded. "Palpatine is in my corner, as it were."

"I was afraid of that." His father regarded him for a long moment. "I urge you think back to the Carrion, Wilhuff. When a pride's territory is threatened, the dominant beast stands its ground. It doesn't run off to enlist in a larger cause. You must think of Eriadu itself as the plateau."

Tarkin stared out the window, and then turned to face his father. "Jova told me a story that bears on my decision. Long before you were born—long before even Jova was born—a group of developers had designs on the Carrion and all those resource-rich lands the Tarkin family had amassed. Our ancestors initially attempted to resolve the matter peacefully. They attempted to placate the developers with credits. At one point, as Jova tells it, they were even prepared to offer the developers all the lands north of the Orrineswa River clear to Mount Veermok, but their offer was rejected in the strongest terms. For the developers, it was either the entire plateau and all the surrounding territory or none at all."

His father smiled weakly. "I know how this story ended."

Tarkin smiled back at him. "The Tarkins understood that they weren't going to keep their adversaries at bay by posting NO TRESPASSING signs or encircling the Carrion with plasma fences. Giving all evidence that they were prepared to capitulate, they lured the leadership of the conglomerate to the bargaining table."

"And assassinated them to a man," his father said.

"To a man. And that was the end of it."

His father took a deep breath and loosed a stuttering exhale. "I understand. But you're naïve to think that the Republic has the guts to do that with Dooku and the rest. Mark my words, this war will drag on and on until every world pays a price. And I'm glad I won't be around to see that happen."

The ambassador to Murkhana was waiting at the top of the ornate stairway that fronted the principal building of the Imperial compound. A tall, broad-shouldered woman, she was dressed appropriately for Murkhana, Tarkin thought, in that she was sporting stormtrooper armor.

Seemingly unable to decide whether to salute or bow as he and Vader approached, she simply spread her arms in a welcoming gesture and adopted a cynical smile. Murkhana's acid rain and soupy air had taken a toll on her hair and complexion, but she appeared otherwise healthy.

"Welcome, Lord Vader and Governor Tarkin. I was aware that Coruscant was sending an investigative team, but I had no idea—"

"Has the operative arrived?" Vader interrupted.

She gestured to the residence with a flick of her head. "Inside. I summoned him as soon as I received your comm."

"Show us to him."

She spun on her boot heels and made for the reinforced front door, two stormtroopers flanking the entrance stepping aside and saluting Vader and Tarkin as they passed. The entry hall and main room of the residence were sparsely furnished, and the dry air was artificially scented. A Koorivarn male taller than Tarkin and draped in tattered robes stood silently behind a curved couch. His cranial horn was of average size for his species, but his facial ridges were marred by intersecting scars.

The ambassador gestured for Vader and Tarkin to sit, but they declined.

"May I at least offer you something to—"

"Tell me, Ambassador," Vader interrupted again, "do you ever leave this compound of yours, with its high sensor-studded walls and company of armed sentries?"

"Of course."

"Then no doubt you have seen the obscene scrawlings and defacements displayed on every other building between here and this planet's wretched excuse for a spaceport."

She showed him a sardonic look. "My lord, as quickly as I have them expunged, new ones spring up."

"And what of the criminal rabble that cluster on every corner?" Tarkin asked.

She laughed shortly. "They proliferate even more quickly than the defacements, Governor Tarkin. The moment Black Sun moved out, the Crymorah moved in."

"The Crymorah," Vader said.

"Actually a local affiliate known as the Sugi."

Vader seemed to tuck the information away.

"You need to make an example of them," Tarkin said.

The ambassador looked at him as if he'd lost his mind. "You think I haven't tried?"

Tarkin cocked an eyebrow. "Meaning what, exactly?"

She started to reply, then blew out her breath and began again. "I've made appeal after appeal to Moff Therbon for additional stormtroopers, to no avail."

"And if we see to it that you have additional resources, you'll do what must be done?"

She continued to regard Tarkin with skepticism. "Excuse me, Governor, but I don't think you understand the situation fully. Officiating here has been like serving a sentence for a crime I didn't commit. The stormtroopers have a saying, *Better spaced than based on Belderone,* and we're a far cry from Belderone." She blew out her breath. "Yes, I can leave this compound, but my life is at risk whenever I do. Hence, the white wardrobe." She glanced between Tarkin and Vader. "Maybe you two haven't noticed, but Murkhana isn't Coruscant. The population here *hates* me. I sometimes think *Murkhana* hates me. I'm held responsible for every Imperial tax increase and every minor change to the legal system. The smugglers are the only ones who garner respect, because they're the only ones providing goods—even if at exorbitant rates. As for the crime lords, they're the only ones powerful enough to provide protection from the thieves and murderers this planet has bred since the war ended."

Vader took a step in her direction. "I will be sure to let the Emperor know of your dissatisfaction, Ambassador."

She didn't retreat. "I sure as hell wish someone would. I mean, I'm humbled that the Emperor deemed me worthy to serve him, but this assignment—"

Vader thrust his forefinger at her. "Allowing a cell of dissidents to operate under your watch is not what I would call serving the Emperor, Ambassador."

"Dissidents?" She shook her head in genuine bewilderment. "I don't understand."

Instead of explaining, Vader turned his attention to the Koorivar. "You are the intelligence asset?"

"I am Bracchia," the Koorivar said in little more than a whisper.

Tarkin knew that it was nothing more than a code name, but it was the only name Deputy Director Harus Ison had been willing to provide. "You were a Republic operative during the war."

Bracchia nodded. "I was, Governor Tarkin. I assisted in your anti-Shadowfeed operation here."

Tarkin adopted a thin-lipped expression of wariness. "Tell us about the Corporate Alliance building—the former medcenter."

The Koorivar nodded in deference. "Before entering, I watched the building every day for a week, Governor Tarkin. When I determined it to be unoccupied, I entered and made a quick inventory of the devices as directed."

"As *directed*?" Tarkin asked in surprise.

But before Bracchia could respond, Vader said, "You entered how?"

The Koorivar turned to him. "Through sliding doors, Lord Vader. I'm not aware of any other entrance, and the devices were just where I was told I would find them."

"How could you fail to notice the turbolift?" Vader said.

The Koorivar looked at the floor. "My apologies,

Lord Vader. I was fixated on investigating the devices."

Tarkin placed himself deliberately between Bracchia and Vader. "Are you saying that you didn't make the discovery on your own?"

"No, Governor, I did not. I was merely tasked with verifying a report sent to me from Coruscant."

Tarkin's brow furrowed. "From Imperial Security?"

Bracchia nodded. "From my case officer at ISB, yes."

Tarkin had his mouth open to pursue the matter when his comlink sounded and he prized the device from its belt pouch.

"We're at the building, Governor Tarkin."

Tarkin recognized the voice of Sergeant Crest. "At what building?"

"Back at the Corporate Alliance building, sir."

"You're not at the landing field?"

Crest took a moment to reply. "Sir, you told us to return here after we'd off-loaded the devices at the corvette."

"Who told you?"

"You, sir." Crest sounded as confused as Tarkin.

"I sent no such orders, Sergeant."

"Excuse me, sir, but the order came by holotransmission from you just after we'd transferred the last of the devices you marked for the ship. Without the gunship, we had to commandeer an airspeeder at the landing field."

"Who is with the ship?" Vader stepped in to say toward the comlink's audio pickup.

"Two of our group, Lord Vader, in addition to the corvette's captain and comm officer."

Tarkin felt blood rush from his face. "Sergeant, return to the ship immediately."

"On our way, sir."

Vader looked at Tarkin while he was contacting the *Carrion Spike*'s captain. "A second feature from the makers of the false holovid transmitted to the moon base?"

"In which *I* am now the principal actor," Tarkin said, trying not to sound too rattled. Checking the comlink again, he added: "I can't raise the ship."

"That happens all the time, Governor Tarkin," the ambassador said. "If it's not the city's power grid, it's the communications array."

He glanced at her with his mouth open, an uneasy feeling beginning to coil in his chest. Fingers dancing over the comlink's keypad, he opened a second channel that allowed him to communicate with the corvette itself, and entered a code that commanded the *Carrion Spike*'s slave system to prevent anyone from so much as approaching the ship. But the system didn't respond.

"Nothing," he said to Vader. "Not from the command cabin, not from the ship itself."

Vader whirled on the ambassador. "Contact Coruscant by HoloNet immediately."

She spread her hands in apology. "Lord Vader, Murkhana hasn't had HoloNet communications since early in the Clone Wars." She cut her eyes to Tarkin. "The HoloNet was destroyed during the first Republic assault."

Tarkin recalled. The relay had been destroyed as a means of disrupting Dooku's Shadowfeeds to worlds along the Perlemian Trade Route. His thoughts reeled.

"Send a subspace transmission," Vader was saying.

"Governor Tarkin," Crest said from the comlink, "we're back at the landing field." He fell silent for a long moment, and when he spoke again his voice betrayed astonishment. "Sir, the *Carrion Spike* is nowhere in sight."

Tarkin stared at the comlink. "What?"

"It's not here, sir. It must have launched."

"Impossible!" Tarkin said.

"Where are your troopers, Sergeant?" Vader all but snarled.

Again the reply was long in arriving. "Lord Vader, we have a visual on four bodies—two stormtroopers, the captain, and the comm officer." Crest paused, then added, "Shot through and through, Lord Vader."

Vader clenched his right hand. "You've failed me for the last time, Sergeant."

"I get that, sir," Crest said in a somber voice.

Vader turned to Tarkin. "We sidestepped the smaller trap only to fall into the larger one, Governor. If nothing else, we now know the reason we were lured here." Bringing his left hand to the brow of his helmet, he paced away from Tarkin and the ambassador, then swung back to them. "The ship is still in the Murkhana system."

Tarkin didn't waste time asking how Vader knew that to be the case. Instead, he glanced at one of the stormtroopers. "The Judicial cruiser at the landing field."

The stormtrooper shook his head in a mournful way. "Not spaceworthy, sir. We've been waiting on replacement parts for the hyperdrive motivator for three months, local."

"I know where to procure a ship," Vader said abruptly. He swept his arm in a gesture aimed at the stormtroopers. "All of you—come with me." Then he turned and pointed to Bracchia. "And you."

Tarkin fell in among them as they hastened from the ambassador's residence.

* * *

Tarkin had his doubts.

At Lola Sayu, when Skywalker, Kenobi, and Ahsoka Tano had participated in rescuing him from the Citadel, Tarkin had taken issue with the Jedi strategy of splitting into two teams. Surrendering group integrity for twice the number of potential problems made little sense, and that was precisely the way the mission had unfolded. Tarkin's general, Even Piell, had been killed, and the rest of them had nearly fallen back into the clutches of the Citadel's sadistic Separatist prison warden. Now, all these years later, Vader had split their forces, and here they were allowing themselves to be herded at blasterpoint into the den of a Sugi crime lord while the stormtroopers were elsewhere in Murkhana City carrying out their part of Vader's plan.

So Tarkin had his doubts.

But with the *Carrion Spike* apparently in the hands of shipjackers, and his captain, comm officer, and two stormtroopers dead, he had little choice but to go along with the subterfuge, in the hope that it would succeed.

"I *still* don't like splitting up the team," he said to Vader as one of the Sugi was shoving him from behind.

Vader glanced over at him, but as ever it was impossible to tell what was going on behind the black orbs and muzzle of his mask.

The headquarters building was in better condition than most in Murkhana City, its graceful swirls of coral and undersea colors having either survived the war or been restored since. Initially Tarkin had taken the Sugi for an insectile species, but in fact they were short bipeds who affected armored powersuits. The suits provided them with a second set of legs and a segmented, barb-tipped abdomen, which gave them the appearance of mythological creatures. The soldiers, at any rate. Others in the dank hall Vader and Tarkin were escorted into stood on their own two feet and wore cowl-like helmets, with power packs of some sort on their backs. The outsized helmets made their large-eyed skeletal faces seem even smaller than they were.

Twenty soldiers complemented the half dozen who were holding weapons on Vader and Tarkin, with several repurposed Separatist battle droids augmenting the hall group. Their apparent leader lounged on a gaudy throne of coral, clicking orders to his minions.

Vader came to a halt five meters from the throne and spent a moment taking in the overstated surroundings. "You have done well for yourself since the demise of your former competitor, crime lord," he said at last.

"And for that I owe you a debt of gratitude, Lord Vader," the Sugi answered in heavily accented Basic. "That is the sole reason I have allowed you entry to my abode—to thank you personally for killing my predecessor and persuading Black Sun to abandon Murkhana for safer realms."

"You are as insolent as he was, crime lord."

"Given that I enjoy the upper hand here, Lord Vader, I can well afford to be."

Vader folded his arms across his massive chest. "Don't be too sure of yourself."

The Sugi dismissed the warning. "I have been apprised by my associates of your prowess, Lord Vader. But I doubt that even you could triumph over so many." When Vader said nothing, he continued: "Now, what is this drivel about commandeering my starship?"

Tarkin stepped forward to speak. "We take your

meaning about being outnumbered. But perhaps there's a healthier way to persuade you to do as Lord Vader asks."

The Sugi's large eyes expanded. "I have not had the pleasure . . ."

"Meet Moff Tarkin, crime lord," Vader said. "Sector governor of Greater Seswenna and more."

The Sugi sat back in his chair. "Now I am impressed. That Murkhana should play host to two such luminary Imperials . . . Though many might say I would be doing the galaxy a favor by eliminating you here and now." He fixed his gaze on Tarkin. "But you were saying, Governor Tarkin . . ."

"That in meetings of this nature there are always alternatives to using brute force."

"I can't imagine any alternatives that will convince me to surrender my fanged beauty of a starship, Governor Tarkin."

Cautiously, Tarkin drew a portable holoprojector disk from the pocket of his tunic. "If I may?"

The Sugi waved permission.

"Sergeant Crest," Vader said toward the device. "Are you in the crime lord's warehouse?"

"Yes, Lord Vader. Ready to bring the entire place down on your command."

"Then you have redeemed yourself, Sergeant."

"Thank you, Lord Vader."

The crime lord's expression approximated entertainment. "You can't be serious. Or do you actually believe that I would surrender my ship for a warehouse full of weapons?"

"Your Crymorah associates on Coruscant might encourage you to do just that."

"I'll take my chances, Lord Vader."

"You're right of course," Tarkin said quickly. "But just now your warehouse contains more than weapons. We've arranged for your wives and brood to be present as well." He called up an image of the Sugi's family members huddled in a circle on the warehouse floor and surrounded by stormtroopers with raised weapons. "We understand that you are very attached to them. A product of your genetics, I suspect."

"You wouldn't!" the Sugi said.

His earlier doubts about Vader's plan beginning to fade, Tarkin lifted an arrogant eyebrow. "Wouldn't we?"

The Sugi fidgeted in apprehension. "I can have both of you killed where you stand!"

"We'll take our chances," Tarkin said, grinning slightly. "Your ship for their lives."

After a long moment of rapid clicking and nervous hand wringing, the Sugi broke the tense silence. "All right, take the ship! I will purchase a replacement. I will purchase twenty replacements. Just let them live— let them live!"

Tarkin's face grew deadly serious. "You'll need to furnish us with all the necessary launch codes and order all of your underlings to leave the landing field at once."

"Then I will do it," the crime lord said. "Whatever you ask!"

Vader leaned slightly in the direction of the com-link. "Sergeant Crest, transport the crime lord's family to the landing field and let me know when your troops are in possession of his ship."

"Let them live," the Sugi repeated, rising halfway out of his throne in supplication.

"Take heart," Tarkin said. "They most certainly will survive you."

12

BURYING THE LEAD

OUTBOUND FROM MURKHANA, the *Carrion Spike*'s new pilot and three members of the new crew were gathered in the command cabin marveling at the wonders of the ship. The shipjackers—a human, a Mon Calamari, a Gotal, and a Koorivar—some standing, others seated in the chairs that fronted the curved instrument console, could hardly keep still, having pulled off an act of piracy that had been close to two years in the planning.

The human, Teller, was a rangy, middle-aged man with thick dark hair and eyebrows to match. His long face was perpetually shadowed with stubble, and his chin bore a deep cleft. Dressed in cargo pants, boots, and a thermal shirt, he stood between the principal acceleration chairs, watching as the Gotal pilot and the Koorivar operations specialist familiarized themselves with the ship's complex controls. The bulkhead left of the forward viewports bore traces of carbon scoring and blood from the brief blaster fight that erupted when the shipjackers had had to burn and battle their way through the command cabin hatch to deal with Tarkin's defiant captain and comm officer.

"Getting the hang of it?" Teller asked the Gotal, Salikk.

The twin-horned, flat-faced humanoid nodded without taking his heavy-lidded scarlet eyes from the instrument array. "She flies herself," he said in accented Basic. A native of the moon Antar 4, he was short and dark-skinned, with tufts of light hair on his cheeks and chin. He wore an old-fashioned but serviceable flight suit that left the clawed digits of his sensitive hands exposed.

"It will fly itself, but we're going to tell it where to go," Dr. Artoz told him.

The Mon Cal wore a flight suit whose neck had been altered to accommodate the amphibious humanoid's high-domed, salmon-colored head, and whose sleeves ended mid-forearm to allow passage for his large webbed hands. Pacing the length of the instruments console, Artoz was pointing out individual controls, his huge eyes swiveling independently of each other to focus simultaneously on Salikk and the ops specialist, Cala.

Teller had known all three of them for years, but what with Salikk's sweaty scent and the saline smell Artoz emitted, he was grateful for the spaciousness of the *Carrion Spike*'s command cabin. Then again, from what he'd been told by his nonhuman friends, humans weren't exactly a picnic when it came to body odor.

"Computer-assisted fire control for the lateral lasers and in-close weapons," Artoz was saying, indicating one set of instruments after the next. "Full-authority navicomp, stealth system initiator, sublight ions, hyperdrive."

"State-of-the-art Imperial technology," Cala said.

Jutting from a headcloth that fell past the Koorivar's shoulders, his spiraling cranial horn was twice the height of Salikk's conical projections and thicker than both of them combined. He wore pouch-pocketed pants not unlike Teller's under a roomy tunic that reached his thick thighs. "This corvette will easily exceed a Star Destroyer."

"Nothing less than what I promised," Artoz said, though without a hint of self-importance. He gestured to the auxiliary controls. "Sensor suite, rectenna controls, alluvial dampers, reverse triggering acceleration compensator—"

"Which one empties the toilets?" a second human asked as she stepped through the scarred cockpit hatch. Fit and scrappy looking, she had a narrow frame and skin the color of a tropical hardwood. Her short curly hair was naturally black but had been lightened to a mishmash of brown and blond. She wore a white utility suit and ankle-length ship-tread boots. The Zygerrian female who followed her into the command cabin was also slender, though somewhat taller, and distinctly feline in appearance. Pointed, fur-covered ears sprang straight up from the sides of a narrow-nosed, triangular face. Her innate exoticism was enhanced by reddish coloring.

Teller turned to them. "Everything locked down back there?"

The woman, Anora, nodded. "The outer hatch is fully sealed. The air lock, not so much." She gestured with her pointed chin to the Zygerrian. "Hask's going to keep working on it—since it was her blaster that did the damage."

Hask snorted. "When she slammed into me." She spoke Basic flawlessly, but with a thick accent.

Anora showed her a long-suffering look. "You were supposed to keep the safety on."

"For the last time," she said, "I'm not a soldier, and I'll never be one."

"Plenty of blame to go around," Teller said, cutting them off. "The holocams survive?"

Enthusiasm informed Hask's nod. Her head bore a symmetrical pattern of small spurs. "They're in the main cabin. I'll get started slaving them to the Holo-Net comm board—"

"As soon as she's repaired the air lock," Anora said, blue-gray eyes bright over her smile.

Hask ignored her. "Nice of Tarkin's stormtroopers to carry some of the storeroom components aboard. I thought we were going to have to sacrifice them."

"We have Tarkin to thank for a lot of things," Teller said. He swung forward in time to catch the end of Artoz's instrument rundown.

"Air lock overrides, blast-tinting for the viewports . . . What else?"

"Do all the Emperor's Moffs rate one of these?" Anora asked, running a hand over the console in appreciation.

"Only Tarkin," Artoz said, "as far as we know."

"A testament to his friendship with Sienar," Teller said.

"Sienar Fleet Systems wasn't the only contributor," Artoz amended. "The company's design sense is all over the corvette, but every shipbuilder from Theed Engineering to Cygnus Spaceworks played a part in outfitting it."

"Not to mention Tarkin himself," Teller said. "The Moff was designing ships for Eriadu's Outland Security Force when he was nineteen."

Hask made a sour face. "More Prefsbelt Academy legends."

Anora shook her head negatively. "True by all accounts."

Teller perched on the arm of one of the secondary acceleration chairs. "The way I heard it, Eriadu was losing a lot of its lommite shipments to a pirate group that had fortified the bow of one of their ships to use as a rostrum—a kind of battering ram—after destroying too much cargo with their lasers."

"The pirates weren't acquainted with ion cannons?" Salikk said from the pilot's seat.

Teller glanced at the Gotal. "Seswenna's ships were too well ray-shielded for that—another Tarkin innovation, I might add. Anyway, he designed a narrow-profile ship with cannons that could swivel on pintles to direct all firepower forward. Confronted the rammer bow-on."

"Damn the particle beams, full speed ahead," Hask said, still refusing to buy into the legend.

Teller nodded. "Burned through the pirates' armor like a knife through butter and blew the ship apart." He turned to point to toggles on the control console. "Same system here."

Cala grinned. "Should come in handy."

"We can hope," Artoz said, giving the console a final appraisal with his right eye while his left remained fixed on Salikk. "Proximity alarms, hypercomm unit, Imperial HoloNet encryptor . . ."

"Why is it called the *Carrion Spike*?" Anora said.

Teller drew his lips in and shook his head. "Not a clue."

Everyone fell silent for a moment, gazing through the viewports at the Murkhana system's small outermost planet and the vast starfield beyond.

"I still can't get over Vader being there," Hask said finally. "I mean, why would the Emperor send him to escort Tarkin?"

"Vader paid Murkhana a visit just after the war

ended," Cala said. "Executed a Black Sun Twi'lek racketeer, among other acts."

"Still," Hask said. "Vader . . ."

"Stop calling him by name," Anora said harshly; then softened her tone to add: "He's a machine. A terrorist." She looked at Teller. "You took a real risk having him and Tarkin walk right into that sliding door ambush."

Teller shrugged it off. "We had to make the scenario ring true. Besides, their getting themselves blown up wouldn't have affected our plans one way or another."

"The Emperor wouldn't have been happy losing two of his top henchmen," Cala pointed out.

"He's not going to be happy either way," Teller said.

The console issued a loud tone, and Cala lifted his eyes to the display. "Uh, Teller, we've got a starship on our tail."

Teller's dark eyebrows quirked together. "Can't be. You certain you have the stealth system enabled?"

The Koorivar nodded. "Status indicators say so. We should be invisible to scanners."

Everyone crowded around the sensor suite. "Put the ship on screen," Teller said.

Cala's stubby-fingered hands raced across the keypad, and a black ship with forward fangs resolved on the display. "Waiting for a transponder signature . . ."

"Don't bother," Salikk said. "That's Faazah's ship. The *Parsec Predator*."

Teller nodded. "The Sugi arms dealer."

"Murkhana's most wanted," Salikk said.

Cala ran his gaze over the sensor indicators. "Matching our every move."

Teller stared at the screen and scratched his head in bafflement. "I'm willing to entertain explanations."

Artoz spoke first. "Perhaps this Sugi is simply heading for the same jump point we are."

Teller nodded to Salikk. "Put this thing through some maneuvers, and let's see what happens."

The corvette changed vectors, slewing to port, then to starboard before rocketing through an abrupt, twisting climb that delivered them swiftly to the dark side of the impact-cratered planet.

Everyone fell silent again, waiting for the Koorivar's update. "The *Predator*'s still with us, just emerging from the transitor." Cala swiveled to Teller. "And here's something strange: We're not being scanned."

Teller and Artoz looked perplexed. "You stated that it is matching our every maneuver," the Mon Cal said.

"It is," Cala emphasized. "And I repeat, we're not being scanned. No sensor lock, no indication that we're being observed."

Teller traded glances with Artoz. "A homing beacon?" he suggested.

The Mon Cal's confusion didn't abate.

Teller looked at Hask. "It was your job to check for trackers."

"I did," the Zygerrian all but snarled. "There weren't any."

"Or you didn't find any," Teller said.

"Why would this Faazah attach a locator to Tarkin's ship?" Anora said. "Or is that just a Sugi thing to do?"

"Offhand, I can't imagine a reason," Artoz said. "But we can certainly outrace the *Predator* if we have to."

Teller considered it. "That doesn't make me feel a whole lot better, Doc. Not if we've got a faulty stealth system."

"Teller, we are *not* being scanned," Cala repeated.

"The stealth system is operating impeccably. Check the status displays for yourself if you don't trust me."

Teller made a placating gesture. "Of course I trust you. I just don't get it."

"Should we contact our ally?" Salikk said.

"No, not yet," Teller said. "We'll be updated soon enough, in any case."

"Unless . . . ," Hask began.

Anora aimed a faint smile at the Zygerrian. "I'll bet I know what you're going to say, and yes, that occurred to me, too."

Teller and the others looked at the two of them. "What am I missing?" Teller asked.

"Vader," Hask said, exhaling. "Vader and Tarkin."

Teller continued to regard them. "What, the Sugi is giving them a ride?"

Anora rocked her head from side to side. "Or they appropriated his ship."

"They could have." Teller plucked at his lower lip. "Still doesn't make sense, though—not if we're invisible to the *Predator*'s sensors. Or are you saying that Tarkin's got some secret way of locking onto us?"

Cala spoke to it. "We disabled the slave circuit when we silenced the stormtroopers' comlinks and the ship's comm."

"Maybe Tarkin is a telepath, along with being a ship designer," Salikk said.

"Vader," Hask rasped. *"Va-der."*

Teller locked eyes with her. "Vader has a way of neutralizing stealth technology?"

Hask spread her slim, furry hands. "Who knows what's inside that helmet of his? Besides, what other explanation is there?"

"We should have launched sooner," Cala said. "We'd be out of the system by now."

Teller shot him a gimlet look. "A couple of jumps

from here, I'm going to remind you that you said that." He glanced at Salikk. "How soon until we can go to lightspeed?"

The Gotal studied the navicomputer display. "As soon as you give the word."

Teller took a breath and let it out. "Let's see them try to track us through hyperspace."

"Is this ship fast enough to close the distance?"

Darth Vader pulled the yoke toward him. "It is faster than most, Governor, but unfortunately not as fast as yours. We need to disable the corvette before it can elude us."

Tarkin despaired. As disturbingly well armed as the late crime lord's ship was, disabling the *Carrion Spike* was easier said than done. If the ship was, in some sense, a measure of his standing in the Imperial hegemony, then his vaunted reputation just might go down with her.

They were at the edge of the Murkhana system, the eponymous world well behind them, already a memory, and a bitter one. He and Vader were sharing the controls, Vader wedged into an acceleration chair made for a much smaller being, Tarkin strapped into the copilot's chair. Crest and the other stormtroopers were amidships, manning the ship's quad laser cannons.

Never having shared a cockpit with Vader, Tarkin was astonished by the Dark Lord's piloting skills. Though perhaps he shouldn't have been.

The sound of Vader's slow, rhythmic breathing overwhelmed the cockpit as he indicated an area dead ahead and slightly to port. "There."

Tarkin saw nothing but star-studded blackness. Nor did the ship's instruments register the *Carrion*

Spike, which was obviously running in stealth mode. He couldn't imagine how Vader was managing to track the ship, but was for the moment content to be mystified.

"Why are they still in system?" he said. "They can't have shipjacked it for a joyride."

Vader glanced at him across a center console. "They were convinced we couldn't follow them. They are merely taking time to familiarize themselves with the instruments."

"Then they must know that we're tracking them."

"Indeed they do."

Tarkin found himself actually warming to Vader, especially after what had happened in the Sugi's headquarters. No sooner had word arrived that Sergeant Crest and his stormtroopers were in possession of the *Parsec Predator* and the codes necessary to launch her than Vader exacted his revenge on the crime lord for having been kept waiting. Tarkin knew merely by the gasping sounds that began to erupt from the Sugi that Vader was performing that thumb-and-forefinger dark magic of his to crush the crime lord's windpipe. By then, too, the ambassador's stormtroopers had rushed into the headquarters, unleashing flash grenades and blaster bolts that had caught the Sugi's underlings by surprise. At one point Vader had asked them whether they actually wanted to die for their leader, and it was when they replied with weapons that Vader drew his crimson-bladed lightsaber from beneath his cape. Tarkin had witnessed numerous Jedi wield lightsabers during the Clone Wars, but he had never seen anyone put an energy blade to such determined purpose or achieve such rapid and lethal results. Two stormtroopers had died in the exchange, but all the Sugi had paid with their lives; Vader's blade had even reduced the repurposed battle droids to useless parts.

"The ambassador owes you a big favor," Tarkin had told Vader at the time.

Now he said: "Surely we weren't lured all the way to Murkhana just so the *Carrion Spike* could be shipjacked."

"And why not?" Vader said. "Stealth, firepower, alacrity." He paused as if he were about to ask a follow-up question, but said nothing further.

"Granted it's one of a kind, but what is their plan? To strip and sell it for parts? To have it dissected and replicated?" Tarkin heard the words tumbling from his mouth in a rush and got control of himself.

"A flotilla of *Carrion Spike*s," Vader said, clearly dubious.

Tarkin gestured in dismissal. "Not without the help of the top engineering conglomerates in the galaxy. More to the point, whoever they are, they now have the corvette, as well as a capital ship."

"You are convinced that the piracy was carried out by the same beings who attacked Sentinel."

"I am. Anyone with skill enough to create counterfeit holovids of ships and beings and to interrupt Imperial HoloNet signals would also have the skill to wrap the *Carrion Spike* in a mantle of silence, disabling not only the ship's slave system but also her various communications systems, including comlinks and helmet radios." He paused briefly. "Vice Admirals Rancit and Screed were correct about the cache being part of a more far-reaching plan. If the cache was merely the lure, then the plot is still unfolding."

"Then tell me how to disable your ship, Governor."

Tarkin firmed his lips. "There is a weakness. If the thieves can be persuaded to lower the shields, concentrated fire on the spine where the main fuselage meets the aft flare should do the trick. We were never able to resolve the problem of properly safeguarding the hyperdrive generator while the power plant is supplying the ion drives, the deflector shields, and the weapons. It's not so much a design flaw as an accommodation to the ship's size in relation to her armament. Even Sienar Fleet was at a loss."

"I will bear that in mind," Vader said, though mostly to himself.

"Frankly, Lord Vader, I'm more concerned about what the *Carrion Spike*'s weapons can do to us while we're attempting to line up what has to be a very precise laser blast."

"Leave that to me, Governor."

"Do I have a choice?"

Abruptly Vader poured on all speed, accelerating away from the system's outmost planet and taking the crime lord's ship into the starry space he had indicated earlier. But then only to loose a guttural sound of anger and frustration.

"They've jumped to lightspeed!"

Tarkin ground his teeth. The situation was growing worse by the moment. In star systems lacking nearby hyperspace relay stations, a ship's pilot had to navigate by beacon or buoy, unless the ship was equipped with a sophisticated navicomputer of the sort the *Carrion Spike* boasted, which could plot jumps well beyond the next beacon, all the way to the Core if necessary. According to the *Predator*'s inferior device, the Murkhana system had no fewer than a dozen jump egresses, and most of those were into other Outer Rim systems where beacons were still more plentiful than hyperspace relay stations.

Vader broke his protracted silence to say, "They have jumped, but not far." He stretched out his left hand to enter data into the ship's navicomputer.

Tarkin was nonplussed. Then it dawned on him: Vader wasn't tracking the ship; he was tracking the mysterious black sphere he had had transferred to the *Carrion Spike*!

Even so, his optimism was short-lived, undermined by a memory of something Jova used to say when they had turned the tables on a predator, making it the hunted rather than the hunter.

"Think first when you're in pursuit: Is your prey trying to escape, or is it going for reinforcements? Is it perhaps looking for a temporary hiding place from which to spring at you, or—still driven by hunger—has it decided to search out a more vulnerable target?"

13

SOFT TARGETS

DARTH SIDIOUS WAS ANNOYED about having been disturbed from his meditations at the shrine. By the time he ascended to the pinnacle of the Palace spire to meet with Mas Amedda, he was ready to take someone's head off.

"Must I attend to every trivial matter, Vizier?"

"I apologize, my lord. But I believe you will want to attend to this one."

Sidious eyed him for a moment. "Murkhana," he said in arrant disgust.

The Chagrian bowed his horned head in acknowledgment. "Just so, my lord."

Sidious took to his tall-backed chair while Amedda readied the table's holoprojector, then moved to stand silently by the window-wall. In the hologram that emerged, several members of Military Intelligence and the Imperial Security Bureau were grouped before a positioning grid in one of the ISB's situation rooms.

"My Lord Emperor," Harus Ison of ISB began, "I'm sorry—"

"Reserve your apologies for when they are most needed, Deputy Director," Sidious said.

"Of course, my lord." Ison swallowed hard and found his voice. "We thought it prudent to apprise you of recent developments on Murkhana."

"I'm well aware that Lord Vader and Governor Tarkin found and investigated the cache of communications devices."

"Of course, my lord," Ison said. "But we have since received a subspace transmission from Lord Vader and Governor Tarkin informing us that the *Carrion Spike* has been seized."

Sidious sat straighter in the chair. "Seized?"

"Yes, my lord. From a landing field on Murkhana— by unknown parties."

Sidious used the chair's armrest controls to mute the audiovisual feeds and swiveled to Amedda. "Why have I heard nothing of this from Lord Vader?"

"Without the *Carrion Spike*, neither Lord Vader nor Governor Tarkin has access to the Imperial HoloNet or other suitably encrypted communications devices. The first subspace message originated from the ambassador's residence in Murkhana City. The second was sent from a starship in the Murkhana system."

"Lord Vader has procured a replacement ship?"

"Yes, my lord."

Sidious re-enabled the holofeeds to the situation room. "Proceed with your report, Deputy Director."

Ison bowed his head once more. "Lord Vader and Governor Tarkin have commandeered the starship of a local crime lord and are in pursuit of the *Carrion Spike*. In their most recent transmission, they stated that they were jumping the commandeered ship to the Fial system, Coreward of Murkhana, though still far removed from the Perlemian Trade Route."

"Do we have a military presence in that system?"

Vice Admiral Rancit stepped forward to address it. "No, my lord, we don't. We do, however, have a presence in the Belderone system, which is nearby."

"My lord, if I may interrupt briefly," Ison said.

Sidious motioned with his right hand.

"My lord, most of the star systems in that region of the Tion Cluster lack hyperspace relay stations. Given the likelihood that the ship Lord Vader commandeered has only a standard navicomputer, he and Governor Tarkin will be forced to navigate buoy-to-buoy."

"Your point?"

"Only that we face a hopeless task in trying to establish a rendezvous while the pursuit is in progress."

Sidious swiveled the chair slightly. "Vice Admiral Rancit?"

"Military Intelligence is even now calculating and prioritizing possible jump and egress points in those local systems, and on into the Nilgaard sector. Ships can be dispatched accordingly, my lord."

Sidious muted the feed once more, steepled his fingers, and brought them to his lips. During his meditations he had tried without success to trace a snaking current of the dark side to its source. What had it been trying to communicate to him?

No doubt Vader was tracking the *Carrion Spike* by focusing his attention on his meditation chamber. But why had he not sensed a disruption in the Force when Tarkin's ship had been taken? In the private transmission he had sent from Murkhana he had dismissed the communications cache as inconsequential; nothing more than misplaced hardware left over from the war. So did his inattention owe to a lingering sense of frustration about the mission? Perhaps he was at odds with Tarkin. Or had he allowed himself to step willingly into the trap, as Sidious had encouraged him to do?

"Tell me, Deputy Director Ison," he said when the audio feed was reestablished, "do you suspect any link between the communications devices and the theft of Governor Tarkin's ship?"

"My lord, we are investigating the recorded evidence and serial numbers in an effort to ascertain the identities of those who gathered the components. At the moment, however, we have no leads."

"There has to be some link, my lord," Rancit said. "Those now in possession of the *Carrion Spike* had to have sliced into the ship's security systems, and are likely the same assailants who launched the attack on Governor Tarkin's base. That means they have now added one of the navy's most sophisticated ships to their arsenal of warship and droid fighters."

Harus Ison was shaking his head. "There's no proof of that. We don't have enough information to establish a solid connection."

Sidious took a moment to consider the options, then said, "Vice Admiral Rancit, instruct your analysts to continue their calculations. You will also inform the Admiralty that their resources in the Belderone system should be prepared to jump to whatever target systems Lord Vader and Governor Tarkin deem significant." He leaned toward the holocam's lens. "Deputy Director Ison and the rest of you are to devote yourselves to unraveling the intentions of our new enemy."

"Imperial Security will not rest until it has done so," Ison said with a stiff bow of his head.

"We will apprehend them, my lord," Rancit added. "Even if that requires repositioning half the capital ships in the fleet."

* * *

The *Carrion Spike* reverted to realspace in the Fial system with the eyes of the six shipjackers focused on the main display of the sensor suite.

"Anything?" Teller asked Cala.

"No sign of the *Predator* so far."

Teller waited a long moment, then breathed a guarded sigh of relief and got to his feet. "Time to get down to business." He turned to Salikk. "Coordinates for Galidraan?"

Salikk watched the navicomputer. "Coming up."

The words had scarcely left the Gotal's full-lipped mouth when Cala said, "Teller!"

"I knew it, I knew it," Hask said, pacing through tight circles while Teller hurried back to the sensor suite.

Cala was sitting stiffly in the chair, staring fixedly at the display. "The *Predator*!"

"Right on cue," Artoz said from the far side of the command cabin.

Teller blinked in disbelief.

In a gesture of concern, Cala touched his forehead below the dangling headcloth. "It's the *Predator,* and she's coming for us all speed."

"Not even Vader could do this," Teller said. "There's a tracking device hidden somewhere aboard this ship."

"Or on the hull or concealed in a landing strut or just about anywhere," Hask said. "But unless you want to power down and perform a full EVA search you better come up with a revised plan."

Teller clenched his jaw. "We're not revising anything. Not now, not anytime." He glanced around him.

Artoz and Salikk nodded, then Cala and Anora, and finally Hask.

Teller rolled his head through a circle to work the kinks out of his neck and nodded to Hask. "You've got the comm board." As Cala stood up from the chair, Teller added: "Doc, you and Cala better get yourselves positioned." Then he turned to Salikk to say: "Jump us to Galidraan."

Seated in the copilot's chair, Tarkin watched Vader expectantly as the *Predator* emerged from hyperspace.

"Full ahead," the Dark Lord said.

Tarkin was glad to oblige, though he saw nothing through the viewports but star-strewn space and nothing on the sensor screens but background noise.

One moment Vader's gloved hands were clamped tight on the yoke, then they flew to the navigation console. "They've jumped to lightspeed again."

"Just as I would have," Tarkin said.

Vader fell silent, then lifted his head as if just roused from a nap and swiveled to the navicomputer display, the fingers of his left hand punching the control pad keys.

"Galidraan," he said at last.

Tarkin gave him a moment to complete the request for jump coordinates. "The chamber," he said. "That's how you're tracking them."

Vader glanced at him, as unreadable as ever, but said: "Very discerning of you, Governor."

Tarkin called up a star map of the Galidraan system and began to study it. "An even shorter jump. Two populated planets." He frowned in uncertainty. "Why not jump farther afield? An error in judgment?"

Vader made no reply.

Tarkin retrieved additional information on the system. "An Imperial space station in fixed orbit at Galidraan Three." The onscreen image of the station showed it to be an outmoded wheel with numerous space docks radiating from the perimeter.

"There is little point in alerting the station," Vader said, "as we will arrive long before a subspace transmission."

"The station won't be able see the *Carrion Spike* coming, in any event."

Vader grunted and reached for the hyperdrive control arm. Beyond the viewports the starfield elongated, and the *Predator* leapt to lightspeed.

Tarkin sat back in his chair, allowing his vision to adjust to the mottled corridor the ship had entered. No past or future here, he told himself. Time's blank canvas. And yet he couldn't keep his thoughts from running wild and in all directions.

Reflecting on Jova's sage advice, he could recall countless instances of each scenario playing out during his years of training on the plateau. Animals had escaped despite the team's best efforts to track and hunt them down. Others had hidden and sprung from concealment, on one occasion nearly making a meal of the Rodians had Jova, Tarkin, and Zellit not come to their rescue. Some with braying calls had summoned reinforcements too numerous for the humans and Rodians to compete with, and they had been the ones to go hungry. And yes, there had been numerous instances of hunted animals skulking off to sniff out more vulnerable game, softer targets. In deep space, similar circumstances had transpired. Pirate groups had gone hungry, sounded calls for support, abandoned the Greater Seswenna for less fortified zones, and employed every method of concealment, taking every advantage of the glower of starlight, the glittering tails of comets, iridescent clouds of interstellar gas.

Again Tarkin tried to assemble all the pieces: the

counterfeit distress call, the sneak attack on Sentinel, the bait set out on Murkhana, the theft of the ship, and now the flight.

But to where? To what end?

Out of the corner of his eye, he saw Vader prepare the *Predator* for the transition to sublight. The timeless corridor narrowed and vanished and the starlines compacted to pinpoints of light, skewing slightly as the ship reverted to realspace. No sooner had Vader engaged the ion drives than proximity alarms began to squeal and something large and white caromed off the forward deflector shield.

Tarkin quickly captured an image of the object on one of the display screens. It was the mangled and frosted body of a stormtrooper.

In the middle distance, fiery explosions flared at the edge of Galidraan III's atmospheric envelope. Plumes of incandescence, like stellar prominences, erupted into space.

Vader firewalled the throttle and the *Predator* raced deeper into the system, the space station coming into unassisted view, an arc of its silvery rim blown wide open and hemorrhaging gas, flames, objects, and bodies. The source of the destruction was invisible to the naked eye and the *Predator*'s scanners, making it appear as if green packets of bundled energy were being fired from deep space. Even so, particle-beam weapons emplaced along the station's curved outer surface were returning fusillades that streamed futilely into the void. Like some sea creature lunging forward to chew flesh and withdraw before it could be counterattacked, the invisible menace continued to advance and retreat, its lasers opening surgical lacerations along the spokes of the wheel as if intent on separating the rim from the hub. Larger explosions blossomed, along with dense clusters of superheated ejecta.

Tarkin bent to the controls, searching for a heat signature, gravitational flux, evidence of propellant glow, anything that might pinpoint the location of the *Carrion Spike*, all the while well aware that the ship was beyond his efforts to track. She could conceal herself from any sensor, contain her own reflection and heat, accelerate out of danger, maneuver beyond the capacity of any ship her size. But worse still was Tarkin's realization about her new crew: They weren't mere shipjackers; they were, as Vader had intuited early on, dissidents. Partisans with a deadly agenda to fulfill.

Flights of ARC-170 and V-wing starfighters, like swarms of stinging insects, were accelerating from the station's launch bays in search of the veiled thing that was pummeling their nest. Keeping to the edge of the battle to avoid being inadvertently targeted, Vader abruptly veered the *Predator* starboard in an obvious attempt to parallel the curving storm of destruction the *Carrion Spike* was sowing.

Tarkin saw a rash of melt circles erupt along the station's already pockmarked hull, an efflorescence of globular explosions.

Vader changed vectors and decelerated to match the *Predator*'s speed to that of the *Carrion Spike*. "We have you now," Tarkin heard him mutter.

Through the viewports, he could see the ARC-170s and the V-wings playing a dangerous game with their opponent, speeding directly into hails of energy bolts in the hope of forcing the *Carrion Spike* to betray her location, and sacrificing themselves in the process.

His hands tight on the yoke, Vader called out, "Sergeant Crest, prepare to fire."

The stormtrooper's voice crackled from the cockpit

nunciator. "Standing by, Lord Vader. But we have no visual on the target."

"Follow the tracers back to their source, Sergeant, and pour all the power of those quad lasers toward the point of origin."

"Shots in the dark," Tarkin said.

"Only from your vantage," Vader said; then he took his hands from the steering yoke and turned to him to add: "Your ship. Flank speed."

Tarkin pulled the copilot's yoke into his lap and began to slalom the *Predator* through the debris field spewed by the crippled station. At the same time, Vader swiveled to position himself at the controls for the forward guns. Wary of allowing the ion engines to overheat, Tarkin slued the ship through clusters of slagged alloy, incinerated starfighters, and tumbling bodies.

Far to starboard the explosions were thinning. The *Carrion Spike* had enough firepower to destroy the entire station, but the dissidents were tapering off the attack, perhaps to reserve energy for future targets. Was that the goal? Tarkin wondered. To use his ship to inflict as much damage as possible?

The thought of having the *Carrion Spike* leave such a legacy hollowed him.

"Commence fire," Vader said.

Hyphens of raw energy surged from the *Predator,* the chuddering of her reciprocating quad lasers loud in the cockpit. Ahead, fire spattered against the *Carrion Spike*'s ray and particle shields, and for the briefest instant the ship was revealed. Quickly, then, the *Predator*'s beams were streaking into empty space.

Tarkin yawed to port, hoping to evade the *Carrion Spike*'s response, but the shipjackers yawed with him and their first salvo nearly overwhelmed the *Predator*'s inferior shields. Tarkin pushed the yoke away from him, skimming the atmosphere of Galidraan III with the *Carrion Spike* hewing to his trajectory and preparing to pounce. In the grip of a second barrage, the *Predator* shook in his grip and the console lights began to flicker.

"Drop behind them," Vader said.

Tarkin rushed a deceleration burn and starboard feint, hoping to trick the shipjackers into overflying the *Predator*. Instead the *Carrion Spike* leapt and spun through a half turn—which Tarkin grasped only when he saw a tempest of energy beams converging on the cockpit.

Tarkin's sudden swerve and spin almost threw Vader from his chair.

"They're employing the pintle guns," Tarkin said in a rush. "They'll burn right through us." He risked a glance at Vader. "We've one chance to survive this. Redirect all power to the aft shields."

Vader took Tarkin at his word, and the *Predator* slowed significantly as a result. The *Carrion Spike*'s beams found their mark, all but driving the smaller ship forward.

"Shields at forty percent," Vader said.

Tarkin pulled on the shuddering yoke, taking the *Predator* into a sudden climb, but there was no escaping his own ship. Another barrage rattled the *Predator* to her rivets.

Vader slammed his fist on the console. "They have jammed our instruments. Shields at twenty percent."

A powerful explosion aft worked its way forward to the cockpit, conjuring fire from the sparking instruments, stripping the ship of shields and propulsion, and leaving the *Predator* dead in space.

"Damage assessment!" Teller called toward the audio pickup as he scrambled to his feet in the *Carrion*

Spike's command cabin. Still strapped into the pilot's chair, Salikk was in the midst of bringing some of the stunned systems back to life, tufts of his fur wafting through the cabin on currents of recycled air.

Anora's voice issued through one of the speakers. "Air lock controls for the escape pods are fried."

"We're not going to be needing the pods, Anora. Move on."

Hask's voice was the next to ring out. "Fire in cargo hold three has been extinguished."

"Lock down the hold and disable the exhaust fans," Teller said quickly. "I don't want us venting any smoke or fire-suppressant foam." Clapping grit from his hands, he dropped himself into the comm officer's chair. "Cala, where are you?"

The speaker crackled. "Aft maintenance bay. The hyperdrive generator seems to be operable, but it's making some awfully strange noises. Don't know what it will do when we jump. Can't now, anyway, until self-diagnostics are complete."

"How long?"

"Ten minutes. Fifteen at the most." Cala's forced exhalation could be heard through the speaker. "They knew just where to hit us, Teller."

"Of course they did—it's Tarkin's ship!"

"And they tracked us through hyperspace again."

Salikk spoke before Teller could reply. "The station has launched another squadron of starfighters. They're flying search formations, radiating out from the *Parsec Predator*."

Teller called up a magnified view of the incapacitated ship. "I was hoping they'd mistake the *Predator* for us, but Tarkin must still have limited comm." He shook his head in vexation. "We must have put on quite a show for the station personnel."

"The starfighters," Salikk repeated.

Teller watched the ARC-170s and V-wings begin to fan out. "Do we have sublight?"

"We do. But I'm worried those starfighters will sniff out our ion signatures."

"Worry more about Vader. He's probably guiding them right to us." Teller thought for a moment. "Take evasive action. Full silent running."

Salikk glanced at him. "Shouldn't we finish them off? I mean, when will we have another chance like this—to kill two of the Empire's chief commanders?"

"They're replaceable."

"Tarkin, maybe. But Vader?"

"For all we know the Emperor has a dozen more like him in deep freeze. Besides, we need to make the most out of this ship while we've got her."

Salikk nodded. "I reluctantly agree."

"Reluctance is fine." Teller swung toward the audio pickup. "Doc, where are you?"

"Cargo hold one," Artoz said. "And there's something here you need to see before we go to light-speed."

Teller looked at Salikk. "You okay here?"

"Go," the Gotal said, fairly bleating the word.

Teller pushed himself out of the chair and hurried through the command cabin hatch into the afterdeck. Racing through the conference cabin, he took the starboard connector to the turbolift, only to find it unresponsive. He hurried back to the main cabin and took the emergency stairwell down one level to the engine room, then wormed his way through a narrow cofferdam that accessed the cargo holds. As he came through the hatch of cargo hold one, he saw Artoz crawling out from around a large black sphere set into a hexagonal dais that took up most of the hold.

"What's so important I need to see it?"

The Mon Cal got to his big feet and gestured to the sphere. "This."

Teller regarded the sphere from top to bottom. "Yeah, I saw this during our initial recon. What of it?"

"To begin with, do you know what it is?"

"Cala thinks it's a component of the stealth system—"

"No, it is not," Artoz cut in. "If the cloaking device was powered by hibridium, then yes, that would provide a possible explanation. But this ship's stealth system runs on stygium crystals, which obviates the need for a device of this sort."

"Okay," Teller said in a tentative way.

Artoz indicated the sphere's vertical seams. "The hemispheres are designed to separate longitudinally, but I can't find a control panel or any way to prompt the device to open."

Teller walked partway around the sphere. "You think it's housing a tracker of some sort?"

"Our scanners haven't detected any."

Teller made his eyes bright with mystification. "So?"

"I think this *is* the homing beacon."

Teller gaped at him.

"What I mean to say is that I think this belongs to Vader, and that Vader was able to follow us to Fial, then Galidraan, by tracking his *property.*"

Teller's brow wrinkled. "Look, he may be more machine than man, but—"

"We've combed the ship forward-to-aft and belly-to-spine and found nothing in the way of a locator capable of tracking us through hyperspace."

Teller's comlink chimed before he could answer.

"The hyperdrive generator's completed its self-test," Cala updated. "It's still protesting, but we should be good to go."

"Then get down here." He commed the cockpit. "Salikk, navigate to the jump point, but hold there until I give you the word. We've got something to take care of before we go to hyperspace."

"Understood," Salikk said.

"Oh, and one more thing: Destroy Galidraan's hyperspace buoy on the way out. We don't want anyone following us this time."

Vader stood unmoving at the *Predator*'s forward viewports, the scarlet light of emergency illuminators reflecting off his helmet, the black orbs of his helmet mask seemingly fixed on the escaping *Carrion Spike*.

"Galidraan Station is dispatching a shuttle and readying their fastest corvette for pursuit," Tarkin said from the copilot's chair. "Sergeant Crest reports three dead."

"Your ship is still in the system," Vader said slowly. Then, turning his head, he barked, "Squadron Commander, are you hearing me?"

A warbling voice drifted from the cockpit nunciator. "Loud and clear, Lord Vader. Awaiting your orders."

"Commander, direct your starfighter squadron toward the bright side of Galidraan Four's outermost moon."

"My scanners aren't showing anything in that vicinity, Lord Vader."

"I will supply all the targeting data you need, Commander."

"Affirmative, Lord Vader. We're keeping the battle and tactical nets open."

Tarkin pressed the padded speaker of a comm headset to his left ear. "Station navicomputers are calculating all possible egress points."

Vader clasped his hands behind his back. "The Perlemian Trade Route is a short jump from this system."

"Escape is not their intention," Tarkin said.

Vader turned away from the viewport to look at him.

"If escape were their plan," Tarkin said, "they would have already done so." He cleared his throat meaningfully. "No. They have something else in mind. Perhaps to strike at another target." Once more he pressed the headpiece speaker to his ear, then toggled a switch that routed the audio feed to the enunciator.

"—calculations are ready, Governor Tarkin," a deep voice announced. "We're transmitting them to the shuttle, so that you and Lord Vader will have immediate access to them."

"Thank you, Colonel," Tarkin said into the headset mike. "In the meantime, I want a list of local systems that host Imperial resources."

"I can provide that information now, Governor. We have a large garrison in the Felucia system. Rhen Var has a small dirtside outpost. Nam Chorios has both a mining colony and a small Imperial prison facility. We have additional outposts at Trogan and Jomark. And of course, the naval base and R/M Facility Four deepdock at Belderone."

"What do we have parked at R/M, Colonel?"

"Several CR-ninety corvettes, two *Carrack*-class light cruisers, a couple of Victories, and a *Venator*-class destroyer—the *Liberator*."

"Stand by, Colonel." Tarkin muted the audio feed and swiveled toward Vader. "Are you reasonably certain that our particle beams wounded them?"

Vader nodded.

"If the hyperdrive is damaged, they might opt to lie low to effect repairs," Tarkin said.

Vader nodded again. "Or go in search of replacement parts."

"And if they're not wounded?"

"Continue their mission," Vader said with finality.

Tarkin fell silent for a long moment. Never having had an opportunity to put the *Carrion Spike* through her paces, the recent engagement had left him with an even more profound appreciation for the ship. "Why didn't they kill us when they had the chance? Could it be they believe they were being pursued by the Sugi crime lord?"

"No," Vader said sharply. "They know that *we* are here."

"Then perhaps they didn't kill us because they have a rendezvous or a schedule to keep?"

"Perhaps," Vader said.

Tarkin swiveled in place. "Belderone?"

"Too heavily fortified—even for your corvette."

"Felucia, then—in reprisal for the way the Republic left it."

"Of no significance."

"Rhen Var is merely an outpost . . . So: Nam Chorios?"

Vader took a moment to respond. "Instruct Belderone to send the *Liberator* there."

Tarkin activated the headset microphone. "Colonel, we need to contact Belderone and Coruscant," he started to say, then cut himself off on hearing Vader growl.

"What is it?"

"Whoever they are, they are resourceful." The Dark Lord turned slowly from the viewports. "They have jettisoned the meditation chamber."

The voice of the starfighter squadron commander issued from the enunciator. "Lord Vader, our scanners have detected an object—"

"Commander, order your pilots to open fire along that vector—lasers and proton torpedoes if they have them."

"Lord Vader, we have a detonation," the commander said a moment later.

Tarkin leapt from the chair to stand alongside Vader. "Did they hit the *Carrion Spike*?"

The answer was slow to arrive. "Lord Vader," the commander said, "the enemy has taken out the system hyperspace buoy. Our sensors are also picking up wake rotation readings."

"They have jumped to lightspeed," Vader said.

Tarkin ran a hand over his high forehead. "Then they've managed to make themselves untraceable, as well as invisible."

14

A CASE OF DO OR DIE

ITS TIERED ROOF a canopy of scanner, sensor, and communications arrays, Naval Intelligence headquarters heaved from Coruscant's metallic crust as if thrust up by tectonic forces from the depths of the planet. Along with the Palace and the byzantine COMPNOR arcology—which housed the Imperial Security Bureau, the Ubiqtorate, and other ambiguous organizations—Naval Intelligence was the third point of the Federal District's supreme triangle. The fact that the shielded, hardened, near-windowless complex more resembled a prison than a fortress had given rise to speculation that its sheer walls were designed as much to keep the agency's staff of tens of thousands of military officers inside as to keep ordinary Coruscanti out.

Constructed soon after the end of the war atop monads that had once made up the Republic's strategic center, Naval Intelligence was a nexus for gathering and analyzing transmissions that poured in from across the ecumenopolis and from all sectors of the expanding Empire. And yet its operations were not conducted in complete secrecy. During the construction phase, micro-holocams had been installed in every nook and cranny so that the actions and conversations of every staffer could be monitored at any hour of the day or night; not by the members of the Senate's various oversight committees, however, but by the Emperor and the most trusted members of the Ruling Council. Everyone involved with Naval Intelligence knew that the cams were there and had gradually grown accustomed to their presence. While the officers and others no longer played to the spy eyes as they had early on, they went about their business well aware that at any given moment they might be on stage.

Just now the Joint Chiefs of the Empire's military were gathered—Admiral Antonio Motti, General Cassio Tagge, Rear Admirals Ozzel, Jerjerrod, and others—along with several top officers from COMPNOR, including Director Armand Isard, ISB deputy director Harus Ison, and Colonel Wullf Yularen. Naval Intelligence was represented by Vice Admirals Rancit and Screed, who had requested the meeting.

With the bright light of late afternoon pouring through the tall windows of the Palace spire's pinnacle room, Sidious studied their holograms from his chair, using controls in the armrest to choose from among several cams and to provide alternative vantages. The droid, 11-4D, stood by him, one of its appendages plugged into an interface socket that routed holofeeds to the summit from what had been a Jedi communications suite in the base of the spire.

"Tint the windows," Sidious said without taking his gaze from the projected holograms.

"Of course, Your Majesty."

With the daylight dimmed, the cyan-hued holograms acquired more detail. The intelligence officers had asked for an audience in the Palace, but Sidious had turned them down. Similarly he had declined to attend their meeting virtually. As nettlesome as it was to have learned that the dissidents in possession of Tarkin's starship had embarked on a killing spree in the Outer Rim, Sidious found the cachet-driven spitefulness of the intelligence chiefs to be even more tedious. So he had dispatched Mas Amedda and Ars Dangor in his stead.

"I accept the dissidents have managed to wreak havoc in an isolated star system," Ison was saying, "but the fact remains that they brought only one ship to bear on our facility."

"One ship capable of hiding itself from scanners," Rancit said, "outmaneuvering our starfighters, outracing a Star Destroyer . . ."

"Permit me to amend my statement, then," Ison continued as Rancit allowed his words to trail off. "One fast and powerful ship. Still, they used it to launch an attack on an unimportant outpost."

"The start of a campaign of destruction," Screed interjected.

The officers were grouped around a large circular table, with Mas Amedda and Ars Dangor occupying prominent seats. Above the center of the table floated 3-D star maps, wire-frame displays, and plotting panels, some showing the locations of Outer Rim bases and installations, others the disposition of ships of the fleet, with symbols denoting Star Destroyers, Dreadnoughts, corvettes, and frigates, on down to pickets and gunboats.

"We've no proof that the shipjackers are on a campaign," Ison said, taking up the challenge. "Targeting the space station may have been their way of evading capture by Governor Tarkin and Lord Vader."

"As a diversion, in other words?" Screed said in elaborate disbelief, his ocular implant glinting in the light from the holograms. "Governor Tarkin came close to losing his life to his own ship. Given his experience and expertise, we have to assume that the *Currion Spike* is in the hands of a very competent and dangerous group."

"I've known Governor Tarkin for over twenty years," Rancit said in reinforcement, "and I can assure you that if he considers the group to pose a serious threat to the Empire, then they are nothing less."

Ison blew out his breath and shook his head. "Repositioning our resources from Belderone to fortify a couple of minor installations was reckless. We can't run the risk of curtailing pacification campaigns or hunting down former Separatists for a strategy of defeat-in-detail at the edge of civilized space."

"And what if the shipjackers' campaign should expand into the Mid Rim?" Rancit said. "The ship gives them the ability to strike almost anywhere in the galaxy."

Ison gaped at him for a long moment. "Is it the navy's aim, then, to redeploy the entire fleet to effect system-denial to a handful of dissidents?"

"In major star systems, yes," Rancit said. "Should the situation warrant it."

Rear Admiral Motti spoke to it. "At the risk of sounding too cavalier about this, Governor Tarkin's ship does not have unlimited firepower." The traditional cut of his brown hair and the boyish features of his clean-shaven face belied an attitude of perpetual sarcasm. "Whatever course we take, the ship will eventually cease to be a threat."

"I concur," Ison chimed in. "It's one ship. I recommend we let it go."

Mas Amedda came to his feet in anger. "Clearly all

of you are oblivious to the real danger posed by this group of privateers. We are not concerned about remote outposts or even important installations. The ship must be captured or destroyed because of the danger it poses to the Emperor's unchallengeable reign!"

"That is just the point I was about to make, Vizier," Rancit said when voices around the table had quieted. He was facing Amedda, but in such a way that he seemed to be speaking more to one of the monitoring cams, as if aware that Sidious was observing, and addressing him directly. "Imperial Security initially stressed that the communications cache on Murkhana could potentially be used to disseminate anti-Imperial propaganda. Now Deputy Director Ison fails to grasp that the intent of the dissidents may be to use Governor Tarkin's ship for that very purpose."

Raven-haired man's man Director Armand Isard was about to intervene when a junior intelligence officer seated at a comm board spoke first. "Sirs, sorry to interrupt, but we're receiving reports of another unprovoked attack in the Outer Rim."

"Nam Chorios," Screed said. "Just as Governor Tarkin predicted."

"No, Admiral," the comm officer said. "Lucazec."

It was General Tagge's turn to rush to his feet. The scion of a wealthy, influential family, he was tall and thickly built, with a broad face defined by long, flaring sideburns. "TaggeCo has operations at Lucazec!"

"We're in reception of a live holofeed," the junior officer updated.

Rancit had amplified an area of the star map and was gazing up into it. "They've jumped clear across the sector, inward of the Perlemian Trade Route!" He looked at Motti. "Do we have any resources there?"

Motti had a datapad in hand and was gazing at the device's display screen. "A small garrison of ground troops and a squadron of V-wing starfighters protecting TaggeCo's mining interests."

"The holofeed is streaming," the junior officer said.

Above the table's inset projector a holographic video of the attack resolved and stabilized. Centered in the field floated TaggeCo's city-sized orbital processing plant, an entire section of it engulfed by spherical explosions, the company logo effaced by melted metal. Quanta of unleashed energy were raining down on the facility, blowing chunks of it into local space. Drifting into view between the continuous barrage of beams were pieces of V-wing starfighters and prosaic ore haulers, one of which was falling toward dun-colored Lucazec in flames, its ablative shields glowing red hot. Farther below, clouds of thick black smoke were coiling into the smudged sky.

"They've targeted surface operations, as well," Tagge said, still on his feet and clenching and unclenching his hand.

Ison glanced from him to the junior officer at the comm board in visible alarm. "Who's transmitting this holovid? Is it being sent live by an orbital facility? An outlying ship?"

"The transmission is arriving on an Imperial HoloNet frequency," the junior officer said.

"Yes," Ison said, "but the point of view . . . It looks as if one of our own ships is the aggressor."

Screed and Motti traded worried glances.

In the summit of the Palace spire, Sidious sat back into his chair, folding his arms across his chest as sinuous currents of the dark side played through him, and as if he meant to contain them.

"Have you puzzled out what is happening, droid?" he asked.

"Yes, Your Majesty," 11-4D said, simultaneous with a further update from the junior officer.

"Sirs, we have confirmation that the holovid is being transmitted by the *Carrion Spike*."

Sidious swiveled toward the tinted windows, behind which the sky above and Coruscant below were the color of ash. Narrowing his gaze, he reached out for Darth Vader, whom he sensed was observing the holovid, as well.

Yes, Lord Vader, Sidious sent through the Force, *you shall have your starfighter.*

Moving with fierce purpose, Tarkin exited the *Liberator*'s hangar command post and walked briskly along the dorsal flight deck, passing starfighters and ground-effect vehicles as he closed on the shuttle craft awaiting him. The Star Destroyer's massive overhead doors were closed, and the light on the flight deck was dim. The captain of the *Liberator* was standing at the foot of the shuttle's boarding ramp. A short man with gray hair and a meticulously trimmed beard, he saluted as Tarkin approached.

"Sorry we couldn't be of more help, Governor Tarkin."

Tarkin gestured in dismissal. "You're not to blame, Commander. You came when called, and for that alone you have my gratitude."

The commander nodded. "Thank you, sir."

Tarkin extended his hand, and the commander shook it decorously. "Are you returning to Belderone base?" Tarkin asked.

"No, sir. Coruscant has ordered us to jump directly to Ord Cestus."

Tarkin's brow furrowed in question. "Why so far down the Perlemian?"

"Triage redeployments," the commander said, "as a result of what happened at Lucazec, I suppose. The

same at Centares and Lantillies. No telling where
your—uh, the missing ship is going to revert next."

"Perhaps," Tarkin said, and let it go at that.

He ascended the boarding ramp and walked aft,
settling into a seat in the main cabin, the *Theta*-class
shuttle's only passenger. High overhead, the *Liberator*'s hangar doors parted down the middle and retracted, and the shuttle rose off its skids on repulsorlift
power, dropped its wings, and sped toward its rendezvous point, a pod-shaped support carrier named
the *Goliath*, which had recently arrived from deepdock at Ord Mantell. Tarkin had a port-side glimpse
of bleak Nam Chorios as the shuttle angled away
from the Star Destroyer, the system's sun providing
barely enough light to illuminate the planet let alone
warm it to human standards.

Tarkin turned inward to consider the commander's
remarks. Capital ships redeploying from bases as distant as Centares and Lantillies, all because of the *Carrion Spike*. He trusted that naval command knew
better than to disperse the fleet too thinly, though
there was no denying that the shipjackers had once
again taken everyone by surprise.

That might not have been the case if Coruscant had
placed Lucazec on alert, but no one, including Tarkin, had given much thought to the possibility that
the dissidents would target a lightly defended TaggeCo
mining concern. Entering the star system with an altered transponder signature but transmitting authen-
tic Imperial codes, the *Carrion Spike* had opened fire
on both the orbital facility and groundside operations before Lucazec could react. Jova would have
applauded the shipjackers' tactics, the idea of masking oneself in the scent of one's enemy.

He could still summon the odors of musky excretions he had been forced to smear over himself during

hunts or surveillance exercises on the plateau. The rodent Jova had struck with the airspeeder one night had only been the beginning. After that had come the dizzying, often nauseating scents of sly vulpines, antlered ruminants, squat felines . . . But in countless situations the excretions had given them the upper hand, allowing them to kill or infiltrate as needed.

Except at the Spike. But of course that wasn't the idea.

At Lucazec, the shipjackers hadn't even bothered to activate the *Carrion Spike*'s stealth systems until they had reached their target. They were experimenting, perhaps in preparation for their next attack. Deflector shields had protected the mining facility for a time, but its fate had been sealed. The destruction and casualties the ship had left in her wake were consistent with what she had wrought at Galidraan.

When the shipjackers' HoloNet transmission had been received by the *Liberator*, Tarkin had tried to convince himself that it was another counterfeit, that the holovid had been cobbled together from wartime news feeds and created images, as had been the case at Sentinel and on Murkhana. In his eagerness to prove himself correct—and to the bewilderment of some of the *Liberator*'s petty officers—he had practically placed himself inside the blue holofield, searching for evidence of corruption that would have identified the feed as a fake. But he found no such signs. It had taken some time to disabuse himself of the notion that the shipjackers were deliberately provoking him, and to accept that they were merely making use of the *Carrion Spike*'s sophisticated communications suite to call attention to their agenda, as Count Dooku had managed to do early on in the Clone Wars. And like Dooku, the shipjackers had succeeded in broadcasting the Lucazec holovid live over civilian HoloNet frequencies to thousands of Outer and Mid Rim star systems before Coruscant was able to shut down vast portions of the communications grid.

Still, the damage had been done. According to the latest reports from Naval Intelligence, the shipjackers were already attracting media attention in some of the outer systems, and certain members of the Ruling Council were worried about blowback: that disaffected factions might begin to think that the Empire was vulnerable, and that imitators would spring up, convinced that they, too, could make themselves heard far and wide.

Tarkin had also learned that the contentious debate between Imperial Security and Naval Intelligence on how best to proceed had yet to subside, especially with the *Carrion Spike* on the loose once more, hiding in hyperspace or lurking in some remote or unpopulated star system. It appeared, however, that Vice Admirals Rancit and Screed were currently the gears getting the most grease, as the Admiralty had been granted permission by the Emperor to deploy forces to unprotected worlds along the Perlemian Trade Route and the Hydian Way. That, in any case, was how the *Goliath* came to be at Nam Chorios, and apparently why the *Liberator* had been deemed needed at Ord Cestus.

No sooner had the support carrier arrived than Vader had had himself ferried aboard, as it had brought from Coruscant his personal starfighter.

Tarkin had been busy since he and Vader had parted company, speaking with Commander Cassel at Sentinel Base, with intelligence assets on Murkhana, and with the commanders of Imperial posts throughout the sector; and as well with Wullf Yularen—who had his hands full keeping the peace among the intelligence agencies. Tarkin had spent the past ten hours in the *Liberator*'s data center, poring over star maps and charts and performing complex calculations.

He needed sleep, but sleep would have to wait until after he met with Vader.

The shuttle's wings folded upward as it lazed through a magcon field into the support escort's main hangar. The ship's commander and a dozen of his top officers and black-uniformed noncoms were standing eyes-front on the deck as Tarkin descended the ramp. Alongside the group stood a full company of stormtroopers, in addition to Sergeant Crest and the remaining six members of Vader's personal detail.

"Welcome aboard, Governor Tarkin," the commander said, stepping out of line to greet him.

"Good to see you again, Ros. I wish it were under better circumstances."

"We'll just have to make them better."

Tarkin smiled without amusement. "Where is Lord Vader?"

"Starfighter bay. I'll escort you." The commander turned to dismiss the others, then gestured politely to Tarkin and set off across the deck.

It took only moments to reach the starfighter bay, where the commander left Tarkin to his business. Tarkin didn't need to look far for Vader's starfighter, as it was the only Eta-2 among a squadron of V-wings. The absence of color might have struck Tarkin as a dramatic choice had black not been the Dark Lord's preferred color. What's more, many pilots during the war had made an effort to distinguish themselves, so why not Vader now?

Vader was standing between the weapons arms of the craft's split prow tinkering with something, while a silver astromech droid stood by, plugged into a portable diagnostics unit. Without so much as a word of greeting from Tarkin, Vader turned and stepped out from between the forward laser cannons.

"I trust that your fighter weathered the jump from Ord Mantell in good repair," Tarkin said.

"Not entirely, Governor, but the starfighter's troubles do not concern me at the moment. What have you learned?"

Tarkin lifted an eyebrow. "An interesting question, Lord Vader."

The foul humor Vader had been in since the attack at Lucazec hadn't faded. "I am not referring to *lessons*, Governor. Do you have new information?"

Tarkin nodded. "Something we need to discuss in strict confidence."

Vader turned to respond to a series of urgent twitters from the droid, then wordlessly led Tarkin to a small unoccupied situation room adjacent to the starfighter bay. The room featured a holotable and an array of communications modules.

"Our isolation is assured," Vader said. "Now: What have you learned?"

"I believe I have discovered a way to predict where the *Carrion Spike* will next emerge."

"Your prediction will need to improve greatly on our hunch at Galidraan, Governor."

"I've removed some of the guesswork."

Vader waited.

"Several things before I speak to my forecast. First, the device serial numbers we recorded on Murkhana indicate that the components were in fact part of a Separatist communications cache confiscated by the Republic during the war and warehoused in an Imperial depot until they disappeared sometime within the past three years."

"Disappeared," Vader said. "Like the warship modules and droids you traced from Sentinel Base."

"Precisely. Sold, stolen, or perhaps given away."

"All three possibilities imply the conspiracy of insiders."

Tarkin smiled with purpose. "There's more. The dissidents' attack on the Galidraan wheel was especially well timed, in that a *Victory*-class Star Destroyer had jumped from the system not an hour before the *Carrion Spike* arrived."

Vader considered it. "The dissidents knew."

Tarkin nodded. "They may be working in tandem with a scout ship. Or perhaps with the warship observed at Sentinel Base."

"Or receiving help from the same insiders who provided them with confiscated equipment." Vader paused. "The Emperor wishes to make an example of them, Governor. But he demands that we reel *all* of them in, not simply those who pirated your ship."

"And so we shall, if my calculations are correct."

Again, Vader waited.

Tarkin prized his datapad from the pocket of his tunic and tasked it to interface with the holoprojector table. A rotund star map resolved in midair, which Tarkin manipulated from the datapad. The *Carrion Spike*'s movements were indicated by a zigzagging red line, annotated by measurements and calculations.

"Fuel consumption," Vader said after a moment.

"I should have known you'd be ahead of me."

"I am not unfamiliar with the method, Governor."

Vader didn't offer an explanation, so Tarkin went on, using his forefinger to highlight his statements.

"The ship was fully fueled when it left Sentinel Base. We didn't bother refueling on Coruscant for the jump to Murkhana, as there was more than an ample supply for the round trip. From Murkhana, however, the ship jumped first to Fial, then to Galidraan, and then to Lucazec. We have no way of assessing let alone knowing where the corvette is at present—whether it is in hyperspace or parked in some local star system—but either way its fuel is in short supply. And unless the shipjackers have completed their mission—a supposition I find highly unlikely—fuel has to be their next priority."

Tarkin made adjustments to the star map, magnifying an area of the local sector. "Fuel requirements for the *Carrion Spike* are not ordinary, and replenishment sites out here are few and far between. In fact, calculations suggest only two options: here"—Tarkin pointed—"at Gromas, in the Perkell sector, or here, at Phindar, in the Mandalore sector."

Vader circled the star map twice before coming to a halt and looking at Tarkin. "As it happens, Governor, I am acquainted with both worlds."

Now Tarkin waited, but once more the Dark Lord offered no explanation.

"Like Lucazec," Tarkin continued, "Gromas supports a mining operation—for phrik, I believe—"

"Yes," Vader said.

"The Empire has a depot there that includes a full range of fuel options. Phindar, by contrast, was attacked by Separatists during the war, and hosts what is little more than a large tanker in fixed orbit. The property of a criminal cartel some twenty years ago, it is now operated by subcontractors as a fuel and service facility for Imperial starships."

"Two options," Vader said, "Gromas presenting more difficulties."

"The shipjackers chose Lucazec over Nam Chorios or even Belderone, and they transmitted their attack live over the HoloNet. If, then, their plan is to spread both destruction *and* propaganda—"

"Gromas would be the expected choice, if only because of its relative importance."

Tarkin nodded slowly. "It's certainly the target we should provide to the intelligence agencies."

Vader nodded slowly, in full understanding of Tarkin's implication. "I'll inform the Emperor."

"The *Carrion Spike* may already be in motion," Tarkin said, squaring his shoulders.

As if in echo of Tarkin's posture of readiness, Vader planted his fists on his hips. "Then we have no time to spare."

15

NEGATIVE CAPABILITY

THE *CARRION SPIKE* DRIFTED above a lifeless, volcanic planet in a star system designated by number rather than by name. The crew was already assembled in the conference cabin when Teller entered, wearing the uniform of an Imperial commander.

"Turn around so we can get the full effect," Anora said from one of the chairs that surrounded the cabin's circular table.

"Doesn't fit you like it used to," Cala said.

Teller stared down at himself in disappointment. "Poverty will do that to a being." He raised his head to speak to all of them. "But I've got good news—"

"Good news from a human dressed as an Imperial," Salikk interrupted, fingering the tuft of fur on his cheek. "That has to be a first."

"What did our ally have to say?" Dr. Artoz asked.

"A task force has jumped for Gromas."

Artoz's side-facing eyes grew vivid with interest. "Confirmed?"

Teller nodded once. "From multiple sources."

"Then you were right about Tarkin," Hask said.

Teller hitched up his trousers and straddled a chair. "When he was with Outland in the Greater Seswenna, they used to track pirates by calculating fuel consumption. Outland would track them to a fuel depot and swoop in. The Jedi did the same. You just have to know how much fuel a ship started out with and you have to be reasonably certain of its itinerary. Doesn't always work, but when it does, it works like a charm." He glanced at Cala. "You glad now about taking the extra time on Murkhana?"

The Koorivar wrinkled his face but nodded.

"Even with Imperials jumping for Gromas," Hask said, "every depot between here and Centares has got to be on the lookout for this ship."

Teller compressed his lips. "I never promised a sure thing. The altered transponder signature worked at Lucazec, and there's no reason to think it won't work again. To most Imperial installations, we're just another corvette running low on fuel. But that doesn't mean something can't go wrong. If that happens, we have enough fuel to jump at the first sign of trouble."

"To where, and then what?" Salikk said.

"Let's not get ahead of ourselves," Teller told everyone. "For now, we follow the plan."

Hask was shaking her head, her slanted eyes narrowed. "We should have stashed fuel somewhere. Refueled ourselves."

Teller scowled at the Zygerrian. "We broke the bank getting that shipment to Murkhana." He gestured to himself. "Like I said, poverty wreaks havoc with a diet."

Hask looked away from him, a frown contorting her angular features, so Teller turned to Anora. "Good job with the holovid. It's getting attention all over."

She shrugged. "Just doing my job, Teller. Same as ever."

Teller grew serious as he swung to Cala. "Speaking of jobs . . ."

"Done," the Koorivar said. "Although I had to spend extra time in decontamination."

"I thought your complexion looked ruddier than usual."

"No joke, Teller," Cala said. "That stint could cost me a couple of years."

"If it's any consolation, there'll be a higher cost to the Imperials."

"That part doesn't bother you at all, does it?" Hask said with a sneer. "The indiscriminate killing, I mean."

Teller frowned. "Indiscriminate? What, because not all of them are soldiers? This is where you draw the line?"

"People have to work, Teller," the Zygerrian said.

"Don't kid yourself, Hask. These aren't civilian targets. They're Imperial installations staffed by people who have bought into the Emperor's sick vision of the future—for you, your queen, me, and everyone between here and the Unknown Regions. You've seen the recruitment posters: Serve the Empire and be a better being for it! That doesn't turn your stomach? Anyone who willingly serves is a traitor to *life*, Hask. And don't tell me they don't know what they're signing up for, because it's as clear as those posters on the wall. It's enslavement, suppression, military might the likes of which none of us has ever seen." He worked his jaw. "I won't go peacefully into that future, and neither should you. Hell, why are you even with us if you haven't thought this through by now?"

Anora made a conciliatory gesture. "She knows.

She just forgets sometimes." She glanced at Hask. "Don't you?"

Hask returned a brooding nod.

But Teller wasn't through. "Look, whether they're mining ore for TaggeCo or refueling Imperial warships, it comes down to the same thing: standing with the Emperor. Our high-minded leader, who on his most benevolent day is still worse than Vader. The idea, Hask, just in case you've forgotten, is to put the fear into anyone who's even contemplating joining up. To slow the death toll, Hask. And as payback. Do you get it or not?"

"I get it," Hask said finally.

Anora slapped the tops of her thighs and laughed shortly. "Teller, sometimes you are so straight out of a holodrama I can't decide whether to cheer or applaud. My production team on Coruscant would have made good use of you."

Teller glanced from her to Hask and snorted in derision. "Artists. If the Emperor has his way, you'll be the first ones targeted for eradication." He waited a long moment. "Are we done?"

Heads nodded in assurance.

Teller looked at Anora. "Speaking of holodramas, let's see how I look with red hair."

Tarkin, dressed in a black flight suit, was waiting in the hangar command center when the ship reverted to realspace at the Rimward edge of the Phindar system. Floating above a holoprojector was a one-quarter-scale holopresence of the tanker facility's administrator, a yellow-eyed, lugubrious-looking humanoid sporting a pair of thin green arms that dangled past his knees.

"Refueling has been completed, Governor Tarkin,"

the Phindian rasped in Basic. "The corvette is preparing to detach as we speak."

"Good work, Administrator. You performed the refueling according to my instructions?"

"We did—though it took considerable effort."

"The Empire looks kindly on those who cooperate in such matters."

"And I look forward to whatever kindness you're willing to dole out, Governor. But you should know that the ship is assailable. My workers and the stormtroopers here are more than willing to take the crew head-on."

"No, Administrator," Tarkin said in a way that brooked no argument. "You mustn't raise any suspicions. What's more, the people aboard that ship have had plenty of time to prepare for this. You and your workers would be killed."

"If you say so, Governor."

"I do say so. Have you a recording of the commander?"

The Phindian nodded his huge, snub-nosed head. "Transmitting it now."

Tarkin squinted at the hologram that appeared alongside the holopresence of the facility administrator. Dressed in an Imperial uniform, the man was tall and lean, with thick red hair and a raised scar on his left cheek that ran from the corner of a full mouth to a bionic eye not unlike the one worn by Vice Admiral Screed.

"His code cylinder identified him as Commander LaSal."

"One moment, Administrator," Tarkin said, stepping out of cam range and turning to the nearest specialist in the command post. "Run the hologram through the roster database. If indeed there is a Commander LaSal, find out where he is currently deployed."

"Yes, sir," the specialist said.

Tarkin moved back into view of the holocam. "You were saying, Administrator . . ."

"Only that LaSal's rank plaque insignia and command cap disk looked legitimate."

Tarkin wasn't surprised. With all the shipjackers had already accomplished, forging command cylinder codes and insignias must have been child's play.

"Sir," the specialist said from his station, "the roster shows a Commander Abel LaSal deployed aboard the Star Destroyer *Sovereign,* currently docked at Fondor. But the likenesses don't match up the way they should. Shall I contact the *Sovereign?*"

Tarkin shook his head. "That won't be necessary."

The words had scarcely left his mouth when a starfighter signals officer entered in a rush. "Governor Tarkin, Lord Vader requests that you join him in the bay soonest."

Tarkin ended the duplex transmission and hurried through the hatch and across the deck to where a yellow-and-gray V-wing was powering up. The canopy was open, and a red astromech occupied a socket aft of the cockpit. Vader's black Eta-2 warmed nearby. Catching sight of Tarkin, the Dark Lord grabbed a flight helmet and life-support chest pack and carried them to him.

"Highly recommended," Vader said, handing over the gear.

Tarkin began to slip into the chest pack.

"It seems your calculations were correct, Governor."

"Yes, but coming all this way had to be a stretch for them. There's good reason to suspect that they did in fact refuel before launching from Murkhana."

"Then someone may have warned them away from Gromas."

"A point worth considering," Tarkin said. "In addition, they've betrayed themselves in other ways. Not only are they conversant with the *Carrion Spike*'s instruments, they are also well acquainted with Imperial procedure. The self-styled commander looks every bit an officer, and he used code cylinders to requisition the fuel cells." He looked up at Vader. "Some of the Empire's own?"

"The Emperor has limited patience for puzzles, Governor. Whoever they are, we need to put an end to their game."

The tanker orbited above hospitable Phindar. A lengthy cylinder of unshielded alloy, the enormous station's aft bridge was elevated above a trapezoid of shielding that protected a quartet of sublight engines and a generic hyperdrive. Pressurized radioactive gas, liquid metal, and composites were housed in proprietary sections. Extravehicular droids of several varieties carried out refueling operations by installing fresh fuel cells in starships and removing and transporting spent cells to storage bins anchored along the tanker's starboard side. The *Carrion Spike* was still umbilicaled to the station, its bow facing the huge tanker's trapezoidal stern, as Teller hastened through the docking ring air lock and into the main cabin.

"Retract the transfer tube and get us out of here," he shouted toward the command cabin.

"Trouble?" Anora asked, leaping from her chair.

Teller shook his head while he peeled the scar from his cheek and the fake implant from his left eye. "That's the problem. Everything went way too smoothly. The

Phindian didn't question anything, didn't even ask about the ship or the special fuel cells."

"You said yourself we're just another corvette out here," Anora said.

"Not up close we're not." Hearing the segmented umbilical retract into the hull, Teller hurried for the command cabin, Anora right on his heels.

"Easing us away," Salikk said from the captain's chair.

The corvette lurched slightly as maneuvering jets separated it from the tanker. Teller moved to the forward viewports to sweep his gaze over local space.

"What are you looking for?" Artoz asked from one of the other chairs.

"I won't know till I see it," Teller started to say when Cala cut him off.

"Ship reverting Rimward!" He paused to study the sensors. "Imperial escort carrier. On screen."

Teller, Anora, Hask, and Artoz crowded behind Cala's chair as an image resolved of a boxy vessel with a curved upper hull and a flat ventral one. Aft, the hull extended over the carrier's engines.

"Transponder signature identifies it as the *Goliath*," Cala continued. "Capable of carrying a wing of starfighters. Armed with ten Taim and Bak H-eights and a Krupx missile delivery system. Not much in the way of shields—"

"I'm not interested in testing its mettle," Teller said.

"It could be here simply to refuel," Artoz said, sounding unconvinced.

Abruptly, the escort vanished from the screen.

"Where'd it go?" Anora asked.

And just as abruptly the escort reappeared—now visible through the forward viewports.

"Microjump!" Cala said. "And deploying starfighters!"

Teller watched as starfighters dropped from the escort's deployment chute. "V-wings, led by an Eta-Two Actis."

"Bets on who's piloting the black one?" Hask said.

Anora was shaking her head in dismay. "How did they know?"

Teller's dark eyes were wide with surprise. "Tarkin may have figured if he could scare us away from Gromas by sending ships, we'd come to Phindar."

"Or he hedged his bet," Artoz said. "Capital ships at Gromas, he and Vader here."

Teller shook himself alert. "Doesn't much matter now." He turned to Cala. "How much time do we have?"

"A quarter hour," the Koorivar told him.

"Marking that," Artoz said.

"How far to the nearest jump point?"

Salikk swung to the navicomputer. "We need to get out of the way of Phindar and the principal moon."

"Then you've got some fancy flying to do first," Teller said. "Keep us as close to the tanker as possible and protect the hyperdrive generator at all costs. A couple of errant beams and everything's toast."

"Don't we know it," Cala said.

Salikk laughed shortly and madly. "If you think that'll keep Vader and Tarkin from firing, you're your own worst enemies."

Teller ignored the remark and looked at Anora. "Get your cams ready."

"Stay on my left wing," Vader told Tarkin over the tactical net as they fairly fell out of the escort, five additional pairs of V-wings at their backs.

The mammoth cylindrical tanker was straight ahead of them, profiled against the planet and with the

Carrion Spike just beginning to drop beneath it, the shipjackers intent on putting the tanker between themselves and the approaching starfighters. With the corvette all but wedded bow-to-stern to the tanker, there was little point in enabling the ship's stealth system.

Schematics of the *Carrion Spike*'s airframe and hyperdrive generator had been uploaded into the targeting computer of each starfighter and astromech, as well as into the fire-control systems of the *Goliath,* a precise strike from whose larger guns could be enough to immobilize the corvette.

The squadron pilots reported in by call signs—Yellows Three through Twelve—as they formed up on Vader's black starfighter and accelerated toward the tanker.

"Our goal is to force the corvette to lower its deflector shields before we return fire," Tarkin said through his helmet headset. "Once we've done so, our priority will be to target the hyperdrive generator, which is aft of the main guns along the corvette's spine."

A chorus of distorted voices acknowledged the directives.

"Affirmative, Yellow Two."

Tarkin's right hand nudged the joystick while his left made adjustments to the instruments. Little more than a single-pilot fuselage pod sitting on vertically stacked ion engines and flanked by deployable heat-radiating stability foils, the V-wing had been designed for speed and nimbleness, at the expense of a reliable life-support system or hyperdrive. Twin ion cannons bracketed the long, wedge-shaped prow. It had been years since he had piloted one, and despite the spaciousness of the cockpit and the broad view through the paned transparisteel canopy, he felt claustrophobic, strapped into the seat by safety webbing and encumbered by gloves, flight boots, and helmet. With the hinged targeting computer intruding on his portside view, the cockpit seemed more suitable to a double-jointed Geonosian. The old Delta-7 Aethersprite was roomy by comparison, the ARC-170 luxurious. Things could have been worse, however. The *Goliath* could have been carrying a squadron of the new—and seemingly disposable—TIE fighters.

"Commencing attack run," Vader said.

With the astromech chirping commands to the inertial compensator, Tarkin fed more power to the engines to stay abreast of and slightly behind Vader, and plummeted toward the tanker. Immediately he realized that the shipjackers were not simply attempting to hide; they were executing what amounted to a slow roll that was keeping the vulnerable dorsal surface of the *Carrion Spike* facing the curved hull of the much larger vessel. As the corvette disappeared behind the port side, Vader climbed, determined to fall on the ship, only to find when he and Tarkin arrived that the *Carrion Spike* was showing them her belly rather than her spine. They unleashed a hail of ion cannon fire regardless and came about for another rapacious run, the corvette upside down on top of the tanker by then and beginning to arc down along the vessel's starboard hull, her positioning jets flaring.

Descending, the *Carrion Spike* fell prey to four starfighters, which unloaded on her, taxing the resiliency of her powerful shields but emerging from the confrontation unscathed. Not until the corvette was tucked safely beneath the tanker once more did she reply, with powerful volleys from the lateral laser cannons that caught Yellows Seven and Eight and disintegrated them.

Jinking at the outer edge of the field of fire, Vader

and Tarkin followed the ship into her second revolution, hammering away at her as she crawled out from beneath the tanker, but with no tangible results.

With Tarkin still clinging to the Eta-2's left wing, Vader powered out of his dive, rolled over, and rushed to re-engage, coming dangerously close to the tanker in an effort to squeeze himself between it and the ascending *Carrion Spike* and forcing Tarkin to decelerate into a tandem position. Fire from Vader's ion cannons coruscated across the corvette from bow to stern, but the shields continued to hold, strengthened, Tarkin guessed, by rerouting power from the cannons and sublight maneuvering jets.

The *Carrion Spike* slowed considerably as she reached the crest of her tortuous loop, but once arrived the ship delivered a triple barrage of laserfire that forced four of the starfighters to diverge, one of them shearing away a piece of the tanker's elevated aft bridge before spinning out of control and exploding.

Vader's voice boomed through the net. "Yellows Three and Four, Ten and Twelve, form up on Yellow Two and follow our attack run. Direct continuous fire at the corvette's command center."

Tarkin mimicked Vader's evasive maneuvers while the four starfighters raced in to join them; then the half dozen banked as one to begin their runs. Maintaining fire discipline, Tarkin tightened his hand on the joystick and swooped in, the astromech transmitting targeting data to the cockpit's display screen. Beams began to find their way through the shields and pock the corvette's gleaming hull. One after the next, the starfighters harried the larger ship, drenching the shields with ion fire as she dropped under the lightly armored hull of the tanker for a third time.

"They can't hide inside those shields for much

longer," Vader said over the net. "Echelon formation on Yellow Two, and re-engage."

They launched their attack as the *Carrion Spike* was drifting up alongside the tanker's starboard side. Tarkin's targeting reticle went red and a laser-lock tone filled the cockpit. He dived and was going for a kill-shot when proximity alarms began to blare, and he glanced up in time to see six ARC-170s spring from one of the tanker's forward bays. Leaning on the joystick, he slued hard to starboard, his shots going wide of their mark as the tactical net grew cacophonous with shouts of caution. Vader's Eta-2 and the rest of the V-wings fanned out in search of clear space as the ARC-170s reeled into their midst, narrowly avoiding collisions.

"Abort the run," Vader told everyone.

Tarkin opened the battle net to the *Goliath*. "Contact the tanker administrator. Order him to recall his fighters at once. They're creating chaos out here."

The specialist at the far end of the communications link acknowledged the request, then returned a moment later to deliver the bad news. "Governor Tarkin, the administrator has refused the order."

"Refused? On what pretext?"

"Sir, he replies that the tanker is his property and that you are not *his* governor."

"*Goliath*, do you have a clear visual on the *Carrion Spike*?"

"Affirmative, sir."

"Then ready your proton torpedoes to target the corvette as soon as she appears at the crest of the tanker hull."

"All due respect, sir, the tanker and the corvette might as well be joined at the hip." It was the voice of the *Goliath*'s commander. "And with our starfighters all over the field, one stray torpedo—"

"I'm well aware of the risk, Commander," Tarkin said, giving full vent to his anger. "Inform your casualty notification officers that I'll assume personal responsibility for any collateral damage."

"Execute Governor Tarkin's orders, Commander," Vader said in a calm voice that at once managed to be full of menace.

"Yes, Lord Vader. Readying the warhead launch system."

The *Carrion Spike* was just short of crowning when her ion engines blazed to life and the ship hurtled away from the tanker in the direction of the escort carrier, firing all guns as she fled. All vigilance abandoned, Vader and Tarkin broke Rimward in a flurry of evasive maneuvers while lines of destruction probed for them.

Vader ordered what remained of the squadron to tighten up their ragged formation. "Enable countermeasures and pursue. That ship must not be allowed to jump."

But the *Carrion Spike*'s laser cannons were already beginning to find their marks. Yellows Five and Twelve vanished in blinding explosions, adding debris to the obstacle course Vader and Tarkin had embarked on.

Tarkin reopened the battle net to the *Goliath*. "What are you waiting for? Why aren't you firing?"

"Sir, the corvette has disappeared from our scanners!"

"Fire along the path of her last logged vector," Tarkin said. "Engage the tractor beam."

The escort carrier began firing at extreme range, its energy beams lancing off into local space.

Vader and Tarkin were still spearheading the chase when a massive, rippling explosion erupted behind them. Tarkin looked over his left shoulder to see the tanker burst open in a roiling outpouring of fire and gas that annihilated all the ARC-170s and singed the tails of Yellow Squadron's trailing starfighters. When the expanding shock wave caught up with him, it overwhelmed the V-wing, propelling it through end-over-end spins and lateral gyrations that refused to abate.

After a long moment, the starfighter's systems came back online and he heard Vader's voice over the tactical net. "The *Carrion Spike* has jumped to hyper-space."

"Anyone else survive?" Tarkin managed to ask.

The *Goliath* responded: "Two starfighters. In addition to the escort carrier."

Tarkin lifted his face to the canopy to find that he was facing what was left of the tanker, still belching fire and beginning a spiraling death plummet into Phindar's atmosphere.

What struck him, however, as he regained his senses, was that neither the *Carrion Spike* nor the *Goliath* had fired the shot that had doomed it.

16

HAZARD MITIGATION

THE *CARRION SPIKE* DRIFTED aimlessly between worlds in another nameless star system, an unscheduled stop this time, the result of a split-second decision on Salikk's part, executed as the corvette was scudding away from the exploding fuel tanker, chased by starfighters and with the escort carrier's cannons, tractor beam, and torpedoes desperately trying to find it.

The ordeal at Phindar had left the corvette battered, bruised, and shaken. The armored hull was rashed with melt circles, and most of the exterior lights were molten heaps. The effects of the tractor beam, which had grabbed the ship more by chance than as the result of any skill on the part of the *Goliath*'s crew, had ripped away part of the rectenna array. The interior looked as if a whirlwind had blown through, and surges of energy had fried most of the appliances in the galley and medical bay. Areas of the ship were now off limits because of air lock damage and radiation leaks. The toilets and showers had stopped working, and emergency illumination prevailed. Most of the alarms had been disabled to prevent them from sounding. Telltales were flashing across the command center's console, and some of the comp routines were refusing to reboot. Weapons and stealth systems, sensor suite, hyperdrive, and navicomputer had fared better, but the shield generators were functioning only at fifty percent capacity.

"On the bright side," Teller was telling his fellow shipjackers, "close calls make for captivating holovids."

All six of them were in the dimly lighted command cabin, nursing their wounds when they weren't fiddling with various instruments. Anora's forehead bore a square of bacta patch, and some of her brownish curls had been clipped away to accommodate a second patch on her scalp.

"The Empire has suspended HoloNet service to most of the sector," she said in a weak, defeated voice. "I doubt our transmission reached more than half a dozen systems."

"We only need to've reached one," Teller said, trying to sound encouraging. "Give it time and the holovid will spread to other sectors."

"I didn't have a chance to edit out the lag before the tanker explosion," Hask said. "But there's one sequence showing the starfighters ganging up on us."

Cala emerged from an access hatch in the deck plates. "The explosion would have taken out the Eta-Two and all the V-wings if the charge hadn't been late in detonating. It's possible the tanker's containment bins were equipped with sensors that monitor whether fuel cells are fully depleted. A sensor in the bin might have detected the bomb and initiated attempts to neutralize or contain the detonation."

"Not our concern," Salikk said from the command

chair. The low light had little effect on his ability to see, and he was scanning the instruments as he spoke. "We're lucky we got away when we did. The *Goliath* had us in target lock."

Hask fixed her gaze on Teller. "You think Tarkin and Vader would have given the order to fire, knowing they might have blown up the tanker?"

"Are you asking seriously?" Teller said.

Hask frowned. "Maybe not about destroying the tanker. But his own starfighter pilots were in harm's way."

Teller leaned back against the port-side bulkhead. "Remember what I was telling you about Tarkin's days with the Outland Regions Security Force, and that special ship he designed with the swing and pintle-mounted front guns?"

"I remember."

"Well, he didn't only deploy it against the pirates," Teller said. "You'd think he would have blamed Eriadu's troubles on the Core Worlds, which were skimming most of the profits from the Seswenna's lommite trade. But he really had it in for the outlaws who were harassing the Seswenna. When Outland's counteroffenses stopped yielding the desired results, Tarkin decided to extend the militia's reach by targeting any groups that were supporting or harboring the Seswenna's foes. It didn't matter to him that the support groups were caught in the middle, threatened by pirates on one side and menaced by Outland on the other. Civilian casualties you might say, Hask, but not to Tarkin. They were allies of his enemies, and that meant enemies of his and deserving whatever he decided to level against them."

Teller firmed his lips and gave his head a mournful shake. "Outland was brutal in what its warships dished out. No one knows how many were killed or where the bodies were buried. But even with the flotilla they'd amassed, Outland couldn't be everywhere at once, so Tarkin came up with the idea of making the supporters responsible for their own protection by arming them against the pirates. That way, they managed to open a separate front against the pirates, and eventually turned one group of supporters against another. With everyone suspicious about who was secretly siding with or supporting whom, they began to turn on one another, out of fear of reprisals from Outland. It was a kind of mutually assured annihilation, and ultimately Tarkin rid the Seswenna of its problems."

Teller fell silent for a moment. "You never know what events give shape to someone's life, to someone's moral choices. Maybe it was centuries of having to defend themselves against the predators, or the centuries of raids by pirates, slavers, and privateers that shaped the Eriaduan character. Maybe the history of the place seeped into their genetic makeup, resulting in an appetite for violence. But even that doesn't fully explain Tarkin, because most of the Eriaduans I've met aren't anything like him."

Teller's gaze favored Hask. "When Outland succeeded in chasing off what was left of the groups they hadn't killed, Tarkin turned his wrath on anyone who had come to Eriadu in flight from intersystem conflicts or in search of new lives, employment—you know, the ones taking jobs from native Eriaduans, crowding the cities, ruining the economy. The entire Tarkin clan waged a campaign against them. It didn't matter if they were human or other than; the point was that these social parasites were cheating Eriadu out of its just and hard-won rewards, and keeping the planet from attaining the status of the Core Worlds. By this time Tarkin was Eriadu's governor, and prob-

ably the most popular one the planet ever had. Fresh
from Outland and years of academy life, he had the
support of a cabal of influential officers who had
trained to become Judicials, but in fact were just itch-
ing for galactic war to break out.

"Palpatine turned a blind eye to what was going on
in the Seswenna—the deportations, the purges, the
atrocities committed against any who found themselves on the Tarkins' extermination list. And not sur-
prisingly, under Tarkin's rule, Eriadu finally achieved
the celebrity it had been clamoring for. It became
the rising star, the planet other eager-to-be-exploited
worlds began looking up to. So of course the invisible
players who had put Palpatine in power were just as
eager to embrace Tarkin. Hell, he had already formed
a military. It was to Eriadu that *Coruscant* looked
when embarking down the same path. Why else do
you think he attained so much in so few years and
became such fast friends with Palpatine, those senators who were pushing for passage of the Military
Creation Act, the members of the Ruling Council?
Why do you think he makes such a perfect partner for
Vader?"

Teller answered his own question. "Because all of
them share the same vision. They're the entitled ones
who know what's best for the rest of us—who should
live, who should die, to whom we should bow and
how low." He glanced at Cala, Artoz, and Salikk. "I
don't need to remind any of you what Tarkin did at the
end of the war when there weren't Jedi around to keep
a lid on the violence and retribution. We wouldn't be
aboard this ship otherwise. The Emperor is going to
winnow the populations of the galaxy until the only
ones left are the ones he can control. And he and
Vader and Tarkin are going to accomplish that with
an army of steadfast recruits who might as well be

clones for the little independent thinking they do, weapons that haven't been seen in more than a thousand years, and *fear*."

Teller stepped away from the bulkhead, limping slightly as he found his way in the scant light to one of the acceleration chairs. "You can think of the *Carrion Spike* as just a ship, but she's more than that. She's an expression of who Tarkin is; a small-scale example of the lengths he's willing to go. Stealth, speed, power . . . That's Tarkin, the omniscient, ubiquitous Imperial enforcer. And that's why we're turning her into a symbol of something else: of *resistance*."

Hask narrowed her feline eyes and nodded in an uncertain way. "You know, it's funny, Teller. The last time you uncorked one of these lectures, you were saying how none of those we've killed were civilians because they were serving the Empire. To me, it sounds a lot like Tarkin's targeting of anyone who was aiding the pirates."

Teller nodded back at her. "Yeah, Hask, except for one thing—"

"We're the good guys," Anora said, pinning Teller with a sardonic look.

Back in uniform and hands clasped behind his back, Tarkin stood side by side with Vader at the center of the *Goliath*'s bridge, their presence imbuing the cabinspace with a sense of uncharacteristic urgency.

"Anything?" Tarkin sharply asked the noncom seated at the communications board.

"Nothing, sir."

"Keep trying."

The escort carrier was still in Phindar space, in part so that Tarkin could iron out responsibility for the tanker's destruction with the planetary leadership.

Off to his left sat the ship's ashen-faced commander, not yet over the fact that he had nearly been made answerable for the deaths of the few starfighter pilots who had survived the fierce engagement with the *Carrion Spike*.

While he didn't show it, Tarkin felt more accountable than the commander realized. He and Vader had been baited and had come close to paying the price for rushing headlong into a trap. He took himself to task for his overconfidence at having predicted where the shipjackers would turn up, and promised that he wouldn't allow himself to make the same mistake twice. That the *Goliath*'s arrival had taken the shipjackers by surprise only made their cunning escape all the more impressive.

A tone sounded from the comm board and Tarkin stepped forward in a rush, realizing at once that he had been premature.

"Report from Phindar's rescue-and-recovery operation, sir," the noncom said after listening to her headset feed for a moment. "They suspect that the tanker was destroyed by an explosive device concealed inside a spent fuel cell."

"Then the dissidents weren't merely attempting to use the tanker as cover," Tarkin said. "They were hoping to draw us in, as much to avoid having to face the storm of our unexpected arrival as in the hope that we, too, would be caught up in the explosion."

A short holovid of the clash, the ensuing chase, and the explosion had been received three hours earlier by a couple of local systems. The delayed transmission of the holovid told Tarkin that the shipjackers had waited until the *Carrion Spike* emerged from hyperspace, which also provided him with some idea of the distance the ship had traveled, though not in which direction.

Turning to Vader, he said, "Perhaps it would have been wiser to target the tanker from the start."

Vader folded his arms across his chest and shook his head. "The Emperor would not have approved."

Tarkin regarded him. It was an odd comment coming from Vader, given the atrocities he had perpetrated for the Emperor since the end of the war. He wondered if Vader was testing him, just as he felt the Emperor had been doing during their most recent meeting.

"If we aren't willing to do whatever is required," he said finally, "then we risk losing what we have been mandated to protect."

The remark paraphrased something Skywalker had said to him following the Citadel rescue. But it got no reaction from Vader beyond his saying, "You misunderstand, Governor. As I said, we need to gather *all* of them in our net."

The comm board chimed again, this time with better and more anticipated news.

"Sir, we're receiving location coordinates from the tracking device."

Tarkin didn't bother to hide his excitement. "The Phindian administrator did one thing right. I was almost certain he lied to me."

Vader nodded. "He served the Empire well in his final moments."

Tarkin stood behind the noncom at the comm board. "What is the source of the transmissions?"

The noncom waited for interface data to arrive from the *Goliath*'s navicomputer. "Sir, the source is sector-designated as LCC-four-four-seven. Parsec equidistant from the Sumitra and Cvetaen systems."

"Those are Coreward—in the Expansion Region," Tarkin said, with genuine unease.

"Yes, sir. Closest principal planets are Thustra and Aquaris."

Vader looked at Tarkin. "Now, Governor, *we* get to spring the trap."

One of the few areas of the former Jedi Temple that had not undergone renovation was the holographic galactic map, an enormous globular representation of the galaxy located mid-level in what had been the Jedi Council spire. The Order had used the map to keep track of its far-flung members; now it served to identify trouble spots in the Emperor's realm.

The Emperor had consented to allowing the members of his Ruling Council to confer with representatives of the intelligence services in the hope that Tarkin and Vader's latest strategy would conclude the search for the Moff's ship and bring the shipjackers' co-conspirators to light. While no less irritated by the fact that a group of insignificant mutants from the galactic underbelly were scurrying about trying to stir up trouble, curiosity had gotten the better of him. Mere eddies in the current of the dark side had transformed into rapids and whirlpools.

He sat in a simple chair atop a podium not unlike the one in the audience chamber, with some of his colorfully clothed advisers arrayed beneath him—Mas Amedda, Ars Dangor, Janus Greejatus, and Kren Blista-Vanee. Intelligence chiefs Ison and Rancit stood opposite the Ruling Council members, making their cases from a circular walkway secured to the curved wall of the spire at the base of the holographic globe.

"My lord, Vice Admiral Rancit and I do find ourselves in agreement on one issue," Ison was in the midst of saying. "If Governor Tarkin is going to continue to make unilateral decisions of the sort he made at Phindar, then he should be doing so on Coruscant, coordinating the efforts of the Imperial military instead of chasing his errant corvette all over the Outer Rim."

Rancit waited until he was certain that Ison had spoken his piece. "My lord, with the *Carrion Spike* now reported to be in the Expansion Region, this crisis takes on greater exigency. It's possible that the dissidents' plan calls for the corvette to be joined by the warship—"

"I'm not interested in what is *possible,* Vice Admiral," the Emperor interrupted. "I'm interested in knowing your plans for dealing with the possibilities."

Rancit bowed his head. "Of course, my lord. Though I must stress that Naval Intelligence has detected unusual activity throughout that sector of the Expansion Region, as if unknown parties are attempting to flood certain star systems with traffic."

The Emperor leaned toward him. "As you are flooding star systems with our warships."

Rancit blinked and stood tall. "My lord, we are simply attempting to safeguard our interests in those systems. Given the path the dissidents have pursued, it is—that is, we think it reasonable to assume that they are intent on targeting systems in the Inner Rim, from which potential hyperspace jump points and destinations will multiply beyond measure. We have taken the liberty of declaring some key systems no-entry zones, but the need to allocate resources to other systems grows only more complicated."

The Emperor's gaze favored Ison. "Do you disagree with the vice admiral, Deputy Director?"

"Not entirely, my lord. The increased activities Vice Admiral Rancit alludes to could be the result of holovids transmitted from the *Carrion Spike.*

COMPNOR surveillance and investigation operatives in several sectors have noted an increase in both anti-Imperial propaganda and mobilization among malcontent groups. ISB is making arrests and interrogating prisoners in various Imperial facilities in an effort to learn the identity of the culprits. As odd as it sounds, my lord, we have also been receiving intelligence from the Crymorah syndicate, which apparently shared some nefarious affiliation with the criminal subcontractors who operated Phindar's fueling station."

The Emperor steepled his fingers. "My instructions to Lord Vader and Moff Tarkin were to make an example of the shipjackers, not to allow the shipjackers to make a laughingstock of the Empire's intelligence chiefs." Turning his hooded gaze on Rancit, he made a beckoning motion with the fingers of his right hand. "Enlighten us as to what you would have us do, Vice Admiral."

Rancit cleared his throat before beginning. "My lord, rather than engage the dissidents at the present location—which Governor Tarkin has yet to make known to us—he proposes waiting for them to plot a course to their next target and ensnaring them there."

In fact Vader and Tarkin *had* made the location known, but the Emperor kept that to himself. Instead he said: "Given that they have successfully escaped each such attempt, just how do you propose to ensnare them?"

"By utilizing Interdictor cruisers, my lord— precisely placed to yank the *Carrion Spike* from hyperspace short of its destination system and reversion point. Governor Tarkin assures us that any jump from the dissidents' current location will require at least two reversions to reach potential Imperial targets. Thus, Interdictors can be positioned in advance of the *Carrion Spike*'s arrival."

The Emperor looked down at Kren Blista-Vanee.

"The requested Interdictors are being developed as part of the Deep Core Security Zone, my lord." Fond of wearing flamboyant hats and frequenting the opera, Blista-Vanee was a relative newcomer to the Ruling Council, but had already proven an asset in blazing hyperspace routes into the Deep Core star systems. "I hasten to add, however, that the ships' gravity well projectors have not been tested in scenarios of this sort."

The Emperor mulled it over for a moment, then looked at Rancit once more. "Tell me about these 'potential' targets."

"Permit me, my lord," Rancit said, gesturing to the star map and amplifying a portion of it. "Our main concerns are Lantillies, from which we have already repositioned many of our resources. Also, the Imperial facility on Cartao, and Ice Station Beta on Anteevy. An attack on Taanab—though on the Perlemian Trade Route—would earn the dissidents more condemnation than praise, as Taanab's agricultural projects feed billions in the Mid and Outer Rim. The same holds true for an attack on Garos, because of the university, though there is also an Imperial facility onworld." Rancit paused. "Do you wish me to go on, my lord?"

By way of answer, the Emperor glanced at Ison.

"As I've said on countless occasions, my lord, the fleet is already too scattered. On the Admiralty's counsel, the navy is now redirecting resources from as far away as Rothana and Bothawui."

"And at the risk of repeating *myself*," Rancit said, "Imperial interests must be protected."

The Emperor spent a long moment studying Ison

and Rancit, stretching out with his powers to discern alignments, configurations, some syzygy of events. Then his thoughts turned to Vader and Tarkin. He appreciated how well they were working together, but he began to wonder if they were perhaps too close to the details of the dissidents' scheme to recognize their ultimate objective. One needed to have a safe remove, as he felt he had, gazing into the 3-D representation of the galaxy he had made his own. How Plagueis would have mocked him for allowing himself to become personally involved in such a seemingly trivial matter; but then his Master had never foreseen that his onetime apprentice would become *Emperor*.

With a subtle gesture he signaled Mas Amedda to join him on the podium. When the Chagrian arrived, he said: "Tell me again how the cache of communications jammers was discovered on Murkhana."

"One of Imperial Security's assets was tasked with investigating the find by his case officer," Amedda said in a little more than a whisper.

The Emperor considered this. "His ISB case officer, here on Coruscant?"

"Yes, my lord."

The Emperor collapsed the steeple he had made of his fingers. "Summon them, Vizier. I suspect some benefit will accrue from my speaking personally with both."

ZERO DEFECTS

WEAPONS RECHARGED, the interior made as ship-shape as possible, the *Carrion Spike* waited for instructions regarding when to launch and where to jump. From the copilot's chair Teller, back in boots and cargo pants, watched Salikk run through a preflight check of the instruments and systems. When the Gotal's hand reached the navicomputer, however, it hovered in hesitation.

"Problem?" Teller asked.

Salikk kept his eyes trained on one of the status displays. "It's probably nothing, but . . ."

Teller sat bolt-upright in the chair's webbing. "It's probably nothing, but I've had this pain in my side . . . It's probably nothing, but my girlfriend's been acting distant lately . . ." He gave his head an aggravated shake. "Whenever I hear that phrase—"

"It's the fuel capacity," Salikk cut in. "Factoring in the cells we took on at Phindar, something doesn't add up."

"That Phindian cheated us!" Teller exclaimed. "No wonder he was being so nonchalant."

Salikk's twin-horned head was shaking back and forth. "That's not it."

Teller leaned toward the console. "Maybe you didn't notice we weren't full up when we separated from the tanker."

The Gotal's head continued to shake. "I checked—at least I think I did. But even if I overlooked a detail, the discrepancy doesn't make sense."

"We had to override that tractor beam—"

"No."

Teller looked at Artoz, who was sitting quietly in the comm officer's chair, watching both of them. "Any ideas?"

The Mon Cal thought for a moment, tapping his webbed hand on the console. "The hyperdrive motivator may be addled. We could try recalibrating the synchronization relays."

Salikk forced an exhale. "It's probably nothing." His hand was reaching for the navicomputer controls again when Teller told him to hold off, and then shouted through the ruined hatch for Cala, who was in the conference cabin.

"You've gotta put the hazmat suit back on," Teller said as the Koorivar entered from the afterdeck.

Cala stared at him. "You're trying to overdose me on rads, is that it? You've decided I'm expendable."

"Calm down," Teller said, gesturing. "I just need you to go into the fuel bay and run tests on the fuel cells we took on at Phindar. You'll know them because they're Wiborg Jenssens, marked with the tanker's logo—a kind of triple S."

Cala's shoulders sagged in defeat. "What am I supposed to be looking for?"

"With any luck, nothing more than an empty or faulty cell," Artoz said.

Cala scowled. "That Phindian cheated us!"

"Let's hope so," Teller said, freeing himself from the chair's safety webbing and getting to his feet. "Come on, I'll help suit you up."

Frozen hatches and malfunctioning air locks forced them to follow a circuitous route to the fuel hold. Once sealed into the hooded, face-shielded hazmat suit, Cala disappeared through the air lock and Teller returned to the command cabin, where he found Anora seated in the copilot's chair.

"What's going on?" she asked, her words more a demand than a question.

"It's probably nothing," he started to say, then stopped himself. Enabling the intraship comlink, he said: "Cala, you inside?"

"I'm checking them now. Power-level indicators look good."

Teller had turned toward Anora when Cala added: "Wait. The sensor found one. The cell is reading empty."

"One of the Phindian's?"

"It has the logo."

"Can you remove it?"

Cala replied with a lengthy curse. "I told you we should have brought a droid along."

"I know you did, but think of the headaches a droid would have caused Salikk." Teller aimed a grin at the magnetically sensitive Gotal. "Besides, we didn't, and you're our best bet. Is the repulsorlift conveyor still in there?"

"Right where I left it after rigging the bomb."

"Task the conveyor to remove the cell," Artoz said toward the audio pickup, "and transfer it into the decontam bay so the diagnostic unit can have a look at it."

"Have a look at it how?" Cala said. "The sensor says it's empty."

"We need to open it up," Teller said.

"Are you out of your mind?" Cala barked. "Suppose there's a bomb inside?"

Teller tried to make light of the idea. "That's something only we do. Anyway, that's why you're letting the diagnostic unit do it. It'll scan the cell first."

"This is the last time I'm putting this suit on," Cala said.

"Deal. Next time I'll have Anora do it."

A gesture from her revealed her feelings on the matter.

Another curse from Cala broke the long silence. "It's not empty."

Teller exchanged nervous glances with Salikk and Artoz. "What's inside?"

Everyone stared at the command center enunciator, as if the Koorivar were there, in the command cabin.

"A device of some sort," Cala reported finally. "Nothing like I've ever seen."

"All right," Artoz said, trying to keep his resonant voice calm. "Task the diagnostic to cam the device, then run the image through the ship's library."

Cala exhaled loudly. "Hold on."

Again the intraship comlink went quiet, and Teller ran a hand down his face.

"It's probably noth—" Anora started to say when he shushed her.

"Damn, Teller, it's an Imperial homing beacon!" the Koorivar said. "Database describes it as a paralight tracker—a kind of HoloNet transceiver that parses commands from the ship's navicomputer."

Salikk swiveled to face the others, his eyes wide

with astonishment. "Tarkin knows not only where we are, but also where we're planning to go. Which means we're essentially marooned, unless you want to get there by sublight, which will only take"—he glanced at a console readout—"on the order of fifty years."

"Maybe we've done enough," Anora said, touching her injured scalp. "We call it quits right here."

Teller shook his head at her. "We haven't done near enough."

Cala's distant voice intruded. "Should I disable this thing?"

"No, don't do anything just yet," Teller told him. "Let it sit in there, and get yourself forward." He glanced around the command cabin. "Let's consider this from Tarkin's side."

"Yes, why don't we," Anora said in plain anger.

"Tarkin knows we're here," Artoz said, "and he is convinced that he has a good read on our intentions."

"With good reason," Salikk said.

"He knows we're here," Teller said, thinking out loud, "but he hasn't come for us." He cut his gaze to Artoz. "Obviously he's waiting to see what we enter into the navicomputer so he can beat us there."

"So he and Vader and whoever else—maybe the entire Imperial Navy by this time—can beat us there," the Mon Cal said. "No doubt they're calculating all possible jump egresses from this system."

Teller nodded in agreement. "Of which there have to be dozens."

"Meanwhile," Salikk said, "the navy's deploying ships to every system where Tarkin thinks we'll show ourselves."

Anora looked up from studying her hands. "Is there a way to enter false coordinates into the navicomputer?"

Salikk shook his head negatively. "Not while that tracker is enabled."

No one spoke for a moment; then Teller said: "At this point, we just need to buy some time, right? So suppose we supply Tarkin with jump coordinates into a very busy star system."

Anora's thin eyebrows formed a V. "I don't see how that helps us, unless you're counting on hiding in a traffic jam."

"We supply the coordinates," Teller said, "but we don't jump."

"You mean—"

"We get someone else to do it."

Standing proudly on the elevated command bridge walkway of the Star Destroyer *Executrix,* Tarkin felt more at home than he had in years. An *Imperial*-class wedge-shaped titan, the warship had just decanted in the Obroa-skai system after a jump from Lantillies, on Tarkin's learning that the *Carrion Spike* was on her way. The panoramic view through the bridge's bay of trapezoidal windows included nearly all the ships that made up the task force. In the distance, positioned against a radiant sweep of stars, floated three Interdictor vessels, a Detainer CC-2200, a newer-model CC-7700 frigate, and—fresh from deepdock in the Corellia system and as yet untested—an Immobilizer 418. Thickly armored, the former two had downsloping bows and stubby winglike lateral projections housing quartets of gravity well projectors. The Immobilizer, by contrast, featured four hemispherical projectors aft on the ship's sharp-bowed hull. Deployed in the middle distance between the Interdictors and the *Executrix* were frigates, pickets, and gunboats. The centermost picket carried Vader,

Crest—promoted by Vader to lieutenant—and some two dozen stormtroopers, who made up a boarding party, in the unlikely event that the *Carrion Spike* could be retaken without a fight or at least put out of commission rather than reduced to wreckage.

A holotable situated starboard and below the elevated command walkway displayed a 3-D chronometer counting down in standard time to the *Carrion Spike*'s estimated moment of arrival. As expected, the dissidents had jumped the ship from her original location to the remote Thustra system, and after spending several hours there had charged the navicomputer to plot a course for Obroa-skai. The ETA was based on the assumption that the *Carrion Spike* had gone to lightspeed at that moment or soon after, and on how quickly the corvette's Class One hyperdrive could deliver her. An earlier-than-expected arrival would find the ship reverting to realspace deeper in system, where other Imperial warships, including the *Goliath*, were positioned to intercept her. A more sophisticated homing beacon would have allowed Tarkin to track the corvette through hyperspace by way of S-thread transceivers, but the stormtrooper squadron assigned to the Phindar fuel tanker had had access only to a basic device that interfaced with a ship's navicomputer.

A specialist seated at a console in the most forward of the sunken data pits got Tarkin's attention. "Sir, the quarry is due at T minus one hundred twenty."

Tarkin angled the microphone of his headset closer to his mouth and opened the battle net to the task force liaison officer, who was aboard the CC-7700 frigate.

"The projectors are powering up to high gain, Governor Tarkin," the commander said. "The field will be initiated, then disabled, in an effort to keep from

dragging vessels other than the quarry from hyperspace. I should caution, however, that that may be
unavoidable, given the heavy traffic in this system."

"I understand, Commander," Tarkin said. "Order
your technicians to be judicious, nonetheless."

"I will, sir. But the power setting of the gravity wells
is dictated to some extent by the relative speed of the
targeted ship, and, well, sir, to be blunt about it, there
aren't many as fast as the *Carrion Spike*."

Tarkin pinched his lower lip in thought. Ideally,
local systems would have been notified that Obroa-
skai had been designated a no-entry zone, but naval
command had opted against issuing the designation
for fear of alerting the dissidents. He had other reasons for concern: chiefly the question of why the
dissidents would jump to Obroa-skai, which lacked
anything in the way of an Imperial target, and was
known mostly for its medcenters and libraries.

"T minus thirty and counting," the specialist in the
data pit announced.

Moving to the forward end of the walkway, Tarkin
fixed his gaze on the trio of Interdictors. Arms folded
across his chest, he counted down in silence even
while the voice of the specialist was doing the same in
his right ear bead.

The countdown had just reached T minus five when
Tarkin was yanked forward, nearly completely off his
feet. Fearing another lurch he spread his hands wide
and so was kept from being slammed headfirst into
the closest viewport panel. Klaxons began to howl
throughout the suddenly trembling command bridge
as the giant ship groaned and lurched yet again in the
direction of the distant Interdictors. Struggling to remain upright, Tarkin caught a glimpse of the middle-
distance frigates and pickets being pulled forward,
almost as if accelerating.

"Commander," he shouted into the headset mouth-piece, "the field is too powerful!"

"Working on it, sir," the commander said with equal volume. "It's the Immobilizer. The overcurrent resistors failed to prevent the gravitic systems from redlining—"

The comlink connection broke.

Close to the Interdictors, ships began to appear where there had only been star-filled space. Tarkin turned from the forward bay and stumbled back to the data pit to study the magnified view on one of the screens. First to drop out of hyperspace was an out-moded, saucer-shaped YT-1000 freighter, followed by two angular transports and a lustrous space yacht. Then another freighter winked into visibility, followed by two passenger vessels.

Abruptly, Tarkin felt as if he'd been shoved toward the rear of the bridge. With the interdiction field neutralized, the ships that had been caught in the invisible web began to whirl out of control. Two of the ships collided and drifted out of view. The magnification screen showed the sublight engines of other ships flashing, but the ships barely had a chance to flee or correct their spins when the field re-initiated, capturing them once again. Tarkin spread his legs wide in an effort to balance himself; then his eyes went wide as well as he turned to face the viewports. Listing on its port side, an enormous ship that more resembled something grown than built decanted, broadsiding the Detainer CC-2200 before careening into a spin that left its dorsal surface impaled on the Interdictor's sloping bow.

"Mon Cal star cruiser!" a voice in his ear said, loud enough to be heard over the head-splitting racket of the klaxons. "The luxury liner *Stellar Vista* out of Corsin. Approximately ten thousand aboard!"

A brief but nova-bright explosion flared in the distance, ferocious enough to leave Tarkin blinking and seeing stars that weren't there. When he was able to focus through the viewport's blast-tinting, he saw that the stern of the organically sculpted passenger ship had disappeared and that the Interdictor had been knocked ninety degrees from its former position. In moments podlike lifeboats and flocks of spherical escape pods were streaming from the stricken liner.

"The *Stellar Vista* reports that it is in imminent distress," the specialist said. "The ship's captain is requesting all the help we can provide."

Tarkin swung toward the data pits, but spoke into the headset. "Order the frigates to render assistance. Instruct the Interdictors to negate the field, and move us into a position where we can utilize the tractor beams to grab the lifeboats."

All at once Vader's voice was booming in his ear. "Where is your corvette, Governor? It is not on any of our scanners. Do you have it?"

Tarkin hurried to the edge of the walkway and gestured to one of the seated noncoms. "Have you located the *Carrion Spike*?"

The spec turned to him. "No sign of the corvette, sir. Could it be in stealth mode?"

Tarkin compressed his lips and shook his head. "Not even a cloaking device could keep it from being detected in an interdiction field."

A second spec called to him. "Sir, the task force commander wants to know if you wish the Interdictors to re-initiate the field. Some of the transports are trying to make a run for it."

Tarkin had his mouth open to reply when Vader said, "I want all those ships corralled. Hold them in place with tractor beams if you have to, but none should be allowed to leave."

Tarkin nodded to the noncoms. "Contain those vessels."

"And the lifeboats, sir?" one asked.

"We'll see to them when we can."

Yet a third specialist joined in. "Sir, one of our frigates is taking fire."

Tarkin moved farther down the command walkway to stand over her. "On screen."

A grainy image of a modified Lux-400 yacht took shape, green hyphens of laserfire erupting from the ship's well-concealed lateral cannons.

"Do we have the transponder signature of that vessel?" Tarkin asked.

"The *Truant,* sir," the tech said. "On the wanted list in several sectors for arms smuggling."

"Draw a bead on it," Tarkin commanded.

The spec relayed the command into her headset, then glanced up at him. "Our gunners report they're having difficulty finding a clear shot because of the lifeboats and the debris field."

Tarkin fumed. "Acquire it and open fire!"

He turned his attention to the screens as turbolaser beams from the Star Destroyer's starboard-side turrets found the Lux-400, and it vanished in a short-lived fireball.

"The *Truant* is no longer on the wanted list, sir. Minimal collateral casualties."

Tarkin strode forward on the walkway to the primary data pit. "Have you confined the rest of those ships?"

"They're not going anywhere, sir, and Lord Vader's picket is currently closing on the group. Still no sign of the *Carrion Spike.*"

"Do the sensors detail any instances of ships jumping to lightspeed?"

"None, sir. No instances of Cronau radiation—

though the interdiction field would make that a long shot, in any case."

Tarkin shook his head in bewilderment. Had the shipjackers had a last-moment change of plans? Or had they been forewarned?

"Is the homing beacon still transmitting?"

The tech attended to his various instruments. "No signal from the tracker, sir. Nothing."

So they *had* discovered it. But when?

Tarkin continued to move forward until he was standing just short of the viewports, just short of the chaos beyond. Vader's voice fractured his introspection.

"Which vessel appeared first?"

"The YT-One-Thousand freighter," Tarkin said.

"Then we'll begin with that one, since it arrived closest to the projected arrival time of the *Carrion Spike*."

"Begin what, Lord Vader?"

"The failure of the corvette to appear does not owe to any impromptu change of plans, Governor. The dissidents are trying to throw us off the scent, and I intend to search each interdicted ship until we have answers."

Tarkin watched the picket accelerate as Vader made haste for the immobilized antique, ignoring the flaming hulk of the passenger liner and the scattering of lifeboats and escape pods to all sides.

Tarkin let his gaze become unfocused, so that the stars and the strewn ships lost all definition. His thoughts returned to the plateau and the lessons he had learned. Sometimes, especially when he, Jova, and the others had gone without food for several days—and despite their best efforts to stalk faultlessly—an elusive hunt took on such desperation that the importance of *thinking* like the prey was abandoned. Vader was cor-

rect: The dissidents hadn't had a last-moment change
of plans; early on they were aware of the trap being
set for them. Creatures understood themselves to
be most vulnerable during flight and evasion. That's
when they paid strict attention to warnings issued by
other animals. Fleeing for their lives, they picked up
scents on the wind; they sharpened their senses, grant-
ing themselves the ability to hear and see their pur-
suers at great distances. They took all advantage of
knowing the territory better than the ones chasing
them. The savannas and jungled areas of the plateau
would perk up when Jova and his band were about,
because they were the intruders, and usually up to
no good.

His loathing and frustration notwithstanding, Tarkin could respect the dissidents for their cleverness
and foresight, but clearly their plan had been hatched
with the aid of confederates, and those allies were
now beginning to play their part in keeping the *Carrion Spike* from being reclaimed.

Tarkin had lost all sense of how long he had been
standing in the viewport bay when Vader's fury
brought him back to the moment.

"This freighter is to be tractored aboard the *Executrix* for a thorough inspection. The crew is to be kept
in detention until I'm through interrogating them."

18

HUNG UPSIDE DOWN

VADER STOOD OMINOUSLY motionless in the illuminated cargo hold of the YT freighter, breathing deeply and looking as if he was ready to draw his lightsaber and cut everything around him to shreds. Tarkin, too, thought it unlikely they were going to discover anything of interest among the haphazardly stacked shipping crates, but he was willing to have a look nonetheless.

The foul-smelling and disheveled old ship sat in the glare of spotlights in one of the Star Destroyer's ancillary hangars, like some stultified and wary insect. Circular in design, with an outrigger cockpit sandwiched between a pair of rectangular mandibles, the *Reticent* had seen better days a century earlier, and was now barely spaceworthy. The cargo ramp beneath the cockpit had been lowered, and glow rods set up inside and out to flood the hold with light. Vader and Tarkin's cursory search had revealed consignments of tools, medical supplies, bolts of fabric, trays of gaudy costume jewelry, tankfuls of alcoholic beverages, and droid parts. Recording devices and scanners in hand, Lieutenant Crest and two other stormtroopers—all three without helmets or armored plastrons—were following Vader and Tarkin as they nosed around.

The *Reticent* was the only ship to have been sequestered following the catastrophe at the edge of Obroa-skai space. The rest that had fallen victim to the faulty interdiction field had been checked out and allowed to go on their way, which for most of them meant directly to the system's namesake planet for repairs, after collisions with escape pods and debris from the wrecked Mon Cal star cruiser. That ship and the Detainer had also been towed to Obroa-skai, with the death toll from the crash estimated at eleven hundred beings. The state-of-the-art Immobilizer whose failsafes had malfunctioned had been returned to Corellian Engineering for reassessment. Legitimate holovids of the events had flooded the HoloNet, most of them cammed by passengers aboard the luxury liner, and by media teams who had received word from unidentified sources of an Imperial operation taking place at the periphery of the star system. As for *Carrion Spike*, she had yet to turn up in any system. By the time the task force's fastest frigate had reached Thustra, Tarkin's rogue ship had already jumped to unknown space.

Crest was reading from a datapad.

"The ship's identification signature doesn't appear to have been altered. It hasn't even changed names in decades. The crew acquired it three years back from a dealer on Lantillies. The itinerary we sliced from the navicomputer corroborates the captain's story. They jumped from Taris to Thustra to pick up replacement parts for a fleet of Sephi flyers that were sold in bulk at the end of the war to an Obroa-skai emergency medevac center."

"How was the pickup and delivery arranged?" Tarkin asked.

"Through a broker on Lantillies—maybe the same dealer in pre-owned ships. He gets a line on what's needed when and where and dispatches crews to make the transfers."

"The *Reticent*'s crew are freelance operators?"

Crest nodded. "They describe themselves as itinerant merchants."

"Where were they bound after Obroa-skai?" Vader wanted to know.

"Taanab," Crest said, "to buy foodstuffs. Parties at Thustra, Obroa-skai, and Taanab have substantiated all this."

"And the communications board?" Tarkin asked.

Crest turned to him. "It isn't set up to record incoming or outgoing transmissions, but the log checks out, at least in terms of supporting the captain's claims about who contacted them and where the freighter was at the time."

Vader scanned the hold, as if in search of something unspecified. "How long did they spend at Thustra?"

"Three hours, Lord Vader."

Vader glanced at Tarkin. "What, I wonder, was their rush?"

Tarkin considered it. "Apparently the goods—the flyer replacement parts—were already crated and waiting for them. The medcenter on Obroa-skai had requested that they expedite the delivery." He fell briefly silent. "The *Reticent*'s hyperdrive is vastly inferior to that of the *Carrion Spike*. No better than a Class Five, I would imagine. That means that even though they arrived in the Obroa-skai system at almost precisely the moment we were expecting the *Carrion Spike*, the *Reticent* had to have gone to hyperspace much sooner than the *Carrion Spike* would have. The timing could owe to nothing more than coincidence, but one question to ask is just what the *dissidents* were doing in the Thustra system for so many hours."

Vader had swung abruptly to Tarkin on the word *coincidence,* and now the Dark Lord was in motion, pushing crates aside as he stormed about—without actually touching any of them.

"This ship rendezvoused with the *Carrion Spike.* I'm certain of it."

Tarkin threw Crest a questioning look.

"If so, Lord Vader," the stormtrooper said, "there's no evidence of the ships linking up. No evidence in the comm board showing intership communication, and no evidence in the docking ring's air lock memory showing that the *Reticent* was umbilicaled to another ship."

Vader took a moment to reply, and when he did it was to pose a question to Tarkin. "Why would the dissidents elect to *send* us a ship, in any case?"

Tarkin smiled faintly, aware that the question was rhetorical. "To throw us off the scent, if I recall your phrase correctly. To give us plenty to deal with while they're busy making plans to strike elsewhere."

Vader turned and proceeded to the cargo hold ramp. "Let us see what the captain of this scrap heap has to say for himself."

"You are not an itinerant merchant, Captain," Vader said, gesticulating with his right hand. "You are in league with a group of dissidents intent on destroying military installations as a means of undermining the sovereignty of the Empire."

A Koorivar with a long cranial horn, the *Reticent*'s naked and shackled captain was suspended a meter overhead, captive of a containment field produced by a device whose prototype had been manufactured on Geonosis long before the war. As far as Tarkin knew, the *Executrix* was the only capital ship in the Imperial fleet to have such an appliance, which created and maintained the field by means of disk-like generators bolted to the deck and to the ceiling directly above. The detention center's version of prisoner interdiction, the field required that the detainee wear magnetic cuffs that not only anchored him in place but also monitored life signs: Too powerful a field could stop a being's heart or cause irreversible brain damage. As well—and as if the field itself weren't enough—the cuffs could be used as torture devices, capable of unleashing powerful electrical charges. Vader, however, had no need to utilize the cuffs. His dark powers had the captain writhing in pain.

"Lord Vader," Tarkin said, "we should at least give him an opportunity to respond."

Reluctantly, Vader lowered his hand, and the Koorivar's ridged facial features relaxed in cautious relief. "I'm a merchant and nothing more," he managed to say. "Torture me as you must, but it won't change the fact that we came to Obroa-skai on business."

"The business of conspiracy," Vader said. "The business of sabotage."

The Koorivar shook his head weakly. "The business of buying and selling. That is what we do, and only what we do." He paused. "Not all of us were Separatists."

Tarkin smiled to himself. It was true: Not all Koorivar population centers and worlds had thrown in with Dooku. Nor had all Sy Myrthians, a pair of which made up the rest of the crew.

But why would the captain say that?

"Why do you make a point of stating that fact, Captain?" he asked.

The Koorivar's bleary eyes found him. "The Empire demands retribution for the war, and so it lumps the innocent with the guilty and holds all of us responsible."

"Responsible for what, Captain? Do you believe that the Separatists were wrong to secede from the Republic?"

"I move about to keep from having to decide who is right and who is wrong."

"A being without a homeworld," Tarkin said. "As your species was once without a planet."

"I'm telling you the truth."

"You're lying," Vader countered. "Admit that you swore allegiance to the Separatist Alliance, and that you and your current allies are the ones seeking retribution."

The Koorivar squeezed his eyes closed, anticipating pain Vader opted not to deliver.

"Tell me about the broker who provides you with leads," Tarkin said.

"Knotts. A human who works out of Lantillies. Contact him. He'll verify everything I've been telling you."

"He helped you procure the *Reticent*?"

"He loaned us the credits, yes."

"And you've been in his employ for three years."

"Not in his employ. We're freelance. He provides jobs to several crews, and we accept jobs from several brokers."

"How did you originally find your way to a human broker on Lantillies?"

"An advert of some sort. I don't recall precisely."

"This time he instructed you to travel from Taris to Thustra?"

"Yes."

"A rush job," Tarkin surmised.

"The medcenter relies on its Sephi flyers for medical evacuations."

"So, in and out," Tarkin said. "No interaction with anyone other than the provider."

"No interaction. Exactly as you say."

"And no ship-to-ship interaction."

"There was no need. The supplies were groundside on Thustra."

Tarkin circled the Koorivar. "In your recent travels, have you seen holovids of attacks launched against Imperial facilities?"

"We try to ignore the media."

"Clueless, as well as homeless," Tarkin said, "is that it?"

The captain sneered at him. "Guilty as charged."

Tarkin traded glances with Vader. "An interesting turn of phrase, Captain," Tarkin said.

Vader loosed a sound that approximated a growl. "We're not in some Coruscant courtroom, Governor. Questions of this sort are useless."

"You'd prefer to break him with pain."

"If need be. Unless, of course, you object."

Vader's menacing tone rolled off Tarkin. "I suspect that our captain will go insane long before he breaks. But I also agree that we're wasting our time. The longer we spend here, the greater the chance that the *Carrion Spike* will elude us entirely." He watched the Koorivar peripherally as he said it.

Vader looked directly at the captain. "Yes, this one is stronger than he looks, and he is not innocent. I want more time with him. For all we know the dissidents abandoned your ship at Thustra and transferred to the YT freighter. He may be one of them."

"Then someone else must have the *Carrion Spike,*

as there was no sign of her there." Tarkin glanced at
the captain a final time and forced an exhalation. "I'll
leave you to your work, Lord Vader."

The Koorivar's anguished screams accompanied
him down the long corridor that led to the detention
center's turbolifts.

Teller found Anora in the corvette's darkened cockpit, swiveling absently in one of the chairs, her bare
feet crossed atop the instrument console. Salikk and
the others were resting, as was the *Carrion Spike*, a
slave to sundry deep-space gravities.

"We're almost done," he said, sinking into an adjacent chair.

Her face fell. "There has to be a more comforting
way of saying that."

He frowned at her. "You're the writer."

"Yes, but you're *talking,* not writing."

His frown only deepened. "You know what I mean.
One more jump and on to the serious business."

Her eyes searched his face. "And then?"

All he could do was shrug. "With luck, live to fight
another day."

She closed her eyes and shook her head. "With
luck . . . There you go again, qualifying every answer."

He didn't know how else to put it; how not to qual-
ify his remarks. In thinking about it, he recalled having made almost the same comment when the *Reticent*
had jumped for Obroa-skai. *With any luck, Tarkin
and Vader will dismiss the ship's arrival as coincidental, and the crew will simply be questioned and released.* But that wasn't what happened. The Imperials
had seen through the ruse, the ship had been im-
pounded, and the crew had been arrested. Word was
that neither Tarkin nor Vader had been able to glean

much information from them, but Teller doubted that Tarkin would leave it at that. Tarkin wouldn't rest until he rooted out connections, and once he did . . . Well, by then it would be too late.

With any luck.

The update on the situation at Obroa-skai had also included a piece of good news. The corvette's crew had been given a target to attack, which had saved him the trouble of having to choose one from among increasingly bad options. The objective was another Imperial facility rather than some more significant objective, but Teller could live with that. No one aboard the *Carrion Spike* nursed any delusions about winning a war against the Empire single-handedly. They were merely contributing to what Teller hoped would one day grow into a *cause*. That, and avenging themselves for what each of them had had to bear; payback for atrocities the Empire had committed, which had inspired them to come together as a group.

"Nice of you to give Cala the privilege of destroying the homing beacon," Anora said.

"He earned it."

Anora put her feet on the cool deck, yawned, and stretched her thin, dark arms over her head. "When do we go?"

Teller glanced at the console's chron display. "We've still got a couple of hours."

"Do you trust your contact entirely?"

Teller rocked his head. "I'd say, up to a point. He's convinced that he has as much to gain as we do."

Anora grinned faintly. "I was expecting you to add, *or lose.*"

"It was implied."

"Any compassion for our stand-ins at Obroa-skai?"

Teller exhaled in disappointment. "Not you, too."

"I'm only asking."

"They knew the risks," Teller said, straight-faced.

Anora took a long moment to respond. "I know I sound like Hask, but maybe I'm just not cut out for this, Teller." She eyed him askance. "It was never an ambition of mine to be a revolutionary."

He snorted. "I don't buy it. You were fighting the good fight in your own way long before I met you. With words, anyway."

She smiled without showing her teeth. "Not quite the same as firing laser cannons at other beings or letting strangers take the fall for you."

He studied her. "You know, I'm actually surprised to hear you talk like this. You practically jumped at the chance to get involved."

She nodded. "I won't deny it. But since we're being honest with each other, I may have been thinking of it more as a career move."

"Fame and fortune."

"I guess. And like our stand-ins, I knew the risk. But I underestimated COMPNOR and the Emperor."

"His reach."

"Not just his reach." Her face grew serious. "His power. His barbarity."

"You're not the only one who underestimated him."

Anora glanced toward the command center hatch and lowered her voice. "I still feel bad about dragging Hask into this."

Teller shrugged. "We could always drop her off somewhere."

Anora's eyes searched his face. "Really?"

"Sure, if that's what she wants."

"Should I ask her?"

"Go ahead. I'll give you odds she says no."

Anora laughed shortly. "I think you're right." She fell silent, then said: "Are we going to win, Teller?"

He reached out to clap her gently on the shoulder. "We're winning so far, aren't we?"

The subsurface Sith shrine wasn't the sole area in the Palace where the dark side of the Force was strong. Rooms and corridors throughout the lower levels still bore traces of the resentful fury Darth Vader had unleashed in the final days of the Clone Wars. In one such room a human and a Koorivar knelt in separate pools of ruthless light trained on them from hidden sources in the vaulted ceiling. To Darth Sidious, however, they were not so much living beings as whirlpools in the befuddled waters he had been negotiating since the cache of communications gear found on Murkhana had been brought to his attention; obstacles he needed to maneuver past in order to reach an untroubled stretch of current.

Sidious occupied a simple chair well removed from the twin pools of light, the droid 11-4D off to one side and, slightly behind him, Vizier Mas Amedda close at hand as well. Opposite him across the barren room, a pair of Royal Guards flanked the carved stone doorway.

The Koorivar—Bracchia—was an Imperial intelligence asset assigned to Murkhana; the human—Stellan—the Koorivar's Security Bureau case officer stationed on Coruscant. Sidious already knew all he needed to about their separate backgrounds and records of service. He sought nothing more than to observe them through the Force, and to evaluate their responses to a few simple questions.

"Koorivar," he said from the chair, "you served the Republic during the war, and more recently you provided some assistance to Lord Vader and Governor Tarkin on Murkhana."

Light reflected off the Koorivar's spiral horn as he lifted his head a bit. "I helped them rid Murkhana of arms smugglers, my lord."

"So it seems. But tell us what you told them at the time about your initial survey of the HoloNet jamming devices."

"My lord, I stated that I did not chance upon the devices on my own, nor was I cognizant of any rumors indicating that such a cache existed in Murkhana City. I was merely executing a directive I received from Coruscant."

Viewing him through the Force, Sidious saw the eddying waters began to relax and surrender themselves to the current.

"Case officer," he said to Stellan, "by '*Coruscant*' he means *you*, does he not?"

"Yes, my lord. The investigation was carried out at my request." A thickset human man of indeterminate age, he had brown wavy hair and large ears set low on a blockish head.

"Then tell us how you came to learn of this cache."

The man lifted his nondescript face to the light, squinting and blinking in puzzlement. "My lord, forgive me. I assumed you were aware that the information was provided to ISB by Military Intelligence."

Sidious's pulse quickened. Instead of smoothing out, the hydraulic tightened on itself and began to spin more rapidly, as if summoning Sidious to follow the swirling funnel beneath the surface to whatever irregularity below had given rise to it.

It may as well have been the dark side that rasped: "Explain this."

Humbling himself, the case officer lowered his head. "My lord, Military Intelligence was in the process of conducting an inventory of caches of armaments, vehicles, and supplies that had been left abandoned during the war on a host of contested worlds, from Raxus all the way to Utapau. In the case of the Holo-Net jamming devices, MI wasn't certain if the cache had been on Murkhana for several years, or if it was of more recent origin, and worthy therefore of further investigation. Given that an investigation of that sort fell outside its purview, MI relayed the matter to Imperial Security."

"To you," Sidious said.

"Yes, my lord, I received a crude holovid that showed the devices."

"A holovid? Cammed by someone in Military Intelligence?"

"That was my assumption, my lord. I didn't see the need to pursue the matter, nor did the deputy director. We simply instructed . . . Bracchia to conduct a survey."

Sidious thought back to the initial briefing that had taken place in the audience chamber. Defending ISB's apprehensions that the jammers could be used to spread anti-Imperial propaganda, Deputy Director Ison had wondered aloud why Naval Intelligence was suddenly so troubled by the cache when on first learning of it they had expressed no such concerns. None of the admirals—not Rancit, Screed, nor any of the others—had replied to Ison's question.

Without taking his eyes from the case officer, Sidious said in a low voice, "Droid, locate this holovid sent by Military Intelligence to ISB."

OneOne-FourDee extended its interface arm into an access port behind Sidious's chair. After a long silence, the droid said: "Your Majesty, I find no record of the holovid."

"As I suspected," Sidious said. "But you will find it in ISB's archives."

Another moment passed before 11-4D said, "Yes, Your Majesty. The holovid is archived."

And when projected, Sidious thought, it would show corruption of a telltale sort. Because the holovid was counterfeit; faked by someone with access to Imperial codes and to devices capable of subverting the HoloNet.

Deep beneath the surface he had found the irregularities responsible for the turbulence above. And it was apparent now that they were closer at hand than even he had realized.

FOOTPRINTS

IN THE MOST SECLUDED of the *Executrix*'s several tactical rooms, Tarkin closed myriad programs running on the immense battle analysis holotable, and entered a restricted Imperial code that tasked the projector to interface with the HoloNet. He then submitted himself to a series of biometric scans that allowed him to access a multitude of top-secret Republic and Imperial databases situated on Coruscant. He had already issued orders that he was not to be disturbed, but he double-checked that the door had sealed behind him and that the tactical room's security cams were offline. He called for the illumination to dim, set himself atop a tall castered stool within easy reach of the table's complex controls, and allowed his thoughts to unwind.

The Star Destroyer was holding at Obroa-skai, awaiting redeployment orders from Coruscant, now that the Emperor had given Vice Admiral Rancit command of the task force created to capture or destroy the *Carrion Spike*. Only a few hours earlier the dissidents had attacked an Imperial facility at Nouane, a client-state system in the Inner Rim. To Tarkin, the dissidents' choice of targets seemed as illogical as would have been their showing up at Obroa-skai. But with major systems becoming so heavily reinforced, perhaps the choice merely reflected the fact that their options were dwindling. At Nouane the rogue ship had been prevented from inflicting serious damage and had nearly become a fatality. The win had gone to Rancit, who through a painstaking process of elimination had predicted where the *Carrion Spike* would strike and had dispatched a flotilla in advance of the corvette's arrival. Even stealth had failed to allow the corvette to evade a continuous onslaught of long-range lasers. From what Tarkin had been given to understand, there was good reason to believe that the *Carrion Spike* had sustained heavy damage before a last-ditch retreat to hyperspace. The rumor mill had it that Rancit's assignment—some called it a promotion—was an indication of the Emperor's disappointment with Tarkin, but Vader had assured Tarkin that the Emperor was merely trying to free him from having to wear too many hats. Tarkin was to leave the chase to others for the time being, and devote himself instead to ascertaining the dissidents' ultimate objective.

And so he was.

When stalking game on the plateau, Jova would tell him that a careful study of prints on a trail could reveal not only the species of animal that had left them, but also the animal's intentions.

With a flourish of input at the holotable's keypad, Tarkin created an open field above the table and instructed the computer to render his voice into lines of text and place them in order in the field. Then he turned slightly in the direction of the nearest audio pickup.

"Access to confiscated warship modules, Separatist weapons, and HoloNet interrupters—either through salvagers, crime syndicates, or other sources," he began. "The ability to make use of purchased or pirated Separatist technology. The ability to transmit real-time holovids through the HoloNet, and the ability to create and transmit counterfeit holovids by accessing public HoloNet archives and other media sources. Knowledge of the existence of Rampart and Sentinel bases. Knowledge of Lieutenant Thon's assignment to Rampart Base. Knowledge of the existence of the *Carrion Spike,* and familiarity with her sophisticated systems. A crew of spacers conversant with Imperial procedures and with a knowledge of Imperial facilities. Possible assistance from Imperial assets with high clearance."

One by one the lines of text appeared in the field and Tarkin studied them for a long moment, his elbow planted on his raised left knee and his chin cupped in his hand.

Vader's interrogation of the *Reticent*'s crewmembers hadn't resulted in anything more than heart failure for the freighter's Sy Myrthian navigator. However, as a recompense of sorts, the Dark Lord had received a significant piece of information from one of his sources inside the Crymorah. A lieutenant in the crime syndicate claimed to have negotiated a deal with Faazah— the Sugi smuggler on Murkhana—for a supply of custom fuel cells, which had been shipped to the planet shortly before Tarkin and Vader's arrival. This in itself wasn't entirely surprising, considering that the *Carrion Spike*'s stop at the Phindar fuel tanker was evidence enough that the dissidents had added fuel to the ship before absconding with her. What *was* surprising was that the deal for the fuel cells had been arranged through an agent on Lantillies, whom Tarkin suspected was the same human the captain of the *Reticent* had named as their broker.

Knotts.

Tarkin instructed the HoloNet database to launch a search for Knotts, and in moments the hologram of a silver-haired human with a deeply lined face was rotating in place above the projector. Knotts had a world-weary look Tarkin associated with veteran soldiers who had seen more than their share of tragedy. Extracting the holoimage, he saved it off to one side of the table and regarded it in silence while machines hummed, chirped, and beeped around him.

What he read in the concise précis accompanying the holoimage supported the fact that Knotts had resided on Lantillies for some fifteen years. Digging a bit deeper, Tarkin was able to retrieve Knotts's documents of incorporation, his Republic and Imperial tax records, court proceedings of his divorce agreement, even images of the modest apartment he owned on Lantillies. Native to the Core, he had relocated to the Outer Rim and established himself as a middleman, bringing clients in want of goods or services together with groups of freelance spacers who could fulfill those needs. He was something of a dispatcher and an agent, taking what struck Tarkin as a fair credit percentage on each transaction.

The eyes-only Coruscant databases —which Tarkin hadn't had reason to access since his days as adjutant general of the Republic Navy—provided a more complete and compelling portrait of Knotts. Yes, for fifteen years he had operated a profitable if minor Outer Rim enterprise, but during the Clone Wars he had also functioned as a subcontractor for Republic Intelligence, responsible for the covert transport of arms and other materials to resistance groups operating on Separatist-occupied worlds, one of which happened to figure prominently in Tarkin's past, as well: the Mid Rim moon Antar 4.

Tarkin sat taller on the stool. The discovery of Knotts's secret past stirred a memory of the excitement he had felt on the plateau when encountering a sudden, unexpected turn along a game trail. Had his quarry gotten wind of him? Had a different threat presented itself? Was his prey keen on reversing the situation by circling behind to stalk him in his own tracks?

Antar 4 had been a member of the Republic almost from its inception, but the Secessionist Movement that preceded the Clone Wars had created a schism among the moon's indigenous humanoid Gotals and given rise to terrorist groups aligned with the Separatists. Shored up by the Republic, Gotal loyalists had managed to retain power until shortly after the Battle of Geonosis, when the moon had fallen to Separatist forces and, for a brief period, become a headquarters for Count Dooku. Tens of millions of Gotal refugees had fled to their colony world, Atzerri, replaced on Antar 4 by an influx of Koorivar, Gossams, and other species whose homeworlds had joined the CIS. As a result, the moon became a political imbroglio, and had spawned one of the first resistance groups, made up of loyalist Koorivar and Gotals whom the Republic supported with tactical advisers and secret shipments of arms and matériel. Though the resistance was successful in carrying out hundreds of acts of sabotage, the moon remained in the grip of the Separatists for the length of the war.

Tarkin recalled the Koorivar captain's words to Vader: *Not all of us were Separatists.*

With the deaths of Dooku and the Separatist

leadership, and the deactivation of the droid army, Antar 4—like many CIS worlds—had soon found itself in the Empire's crosshairs. More to the point, in the crosshairs of Moff Tarkin, who had been given Imperial orders to make an example of the moon. No attempt was to be made at repatriation, nor was Tarkin to waste time sorting the Separatists from those resistance fighters and intelligence operatives waiting to be exfiltrated to safety.

COMPNOR did its best to cover up the fact that many Koorivar and Gotal loyalists had been swept up in the arrests, executions, and massacres, but the media eventually got hold of the story, and for a while the Antar Atrocity had become a celebrated cause in the Core—this despite the swift disappearances of many beings who had attached themselves to reporting on the story. Instead, the disappearances so fueled the public's hunger for details that the Emperor decided to remove Tarkin from the controversy by assigning him to pacification operations in the Western Reaches and had ultimately installed him as commander of the bases servicing the deep-space mobile battle station project, replacing Vice Admiral Rancit, who was reassigned to Naval Intelligence.

In thinking back to that period, some four years earlier, Tarkin recalled the case of two Coruscanti journalists who had risen briefly to the forefront among a host of anti-Imperial irritants. A quick search of the HoloNet archives conjured their holograms, which Tarkin placed above the table alongside that of Knotts. In the Coruscant database, Tarkin located intelligence reports detailing their activities.

An attractive, dark-skinned human woman with blue-gray eyes, Anora Fair had been the most vocal and volatile of the Core media correspondents who had fixated on the events at Antar. An ambitious journalist, Fair had already attracted attention for her probing interviews with Imperial officials and her editorials critical of Imperial policy, as well as of the Emperor himself. Her unrelenting reports on the Antar Atrocity had been brought to life with holographic re-creations of arrests and executions, produced and directed by a rubicund Zygerrian female named Hask Taff, whom many a pro-Imperial pundit had deemed "a master of HoloNet manipulation."

It was clear to COMPNOR that the two of them knew more than they could possibly have known without the help of an intelligence community insider, and suspicions at the time had focused on a disaffected former Republic station chief named Berch Teller.

A HoloNet archive search for Teller came up empty, but an access-restricted database search returned a decade-old image of a rangy, dark-haired human with thick eyebrows and a cleft chin. Extracting the hologram, Tarkin placed it alongside those of Anora Fair and Hask Taff, then changed his mind and moved Teller's hologram to the center, with Knotts—the broker—to one side, and the two media professionals on the other.

Tarkin contemplated the arrangement and was pleased. With each new set of prints, the trail was beginning to surrender its secrets.

Captain Teller's intelligence network résumé indicated a long and distinguished career. Early in the Clone Wars, Teller had been involved in covert operations on a host of Separatist worlds. That, however, paled in comparison with the fact that Teller had been one of the intelligence officers who had debriefed Tarkin following his rescue and escape from the Citadel, with the plans to a secret hyperspace route into Separatist space.

He and Teller had history.

And there was more.

Assigned to Antar 4 in the war's final year, Captain Teller had helped train and organize Gotal and Koorivar partisans into well-armed resistance groups, which had carried out raids, destroyed armories and spaceports, and generally made a nuisance of themselves for the governing Separatists. Sensing what was in store for Antar 4 after the war's abrupt conclusion, Teller had appealed to his superiors in the intelligence agencies to arrange for the extraction of his principal assets before Tarkin could bring the hammer down on the moon. Republic Intelligence had tried to provide aid in the form of documentation and transport, but COMPNOR, by then on the rise in the Imperial hegemony, had refused to intervene, and so many of Teller's operatives, despite their long-standing loyalty to the Republic, had been arrested and executed.

The Imperial directive to make an example of the moon had made perfect sense to Tarkin at the time. He wasn't a retributionist; it was simply that separating friend from foe would undoubtedly have allowed many Separatists to flee into hiding. Eliminating them en masse on Antar 4 was preferable to having to hunt them down later, in whatever remote regions they found shelter. His actions had conveyed a message to other former CIS worlds that defeat didn't grant them absolution for their crimes, or assure them that the Empire was ready to welcome them back into the fold with open arms. The message had to be made clear to Raxus, Kooriva, Murkhana, and the rest: Surrender all former Separatists, or suffer the same fate as the population of the Gotal moon.

Still, Tarkin could see how a Republic officer like Teller might feel betrayed to the point where he would attempt to wage a campaign of revenge against all odds. The military was filled with those who refused to accept that collateral damage was acceptable when it served to further the Imperial cause. In the absence of order, there was only chaos. Did Teller expect an apology from the Emperor? Compensation for the families of those who had been unjustly executed? It was witless thinking. Multiply Teller by one billion or ten billion beings, however, and the Empire could face a serious problem . . .

He continued to peruse Teller's résumé, wading through the dense text that scrolled in midair in front of his eyes. By the time Teller had made his appeal to his intelligence chiefs, he had already been reassigned to head up security at—

Tarkin stared at the words: *Desolation Station*.

The clandestine outpost responsible for overseeing much of the research for the deep-space battle station.

But Teller wasn't there for long; he had vanished shortly after the events at Antar 4 and hadn't been seen since. Some in Military Intelligence believed that he had been assassinated by COMPNOR agents, but others were convinced that it was Teller who had not only fed information about Antar 4 to Anora Fair and Hask Taff, but also been instrumental in spiriting the media partners to safety hours before they were to have been disappeared by COMPNOR.

Tarkin eased off the castered stool and began to pace the length of the massive table, all the while regarding the four projected holoimages. Was it possible that some or all of them were involved in the pirating of the *Carrion Spike*? He stopped to mull it over, and shook his head. The odds were good that Teller and Knotts knew each other, in that they had answered to the same case officer at Republic Intelligence; also that Teller had approached the journalists with his story. But none of the four was a starship pilot, much less an engineer capable of managing the corvette's sophisticated instruments and systems.

Returning to the stool, Tarkin re-summoned the lengthy file devoted to Antar 4.

The Republic databases were difficult to navigate, as much of the information had been deleted or redacted, or was in the process of being altered and "reinterpreted." Once he had successfully wormed his way into the appropriate archives, however, he was able to narrow the parameters of his search for Republic assets associated with the resistance. Ultimately the distant computers provided the names of several of Teller's partisan subordinates who had escaped execution on the moon and were at least worthy of consideration. There was, for example, a Gotal starship pilot, identified in the archives only as "Salikk," and a Koorivar munitions and surveillance expert listed only as "Cala."

Tarkin extracted holoimages of the twin-horned humanoid and the single-horned near-human and placed them on the far side of the holograms of Fair and Taff; then, changing his mind, he moved them to float between those of Teller and Knotts.

A tremor of excitement coursed through him.

He propelled the castered stool to the HoloNet array and contacted the escort carrier, *Goliath,* ordering the specialist he eventually spoke with to forward from the ship's database a record of his transmission with the Phindian administrator of the fuel tanker. When the recording arrived, he extracted the image of the scar-faced, red-haired human who had requisitioned fuel cells and ordered the computer to compare the hologram of Teller to the bogus Imperial commander with the ocular implant.

In short order, text flashed above the holotable between the two holograms:

MATCH: 99.9%

Tarkin's jaw fell open in wonder as he stared at
the man who had stolen his ship.

Shifting his gaze between his dictated text and the
holograms of the suspects, he began to think through
everything from scratch.

Yes, Teller could have learned about the *Carrion
Spike* during his short tenure at Desolation Station.
And it would have been easy enough for him to persuade "Salikk" and "Cala" to join him, since he had
probably been responsible for exfiltrating them from
Antar 4—just as he'd been responsible for saving the
lives of Fair and Taff by whisking them from Coruscant. At that point, Teller would have had a pilot, an
operations and munitions specialist, and two Holo-
Net experts.

Tarkin ran a hand down over his mouth and took
hold of his chin.

Something was missing; some*one* was missing.

He reentered the top-secret database to scan the
few reports he could access relating to Desolation
Station.

Teller wasn't the only being who had disappeared
from the secret facility. Motivated by grievances against
the Empire, many had fled and become fugitives. The
count was so high, in fact, that COMPNOR had
compiled a most-wanted list of missing scientists and
technicians who had held high-priority security clear-
ances. The disappearances were often offered up as
an explanation for harassment attacks against Imperial bases and installations.

Tarkin scrolled through the list several times, returning after each read-through to a Mon Cal starship systems engineer named Artoz, who had gone missing shortly after Teller. "Dr. Artoz," as he was apparently affectionately known, was a former member of the Mon Cal Knights, a group that had fought against his planet's Separatist-aligned Quarren. Artoz certainly would have known about the *Carrion Spike,* as parts for the corvette's stygian crystal stealth system had been manufactured at Mon Cal shipyards after the concept-design team had given up on attempts to utilize hibridium.

Tarkin blinked, rubbed his eyes, and stared at the midair holograms.

What about Bracchia, the Koorivar asset on Murkhana? Was he involved in the plot, despite the part he had played in procuring a replacement starship?

Were the Crymorah crime families involved?

What about the crew of the freighter *Reticent*? Had they perhaps been aboard the cobbled-together warship that had attacked Sentinel Base?

Then there was the matter of the warship itself. Who had funded the purchase of the modules, droids, and starfighters? Where and by whom had the ship been assembled? Just how wide reaching was the conspiracy? Did it involve only former Republic Intelligence operatives, or did it penetrate Imperial agencies, as well?

Sentients, like animals, have their fussy behaviors, Jova would say. *Learn the particulars of one, and you begin to understand the entire species.*

If Tarkin's hypothesis about Antar 4 being the nexus of the conspiracy was correct, could the involvement of the *Reticent*'s crew owe to something as simple as having lost friends or relatives to the mass executions? Relatives who were perhaps affiliated with Teller's partisans?

Tarkin continued to scan the 3-D images.

If he was right and he was actually looking at those who had stolen his ship and discovered how to replicate the Clone Wars Shadowfeeds, then as it happened they were not former Separatists nursing a grudge against the Empire, but rather former Republican *loyalists* with a vendetta.

Supreme Chancellor Palpatine's onetime allies had become the Emperor's new foes.

Saving his research to an encrypted file, Tarkin thought: *The trail continues beyond where you lose it.*

Were the dissidents leading him on a chase calculated to disguise their actual objective?

The thread that had begun to unspool at Sentinel Base could end at only one point.

The *Carrion Spike* stumbled out of hyperspace to an interstellar reversion point ten parsecs from Nouane. The near miss in the autonomous region had left the corvette so rattled that, for a long while, the damaged navicomputer couldn't even establish where the ship was. It was easier now to list the instruments that were still functioning than those that were damaged beyond repair.

"We have two forward laser cannons and one starboard battery," Cala reported to the others in the corvette's main cabin, where Artoz was tending to Salikk's facial injuries. "Shields are down to nothing. Hull armor's the only thing protecting us from a collision with space dust. Hyperdrive motivator is marginal, but probably good for one, possibly two more jumps—"

"One is all we need," Teller said, while the ship groaned like a wounded animal and Salikk's shed fur wafted in all directions.

"Stealth systems and sublight drives are hit or miss," the Koorivar continued. "Same with communications and the HoloNet."

Hask gave her pert-eared head a woeful shake. "We don't come off very well in the vids the Empire released of the Nouane engagement."

"There go our ratings," Artoz said.

Anora scowled at him and threw Teller a peeved look. "So much for trusting your ally to hold up his end of the bargain."

"I said I trusted him up to a point," Teller shot back. "If I trusted him entirely, we wouldn't even be having this conversation."

The remark was not an exaggeration. Had the *Carrion Spike* decanted in the Nouane system at the anticipated reversion point, she would have been instantly annihilated by Imperial fire. Instead, Teller had had Salikk decant the ship deeper in system, as far from the capital ships as was feasible. Regardless, they had been forced to make a run for it without firing a beam at the star system's Imperial facility, its inconsequence notwithstanding. Boxed in and pounded by laserfire, they had jumped to lightspeed with a maneuver that in itself had been no mean feat.

"Besides," Teller went on, "he had to make it look real."

Anora loosed a bitter laugh. "They weren't just making it *look* real, Teller. Face facts: We've been betrayed."

Teller snorted a bitter laugh. "Probably. But in the end it won't matter." He looked at Salikk, then Artoz. "Is he going to be all right, Doc?"

"I'll live," Salikk said for himself. "At least for long enough to finish this."

"The autopilot also survived," Cala said.

Teller blew out his breath and nodded. "Then we're

good to go on that score. Plus, we've been assured of clear skies."

"As long as he's still convinced we're on our way," Anora said.

Teller nodded. "The *Carrion Spike* will arrive on schedule."

"You realize that the Empire won't rest until we're found and dealt with," Artoz said.

Hask glanced around. "Assuming anyone's figured out who we are."

"I wouldn't put it past Tarkin and Vader—not with the *Reticent* crew in hand." Teller compressed his lips. "Even if not, we'll be given up at some point."

Cala grinned. "Fortunately, we've all grown accustomed to looking over our shoulders."

20

THE CARRION SPIKE

ON THE COMMAND WALKWAY of the *Executrix*, Tarkin waited for Vader to conclude a private holo-communication with the Emperor.

"Vice Admiral Rancit is convinced that the dissidents intend to attack the Imperial academy at Carida, martyring themselves in the process," Vader said when he emerged from one of the data pits. "The vice admiral has been given permission to redeploy as many vessels as he sees fit, and he himself will be commanding all elements of the task force."

Tarkin scoffed. "The dissidents' last stand?"

"Someone's last stand," Vader said. "The Emperor has given careful thought to your premise that his onetime allies have now become his foes."

"I'm relieved to hear that, Lord Vader. Then we three are in agreement?"

Vader nodded solemnly. "We are."

Tarkin smiled in a self-satisfied way. "A shuttle is waiting to take you to the frigate."

Vader nodded again and started to move off, only

to stop and turn back to Tarkin. "Tell me, Governor Tarkin, why did you choose to name the corvette the *Carrion Spike*?"

Tarkin allowed his surprise to show. "The ship is named for a unique geographic feature on Eriadu, Lord Vader." When he realized that Vader was waiting for a more complete explanation, he said, "Allow me to accompany you to the shuttle bay."

As they set off side by side, Tarkin began to tell Vader about his annual visits to the Carrion Plateau as a teenager, about the tests he had endured there, and about the training he had undergone at the hands of his wilderness-experienced elder relatives and various guides. Vader paid close attention, interrupting him several times to ask for clarification or additional detail. As Tarkin obliged, one part of him took note of how strange it felt to be having an actual dialogue with the Dark Lord. In the recent days they had spent together, their exchanges had been limited to a few sentences, and more typically had been one-sided. Vader's mask was responsible for some of that, complicating the process of conversation. But just now Vader's frequent downward glances suggested that he was actually listening; so Tarkin went on talking, opening up about his experiences on the plateau while they continued down the *Executrix*'s broad central corridor toward the waiting shuttle.

"By the time I was sixteen, I had come to know the plateau almost as well as I knew the grounds of my parents' home in Eriadu City," Tarkin said. "There was one area that we avoided, however— a vast stretch of savanna interrupted by stands of thick forest. It wasn't precisely off limits. In fact, on several occasions I understood that my uncle was taking us well out of the way simply so I could get a glimpse of the territory. Each time he did so he would explain that we were not alone in being the plateau's reigning predators. And while there was no denying that our blasters were capable of eliminating all competitors, an act of that nature would have flown in the face of keeping the plateau pristine. One goal of the training was to help me understand how to place myself at the top of the food chain through fear rather than force, and how best to maintain my position. The territory we always seemed to skirt was there to provide me with another lesson, as it was ruled over by our chief competitors on the plateau, a one-hundred-strong troop of especially vicious primates."

He paused to glance up at Vader. "Are you familiar with the veermok?"

Vader nodded. "I've had some experience with the species, Governor."

Tarkin waited for more, but Vader said nothing. "Well, then, you know how ferocious they can be on their own, let alone in a group. There's scarcely a creature they can't outwit or outfight when they set their minds to it. But the species on Eriadu is probably not the one you are familiar with. The Eriadu veermok stands a meter high, but is sleek-skinned rather than woolly, is social rather than solitary, and is ardently territorial. It has adapted to the dry conditions of the plateau, rather than to swamps and moist woodlands. Like the more ordinary species, it has razor-sharp claws, equally sharp teeth in its canine muzzle, and the strength of ten humans. Its powerful arms and upper torso appear made for climbing, but the Eriadu veermok is generally not arboreal. Like all its brethren, however, it is a swift and voracious carnivore.

"At the center of the terrain the troop controlled stands a one-hundred-meter-tall hill that more resembles a rock fortress. Crowning it is a four-sided spire of black volcanic glass, some twenty meters high and flat at the top. A time-eroded shaft of quickly cooled magma, to be sure, as are the boulders that support it."

Vader looked at him. "The Carrion Spike?"

"Just so," Tarkin said. "Without Jova having to say as much, I began to grasp that the Spike was to be the site of my final test."

Vader interrupted his rhythmic breathing to make a sound of acknowledgment. "Your trial."

Tarkin nodded. "I was in the midst of my second season on the plateau when Jova first pointed the Spike out to me, but my . . . trial, as you say, wouldn't take place for four years to come. When that time arrived, he explained what was expected of me: I merely had to spend an entire day at the Spike, on my own. I would have neither food nor water, but I would be allowed to carry a vibro-lance of the sort we used in some of our hunts."

"A vibro-lance," Vader said.

"An electroshock weapon longer and lighter than the force pike. It has the same vibro-edged head but is balanced in such a way that it can also be hurled like a spear. Mine would be primed with a limited number of charges, though Jova didn't specify how many. In any case, if I could accomplish that—spend a single day at the Spike—my final test would be behind me, and I would no longer be compelled to visit the Carrion Plateau, unless of course it was my desire to do so."

"You must have thought it a simple task," Vader said.

"Initially, indeed," Tarkin said. "Until Jova allowed me to observe the hill and the spire through macro-binoculars."

"Your eyes were opened."

"Jova said that I could take as much time as I

needed to assess the situation and decide on a course
of action, and I spent the better part of my sixth season on the plateau doing just that. The first order of
business was to get to know my enemy, which I did
over the course of the first couple of weeks. I would
conceal myself in areas of forest or in the tall savanna
grass and observe the routines of the veermoks, which
rarely varied from day to day—or perhaps it's better
to say night to night, since that was when they would
emerge from their hill caves and set out on communal
hunts. The feasting that resulted from their hunts
would continue for most of the night, sometimes at
the site of their kills or sometimes back at the caves,
where the females fed their gray-skinned young. With
the return of the light and the heat, the males would
ascend to the top of the hill and sprawl on the rocks
at the foot of the Spike, which I was never able to
get a good look at, even through the macrobinoculars, as the hill was the tallest feature for kilometers
around in every direction. Midafternoon, the veermoks
would make their descent, gathering at a watering
hole to drink before repeating the entire routine.

"The water hole became my preferred place for observing them, and it was there where I began to get to
know some members of the troop individually. Their
dominant member was a dark-striped male, large and
battle-scarred, to whom I gave the name Lord. During my weeks of stealthy observation, I saw him
challenged at regular intervals. Sometimes the fights
would be to the death, but more often Lord would
allow challengers to limp away in shame but remain
part of the troop. Since it was impossible to defeat
him, there was much competition among his subordinates to get close to him. In some sense, the fights
were as much about training as they were displays
of supremacy. Lord was teaching the weaker males,

aware that he would eventually have to yield his position for the sake of the troop. The rest understood this and as a result followed his lead in all matters. I don't think the species is capable of abstract thought, much less truly sentient, but they do communicate with one another through a complex language of displays and vocalizations.

"There was a second male that caught my attention—a younger and smaller veermok who always seemed to be in Lord's shadow, so that was how I began to think of him. Shadow would tag behind and watch Lord from a respectful distance. Sometimes Lord wouldn't abide the scrutiny and would run Shadow off; at other times he tolerated the younger veermok's attempts to learn from him. What interested me most, however, was that Shadow had a following of his own, a subgroup of some eight young males who accompanied him wherever he went. Lord tolerated them as well, so long as they kept their distance, which they always did, retreating if he so much as turned in their direction.

"It was at the water hole that Shadow and his group began to take an interest in me. They observed me observing them, and began to study me as something curious that had showed up at the edge of their carefully defined domain. Sated from the previous night's hunt and having dismissed me as a threat, they demonstrated no immediate interest in killing me. At that point in my life, I had never heard of a veermok being domesticated, but I had heard of people who used the creatures as watchbeasts, and I imagined that it was possible to enter into some sort of partnership with them. I thought that perhaps I could make use of them as allies of a sort, either when I was at the Spike or in making my escape; and so each day I would try to edge closer to them, only to have them challenge me on every occasion, forcing me back across the invisible line of their hunting grounds.

"When I determined I had seen enough, I set myself to the task of thinking through the separate challenges I faced: getting to the top of the hill; climbing the Spike; and getting away—assuming I even survived the ordeal. Neither Jova nor any of the others offered help.

"Getting to the hill was going to require nothing more than moving while the veermoks were in the caves. I would emerge from the copse of forest closest to the hill, cross an expanse of savanna, and pick my way through the boulders to the top. There would be no shade and no rest, and some of the crevasses between the boulders appeared deep enough to swallow me whole. If I wasn't safely at the top by the time the veermoks emerged from the caves, I'd likely be torn apart on the hill.

"The spike itself presented problems of a different sort. The edges of the black glass column appeared sharp enough to cut through cloth or hide or human flesh. So I devised a strap made from a duranium-threaded belt I found among replacement parts for the old speeder we used from time to time; and from that same belt I also fashioned thick soles for my boots and protective pads for my hands. I knew that even the veermoks' muscular legs weren't powerful enough to propel them to the top of the Spike, but there was still the matter of my remaining on the flat summit for the entire day. Especially after Jova allowed that the veermoks might delay their nocturnal hunt until they had dealt with me. The vibro-lance was meant to counter that eventuality, though the lance wouldn't contain enough charges to kill or stun all of the males. Worse still, they weren't frightened of the vibro-lance. In run-ins we'd had with solitary veermoks, they had evinced no fear even of blasters and had often proved agile enough to dodge beams. Add to this that I would have to scramble down and fight my way to the bottom of the hill and cross the savanna in darkness. That was where some of my predecessors had failed their initiations. Jova said that I would see what remained of their bones scattered about, as if the Spike were some sort of Tarkin reliquary.

"To provide myself with an advantage, I spent days working with a shovel—while the males were lazing on the hill and the females were in the caves tending to the young—to excavate a series of traps and pits along what would be my escape route, some little more than deep holes, others with floors of sharpened stakes.

"Then the day came.

"I made my crossing through the tall grass and scampered up onto the porous, fine-grained rocks. One slip and I could have broken an ankle or become permanently wedged between the boulders. Venomous insects attacked me from hidden nests; stinging ants streamed out from hills of their own making; serpents rattled in forewarning. The heat beat down on me. Nature had conspired to make the hill a last stand against technology and civilization; a place engineered to test a sentient's resolve to conquer and survive. But I endured.

"The Spike loomed above me like a lightning rod, a solidified puddle of black glass at its base. I threw the strap around it, planted the thick soles of my boots against the edges, and hauled myself up centimeters at a time. The ascent took much longer than I had anticipated, and I had scarcely reached the flat, slightly angled top when the first of the veermoks arrived.

"Seeing me there sitting cross-legged atop the Spike,

the vibro-lance hanging over my shoulder, they began to hop and circle round in mounting, growling agitation, uncertain, perhaps awaiting instructions from Lord. Alone among them, however, Shadow merely sat on his haunches to watch me, communicating with members of his clique by clacking vocalizations. Finally Lord made his appearance, gazing up at me with fury in his eyes—and what struck me as hatred at having to be put to a test so early in the day. I wondered if some of my ancestors had survived by killing the dominant veermok, thinking that would dissuade the rest. But I didn't believe that would work; not with Shadow standing by to assume leadership.

"As if by the power of voice alone he could dislodge me from my perch, Lord barked louder than the rest combined. After all, it was incumbent on him to deal with this intruder. But before he had a chance to act, Shadow issued another series of vocal clackings that prompted his followers to launch an attack on the Spike from all sides, their lethal claws scoring the volcanic glass with a sound that made every nerve in my body jangle. As if intent on splitting my attention, some feinted while others leapt as high as their legs could carry them. They roared and gnashed their big, triangular teeth, but I refused to give in to fear. Moreover, something unusual was going on. The attacks by Shadow's minions were chaotic, nothing at all like the well-coordinated exercises I had watched them utilize during hunts. The turmoil sent Lord into a rage. Desperate to restore order, he batted at the young males who were charging back and forth or trying to gain purchase on the glass. He drew blood from a few but was unable to control them.

"I glanced at Shadow in time to hear him issue a low, warbling groan, and at once the young males turned on Lord with teeth and claws set to one purpose. For a moment the old veermok champion seemed too confused to respond, almost as if the communal attack violated their code of behavior, some etiquette particular to the species. Quickly, though, he realized that he had to fight for his life, and he gave himself over to defending himself, killing three of the young males before the rest finally got the better of him. And throughout it all, Shadow didn't move a muscle."

"An assassination," Vader said. "With you providing the necessary distraction."

Tarkin nodded. "An opportunity they had long been waiting for."

"And the pretender—Shadow?"

Tarkin forced an exhale. "I gave the veermoks a moment to laud their new leader, then I hurled my lance and promptly killed him.

"I might as well have dropped a bomb on the hill. One moment the young veermoks didn't know what to make of their victory in overcoming Lord; now they behaved as if they had nowhere to turn. Without a leader, a true inheritor, they fell victim to a kind of bewildered grief, an almost existential despair. They dropped to their bellies and stared up at me in almost docile expectation. I didn't trust them, but I had no option but to descend the Spike at sunset, and when I threaded among them to retrieve my lance from Shadow's inert body, not one of them loosed even so much as a growl, and they actually followed me down the hill."

"What was your uncle's reaction?" Vader asked.

"Jova said it was good to see me in one piece, particularly since he and the others had wagered that my bones would be joining those of my ancestors." Tarkin paused before adding: "The following morning,

the veermok troop abandoned the hill and the Spike.
They left the plateau and weren't seen again."

"They failed to realize what they would bring down
on themselves by turning on their leader," Vader said.

"Precisely."

"Then you are the last Tarkin to have passed the
test."

Tarkin nodded. "That particular test, yes."

By then they had reached the shuttle bay. Tarkin
walked alongside Vader to the foot of the ramp.

"Safe journey, Lord Vader. Be sure to give the pretender my regards."

"Rest assured, Governor Tarkin."

With an abrupt nod of his head and a swirl of his
black cloak, Vader disappeared up the ramp and Tarkin started for the Star Destroyer's command bridge.

21

DISSOLUTION

THE *SECUTOR*-CLASS Star Destroyer *Conquest* hung in fixed orbit above the Carida Imperial Navy Deepdock Facility Two, some half a million kilometers from the eponymous planet. On the bridge Vice Admiral Rancit received an update from the ship's commander.

"Sir, the *Carrion Spike* has reverted to realspace, bearing zero-zero-three ecliptic. Target is acquired, firing solutions have been computed, and all starboard batteries are standing by."

Rancit took a final look at the myriad ships that made up the task force, and turned from the bridge viewport. "Prepare to fire on my command."

"Awaiting your word—"

"Belay that command," a voice boomed from the rear of the command bridge.

Rancit, the commander, and several nearby officers and specialists turned in unison to see Darth Vader storming forward on the elevated walkway, his cape billowing behind him, a squad of armed stormtroopers marching in step in his black wake.

"Lord Vader," Rancit said in genuine surprise. "I wasn't informed you were aboard."

"With purpose, Vice Admiral," Vader said, then swung to the bridge officer. "Commander, direct your technicians to scan the *Carrion Spike* for life-forms."

The commander looked to Rancit, who returned a dubious nod. "Do as he orders."

Vader came to a halt in the center of the walkway and put his gloved hands on his hips, fingers forward. "Well, Commander?"

The commander straightened from peering at a console over the shoulder of one of the specs. "The scanners aren't picking up any life signs." He glanced at Rancit in confusion. "Sir, the corvette is deserted, and appears to be astrogating on autopilot."

Rancit shook his head in denial. "But that can't be."

Vader looked at him. "Your co-conspirators abandoned the ship before it jumped to hyperspace, Vice Admiral."

Alarm found its way into Rancit's perplexity. "My co-conspirators, Lord Vader?"

"Don't act surprised," Vader said. "This entire charade was yours from the start."

Rancit tightened his fists and worked his jaw while the warship's commander and the rest exchanged worried glances. When he began to move toward one of the forward chairs, Vader raised his hand and clenched it.

"Stay right where you are, Vice Admiral." Vader pointed his finger at the bridge officer. "Order the commanders of the task force flotilla to stand down from general quarters."

The bridge officer nodded and walked backward

to the communications board. "Immediately, Lord Vader."

Vader turned to Rancit once more.

"You made a deal with some of your former intelligence assets. Displeased with certain events that occurred at the end of the war, they were seeking a way to avenge themselves on the Empire, and you provided one. You allowed them access to confiscated technologies, and you facilitated the theft of Governor Tarkin's ship after luring him into your plot with counterfeit holotransmissions. You supplied them with tactical information along the way, and by doing so you are complicit in the deaths of thousands of Imperial effectives and the destruction of Imperial facilities."

Vader paced to the viewports and returned, positioning himself a meter from Rancit.

"You assured your co-conspirators that they would be allowed to strike at Carida and continue their reign of terror. But in fact you planned to betray them here, seeing to their deaths and so eliminating everyone who had been witness to your treachery. By having predicted where they would show themselves and by having put an end to their campaign, you would have earned the approval of the Emperor and . . . And what, Vice Admiral? Exactly what did you hope to achieve?"

Rancit regarded him with sudden loathing. "You of all people need to ask?"

Vader said nothing for a long moment, then approximated a sniff. "Power, Admiral? Influence? Perhaps you simply felt overlooked, that you, too, should have been named a Moff."

Rancit bit back whatever he had in mind to say.

"If only you had been one step ahead of your co-conspirators rather than one step behind," Vader continued in false lament. "Consider how far you might have risen in the Emperor's estimation had you been able to predict that *they* would betray *you* and go on to execute the plan they had in mind from the beginning."

Curiosity seeped into Rancit's rigid expression. "What plan?"

"This system was never meant to be their final target, Vice Admiral. The deal they made with you merely gave them free rein to carry out a mission of their own. They transferred to a different ship and are now on their way to the actual target."

"Where?" Rancit asked in an insistent tone.

"That is not your concern. Understand as well, Vice Admiral, that the Emperor has long held suspicions about you. He allowed your scheme to unfold as a means of ensnaring everyone involved in your conspiracy."

Rancit's courage returned. "What is the target, Vader? Tell me."

"Your apprehension is misplaced," Vader said in a menacingly calm voice. He lifted his right hand and began to bring his thumb and fingers together, then stopped. "No. You have already determined the method of your execution."

He swung to the squad of stormtroopers.

"Lieutenant Crest, Admiral Rancit is to be escorted to and placed inside an escape pod. I will give the order to launch the pod, and Admiral Rancit, once removed to a distance from this vessel, will issue the fire order that destroys it." Vader glanced over his shoulder at Rancit. "Does that meet with your approval, Vice Admiral?"

Rancit snarled. "I won't beg you, Vader."

"It would not affect the outcome in any case."

Vader nodded to the stormtroopers, who moved forward to surround Rancit.

"One last thing, Vice Admiral," Vader said as Rancit was being escorted aft down the walkway. "Moff Tarkin sends his regards."

A warship lay in wait in the shadow of a cratered, waterless moon in a star system Coreward of the Gulf of Tatooine.

Since it was not the product of a major shipbuilding conglomerate, the vessel lacked both a name and a registered signature. It was instead a farrago—a medley of modules, components, turbolasers, and ion cannons acquired by its assemblers from Imperial surplus depots, deep-space salvagers, smugglers, and others in the business of selling stolen parts and proscribed armaments. Fittingly the ship most resembled the Quarren Free Dac Volunteer Corps's *Providence*-class carrier, but at less than half the length was stubby by comparison and did not boast an aft communications tower. Its belly housed several squadrons of droid starfighters, and its weapons were operated by computer-controlled droids, but the ship was commanded by sentients—in this case a small group of humans, Koorivar, and Gotals, along with a sole Mon Cal starship systems engineer. It was the sort of vessel that would become closely associated with Outer Rim pirates in the postwar years. And in fact, it was the same capital ship that had briefly revealed itself at Sentinel Base weeks earlier.

"We've come full circle," Teller was telling Artoz in the starfighter hangar. Dressed in a flight suit, he had a helmet under one arm and was standing alongside a warming Headhunter retrofitted with a rudimentary hyperdrive—the very model Hask had used in craft-

ing the false holovid that had been transmitted to
Sentinel Base.

For the benefit of Knotts and the handful of other
sentient pilots, Artoz said, "The convoy will revert to
realspace at the edge of this system and continue by
sublight to the Imperial marshaling station at Pii. From
there, supply ships are escorted to Sentinel Base, and
finally to Geonosis."

"Not this convoy," Knotts said. The world-weary
human broker had helped pilot the hodgepodge carrier from its place of concealment near Lantillies.
"Rancit did us a great favor by reallocating the convoy's protection."

"He promised us clear skies at Carida and gave us
just that here," Teller said. "He had no reason to believe he'd be leaving the convoy vulnerable. He was
simply shuffling ships around for show."

"Any word from Carida?" Knotts asked.

"Nothing yet," Artoz said.

"The evidence trail that links him to us is too much
of a maze for anyone to follow," Teller said. "Accusa-
tions will be flying every which way about our not
getting apprehended, but the assumption will be that
we simply abandoned the cause."

"Rancit won't be happy with being denied his expected promotion," Knotts said. "He'll be on the
hunt for us for betraying him."

Teller shrugged that off and glanced at Artoz. "Any
suggestion Rancit makes about our being involved
in the attack on the convoy would only make matters
worse for him for pulling ships away. Rancit'll be
lucky to be removed from Naval Intelligence with his
pension intact, let alone be in a position to pose a
threat to us."

"And Tarkin?" the Mon Cal asked.

"He gets back what's left of his precious corvette," Knotts said before Teller could reply.

"Tarkin won't be held accountable for any of it," Teller added. "He's a Moff. And besides, it wasn't his idea to go to Murkhana." He shook his head with finality. "I'm guessing he retains command of Sentinel Base."

Knotts nodded in agreement. "The question is, will *he* come after us?"

"Oh, you can count on that," Teller said. "We're going to need to scatter far and wide. The Corporate Sector's probably our safest bet."

No one spoke for a long moment; then Knotts said, "Once the convoy is history, how far will we have set them back?"

Artoz replied: "Work on the hyperdrive components alone had been in progress for three years before I was sent to Desolation Station. Even with perfected plans and a redoubling of their efforts, I suspect that we will set them back four years."

Teller smiled lightly. "I wish we had a better sense of what they're up to at Geonosis."

"A weapons platform of some sort," Knotts said. "Do we need to know more than that?"

Teller looked at him. "I suppose not. If we can just keep delaying them with strikes . . . Once the rest of the galaxy gets to know the Emperor as well as we know him, we won't be alone in the fight."

Doubt surfaced in Artoz's huge, glistening eyes. "With shipyards turning out *Imperial*-class Star Destroyers, any revolt will be hard-pressed to make so much as a dent in the Emperor's armor. Even if we can continue to impede construction of whatever they are building at Geonosis, something unexpected is going to have to enter the mix in order for any rebellion to succeed. Yes, people will begin to recognize the truth about the Empire, but numbers alone will never make the difference—not against the likes of the Emperor, Vader, and the military they're amassing. And don't expect the Senate to restrain them, because it is even less effective than it was during the Republic."

Teller gave his head a defiant shake. "We can either decide right now that it's hopeless and call it a day, or we can hold out for hope and do what we can."

"That decision has never been in dispute," Artoz said.

"For Antar Four, then, and for a brighter future," Knotts said.

Heads nodded in concert.

While the assembled pilots were moving toward their starfighters, Cala hurried into the hangar. "The supply convoy has dropped from hyperspace. HoloNet and communications jammers are enabled, and all weapons systems are standing by."

Knotts extended his hand to Teller. "Good luck out there."

Teller shook his old friend's hand and tugged the helmet down over his head. Turning to Cala, he said, "Tell Anora and Hask that we expect nothing less than a galactic-class holovid."

The attack on the battle station convoy was well under way by the time the *Executrix* reverted from hyperspace close enough to a small moon to all but tweak its orbit. Tarkin and several officers were at the viewports as the stars shrank back into themselves. With his booted legs spread, hands clasped behind his back, graying hair swept back from his high forehead as if blown in the wind, the governor might have been the vessel's figurehead, taunting the enemy to face off with him personally in mortal combat.

"Sir, they've jammed the local HoloNet relay," a spec reported from behind him. "That's why our alerts weren't received. For the moment our counter-measures are managing to keep the battle and tactical nets open."

"Can we communicate with any of the convoy transports?" Tarkin asked without turning around.

"Negative, sir. It's possible we're not even register-ing on their scanners."

"Keep trying."

The boxy cargo ships and transports that made up the convoy had drawn together to allow the escort gunboats and frigates to fashion a defensive circle around them, but enemy lasers were chipping away at the perimeter, allowing droid fighters to dart through openings and prey on the larger vessels.

"Sir, battle analysis is showing one capital ship re-inforced by a Nebulon-B frigate, multiple tri-droid fighters, and three—make that four starfighters. Two friendly tugs, two escort gunboats, and more than a squadron of ARC-one-seventies are already out of the fight."

Tarkin took in the scene.

Same cobbled-together *Providence*-class warship, same swarm of droid fighters and antique starfight-ers. Only this time *he* was commanding the counter-offensive, and instead of Sentinel Base the enemy's objectives were the hyperdrive components he had been worried about since leaving for Coruscant.

Pivoting away from the viewports, he made his way down the observation gallery to watch a simulation of the attack resolve above a holotable. The spherical defense mounted by the Imperial escorts was being dismantled by steady fire from the warships; pieces of gunboats and frigates drifted through a frenzied nimbus of ARC-170s and droid starfighters in pitched combat.

"V-wing fighters are away," the noncom who had followed him down the observation gallery updated. "Tactical net is viable, and the wing commander is awaiting your orders."

"They are to engage with the frigate and the carrier and leave the droid fighters to the convoy escorts."

Tarkin regarded the simulation for a moment longer, then paced forward to rejoin the officers at the viewports. By shunting ships to systems imperiled by the *Carrion Spike,* Naval Command and Control had left the convoy defenseless; like Tarkin, taken in by the dissidents' ruse. Had he not been called to Coruscant, he never would have allowed the convoy's defensive escorts to be redeployed elsewhere, and it irked him that he had not made a stronger case for his remaining at Sentinel. He could only hope that the Emperor had made a wise choice in allowing Rancit's and the shipjackers' ploy to unspool, and that all of them were now caught up in the net. He narrowed his eyes at the enemy carrier, wondering whether the crew that had pirated the *Carrion Spike* was aboard, or if the shipjackers had gone into hiding after deserting the corvette.

"The enemy carrier is repositioning," the bridge officer said. "Looks like they're trying to put the convoy between us and them."

Tarkin nodded to himself as he watched the hodgepodge ship disappear behind the convoy and—recalling the tactics the dissidents had employed at the Phindar fuel tank—thought: *Yes, this was the same crew.*

"Wing commander reports heavy resistance from the enemy fighters," someone behind him said. "They're having trouble reaching the capital ships. Assessment scans indicate that two of the convoy transports have sustained significant damage."

Tarkin turned to the spec. "Still no communication with the convoy leader?"

"None, sir. We can't penetrate the jammers."

That was not welcome news. Tarkin couldn't be certain which of the transports was carrying basic supplies, and which contained components critical for the mobile battle station.

Jova's voice whispered in his ear: *Only glory can follow a man to the grave.*

"Commander," he said, with an abrupt turn to the officer central to the rest, "set us on a course into the midst of the battle."

A tall man with a fringe of black hair, the commander stepped away from the viewports to approach him. "With permission, Governor Tarkin, we have no way of warning the friendlies in our path."

Tarkin firmed his lips. "They'll get out of our way or they won't, Commander."

"I won't argue with that. But even if we manage to penetrate the defensive sphere without incident, we've barely enough space to squeeze between the transports."

"We'll worry about that when we have to. I will not chase that carrier in circles." Tarkin's eyes narrowed. "Death or renown, ladies and gentlemen."

"Sir!"

As the commander left his side, Tarkin glanced at the bridge officer. "Our batteries are to refrain from firing until I give the command. Alert the wing commander that for the time being he and his pilots are our artillery. The droid fighters are slow to react to chaos. I want our starfighters to break formation and improvise, firing at will."

"Clear, sir."

Tarkin resumed his stance. This was how the Empire would conquer and rule, he thought: through might and *fear*.

The *Executrix* lumbered through the congestion of starfighters and into the thick of battle, where the cargo ships and transports were being pounded by cannon and turbolaser fire from the Nebulon-B frigate and the carrier. Explosive light pulsed blindingly beyond the viewports.

"All forward batteries are to concentrate fire on the frigate," Tarkin ordered.

Local space lit up as dozens of energy beams loosed by the Star Destroyer converged on the much smaller vessel. In moments the ship's shields were overwhelmed and the beams began to take their toll, obliterating the Nebulon's rudder-like ventral appendage, then severing the spar that connected the main body of the ship to the engine module. Cracked open, the ship spilled its contents into space and imploded, sucking countless droid fighters into its blistering collapse.

"Battle speed," Tarkin said.

The *Executrix* surged forward, slipping like a needle between two of the larger transports, its pointed bow in direct line with the enemy carrier, which seemed to rear up in reaction to the Star Destroyer's relentless approach.

The bridge officer spoke up. "Wing commander reports that his squadrons are being carved to pieces."

Tarkin kept his eyes on the carrier. It wasn't turning tail as it had at Sentinel. This was the moment the scenario would change; this was the moment the dissidents would demonstrate their unshakable commitment.

"Order the starfighters to withdraw into our wake and to protect the convoy at all costs," he said at last.

"Carrier is changing vector," the spec all but shouted into his left ear. "Flank speed at the convoy leader."

Tarkin's eyes tracked the ship's abrupt swing to port and sudden acceleration. "Ten degrees port. Starboard ion batteries go to steady fire. Race to the light of the lasers!"

If Teller wasn't careful, astonishment was going to be the death of him. The sneak attack on the convoy had commenced without incident, with several Imperial support vessels destroyed and the cargo ships themselves jeopardized, until a Star Destroyer—certainly Tarkin's Star Destroyer—had reverted to realspace and turned the battle on its ear. V-wings were decimating the droid fighters, and a Headhunter and a Tikiar had been obliterated, leaving only Teller's ship and the Tikiar piloted by a Koorivar he had trained on Antar 4. The warship itself was now pushing into the heart of the fray, as if intent on going head-to-head with the Star Destroyer, but was in fact on a collision course with the bulkiest of the cargo vessels. Energy began to coruscate across the hull as it continued its desperate charge for the convoy transports.

If it was Tarkin's aim to confound and confuse, he had done so brilliantly. The V-wing fighters were creating such chaos, it was impossible to predict what Tarkin would do next. And where a more cautious commander might have steered a course around the chaos, Tarkin was taking the massive ship right into the middle of it, placing not only himself but his own pilots and everyone else in peril.

Teller had made repeated attempts to raise Salikk and the others on the battle net without success. Abruptly, the interference abated, and Salikk's face resolved in flickering fashion on the cockpit display screen.

Teller got right to the point. "Get clear and jump the ship to hyperspace while there's still time," he told the Gotal.

"Back to you, Teller," Salikk said through a pall of smoke drifting over the warship's bridge.

"Get clear of that Star Destroyer!"

Salikk shook his head. "We're already committed."

"You'd have a better chance flying into a supernova!"

Anora leaned into cam range from behind the captain's chair. "Teller, haven't you ever seen a holodrama? You're the one who's supposed to live to fight that other day."

Teller grimaced for the cockpit cam. "I'm not the one being dramatic. I'm the one who's talking sense!"

"Listen to her," Salikk said. "For my part, I'll always be grateful for the extra years you gave me after Antar."

Teller's nostrils flared. "You dumb, flat-faced space jockey!"

Salikk ignored the insult. "I'm transmitting jump coordinates to your fighter. Ease out of the fight while Tarkin is concentrating on us. The Headhunter's hyperdrive will do the rest."

Anora nodded soberly. "Looks like we're destined to be martyrs after all, Teller."

"Over and out," Salikk said before Teller could reply.

"Carrier's shields are failing," a tech updated.

"The carrier is modular," Tarkin said. "If we can't blow it to pieces we can certainly dismantle it. Order armaments to target the assembly points."

Coherent light from the *Executrix*'s turbolaser batteries stratified local space, skewering the carrier like a beast set upon by lance-wielding hunters. Debris streamed and corkscrewed from jagged breeches in the ship's belly, and illumination systems began to wink out from stern to bow. Two modules blown from the main body pirouetted away from the ship and exploded. The sublight engines flared and died.

"Droid fighters are powering down," the tech updated. "HoloNet signal-to-noise is better than fifty percent."

"Our lasers must have found the master control computer," the bridge officer said.

Its curved bow severed and deflector shields sparking out, the carrier continued to come apart as Tarkin and the others watched, the droid fighters twirling about like storm-tossed leaves. Quartered by the Star Destroyer's cannons, what remained of the vessel listed to starboard and showed its belly to the vanquisher.

"Cease fire," Tarkin said.

The order had scarcely left his mouth when the spec spoke. "Two marks reverting from hyperspace."

For a moment Tarkin thought that he had stumbled into another trap, but then the tech said, "Star Destroyers *Compliant* and *Enforcer* from Imperial marshaling station Pii."

"Sir, we have one Headhunter unaccounted for," a second tech said. "Sensors indicate that it may have jumped to hyperspace."

"We'll find it," Tarkin said. "In the meantime, ready a boarding party. I want the carrier crew taken alive."

Standing alone at the summit of the Palace spire, the Emperor narrowed his eyes as he gazed out on Coruscant, spread below him like a stage set. The sky was clearing after a cleansing of the Federal District by weather control, and the skyscrapers and towering monads shone like new. The power of the dark side coursed through him like a transfusion of unsullied blood.

Out there were people who wished him dead, others who envied his station, and still others who wished merely to be close enough to him to sate themselves on the crumbs he brushed aside. The thought of it was almost enough to transform his disgust to sadness for the plight of the ordinary. But the wretched practices of the Republic endured: corruption, decadence, the lust for prestige. A penthouse in an elite building, a position that opened doors anywhere in the Core, collections of priceless art, the finest foods, the most able servants . . . He never had need for any of it, even when a senator, even when Supreme Chancellor, and had subscribed to luxury only to satisfy juvenile fantasies and, of course, because it was expected of him. Now he had only the dark side to answer to, and the dark side had an appetite for extravagance of a different sort.

A plot had been foiled, a distraction laid to rest. Needless energy had been expended, and resources wasted. Eventually the dark side would grant him infallible foresight, but until such time future events would remain just out of clear sight, clouded by possibilities and the unremitting swirlings of the Force. He had made himself lord of all he surveyed, but he had much to learn. Actions meant to topple him from his lofty perch wouldn't end with the successful containment of this most recent fiasco. But he would deal with any who chose to challenge him with the same precision he had applied to exterminating the Jedi. And he would not allow himself to be sidetracked from his goal of unlocking the secrets many of the Sith Masters before him had sought: the means to harness the powers of the dark side to reshape reality itself; in effect, to fashion a universe of his own creation. Not mere immortality of the sort Plagueis had lusted after, but *influence* of the ultimate sort.

As his Empire swelled, bringing more and more of the outer systems into its fold, so too would his power unfurl, until every being in the galaxy was held captive in his dark embrace.

A search of the carrier's extant module yielded thirteen dead crewmembers—humans, Koorivar, and Gotals—and twice the number of survivors, representing the same mix of humans, humanoids, and nonhumans. Tarkin stepped from one of the module's air locks as the latter group was being herded into a thoroughly ruined cabinspace by the stormtrooper squads who had captured them. The floor was awash in fire-suppressant foam, and the air reeked of fried circuitry and melted components.

Tarkin waited for the prisoners to be shackled and formed up into two lines before conducting an inspection. He began with the inner line, stopping to regard each being before moving on. As he turned to move down the outer line, a smug smile softened his expression.

"Anora Fair," he said, stopping in front of the only human female among the captives. "Though I see you've restyled your hair." Leaning back to glance farther down the line, his eyes settled on a willowy, red-furred Zygerrian female. "And you would be Hask Taff. I trust you found the *Carrion Spike* to your liking?"

Neither uttered a word or altered her forward

gaze—not that he would have expected them to. A sidestep brought him eye-to-eye with a rheumy-eyed middle-aged man.

"Ah, the infamous Lantillies broker himself," Tarkin said. "Nice of you to attend, Knotts."

The broker, too, stared straight ahead and offered no reply.

Tarkin took a few more steps, stopping to look up into the face of a Mon Cal. "Dr. Artoz, perhaps?" He stepped back from the line to address everyone. "But where is Teller?" When the silence had gone on long enough, he said: "Left for dead in some other module? A starfighter casualty?" He paused, then, with an eyebrow arched, added: "Escaped?"

He gave them another long moment.

"Tell me, was it our late vice admiral Rancit who reached out to you, or did you approach him?" Tarkin glanced at Knotts. "Come now, Knotts, both you and Teller answered to him during the war, did you not? Apparently your betrayal took him by surprise, spoiling the betrayal *he* planned for *you*." Again he waited. "Nothing to say? No last moment cheers of solidarity? No verbal abuse for the Empire or for the Emperor himself?"

"You'll fall from your perch soon enough, Tarkin," Anora Fair said, skewering him with an abrupt glare. "And it won't be a soft landing."

He grinned without showing his teeth. "And here I was expecting an apology for the condition in which you left my ship."

She managed to contort her shackled hands into an obscene gesture before one of the stormtroopers slammed her in the back of the head with his blaster rifle.

"So much venom from such a lovely mouth," Tarkin said. He took a backward step to scan the prisoners once more. "Anyone else, or shall I simply assume that she spoke for the lot of you?" When no one replied, he shrugged. "Well, never mind. I'm confident that once on Coruscant we can find ways to loosen all your tongues."

22

RED, IN TOOTH AND CLAW

THE EMPEROR, Vader, and Tarkin—the Empire's newly formed dark triumvirate—met in private in the pinnacle chamber of the spire. The Emperor was in his customary chair, with Tarkin seated opposite him across the table. Vader remained standing, as he usually did when in the presence of his Master. Three weeks had passed since the attack on the convoy, most of which Tarkin had devoted to interrogating the captured conspirators and collaborators, with some assistance from Vader and ISB specialists. None had died during the process, though all had since been executed in secret. The ISB had advocated for making a public spectacle of their deaths, but the Emperor had ultimately rejected the idea, if only to deny the dissidents martyrdom. The details of Rancit's death, too, became a closely guarded secret, even among his peers in the intelligence community. But most got the message: No rank or position was a guarantee of privilege or exemption.

Everyone was expendable.

"It's clear that he felt passed over," Tarkin was explaining to the Emperor. "First he was forced to disappoint his former operatives on Antar Four due to a squabble between Military Intelligence and the ISB, and then he lost command of Sentinel Base, which he perceived as a demotion for having objected to the actions the Empire took on the Gotal moon."

"So the plot began with him," the Emperor said.

Tarkin nodded. "In a sense. He was informed through back channels of the conspirators' attempts to procure proscribed armaments, confiscated Separatist matériel, and communications jammers. When he learned, however, that the prospective buyers were former Republic intelligence operatives, he facilitated their access to Imperial depots and armories."

"The warehouse workers and salvagers who supplied the conspirators have been dealt with," Vader pointed out, "including several scientists at Desolation Station who violated the terms of their security oaths."

Tarkin waited for Vader to finish. "We've also determined that the warship was assembled at shipyards in the Bajic sector, jointly owned and operated by the Tenloss Syndicate and lower-level members of the Crymorah syndicate. Along with those, our operatives discovered two clandestine facilities located elsewhere in the Outer Rim, both of them long abandoned. We did, however, succeed in tracing the whereabouts of some of those involved, and they have since been eliminated."

"Good," the Emperor said. "Let that be a lesson to all of them"—he narrowed his eyes at Tarkin—"including the one who apparently got away."

"The Headhunter was found on Christophsis," Tarkin said, more defensively than he had planned.

"You are certain the starfighter belonged to Teller?" Vader asked.

"His genetic fingerprints were all over it," Tarkin said.

"An intelligence officer of Teller's skill would know better than to leave his ship to be found, much less his fingerprints." Vader paused, then added: "He left us his calling card."

"He's gone to ground," Tarkin said.

Vader regarded him. "You don't believe that any more than I do."

Tarkin took a breath and blew it out. "I don't suppose I do." He paused. "Finally there is the matter of funding for the warship, droids, and other matériel. Evidence points to the fact that Rancit played a role in diverting funds allocated to Naval Intelligence's black budget, but the investigation is ongoing. Others may have been involved."

The Emperor gestured in impatience. "Was it Rancit who brought these malcontents together?"

"No, he wasn't responsible for assembling the cell," Tarkin said. "The idea appears to have originated with Knotts or Teller, or perhaps they were in league with each other from the start. But Rancit may have contributed the names of people known to be on ISB's watch lists for acts of sedition or sabotage. That may explain how the Mon Cal engineer came to be part of the cell, though it's possible that Artoz was enlisted while Teller was head of security at Desolation Station. The Mon Cal's involvement certainly explains their familiarity with the *Carrion Spike,* as well as with the convoy route."

"But not the battle station," the Emperor said.

"No, my lord," Tarkin said. "Many are aware that an Imperial construction project is in progress at

Geonosis, but the mobile battle station is not in jeopardy."

The Emperor steepled his fingers and fell silent for a long moment. "I will give the matter consideration."

"Of course, my lord," Tarkin said. "For Rancit the plan entailed nothing more than allowing the conspirators to attack a few Imperial facilities. He promised them Carida, but he never had any intention of allowing them to fire on the Imperial academy. In fact, he attempted to betray them earlier by incapacitating the *Carrion Spike* at Nouane, but the dissidents managed to escape."

"What case did the dissidents make for attacking the academy?"

"That an attack would send a message to potential enlistees," Tarkin said. "But of course their principal target all along was the convoy. They were counting on the fact that Rancit would go to great lengths to assure that his subterfuge was beyond suspicion, as was his wont during the Clone Wars. Thus, the starship allocations and redeployments. We suspect that the conspirators had a short list of secondary targets, as well, and were monitoring Rancit's ship dispositions. When he inadvertently fulfilled their hope that the battle station convoy would be left relatively unprotected, their decision was made."

The Emperor's furtive smile gave Tarkin pause. Had he actually seen through Rancit's and the dissidents' schemes from the beginning? Had the events of the past few weeks been less about unmasking a cell of traitors than testing Tarkin's ability to foil the plot and to work effectively with Vader?

"Along with planning to betray two of the men he worked most closely with during the Clone Wars," Tarkin went on, "Rancit outwitted the Naval Intelligence's security cams, and also managed to dupe both Deputy Director Ison and Vice Admiral Screed."

"Perhaps I should have made him a Moff, after all," the Emperor said with obvious sarcasm. "He might have had a brilliant career, if ambition hadn't brought him down."

Tarkin adopted a tight smile. "My lord, the fact that you saw fit to promote me certainly figured into his plan to even the score, as it were."

The Emperor nodded. "Ironic, is it not, that his attempts to increase his own cachet should end up benefiting so many of his seeming competitors?"

It was true. Naval Intelligence had been folded back into Military Intelligence, and Colonel Wullf Yularen had been designated to take Rancit's place as deputy director; Harus Ison had been moved into the Ubiqtorate; Admiral Tenant had been made a Joint Chief; Motti, Tagge, and others had received similar upgrades . . . Yularen's promotion, especially, had come as a relief to Tarkin, who had feared that the Emperor might assign *him* to Rancit's former position.

"We need to tighten our hold over the Outer Systems," the Emperor continued. "You will be in charge of that, Moff Tarkin. Or should I say *Grand* Moff Tarkin."

Tarkin gaped in genuine surprise. "Grand Moff?"

"The Empire's first." The Emperor spread his sickly hands. "Was it not you who suggested the creation of oversectors and oversector governance as a means of enhancing our control?"

"It was, my lord."

"Then your wish is granted. The Outer Rim is yours to oversee—and with it, Grand Moff Tarkin, the whole of the mobile battle station project."

Tarkin rose from his chair so he could bow from the waist in frank obedience. "I will not fail you."

When he looked up, he saw that the Emperor was leaning forward in his chair.

"It will be a momentous responsibility," the Emperor said, drawing out the words. "For once the battle station is fully operational, you will wield the ultimate power in the galaxy."

Tarkin's gaze moved from the Emperor to Vader and back again. "I don't believe that will ever be the case, my lord."

Considering that the Emperor had created the title Grand Moff for Tarkin, he had not been promoted so much as escalated. No secret was made of it, in any case, except regarding his oversight of the battle station project, and for the two weeks that he remained on the galactic capital following the meeting with the Emperor and Vader, he was honored and feted wherever he went.

He granted lengthy interviews to top media outlets throughout the Core, announcing his intention to embark on a tour of the major systems of the Outer Rim, beginning with his native Eriadu. None of the interviewers pressed him about where he had spent the past three years, and no one brought up Antar 4. It was as if the postwar events that had occurred on the Gotal moon had passed into ancient history—or mythology. The recent attacks on facilities in the Outer and Mid Rim, as well as the holovids that had been circulated, were made to seem part of an Imperial plan to root out dissident cells.

Tarkin was quoted as saying:

The factor that contributed most to the demise of the Republic was not, in fact, the war, but rampant self-interest. Endemic to the political process our ancestors engineered, the insidious pursuit of self-enrichment grew only more pervasive through the long centuries, and in the end left the body politic feckless and corrupt. Consider the self-interest of the Core Worlds, unwavering in their exploitation of the Outer Systems for resources; the Outer Systems themselves, undermined by their permissive disregard of smuggling and slavery; those ambitious members of the Senate who sought only status and opportunity.

The reason our Emperor was able to negotiate the dark waters that characterized the terminal years of the Republic and remain at the helm through a catastrophic war that spanned the galaxy is that he has never been interested in status or self-glorification. On the contrary, he has been tireless in his devotion to unify the galaxy and assure the well-being of its myriad populations. Now, with the institution of sector and oversector governance, we are in the unique position to repay our debt to the Emperor for his decades of selfless service, by lifting some of the burden of quotidian rulership from his shoulders. By partitioning the galaxy into regions, we actually achieve a unity previously absent; where once our loyalties and allegiances were divided, they now serve one being, with one goal: a cohesive galaxy in which everyone prospers. For the first time in one thousand generations our sector governors will not be working solely to enrich Coruscant and the Core Worlds, but to advance the quality of life in the star systems that make up each sector—keeping the spaceways safe, maintaining open and accessible communications, assuring that tax revenues are properly levied and allocated to improving the infrastructure. The Senate will likewise be made up of beings devoted not to their own enrichment, but to the enrichment of the worlds they represent.

This bold vision of the future requires not only the service of those of immaculate reputation and consummate skill in the just exercise of power, but also the service of a vast military dedicated to upholding the laws necessary to ensure galactic harmony. It may appear to some that the enactment of universal laws and the widespread deployment of a heavily armed military are steps toward galactic domination, but these actions are taken merely to protect us from those who would invade, enslave, exploit, or foment political dissent, and to punish accordingly any who engage in such acts. Look on our new military not as trespassers or interlopers, but as gatekeepers, here to shore up the Emperor's vision of a pacified and prosperous galaxy.

The media took to calling it "the Tarkin Doctrine," and some commentators began to wonder if he wasn't destined to become the new voice of the Empire.

He made it his business to meet with senators representing star systems over which he now had authority. Most seemed relieved about having to answer to him rather than the Emperor or the Ruling Council, but he made clear to one and all that he wouldn't tolerate acts of sedition or anti-Imperial propaganda, and that he would be merciless with all perpetrators.

He met, too, with the Joint Chiefs of the Army and the Navy, and with the directors and top officers in the intelligence agencies. Through them he instituted changes at Desolation Station, replacing many key personnel and altering supply schedules and convoy routes. He authorized reevaluations of every scientist and technician and established new parameters for both secrecy and security. He ordered that no convoys were to move without adequate protection. And to the dismay of countless beings in systems along the supply routes, he limited the HoloNet to Imperial use. The populations of those worlds viewed his actions as the start of an Imperial conquest of the Outer Rim.

At Geonosis, he enacted procedures that would limit contact between workers—whether contractors, employees, or slaves—and the outside galaxy; leaves were canceled and communications of any sort were strictly monitored. He reinforced Sentinel Base and the marshaling stations, and deployed patrol flotillas to the nearby systems. His most trusted officers were sent in search of pirates and smugglers, with orders to eliminate them on sight.

To complement his new station, he designed and had made a gray-green uniform whose thick-belted, round-collared tunic featured four code cylinders and a rank plaque of twelve multicolored squares, six blue over trios of red and gold. In all dealings with the Emperor he was referred to as *Grand Moff,* but for ordinary interactions with military personnel he retained the honorific *Governor.*

His agenda on Coruscant complete, he traveled from the Core to the Greater Seswenna sector aboard the *Executrix,* which was now his personal vessel— "The least the Empire can do to compensate you for the loss of the *Carrion Spike,*" the Emperor had said on awarding him the *Imperial*-class Star Destroyer. In addition to the thousands of troops and technicians who staffed and crewed the massive ship, he had a personal bodyguard of thirty-two stormtroopers who accompanied him wherever he went—or at least when he allowed as much.

Arriving by Imperial shuttle at Phelar Spaceport, he was greeted by cheering crowds, media representatives, and a military marching band. In Eriadu City he visited with family and old friends and granted more interviews. The local governor, who happened to be a relative, awarded him the key to the city and held a parade in his honor. While residing at his former home, he sat for a sculptor who had been commissioned to create a statue that would stand in the city's principal public space.

He had one last mission to carry out before he left his homeworld, and with some effort he managed to persuade his platoon of personal guards that it was an undertaking he needed to fulfill alone, as it was a kind of personal pilgrimage. The stormtroopers were not pleased, as it was their duty to protect him, but they relented inasmuch as he would be spending his time on ancestral ground. Potential assassins notwithstanding, he made no show of secrecy the morning he left for the plateau, in an old airspeeder that had gone unused for years by anyone residing at the family estate. Once removed from the confines of Eriadu City, he relaxed into the journey, almost as if in an attempt to reexperience the annual trips he had made to the plateau as a youth. He even wore clothes of the sort he would have worn in those days, more suited to a hunter or trekker than to an Imperial Grand Moff.

When after several hours of ragged flight the plateau and surrounding volcanic terrain came into view, he felt as if he had never left; and indeed he hadn't, because he had carried the place within him wherever he had ventured. He had been accused by lovers and others of being heartless, but it wasn't true; it was

simply that his heart was here, in this pristine part of
his homeworld. His attachment to the place was not
as one who worshipped nature; rather as one who
had learned to tame it. And he would leave the area
unchanged, the animals and riotous growth, as a reminder of the control he exercised over it.

He took the airspeeder through several passes over
the plateau, observing herds of migrating animals.
The day was bright and clear and he could see in detail everywhere he looked. Ultimately he landed the
antique vehicle on the savanna, close to the hill of
boulders he had come to climb. He set out on foot,
with the legs of his trousers tucked into his high boots
and the sleeves of his lightweight shirt secured at the
wrist as protection against swarms of stinging insects.
Arrived at the hill, he began to pick his way up over
the pitted rocks, leaping over crevasses and finding
finger- and toeholds as he bouldered to the summit.
The hill seemed a lonelier place without its troop
of guardian veermoks, but also a more sacred one—
sanctified by what he had accomplished here.

He was breathing hard when he reached the top, the
hot wind blowing across the rocks and garish light
reflecting from the obsidian pool at the base of the
Spike. He had given thought to scaling the column but
realized now that it was enough simply to stand at its
base and savor his recollections. He lingered for hours,
as a veermok might have, sprawled on the warmed
rocks, allowing himself to become nearly dehydrated
in the heat. He left as that part of the planet was slipping into darkness, carefully picking his way down
the boulders, a task more difficult than the ascent.
One skid, one wrong step or stumble . . .

Returned to the tall grass, he followed traces of
the path left by his earlier transit, then, as if avoiding
obstacles concealed by the stalks, began to pursue a

more zigzag route as he neared the airspeeder and an isolated patch of forest beyond. The noise of his legs swooshing through the grass competed with the buzz and drone of insect life. Otherwise there was only the sound of his respiration and a faint echo of his movements. He was fifty or so meters from the airspeeder when he heard the sound of branches snapping and giving way behind him, and the surprised exclamation of the human who had fallen into the trap.

Pleased with himself, he stopped, turned about, and started for the pit he had excavated so many years earlier.

"Welcome, Wilhuff," someone said from the towering grass off to his left before he reached the pit.

Jova stood from where he had been hiding. He was gnarled, wrinkled, and deeply tanned, but still spritely for his age. Thirty additional years of living on the Carrion didn't seem to have done him too much harm. Parting the savanna grass with leathery hands, he began to make his way toward Tarkin, proffering a sleek blaster when they reached each other.

"He dropped this when he fell in," the old man said. "A WESTAR, isn't it?"

Tarkin nodded as he accepted the blaster, switched off the safety, and tucked it into the waistband of his trousers. "Where's his speeder, Uncle?"

Jova's crooked finger pointed east. "Behind the trees. I thought he might follow you up the hill, but he stayed at the bottom, making a little nest for himself in the grass, then tracked you when you came down and started for your ship."

Together they walked to the pit to gaze down at Teller, some four meters below them, somewhat stunned by the unexpected plunge but squinting up as their heads appeared over the rim. Fortunately for Teller, the sharpened stakes that had once studded the floor of the pit had rotted to mulch. The fall, however, had damaged some of the mimetic circuits of his camouflage suit, and he was alternately blending in with the mulch and visible to the naked eye.

"I made it as easy as I could for you to stalk me, Captain," Tarkin said, using the rank Teller had earned during the Clone Wars. "I even left my stormtroopers behind in Eriadu City."

"Very bighearted of you, Governor—or do I have to start calling you Grand Moff now?" Teller tried to get to his feet, but promptly winced in pain and sat back down to inspect a clearly broken ankle. "I knew you were leading me on," he said through gritted teeth, "but it didn't matter. Not as long as I had a shot at getting to you."

"You had plenty of shots at getting to me, as you say. So why not when we were in the air? And why a simple hand blaster rather than a sniper rifle?"

"I wanted us to be looking each other in the eye when I killed you."

Tarkin grinned faintly. "Sadly predictable, Captain. And so unnecessary."

Teller snorted. "Well, this old fossil would probably have killed me before I got off a shot, anyway."

"You're right about that," Jova said good-naturedly. He and Tarkin stepped back from the rim. Jova stomped down an area of razor grass with his wide callused feet, and they sat facing each other.

"Were you surprised to hear from me, Uncle?" Tarkin asked.

Jova shook his hairless, nut-brown head. "I knew you'd return someday. I had to renovate some of your old traps. Lucky you recalled where you dug them." He paused to grin. "Though I don't suppose luck has much to do with anything."

Tarkin gazed around him. "I remember my time here like yesterday."

Jova nodded sagely. "I've tried to keep abreast of your career. Haven't read or heard much about you the better part of three or four years now."

"Imperial business," Tarkin said, and let it go at that. "But whatever success I've achieved is to your credit for mentoring me. My memoir will make clear your contributions."

Jova gestured in dismissal. "I don't need to be singled out. I prefer being more of a phantom."

"Phantom of the plateau."

"Why not?"

Tarkin got to his feet and returned to the rim of the pit. "How's the ankle, Captain? Swelling, I would imagine."

Teller's glower said it all.

"Need I remind you that we fought on the same side in the Clone Wars?" Tarkin said. "We fought to prevent the galaxy from splintering, and we achieved our goal. But where I've put that war behind me, you appear to be still waging it. You'd have the galaxy fracture again?"

"You haven't put it behind you," Teller said. "That war was nothing more than a prelude to the war the Emperor always had in mind. Subjugating Separatists was practice for subjugating the galaxy. You've known all along. And this time you're going to crush your opponents before they have a chance to organize."

"That's called pacification, Captain."

"It's rule by fear. You're not just demanding submission, you're generating evil."

"Then evil will have to do."

Teller stared up at him. "What transforms a man into a monster, Tarkin?"

"Monster? That's a point of view, is it not? I will

say this much, however: This place, this plateau is what made me."

Teller considered it, then asked: "What is the Empire building at Geonosis?"

Tarkin showed him a faint grin. "Unfortunately, Captain, you are not cleared to know that. But I'm willing to make a deal with you. I'm certain you'll have a difficult time extricating yourself from this trap you stumbled into—what with the depth of the hole and now a broken ankle. But should you succeed, you will find your blaster, just here on the rim." He made a point of setting the weapon down. "The most dangerous of the Carrion's predators don't appear until nightfall. They'll sniff you out, and . . . Well, suffice it to say you don't want to loiter down there. Of course, even if you manage to get out, it's a long way to the edge of the escarpment." He paused in thought, then added, "I'll have Jova park your speeder at the base of the plateau. Should you make it off Eriadu alive, look me up and I'll reconsider what I said about Geonosis."

"Tarkin," Teller said, "you will die horribly because you deserve nothing less. The more you try to coerce the disadvantaged to play by your rules, the more they will rebel. I'm not the only one."

"You're hardly the first to prophesize my demise, Captain, and I could certainly make an equally dire prediction about your death. Because here you are, trapped in a deep hole and crippled, and that's precisely where I intend to keep the others of your ilk."

Teller smiled with his eyes. "Then if I can escape, the rest will."

Tarkin returned the look. "That's an interesting analogy. Let's see how it plays out in real life, and in the long run. Until then, farewell, Captain."

Jova stood up as Tarkin approached, gesturing with

his stubbled chin to the hole. "Broken ankle or no, he seems capable enough to escape. Do you want me to keep an eye on him, perhaps provide a hint or two of the lay of the land to better his chances?"

Tarkin stroked his jaw. "That might be interesting. You be the judge."

"And if he makes it down off the plateau in one piece, and to his speeder?"

Tarkin mulled it over. "Learning that he's actually at large will keep me on my toes."

Jova smiled and nodded. "A good strategy. We're never too old to learn new tricks."

The epicenter of a bustling throng of construction droids, supply ships, and cargo carriers, safeguarded by four Star Destroyers and twice as many frigates, the deep-space mobile battle station hovered in fixed orbit above secluded and forbidding Geonosis. When viewed from mid-system or from even as close as the asteroid belt that further isolated the planet from celestial interchange, one could be fooled into believing that the irradiated world had added another small moon to its collection. Still youthful, the spherical station had yet to grow into the features by which it would be recognized a decade on. The northern hemisphere focus lens frame for the superlaser was scarcely more than a metallic crater; the Quadanium hull, a mere patchwork of rectangular plates, so that one could see almost to the heart of the colossal thing. The sphere's surface city sprawls and equatorial trench might as well have been dreams.

By the time Tarkin arrived, at the conclusion of his travels through the Outer Rim systems, some of the hyperdrive components had been installed, but the station was far from being jump-ready. Nevertheless, work on some of its array of sublight engines had recently been completed, and those were ready to be tested, if only to determine how well the globe handled.

The project's chief scientists and engineers had taken Tarkin on a tour of finished portions of the station that had lasted a week, and yet he still hadn't seen half of it. From the interior of a repulsorlift construction craft, his guides had pointed out where the shield and tractor beam generators would be installed; they had laid out their plans for housing a staff and crew of three hundred thousand; they had described gun emplacements, mooring platforms, and defensive towers that would stipple the gray skin.

Tarkin was in his glory. If he felt at home on the bridge of a Star Destroyer, here he felt *centered*. The station was a vast technoscape, ripe for exploration; an unknown world awaiting his stamp of approval and his mastery.

While most of the construction work was done in micro-g, omnidirectional boosters supplied standard gravity to a large cabinspace near the surface that would one day become the overbridge, with designated posts for Tarkin and various military officers, a conference room featuring a circular table, a Holo-Net booth dedicated to communicating with the Emperor, and banks of large viewscreens. There, in the company of the station's designers and construction specialists, Tarkin gave the order for the sublight engines to engage.

A faint shudder seemed to run through the orb—though Tarkin thought that the vibration could easily be the effect of exhilaration coursing through him in a way he hadn't experienced since his teenage years.

Then, with almost agonizing sluggishness, the battle station began to leave its fixed orbit. Ultimately it surpassed the speed of the planet's rotation, emerging from the shadow of Geonosis and moving into deep space.

Read on for an excerpt from

STAR WARS: Dark Disciple

by Christie Golden

Published by Del Rey Books

1

ASHU-NYAMAL, Firstborn of Ashu, child of the planet Mahranee, huddled with her family in the hold of a Republic frigate. Nya and the other refugees of Mahranee braced themselves against the repercussions of the battle raging outside. Sharp, tufted Mahran ears caught the sounds of orders, uttered and answered by clones, the same voice issuing from different throats; keen noses scented faint whiffs of fear from the speakers.

The frigate rocked from yet another blast. Some of the pups whimpered, but the adults projected calm. Rakshu cradled Nya's two younger siblings. Their little ears were flat against their skulls, and they shivered in terror against their mother's warm, lithe body, but their blue muzzles were tightly closed. No whimpers for them; a proud line, was Ashu. It had given the Mahran many fine warriors and wise statesmen. Nya's sister Teegu, Secondborn of Ashu, had a gift for soothing any squabble, and Kamu, the youngest, was on his way to becoming a great artist.

Or had been, until the Separatists had blasted Mahranee's capital city to rubble.

The Jedi had come, in answer to the distress call, as the Mahran knew they would. But they had come too late. Angry at the Mahranee government's refusal to cooperate, the Separatists had decided that genocide, or as close a facsimile as possible, would solve the problem of obtaining a world so rich in resources.

Nya clenched her fists. If only she had a blaster! She was an excellent shot. If any of the enemy attempted to board the ship, she could be of use to the brave clones now risking their lives to protect the refugees. Better yet, Nya wished she could stab one of the Separatist scum with her stinger, even though it would—

Another blast, this one worse. The lights flickered off, replaced almost instantly by the bloodred hue of the backup lighting. The dark gray metal that comprised the freighter's bulkheads seemed to close in ominously. Something snapped inside Nya. Before she really knew what she was doing, she had leapt to her feet and bounded across the hold to the rectangular door.

"Nya!" Rakshu's voice was strained. "We were told to stay here!"

Nya whirled, her eyes flashing. "I am walking the warrior path, Mother! I can't just sit here doing nothing. I have to try to help!"

"You will only be in the . . ." Rakshu's voice tailed off as Nya held her gaze. Tears slipped silently down Rakshu's muzzle, glittering in the crimson light. The Mahran were no telepaths, but even so, Nya knew her mother could read her thoughts.

I can do no harm. We are lost already.

Rakshu knew it, too. She nodded, then said, her voice swelling with pride in her eldest, "Stab well."

Nya swallowed hard at the blunt blessing. The stinger was the birthright of the Mahran—and, if used, their death warrant. The venom that would drop a foe in his tracks would also travel to his slayer's heart. The two enemies always died together. The words were said to one who was not expected to return alive.

"Good-bye, Mama," Nya whispered, too softly for her mother to hear. She slammed a palm against the button and the door opened. Without pausing, she raced down the corridor, her path outlined by a strip of emergency lighting; she skidded to a halt when the hallway branched into two separate directions, picked one, and ran headlong into one of the clones.

"Whoa, there!" he said, not unkindly. "You're not supposed to be here, little one."

"I will *not* die huddled in fear!" Nya snapped.

"You're not going to," the clone said, attempting to be reassuring. "We've outrun puddle-jumpers like these before. Just get back to the holding area and stay out of our way. We've got this in hand."

Nya smelled the change in his sweat. He was lying. For a moment, she spared compassion for him. What had his life been like when he was a youngling? There had been no one to give him hugs or tell stories, no loving parental hands to soothe childhood's nightmares. Only brothers, identical in every way, who had been raised as clinically as he.

Brothers, and duty, and death.

Feeling strangely older than the clone, and grateful for her own unique life that was about to end, Nya smiled, shook her head, and darted past him.

He did not give chase.

The corridor ended in a door. Nya punched the button. The door slid open onto the cockpit. And she gasped.

She had never been in space before, so she was unprepared for the sight the five-section viewport presented. Bright flashes and streaks of laserfire dueled against an incongruously peaceful-looking blue sky. Nya wasn't sufficiently knowledgeable to be able to distinguish one ship from another—except for her own planet's vessels, looking old and small and desperate as they tried to flee with their precious cargo of families just like her own.

A clone and the Jedi general, the squat, reptilian Aleena who had led the mission to rescue Nya's people, occupied the cockpit's two chairs. With no warning, another blast rocked the ship. Nya went sprawling into the back of the clone's chair, causing him to lurch forward. He turned to her, his eyes dark with anger, and snapped, "Get off this—"

"General Chubor," came a smooth voice.

Nya's fur lifted. She whirled, snarling silently. Oh, she knew that voice. The Mahran had heard it uttering all sorts of pretty lies and promises that were never intended to be kept. She wondered if there was anyone left in the galaxy who didn't recognize the silky tones of Count Dooku.

He appeared on a small screen near the top of the main viewing window. A satisfied, cruel smirk twisted Dooku's patrician features.

"I'm surprised you contacted me," his image continued. "As I recall, Jedi prefer to be regarded as the strong, silent type."

The clone lifted a finger to his lips, but the warning was unnecessary. Nya's sharp teeth were clenched, her fur bristled, and her entire being was focused on the count's loathsome face, but she knew better than to speak.

General Chubor, sitting beside the clone in the pilot's chair, so short that his feet did not reach the floor, likewise was not baited. "You've got your victory, Dooku." His slightly nasal, high-pitched voice was heavy with sorrow. "The planet is yours . . . let us have the people. We have entire families aboard, many of whom are injured. They're innocents!"

Dooku chuckled, as if Chubor had said something dreadfully amusing over a nice hot cup of tea. "My dear General Chubor. You should know by now that in a war, there is no such thing as an innocent."

"Count, I repeat, our passengers are civilian families," General Chubor continued with a calmness at which Nya could only marvel. "Half of the refugees are younglings. Permit them, at least, to—"

"Younglings whose parents, unwisely, chose to ally with the Republic." Gone was Dooku's civilized purr. His gaze settled on Nya. She didn't flinch from his scrutiny, but she couldn't stifle a soft growl. He looked her up and down, then dismissed her as of no further interest. "I've been monitoring your transmissions, General, and I know that this little chat is being sent to the Jedi Council. So let me make one thing perfectly clear."

Dooku's voice was now hard and flat, as cold and pitiless as the ice of Mahranee's polar caps.

"As long as the Republic resists me, 'innocents' will continue to die. Every death in this war lies firmly at the feet of the Jedi. And now . . . it is time for you and your passengers to join the ranks of the fallen."

One of the largest Mahranee ships bloomed silently into a flower of yellow and red that disintegrated into pieces of rubble.

Nya didn't know she had screamed until she realized her throat was raw. Chubor whirled in his chair.

His large-eyed gaze locked with hers.

The last thing Ashu-Nyamal, Firstborn of Ashu, would ever see was the shattered expression of despair in the Jedi's eyes.

The bleakest part about being a Jedi, thought Master Obi-Wan Kenobi, *is when we fail.*

He had borne witness to scenes like the one unfolding before the Jedi Council far too many times to count, and yet the pain didn't lessen. He hoped it never would.

The terrified final moments of thousands of lives played out before them, then the grim holographic recording flickered and vanished. For a moment, there was a heavy silence.

The Jedi cultivated a practice of nonattachment, which had always served them well. Few understood, though, that while specific, individual bonds such as romantic love or family were forbidden, the Jedi were not ashamed of compassion. All lives were precious, and when so many were lost in such a way, the Jedi felt the pain of it in the Force as well as in their own hearts.

At last, Master Yoda, the diminutive but extraordinarily powerful head of the Jedi Council, sighed deeply. "Grieved are we all, to see so many suffer," he said. "Courage, the youngling had, at the end. Forgotten, she and her people will not be."

"I hope her bravery brought her comfort," Kenobi said. "The Mahran prize it. She and the others are one with the Force now. But I have no more earnest wish than that this tragedy be the last the war demands."

"As do all of us, Master Kenobi," said Master Mace Windu. "But I don't think that wish is coming true anytime soon."

"Did any ships make it out with their passengers?" Anakin Skywalker asked. Kenobi had asked the younger Jedi, still only a Knight, to accompany him to this gathering, and Anakin stood behind Kenobi's chair.

"Reported in, no one has," Yoda said quietly. "But hope, always, there is."

"With respect, Master Yoda," Anakin said, "the Mahran needed more than our *hope*. They needed our help, and what we were able to give them wasn't enough."

"And unfortunately, they are not the only ones we've been forced to give short shrift," Windu said.

"For almost three years, this war has raged," said Plo Koon, the Kel Dor member of the Council. His voice was muffled due to the mask he wore over his mouth and nose; a requirement for his species in this atmosphere. "We can barely even count the numbers of the fallen. But this—" He shook his head.

"All directly because of one man's ambition and evil," said Windu.

"It's true that Dooku is the leader of the Separatists," Kenobi said. "And no one will argue that he isn't both ambitious *and* evil. But he hasn't done it alone. I agree that Dooku may be responsible for every death in this war, but he didn't actively commit each one."

"Of course not," Plo Koon said, "but it's interesting that you use nearly the same words as Dooku. He placed the blame for the casualties squarely upon us."

"A lie, that is," Yoda said. He waved a small hand dismissively. "Foolish it would be, for us to give it a moment's credence."

"Would it be, truly, Master Yoda?" Windu asked with a hard look on his face. As a senior member of the Council, he was one of the few who dared question Master Yoda. Kenobi raised an eyebrow.

"What mean you, Master Windu?" asked Yoda.

"Have the Jedi really explored every option? Could we have ended this war sooner? Could we, in fact, end it right now?"

Something prickled at the back of Kenobi's neck. "Speak plainly," he said.

Windu glanced at his fellows. He seemed to be weighing his words. Finally, he spoke.

"Master Kenobi's right—Dooku couldn't have done this completely alone. Billions follow him. But I also stand by my observation—that this war is Dooku's creation. Those who follow him, follow *him*. Every player is controlled by the count; every conspiracy has been traced back to him."

Anakin's brow furrowed. "You're not saying anything we don't already know, Master."

Windu continued. "Without Dooku, the Separatist movement would collapse. There would no longer be a single, seemingly invincible figurehead to rally around. Those who were left would consume themselves in a frenzy to take his place. If every river is a branch of a single mighty one . . . then let us dam the flow. Cut off the head, and the body will fall."

"But that's what we've been—*oh*." Anakin's blue eyes widened with sudden comprehension.

No, Kenobi thought, *surely Mace isn't suggesting—*

Yoda's ears unfurled as he sat up straighter. "Assassination, mean you?"

"No." Kenobi spoke before he realized he was going to, and his voice was strong and certain. "Some things simply aren't within the realm of possibility. Not," he added sharply, looking at Mace, "for Jedi."

"Speaks the truth, Master Kenobi does," Yoda said. "To the dark side, such actions lead."

Mace held up his hands in a calming gesture. "No one here wishes to behave like a Sith Lord."

"Few do, at first. A small step, the one that determines destiny often is."

Windu looked from Yoda to Kenobi, then his brown-eyed gaze lingered on Kenobi. "Answer me this. How often has this Council sat, shaking our heads, saying

'Everything leads back to Dooku'? A few dozen times? A few *hundred*?"

Kenobi didn't reply. Beside him, Anakin shifted his weight. The younger Jedi didn't look at Kenobi or Windu, and his lips were pressed together in a thin, unhappy line.

"A definitive blow must be struck," Mace said. He rose from his chair and closed the distance between himself and Kenobi. Mace had the height advantage, but Kenobi got to his feet calmly and met Windu's gaze.

"Dooku is going to keep doing exactly what he has been," Windu said quietly. "He's not going to change. And if *we* don't change, either, then the war will keep raging until this tortured galaxy is nothing but space debris and dead worlds. We—the Jedi and the clones we command—are the *only* ones who can stop it!"

"Master Windu is right," said Anakin. "I think it's about time to open the floor to ideas that before we would have never considered."

"Anakin," Kenobi warned.

"With respect, Master Kenobi," Anakin barreled on. "Mahranee's fall is terrible. But it's only the most recent crime Dooku has committed against a world and a people."

Mace added, "The Mahran who died today already have more than enough company. Do we want to increase those numbers? One man's life must be weighed against those of potentially millions of innocents. Isn't protecting the innocent the very definition of what it means to be a Jedi? We are failing the Republic and its citizens. We must stop this—*now*."

Kenobi turned to Yoda. The ancient Jedi Master peered at all those present, be it physically or holographically. Saesee Tiin, an Iktotchi Master; the Togruta Shaak Ti, her expression calm but sorrowful;

the images of Kit Fisto, Oppo Rancisis, and Depa Billaba. Kenobi was surprised to see sorrow and resignation settle over Yoda's wrinkled, green face. The diminutive Jedi closed his huge eyes for a moment, then opened them.

"Greatly heavy, my heart is, that come to this, matters have," he said. Beside the Council leader was a small table, upon which burned a single, white taper. Yoda gazed at the soft, steady glow.

"Each life, a flame in the Force is. Beautiful. Unique. Glowing and precious it stands, to bravely cast its own small light against the darkness that would consume it. But grows, this darkness does, with each minute that Dooku continues his attacks." Yoda extended a three-fingered hand, holding it over the candle so that it cast a shadow. As he moved his shadow-hand, the light flickered, almost frantically, then winked out. Kenobi felt his heart lurch within his chest.

"Stop him, we must," Yoda said solemnly. He closed his eyes and bowed his head. The moment hung heavy, and it seemed everyone was loath to break it.

Finally Mace spoke. "The question before us now is—who will strike the killing blow?"

Kenobi sighed and rubbed his eyes. "I, ah . . . may have a suggestion . . ."

Read on for an excerpt from

STAR WARS: Battlefront: Twilight Company

by Alexander Freed

Published by Del Rey Books

THE RAIN ON Haidoral Prime dropped in warm sheets from a shining sky. It smelled like vinegar, clung to the molded curves of modular industrial buildings and to litter-strewn streets, and coated skin like a sheen of acrid sweat.

After thirty straight hours, it was losing its novelty for the soldiers of Twilight Company.

Three figures crept along a deserted avenue under a torn and dripping canopy. The lean, compact man in the lead was dressed in faded gray fatigues and a hodgepodge of armor pads crudely stenciled with the starbird symbol of the Rebel Alliance. Matted dark hair dripped beneath his visored helmet, sending crawling trails of rainwater down his dusky face.

His name was Hazram Namir, though he'd gone by others. He silently cursed urban warfare and Haidoral Prime and whichever laws of atmospheric science made it rain. The thought of sleep flashed into his mind and broke against a wall of stubbornness.

He gestured with a rifle thicker than his arm toward the nearest intersection, then quickened his pace.

Somewhere in the distance a swift series of blaster shots resounded, followed by shouts and silence.

The figure closest behind Namir—a tall man with graying hair and a face puckered with scar tissue—bounded across the street to take up a position opposite. The third figure, a massive form huddled in a tarp like a hooded cloak, remained behind.

The scarred man flashed a hand signal. Namir turned the corner onto the intersecting street. A dozen meters away, the sodden lumps of human bodies lay in the road. They wore tattered rain gear—sleek, lightweight wraps and sandals—and carried no weapons. Noncombatants.

It's a shame, Namir thought, *but not a bad sign.* The Empire didn't shoot civilians when everything was under control.

"Charmer—take a look?" Namir indicated the bodies. The scarred man strode over as Namir tapped his comlink. "Sector secure," he said. "What's on tap next?"

The response came in a hiss of static through Namir's earpiece—something about mop-up operations. Namir missed having a communications specialist on staff. Twilight Company's last comms tech had been a drunk and a misanthrope, but she'd been magic with a transmitter and she'd written obscene poetry with Namir on late, dull nights. She and her idiot droid had died in the bombardment on Asyrphus.

"Say again," Namir tried. "Are we ready to load?"

This time the answer came through clearly. "Support teams are crating up food and equipment," the voice said. "If you've got a lead on medical supplies, we'd love more for the *Thunderstrike*. Otherwise, get to the rendezvous—we only have a few hours before reinforcements show."

"Tell support to grab hygiene items this time," Namir said. "Anyone who says they're luxuries needs to smell the barracks."

There was another burst of static, and maybe a laugh. "I'll let them know. Stay safe."

Charmer was finishing his study of the bodies, checking each for a heartbeat and identification. He shook his head, silent, as he straightened.

"Atrocity." The hulking figure wrapped in the tarp had finally approached. His voice was deep and resonant. Two meaty, four-fingered hands kept the tarp clasped at his shoulders, while a second pair of hands loosely carried a massive blaster cannon at waist level. "How can anyone born of flesh do this?"

Charmer bit his lip. Namir shrugged. "Could've been combat droids, for all we know."

"Unlikely," the hulking figure said. "But if so, responsibility belongs to the governor." He knelt beside one of the corpses and reached out to lid its eyes. Each of his hands was as large as the dead man's head.

"Come on, Gadren," Namir said. "Someone will find them."

Gadren stayed kneeling. Charmer opened his mouth to speak, then shut it. Namir wondered whether to push the point and, if so, how hard.

Then the wall next to him exploded, and he stopped worrying about Gadren.

Fire and metal shards and grease and insulation pelted his spine. He couldn't hear and couldn't guess how he ended up in the middle of the road among the bodies, one leg bent beneath him. Something tacky was stuck to his chin and his helmet's visor was cracked;

he had enough presence of mind to feel lucky he hadn't lost an eye.

Suddenly he was moving again. He was upright, and hands—Charmer's hands—were dragging him backward, clasping him below the shoulders. He snarled the native curses of his homeworld as a red storm of particle bolts flashed among the fire and debris. By the time he'd pushed Charmer away and wobbled onto his feet, he'd traced the bolts to their source.

Four Imperial stormtroopers stood at the mouth of an alley up the street. Their deathly pale armor gleamed in the rain, and the black eyepieces of their helmets gaped like pits. Their weapons shone with oil and machined care, as if the squad had stepped fully formed out of a mold.

Namir tore his gaze from the enemy long enough to see that his back was to a storefront window filled with video screens. He raised his blaster rifle, fired at the display, then climbed in among the shards. Charmer followed. The storefront wouldn't give them cover for long—certainly not if the stormtroopers fired another rocket—but it would have to be enough.

"Check for a way up top," Namir yelled, and his voice sounded faint and tinny. He couldn't hear the storm of blaster bolts at all. "We need covering fire!" Not looking to see if Charmer obeyed, he dropped to the floor as the stormtroopers adjusted their aim to the store.

He couldn't spot Gadren, either. He ordered the alien into position anyway, hoping he was alive and that the comlinks still worked. He lined his rifle under his chin, fired twice in the direction of the stormtroopers, and was rewarded with a moment of peace.

"I need you on target, Brand," he growled into his link. "I need you here *now*."

If anyone answered, he couldn't hear it.

Now he glimpsed the stormtrooper carrying the missile launcher. The trooper was still reloading, which meant Namir had half a minute at most before the storefront came tumbling down on top of him. He took a few quick shots and saw one of the other troopers fall, though he doubted he'd hit his target. He guessed Charmer had found a vantage point after all.

Three stormtroopers remaining. One was moving away from the alley while the other stayed to protect the artillery man. Namir shot wildly at the one moving into the street, watched him skid and fall to a knee, and smiled grimly. There was something satisfying about seeing a trained stormtrooper humiliate himself. Namir's own side did it often enough.

Jerky movements drew Namir's attention back to the artillery man. Behind the stormtrooper stood Gadren, both sets of arms gripping and lifting his foe. Human limbs flailed and the missile launcher fell to the ground. White armor seemed to crumple in the alien's hands. Gadren's makeshift hood blew back, exposing his head: a brown, bulbous, wide-mouthed mass topped with a darker crest of bone, like some amphibian's nightmare idol. The second trooper in the alley turned to face Gadren and was promptly slammed to the ground with his comrade's body before Gadren crushed them both, howling in rage or grief.

Namir trusted Gadren as much as he trusted anyone, but there were times when the alien terrified him.

The last stormtrooper was still down in the street. Namir fired until flames licked a burnt and melted hole in the man's armor. Namir, Charmer, and Gadren gathered back around the bodies and assessed their own injuries.

Namir's hearing was coming back. The damage to

his helmet extended far beyond the visor—a crack extended along its length—and he found a shallow cut across his forehead when he tossed the helmet to the street. Charmer was picking shards of shrapnel from his vest but made no complaints. Gadren was shivering in the warm rain.

"No Brand?" Gadren asked.

Namir only grunted.

Charmer laughed his weird, hiccoughing laugh and spoke. He swallowed the words twice, three, four times as he went, half-stuttering as he had ever since the fight on Blacktar Cyst. "Keep piling bodies like this," he said, "we'll have the best vantage point in the city."

He gestured at Namir's last target, who had fallen directly onto one of the civilian corpses.

"You're a sick man, Charmer," Namir said, and swung an arm roughly around his comrade's shoulders. "I'll miss you when they boot you out."

Gadren grunted and sniffed behind them. It might have been dismay, but Namir chose to take it as mirth.

Officially, the city was Haidoral Administrative Center One, but locals called it "Glitter" after the crystalline mountains that limned the horizon. In Namir's experience, what the Galactic Empire didn't name to inspire terror—its stormtrooper legions, its Star Destroyer battleships—it tried to render as drab as possible. This didn't bother Namir, but he wasn't among the residents of the planets and cities being labeled.

A half dozen Rebel squads had already arrived at the central plaza when Namir's team marched in. The rain had condensed into mist, and the plaza's tents and canopies offered little shelter; nonetheless, men and women in ragged armor squeezed into the driest corners they could find, grumbling to one another or tending to minor wounds and damaged equipment. As victory celebrations went, it was subdued. It had been a long fight for little more than the promise of a few fresh meals.

"Stop admiring yourselves and do something *useful*," Namir barked, barely breaking stride. "Support teams can use a hand if you're too good to play *greeter*."

He barely noticed the squads stir in response. Instead, his attention shifted to a woman emerging from the shadows of a speeder stand. She was tall and thickly built, dressed in rugged pants and a bulky maroon jacket. A scoped rifle was slung over her shoulder, and the armor mesh of a retracted face mask covered her neck and chin. Her skin was gently creased with age and as dark as a human's could be, her hair was cropped close to her scalp, and she didn't so much as glance at Namir as she arrived at his side and matched his pace through the plaza.

"You want to tell me where you were?" Namir asked.

"You missed the second fire team. I took care of it," Brand said.

Namir kept his voice cool. "Drop me a hint next time?"

"You didn't need the distraction."

Namir laughed. "Love you, too."

Brand cocked her head. If she got the joke—and Namir expected she did—she wasn't amused. "So what now?" she asked.

"We've got eight hours before we leave the system," Namir said, and stopped with his back to an overturned kiosk. He leaned against the metal frame and stared into the mist. "Less if Imperial ships come before then, or if the governor's forces regroup. After that, we'll divvy up the supplies with the rest of the battle group. Probably keep an escort ship or two for the *Thunderstrike* before the others split off."

"And we abandon this sector to the Empire," Brand said.

By this time Charmer had wandered off, and Gadren had joined a circle with Namir and Brand. "We will return," he said gravely.

"Right," Namir said, smirking. "Something to look forward to."

He knew they were the wrong words at the wrong time.

Eighteen months earlier, the Rebel Alliance's sixty-first mobile infantry—commonly known as Twilight Company—had joined the push into the galactic Mid Rim. The operation was among the largest the Rebellion had ever fielded against the Empire, involving thousands of starships, hundreds of battle groups, and dozens of worlds. In the wake of the Rebellion's victory against the Empire's planet-burning Death Star battle station, High Command had believed the time was right to move from the fringes of Imperial territory toward its population centers.

Twilight Company had fought in the factory-deserts of Phorsa Gedd and taken the Ducal Palace of Bamayar. It had established beachheads for rebel hover tanks and erected bases from tarps and sheet metal. Namir had seen soldiers lose limbs and go weeks without proper treatment. He'd trained teams to construct makeshift bayonets when blaster power packs ran low. He'd set fire to cities and watched the Empire do the same. He'd left friends behind on broken worlds, knowing he'd never see them again.

On planet after planet, Twilight had fought. Battles were won and battles were lost, and Namir stopped keeping score. Twilight remained at the Rebellion's vanguard, forging ahead of the bulk of the armada, until word came down from High Command nine months in: The fleet was overextended. There was to be no further advance—only defense of the newly claimed territories.

Not long after that, the retreat began.

Twilight Company had become the rear guard of a massive withdrawal. It deployed to worlds it had helped capture mere months earlier and evacuated the bases it had built. It extracted the Rebellion's heroes and generals and pointed the way home. It marched over the graves of its own dead soldiers. Some of the company lost hope. Some became angry.

No one wanted to go back.

A long time ago in a galaxy far, far away. . . .

STAR WARS®

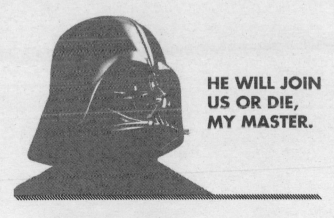

HE WILL JOIN US OR DIE, MY MASTER.

DEL REY